THE JUDAS BATTALION

'I think we are on to something pretty hot,' Roberts said.

'Must you use those confounded Americanisms, Austin?' Kylie protested. 'What is this "hot" something you have?'

'I believe the Germans have succeeded in recruiting a unit from British POWS and that this unit is fighting on the Eastern Front against the Soviet Union.'

Kylie's jaw dropped a fraction.

'During the fighting between German troops and units of Rokossovsky's 49th Army, at a village called Serov, the Russians came across a dead soldier in a Waffen-SS uniform.' Roberts dug into his folder and handed across some photographs. 'I think you will be interested by the uniform.'

Kylie's eyes grew round. '*Britisches Freikorps*?' The wording in Gothic characters on the armband of the dead man's jacket was unmistakable.

D0557476

THE JUDAS BATTALION

Peter MacAlan

A STAR BOOK

published by

the Paperback Division of
W. H. ALLEN & Co. PLC

A Star Book

Published in 1984
by the Paperback Division of
W. H. Allen & Co. PLC
44 Hill Street, London W1X 8LB

First published in Great Britain by W. H. Allen & Co., 1983

Copyright © Peter MacAlan, 1983

Printed in Great Britain by
Cox & Wyman Ltd, Reading

ISBN 0 352 31543 1

For two generous friends –
Rudiger and Sylvia Stetzelberg

'They talk of a man betraying his country, his friends, his sweetheart. There must be a moral bond first. All a man can betray is his conscience.'

– Joseph Conrad
Under Western Eyes, 1911

Chapter One

The bullet struck less than a yard in front of the face of Sergeant Kiril Dobrush as he lay prone in the freezing snow and slush of the roadway. It splintered a protruding rock and Dobrush gasped painfully as he felt something sharp graze his forehead. He raised a hand, felt the warm blood, and swore.

'Sniper!'

The warning cry came from a member of Dobrush's platoon crouching behind a wood pile on higher ground.

Dobrush rolled swiftly to his left, towards a heap of stones which had once been the boundary wall between the road and a field. Once in the shelter of the ruined wall, he rose to a kneeling position and slowly raised his head.

A plain of white rolled away into the distance before him, sparkling and glistening in the pale early morning sun. The snow-covered Belorussian vista was beautiful in the soft winter light. Far to the south the tips of high mountains edged the horizon, while to the north the blue sparkling band of the Pripet River wound its way towards the town of Mozyr. But Sergeant Kiril Dobrush, of the 8th Assault Regiment, 49th Army Group of Lieutenant-General Konstantin Rokossovski's 2nd Belorussian Army, was not appreciative of the scenery which met his searching eyes.

Three hundred yards away, in a slight depression too shallow to be called a valley, sprawled a group of ruined houses which surrounded a half-demolished church – its tower, a jagged piece of shattered masonry. This was the village of Serov, his regiment's main objective and the last fortified German position before the morass of the vast Pripet Marshes, beyond which lay the Polish frontier. Since December, Dobrush's regiment had been pushing the Germans backwards towards Poland, driving the invaders out of Soviet territory. Now, with only a few days of the New Year gone, Soviet forces were already on the Polish border. Moscow was hailing 1944 as the year of total victory over Fascism.

Well, it was a long way to Berlin yet and the village of Serov still stood in the way. Dobrush peered at the war-scarred and blackened buildings, but without curiosity. All he was interested in was pin-pointing the sniper. His platoon commander, Captain Volkov, had informed them that, according to intelligence reports, Serov was being held by units of the 1st Infantry Regiment of the SS Totenkopf (Death's Head) Division – highly trained and fanatical troops. To Dobrush, soldiers were men whatever title they had; their bodies could be hurt and destroyed in the same way as others; they bled, felt pain, they screamed and they died just like anyone else. Dobrush was not given to flights of imagination. He was a stolid farm-worker from Fumanova; placid, thick-set, a steadying influence on his men.

He could see nothing stirring among the buildings.

Two more shots came in rapid succession.

Dobrush threw himself down, cursing that he had not spotted their origin.

One of his men, Fastov, came slithering through the snow on his stomach and reached the safety of the wall.

'One hundred yards down the road, Sergeant,' he gasped. 'The bastard is holed up in that ruined house.'

Dobrush bobbed his head up.

A hundred yards down the road was a stone building. He presumed it had been a cottage. Its roof and one wall were completely missing and large holes had been punched in its crumbling masonry. Dobrush caught a slight movement behind the broken glass of a window and ducked as another bullet came whining through the air. The sniper had placed himself in a good position, Dobrush admitted to himself. Beyond the stone wall, behind which he crouched, there was virtually no cover across the snowfield which separated them from Serov. The sniper could pin down the entire regiment in such a position. Unless he was an amateur and exposed himself for a clear shot, there was no way of eliminating him. Dobrush did not think the man was an amateur.

'I think I can take him, Sergeant,' Fastov interrupted his thoughts in a tone of excitement.

Fastov was young, not yet eighteen. Dobrush gazed down at his fair, tousled hair and flushed boyish face and found himself thinking that the lad ought to be still at school. He shook his head.

'But Sergeant,' protested Fastov, 'there's a gully along the side of the road. I can crawl along it while the rest of you put up a fire to divert his attention.'

Dobrush could see what the boy meant. He hesitated. The advance could not be held up. Captain Volkov had emphasised the importance of getting into Serov as part of the big push. Re-organised and re-supplied, the Red Army was going to roll the Germans all the way back to Berlin. Serov had to be taken.

He gave a grimace of consent to Fastov and then signalled across the road to where Corporal Rudnov and Private Komrat had set up their machine-gun post. He caught Rudnov's eye, pointed to the ruined house and made a gesture with his hand. The machine-gun erupted into a staccato chatter and Fastov, pulling a stick grenade from his belt, started to crawl rapidly along the narrow depression. He had not gone more than twenty-five yards when he stopped moving.

Dobrush gazed at him for a full minute before he realised that the boy had been hit. With a grunt of suppressed anger he turned and waved at Rudnov to cease firing.

Two figures were crawling down the road behind him. Dobrush turned and shouted at them to take cover, his instructions liberally laced with expletives. One of the men was Captain Volkov; the other was his radio operator.

'What's the situation, Dobrush?' demanded Volkov, ignoring his sergeant's lack of military courtesy.

Briefly, Dobrush told him.

Volkov checked his sergeant's assessment and ordered the radio operator to raise the regiment's command post. The soldier fiddled with his instruments and began calling softly.

'Kishinyov Five to Command, come in. Come in.'

There was a pause before he handed the mouthpiece to Volkov.

'This is Kishinyov Five, we need urgent tank support.'

Volkov paused and gave map co-ordinates.

Meanwhile, Dobrush was peering over the wall again. Among the ruined houses of Serov he could now see movement. Through the crisp Janurary morning air he heard a metallic clanking.

'Captain!'

Volkov glanced up, frowning at the tension in Dobrush's voice.

'I think the Nazis have tanks in Serov.'

Volkov reached for his field glasses and trained them towards the ruins. He could see a grey shape moving amidst the rubble. Dobrush was right. The outline was familiar. He had seen such shapes before at Stalingrad. Henschel Tiger Tanks. He frowned. How many tanks were in Serov? He bit his lip as he crouched down behind the wall.

'Panzers,' he said in reply to Dobrush's glance of inquiry. 'The Germans might be preparing a counter-attack. Get me regimental command again.'

The operator soon handed the instrument to Volkov. The captain swiftly explained. He paused, listening to instructions.

'Yes, yes. I'll hold my men back . . . what else can I do?'

He forced a tired grin towards Dobrush.

'They'll be in for a hot time in a minute, you'll see.'

A moment passed before they heard the ponderous note of a heavy engine behind them and the clanking of metal treads. Slowly down the road trundled the heavy brown shape of a T34 tank, its cannon lurching menacingly.

Volkov muttered something inaudible and, crouching below the level of the wall, began to run towards it. Dobrush could see him talking to the gunner, hanging over the rim of the turret, waving his arm towards the sniper's position. Moments later the turret with its black muzzled cannon was swinging. The first shell screamed low overhead, causing Dobrush to wince, and exploded twenty yards behind the building. Dobrush glanced over the wall. A heavy pall of smoke hung between Serov and the house. It occured to Dobrush that the German tanks would not be slow in answering the T34. A second shell screamed overhead and the sniper's position erupted in a shower of flaming masonry and black smoke.

Dobrush half rose but Volkov was yelling for him to get down.

'We still have the Panzers to deal with!' he cried.

'Surely we ought to get in now, under the level of their gunfire?' Dobrush retorted.

'Not yet . . .'

There were several flashes from the ruined buildings. Dobrush could see them clearly. A split second later came the whine of shells. Explosions rocked the earth behind them. Dobrush glanced back and saw the T34 hastily reversing down the roadway, trying to get out of the range of the German fire.

Then Dobrush heard a new sound. Shrieking, screaming wails – one after the other until they merged into a hideous chorus, flashing across the now-acrid sky. Dobrush had seen the Katyusha multiple rocket throwers at work before. For fifteen minutes, rocket after rocket screamed into Serov, exploding with force and volume until Dobrush felt that nothing could be left alive there.

Eventually there came a silence which was almost painful.

'Let's go!' cried Volkov, leaping to his feet and scrambling across the wall.

The cry was taken up by the men of the 8th Assault Regiment as they scrambled from their positions and began to run forward.

Dobrush spat reflectively as he swung over the wall and trotted across the mushy snowfield towards the smoking pile of rubble in which the sniper had hidden. A sporadic rifle fire came from Serov. Dobrush shook his head in wonderment that men could still exist in the inferno caused by the Katyusha rockets. He reached the mess of stones and climbed inside. Rudnov and Komrat followed him, dragging their heavy machine gun with them. Behind them a squadron of T34s were rumbling towards Serov.

'We'll let them mop up,' grunted Dobrush.

Rudnov set down his gun and reached into his tunic, fumbling for a soiled packet of cigarettes, and offered them to the others. Dobrush passed a match around.

As he exhaled he noticed the crumpled bodies of two German

soldiers half hidden by the fallen masonry. Perhaps it was curiosity – a desire to see the face of his enemy – which prompted him to move across and look down on them. One of the bodies lay face down in the rubble, hand flung out still clutching the shattered stock of a rifle with a telescopic sight. The left leg and arm of the body were missing; the entire left side was merely a bloodied pulp. Dobrush was used to such sights. The second body also lay face down a few feet away.

Dobrush was about to turn away when a slight movement stayed him. He would not have noticed anything had not masonry dust been piled on the back of the jacket of the soldier and a slight breathing motion caused some of it to be dislodged. Sergeant Kiril Dobrush did not change his expression as he worked the bolt action of his rifle. Then, with the toe of his boot, he pushed violently at the body, turning it over on its back. A scream of agony came from the mouth of the man, causing Dobrush's nerves to tingle. An expression of distaste moulded his features as he saw the multi-coloured mess that had been the man's stomach and smelt the vile stench of bloodied gore. As he dragged his gaze away, he suddenly realised that the man's eyes were wide open, staring blankly at him in pain and fear. Dobrush had seen such expressions before on the faces of sick animals back on his farm in Fumanova.

Dispassionately, Dobrush saw that he was looking into the face of a boy; a boy not more than eighteen or nineteen. The face reminded him of Fastov. It was a white, gaunt face contorted in fright and agony. Tears stained the dirt-covered cheeks. The mouth was working, blood oozing at the corners. No distinguishable words came from the boy, only terrified animal grunts.

'Poor swine,' muttered Dobrush, raising his rifle and shooting the boy through the head. He turned and dragged heavily on his cigarette.

'Hey, sergeant!'

It was Rudnov, bending and peering at the boy's body with curiosity.

'Have you seen a uniform like this before?'

Dobrush frowned.

'What do you mean, Rudnov?' he asked, turning back. 'It's an SS uniform, isn't it?'

Both Dobrush and Rudnov were old hands, veterans of the struggle for the isthmus between the Don and the Volga back in '42. They could tell most German units by insignia.

'There's an English flag on the sleeve of the jacket.'

Dobrush's eyes widened as he bent to examine it.

The uniform was a field grey German military uniform right enough; there was the usual SS markings and the collar badge had a design of three leopards. On the left sleeve of the jacket, however, was a shield bearing the British flag, while just below, around the cuff, was a black band, silver-edged, on which were stitched, in Gothic characters, the words *Britisches Freikorps*.

Dobrush was puzzled.

During the last two years of fighting across the broad expanses of Belorussia and the Ukraine he had come up against a weird assortment of foreign regiments fighting for the Germans: Rumanians, French, Italians, Flemish, Spanish . . . even Russian emigrés and deserters who stupidly thought that the Nazis would somehow return the Tsar to power. But the British! That didn't make sense.

Dobrush fumbled with the breast pocket of the dead boy's tunic and pulled out a wallet. Inside was a letter written in a language Dobrush didn't understand. He presumed it was English. There were a few creased photographs and, more importantly, there was the dead soldier's paybook, the *Soldbuch* issued to all members of the German Army. Dobrush tried to make out the unfamiliar characters of the Gothic print.

'Edward Small.' He pronounced the foreign name with difficulty. 'Born London, 17 March 1924.'

He glanced at Rudnov in amazement.

'Damned right!' he whistled. 'There must be an English unit serving with the Germans.'

Lieutenant Vaslav Koblenski of the 49th Army Field Intelligence Unit, watched anxiously while two of his men finished photographing the body.

'You made sure that the badges were in focus?' he demanded.

It was the third time he had made the demand. Koblenski was

a former mathematics teacher, precise, methodical, always checking and re-checking the work of his men. It made him a good intelligence officer, but did not endear him to his subordinates.

'Yes, sir,' sighed the photographer. 'Everything will be perfect.'

'It is important,' Koblenski said. 'Moscow wants these pictures by this evening.'

Not only the pictures, he thought moodily. He had to fly with the pictures to Moscow to make a personal report to the Politburo. That Moscow was disturbed by Sergeant Kiril Dobrush's find was an understatement. It was well known in certain quarters that Hitler had secretly been trying to form an alliance with Britain and America against the Soviet Union. Even at this late stage of the war Moscow did not entirely trust her Western Allies. Like most Russians, the men of the Politburo had long memories. After the Bolsheviks had come to power in the October Revolution of 1917, the English had panicked and to secure their capitalist interests had sent armed forces into Russia in an effort to overthrow the infant Communist regime. Winston Churchill, who had been the British Minister of State for War at the time, had been a leading instigator of British intervention in Russia, and had persuaded America, France and Japan to send expeditionary forces to reinforce the British armies. A fierce war had disrupted the country from March 1918, dragging on until 1920 before the fledgling Red Army and Navy had succeeded in driving back the interventionist forces. The Soviets had not forgotten. What Churchill and the British had done once, they could do again. That the British might be allowing the recruitment of men to serve against the Soviet Union on Germany's Eastern Front was not beyond Soviet comprehension.

The report of Sergeant Kiril Dobrush's discovery, when relayed to Moscow, had brought forth immediate demands for action.

'Are you sure everything is in order?' snapped Koblenski again.

His men had finished their gruesome photographic task and

were now removing the dead boy's uniform to preserve the insignia badges.

'Everything is fine,' assured one of his men. 'You'll be in Moscow in time.'

Koblenski blinked.

'It's very important,' he said.

Chapter Two

The black limousine purred quietly out of the centre of Stockholm and sped northward along the Birger Jarlsgatan. In the back seat, Sir Heathcote Grey relaxed and lit his pipe. A tall, wiry man, with a face that was deeply etched and permanently grave, although the grey eyes held a sparkle of humour, he was approaching his sixtieth birthday. His hair was unruly, a salt-and-pepper mix of colour, and was muffled against the cold of the harsh Nordic winter.

'Will it take us long?' he asked the driver, the only other occupant of the car.

'Depends on the condition of the road between here and Uppsala.' The man shrugged. 'It should be fairly clear. The Swedes are fairly efficient about that sort of thing.'

Sir Heathcote grunted and turned to stare out of the back window.

They were just passing the historic landmark of Engelbrekts' church and there was hardly any traffic about.

When he faced front again he saw the driver was smiling at him in the driving mirror.

'Don't worry, sir. I've been keeping an eye open for the opposition. They're probably still tucked up in bed.'

The driver was right. The roads north of the city were clear of snow, although sudden flurries caused them to slow down now and again.

Sir Heathcote drummed impatiently on his briefcase. From

time to time he would glance surreptitiously behind. He hated these cloak-and-dagger episodes. He was a diplomat, not a spy. He sighed and bit hard against his pipe stem. The driver was picking up speed now, passing through a town called Upplands-Väsby.

'I'll detour through Sigtuna just in case we've been followed,' the driver suddenly said.

Sir Heathcote made no reply. The man was an expert at his job – driver and bodyguard at the British Embassy in Stockholm and occasional wet-nurse to visiting diplomats such as Sir Heathcote Grey.

The car turned off the main road and suddenly drew up. The driver left the engine idling and lit a cigarette, while he sat watching the road behind them in his driving mirror. Ten minutes later the man smiled, wound down his window, threw his cigarette out and put the car into gear.

'No sign of anyone following, sir,' he said brightly. 'We shouldn't be too long now.'

Indeed, it was hardly any time before they entered the outskirts of Sweden's historic city Uppsala, home of the country's oldest university, whose great library contained more than a million books and twenty thousand medieval manuscripts. Grey, who considered himself something of a medievalist, found himself wishing he had time to stop off at the library. He would have liked to see the priceless fifth-century AD Bible, the *Codex Argenteus,* the world's only remaining example of a book written in pure Gothic. Even with its shroud of snow, Sir Heathcote could see that Uppsala, dominated by its thirteenth-century cathedral, was a beautiful city. His driver seemed to know it well, as he skirted the cathedral square and turned into a pleasant thoroughfare nearby.

'This is the Svartbacksgatan,' he said, slowing the car.

'Drop me before we get to the house,' called Grey nervously.

'Yes, sir. I know the drill,' the man replied patiently. He pulled into the kerb and Sir Heathcote clambered out.

'I'll be waiting outside the main entrance of the cathedral in two hours,' the driver called out as Sir Heathcote joined the few pedestrians passing along the street. Out of the corner of his eye the British diplomat saw the car draw away into the traffic. He tried to walk nonchalantly along the pavement, his eyes seeking the house he wanted. It was a large one, well set back behind a high wall. The wrought-iron gates looked imposing. He hesitated before them. He was reaching out a hand towards the iron ring-pull of the bell chain when a man in a green baize apron appeared behind the gates and gave him an appraising look. The man said something in Swedish.

'I am looking for the house where Carl von Linné was born,' said Sir Heathcote.

'He is buried in the cathedral,' the man replied in a heavily accented English. 'All the botany students go there.'

'Yet I was told he used to live in Svartbacksgatan.'

The man nodded and unlocked the gate.

'I will enquire at the house,' he said gravely.

Sir Heathcote followed him into the house. The man bade him wait in the hall and disappeared through a side door. The place was decorated and furnished with impeccable taste. A far cry from war-torn Europe, Sir Heathcote reflected, with a sudden nostalgia for the days of ease and opulence that had been his lot before the war.

'Sir Heathcote!'

A chubby, red-faced man bustled through the door, hands extended and with a smile of welcome on his face.

'Good-day, Mr Almsta,' Sir Heathcote responded to the man's hearty handshake. 'Good to see you again.'

Sir Heathcote had last seen Almsta in London three months before. He was a Swedish businessman with a reputation for prominent connections in all the major European countries. It had been Almsta who had arranged this meeting.

'You had no difficulty in reaching here?'

Sir Heathcote sensed an anxiousness behind the question.

'No difficulty at all,' he assured him.

'Good. Then all is in order. The Countess is waiting.'

He turned and led the way into a sitting room. There was only one occupant; a tall, pale blonde girl in her early twenties, sitting nervously on the edge of a chaise-longue. She glanced up with narrowed eyes as they entered.

Almsta bustled forward.

'Permit me. The Countess Helga von Haensel. Countess, this is Sir Heathcote Grey.'

The Countess inclined her head slowly in Sir Heathcote's direction, her grey troubled eyes not leaving his face, examining him as a fencer examines his opponent before the contest.

Sir Heathcote cleared his throat gruffly and nodded.

He was a little surprised. The girl was very young – young and attractive, that sort of haughty beauty that he always associated with the old German aristocracy. He had been expecting them to send someone older, more experienced, more hardened.

Almsta was speaking again.

'A drink? Coffee? A cognac?'

The Countess already had a coffee cup balanced on her knees.

'A cognac,' replied Sir Heathcote as he lowered himself into an armchair. 'It's beastly cold outside.'

No one said anything while Almsta poured the drink.

'And now,' beamed the Swede, 'I shall leave you good people to your talk.'

The uneasy silence continued several moments after the little man had withdrawn and closed the door behind him.

Sir Heathcote suddenly felt sorry for the girl.

'I am told that you represent certain German interests which are opposed to the Nazi regime?' he prompted.

For a moment the girl looked startled, shivered slightly and gave an almost conspiratorial glance around. To Sir Heathcote her actions seemed melodramatic, but then he was not a subject of Hitler's Germany.

'I represent several groups within Germany who would like to know the intentions of the Allies towards our country if Germany were to rid herself of the Nazis.'

She spoke English fluently. Her voice was soft and musical but held a tremulous tone which Sir Heathcote ascribed to her nervousness.

The British diplomat raised his eyebrows. 'I believe that there have already been several attempts to stage an anti-Nazi coup in Germany?' he countered.

The girl shrugged.

'All of which have failed because of a lack of planning, of proper organisation and backing.'

Sir Heathcote decided to be blunt. 'The British Government,' he said, 'have had many approaches over the years from Germans who proclaim themselves to be anti-Nazi, who have talked about a German resistance, about plans for either arresting or even assassinating the top Nazi leaders and seizing control of government. Little has happened, Countess. Prime Minister Churchill and our Foreign Secretary Eden are convinced that a German resistance cannot be taken seriously.'

The Countess's eyes blazed with passion. 'Do they consider all Germans are Nazis?'

Sir Heathcote shrugged. 'I can only relay their opinions, Countess. If there is a strong German resistance, where is it?'

The Countess carefully put down her coffee cup, drew a cigarette case out of her handbag and took out a cigarette. Sir Heathcote rose and lit it for her. She exhaled shallowly, nervously. Her face seemed a conflict of emotions.

'The resistance is there, but it is not co-ordinated,' she replied, making an effort to keep her voice even. 'There are groups all over Germany who would rejoice to see Hitler and his thugs destroyed. But they are isolated, they have no leadership and they have little to promise the people in the place of Hitler's total war. The Allies have demanded the surrender of the German nation. The mass of people see only the continuation of the war as a bulwark between them and total annihilation.'

She paused to gather her thoughts.

'Last month my good friend Elizabeth von Thadden was executed by the Gestapo.' The girl's mouth twisted in bitterness. 'She ran the famous girls' school at Weiblingen, perhaps you have heard of it? She was a good German; an intellectual, a liberal. She hated Fascism. She was a member of a small group who used to meet in the house of Frau Anna Solf, the widow of our former Colonial Minister during the days of the Kaiser. Herr Solf also served as ambassador to Japan during the Weimar Republic.'

Sir Heathcote found himself recalling a handsome diplomat with a boisterous sense of humour. 'I once had the pleasure of meeting Herr Solf in Tokyo.'

The Countess did not seem to hear him.

'At Frau Solf's house, Elizabeth and a group of friends used to gather regularly to discuss the political situation. There was Countess Hanna von Bredow, the grand-daughter of Bismarck; Count Albrecht von Berstorff; Otto Kiep from the Foreign Office; and Father Erxleben, a well-known Jesuit priest. One day my friend met a young Swiss doctor named Reckse. She thought he was anti-Nazi and took him along to a tea party Frau Solf was giving on 10 September. Reckse was a Gestapo agent. Everyone was arrested and executed.'

She paused and stubbed out her cigarette savagely.

Sir Heathcote shifted uneasily in his chair.

'While I can express individual sympathy, Countess, the experience is not dissimilar to what is happening in a million homes throughout Nazi-occupied Europe. The point is, harsh as it may seem, a group of intellectuals discussing matters in the privacy of their drawing rooms does not constitute a resistance movement.'

Countess von Haensel stood up abruptly and walked to the window, staring out at the garden.

'I am the representative of several groups who have now joined together. We represent all walks of German life: trade unionists, Communists, liberals, priests, civilians and the military. I am not at liberty to divulge names, but on our council are two field marshals and many highly placed generals. We are all agreed that the demonic dictatorship of Adolf Hitler is leading our country to absolute ruin. I have been sent to meet you to ask you one important question.'

Sir Heathcote set down his empty glass on a side table and gazed steadily at the girl who turned to face him, her chin thrusting aggressively forward.

'If the German people, by their own volition, removed Hitler and the Nazis from power and established a new government, would the Allies still demand the unconditional surrender of the German nation? When I ask that question, I should perhaps be more precise. Would the *Western* Allies demand that surrender?'

Sir Heathcote rose and stared hard at the girl.

'I can only speak for the British Government, of course,' he began. 'Your question implies that their might be some difference of opinion between Britain and America and our ally the Soviet Union. Let me dispel that notion. The Allies speak with one voice. I shall, of course, pass on your question for a formal reply. Informally, Countess, I cannot see your group receiving any other reply than the one my Government has given to other dissident German groups in recent years. If you are against the Nazi regime which is now in power in your country, the Allies will fully support you. However, while Hitler remains in power with, as it appears to us, the backing of the vast majority of the German people, then there can be no question of our not pursuing the unconditional surrender of Germany and her allies as the outcome to the present conflict.'

There was a long pause before the Countess spoke again.

'The Allies do not hold out encouragement for the German people.' There was a tone of soft rebuke in her voice.

'What encouragement can we give while the German people support such a regime?' countered Sir Heathcote.

'It is rumoured that, should Germany be defeated, the Allies plan to partition and occupy Germany, that most of the country will be handed over to the Soviets. Germany cannot let this happen; yet the only alternative is to support Hitler's policy of total war. Encourage opposition to the Nazis by holding out some hope for the German people, the hope that they can return to democracy and freedom.'

'You still have not convinced me of any widespread opposition,' sighed Sir Heathcote doggedly.

'What do you want?' demanded the girl angrily. 'Names, places, events? What of the Munich students' revolt of last year?'

Sir Heathcote betrayed his ignorance by a frown.

'In February of last year, Paul Giesler, the Gauleiter of Bavaria, convoked a meeting of the students at Munich University and told them that all male students were being drafted into the army. Let me tell you at once that all the able-bodied students had long since been drafted. All female students would cease their studies and produce children for the Fatherland. They were to bear one child annually from Aryan males selected by the Reich. The students started to howl the Gaulieter down. That afternoon, for the first time since Hitler came to power, there was an open anti-Nazi demonstration on the streets of Munich.

'A few days later the student leaders, a medical student named Hans Scholl and his young sister, Sophie, a student of biology, were arrested and executed. Sophie hobbled to her death because the Gestapo broke her leg during questioning. Not long afterwards the senior professor at Munich, Kurt Huber, was also executed.'

The Countess paused to light another cigarette.

'Oh yes, there is resistance among the German people. But it needs fostering; it needs help, encouragement. Each day it grows stronger; each day shattered young men – the lucky ones – return from the various war fronts embittered and disillusioned. And the opposition to the Nazis grows.'

Sir Heathcote made a sympathetic gesture, noting how the nervousness had left the girl as she had warmed to her theme. There was a quality of cold steel behind the attractive face.

'Tell me, Countess,' he said, 'There is one thing which it seems that most dissident German groups have in common; all seem to agree that Hitler must be assassinated as the prelude towards the ousting of the Nazi regime. Surely if Hitler fell, then someone else, Boorman or Goebbels, would simply step into his place?'

The Countess pursed her lips. 'Adolf Hitler is a psychopath surrounded by sycophants. With Hitler destroyed the entire Nazi structure would be in turmoil. For the last ten years Hitler's word has been absolute. No one has dared to question his authority. If he were destroyed then the Nazis would be like a chicken without a head. They might run hither and thither for a brief moment, in their death spasms, but they would die, exactly as the headless chicken would die.'

For a moment Sir Heathcote was shocked at the analogy coming from the attractive young woman; shocked by the sudden undisguised gleam of fanaticism in her eyes.

'Believe me,' Countess Helga von Haensel repeated with vehemence, 'if Hitler were assassinated tomorrow morning then the Nazis would fall in the afternoon and the war would be over by evening.'

Chapter Three

Lieutenant-Colonel Austin Roberts sat back on his creaking wooden chair and surveyed his office in distaste. It was a small, square room with no other features than its bland, pale green walls and ceiling. There were no pictures on the wall except a poster pinned crookedly to the back of the door which warned the British people to 'Keep Mum!' bearing caricatures of Hitler and Mussolini eavesdropping on an old lady while crouched behind a garden wall. A plain wooden table without drawers, two chairs, a steel filing-cabinet and an anonymous black telephone constituted the only furniture. A single unshaded light-bulb hung from the centre of the room while the casement window behind the table was criss-crossed with strips of sticky tape in case of bomb blast.

The room was like hundreds of others in the dark brick building in Kensington Palace Gardens which housed the head-quarters of British Military Intelligence. The staff called these rooms 'interview rooms', a strange euphemism, thought Roberts with wry amusement.

At forty years of age, he was still younger-looking than most of his contemporaries. He had nondescript light-brown hair, which usually hung rebelliously over his forehead. His face was angular, his eyes light brown, and he had a ready smile as if he were always prepared to laugh at what life offered. He was tall and carried himself with a slight stoop by way of compensation – an unmilitary posture. He looked very much what he had been in civilian life, a college lecturer, a university don who had squeezed himself into a badly fitting colonel's uniform by accident.

He was part of a group officially designated as the German Department of Section D, Military Intelligence (Research), whose purposes were vague. The section was to keep itself informed of events within Germany itself and 'investigate any possibility of attacking the enemy within his home territory by means other than the operation of military forces'. In plainer language, the German Department dealt with all forms of German dissidents, organised subversion and sabotage within the Reich, ran agents and generally collected information by listening to German radio, reading German newspapers and interrogating German prisoners of war.

Roberts's qualification for the department was the fact that he had been a German language teacher, almost bilingual. He also had a working knowledge of French and Spanish, and was equally at home in ancient Greek and Latin. Yet his manner was vague, and his boyish indiscipline made the ATS's in his section feel maternal towards him. The vagueness hid a mind that was razor sharp. He was a county chess champion who had written two textbooks on the game, and his brain was one of the utmost clarity, ordered and logical. Some who knew Roberts well felt he went out of his way to cultivate the air of rebellious indiscipline and the appearance, as one senior officer complained, of 'downright scruffiness'.

To Roberts, the games he played in his office in Kensington Palace Gardens were rather like academic problems to be resolved; he hardly ever related them to reality. When he made a decision, he never thought that it might result in someone lying bleeding to death in some cold, dark German backstreet, or someone else fainting with pain in a cold Berlin cellar while the eager young men of the Gestapo set about their work. Roberts managed to insulate himself from the war, seeing it only as some gigantic game of chess; sometimes a piece had to be sacrificed to gain an advantage. It was all a matter of stratagem. Perhaps that was the strength of a man in Lieutenant-Colonel Roberts's position.

He was able to leave his work in his office, return to his comfortable house in Maida Vale and play for an hour with his four-year-old twin boys before settling down with his wife, Maude, for a pre-dinner drink. After dinner he could smoke a pipe, listen to the concerts on the radio, discuss the news in general terms with his wife, or work out new chess problems. Maude never asked him what he did in his work and he never

26

volunteered the information. His work began at nine o'clock when he settled in his office and ended when he locked his office door in the evening.

Roberts finished his customary morning inspection of his office, stifled a yawn and returned his gaze to the large buff folder which lay before him on the table. He reached for the telephone.

'Morning, Doris,' he smiled as the voice of his ATS secretary answered. 'Send in Sergeant Wilkens and two mugs of tea, hot and sweet.'

There was a few seconds' pause before someone tapped on the door. In answer to his 'Come', a slightly built man wearing the uniform of the Green Howards entered and saluted. He wore sergeant's chevrons and the ribbon of the Military Medal on his breast.

Roberts smiled at him.

'Morning, Wilkens. Be seated.'

The sergeant shut the door behind him, crossed smartly to the only other chair in the room and sat down. It squeaked in protest. Roberts tried to keep a grave face as the man contrived to sit at attention.

'Sit easy,' he instructed.

The sergeant relaxed.

Roberts opened the file before him and skimmed through it. As he was doing so, the door opened and a fair-haired ATS came in carrying two steaming mugs.

'Bless you, Doris,' murmured Roberts and pushed one of the mugs towards the sergeant. 'This will help you unfreeze,' he said.

Outside, London lay under a coat of snow, ice and slush. It was the coldest February for two years and the first icy snows of 1944 had fallen on Monday the 17th, accompanied by a bitter wind from the east.

He waited until his secretary had left before slouching back in his chair and grinning apologetically at the sergeant.

'Sorry we had to delay your leave, Sergeant. I'd like to clarify a few points.'

The man waited politely.

'Firstly, let me congratulate you on your escape. How long were you a POW?'

'Since Dunkirk, sir.'

'Had you tried to escape before?'

'Six times, sir. Something went wrong every time.'

'At least you were successful in the end.'

'Just after Christmas we were sent on a work detail to clear some roads. I suddenly saw a chance, dodged behind a hedge and ran like hell. It was easy. It took me a week to get to Switzerland, and here I am.'

'Splendid,' murmured Roberts, knowing it was probably anything but easy. He motioned towards the sergeant's untouched tea.

'Don't let it get cold, Wilkens. Tea is at a premium around here.'

The sergeant obediently sipped at the mug.

'You were at Kaisersteinbuch POW camp in Austria, weren't you?'

'Stalag Eighteen A, they called it, sir.'

'In your initial debriefing you told our intelligence officer about a visit to your camp . . .' Roberts paused and peered at a document in the folder. 'A visit by an Englishman who said he was recruiting for a British Legion to fight the Russians. Is that so?'

Sergeant Wilkens nodded.

'Yes, sir.'

'Tell me about this Englishman. Tell me what he said,' invited Roberts, sitting back.

'Bloody traitor, sir,' the sergeant grimaced. 'About thirty years old, the sort of accent that comes out of public schools, begging your pardon, sir. Fair hair, a bit weedy-looking. A weak bastard . . . er, person, sir.'

Roberts made a gesture of encouragement.

'Well, sir, last October it was. The commandant of the camp called all us English POWs together and said someone of importance was going to address us. When this bas . . . person, sir, showed up we were taken aback. Out he comes with a French tart on his arm, beg pardon, French woman, sir. Stood there as cool as a cucumber and started to prattle away about the Bolshevik menace. "What about the Nazi menace?" one of the lads called out. He was promptly given a dig in the guts by

28

some enthusiastic goon, beg pardon, guard, sir. That's what we called them.'

'Go on, Wilkens.'

'Well, the lads were getting a bit upset at this Englishman telling us we ought to be fighting for the Germans instead of against 'em. There was a lot of muttering and the commandant began to get nervous. He told the bloke to speed up his delivery. He rambled on about the Jews being behind Communism and then said that a British unit was being formed which would fight on the Russian Front. If any prisoners wanted to enlist then they would cease to be POWs and would get pay and privileges, uniforms, leave in town, and so forth.'

The sergeant gazed reflectively at his mug.

'Well?' prompted Roberts.

'There was damned near a riot in the camp and the weedy bastard had to beat it. Him and his French tart.'

'Do you recall anything else?'

Wilkens shook his head.

'Oh, one thing, sir. The French tart called him 'Jean'. I overheard that, but I wouldn't have thought it was his real name. He was English, I swear it.'

Wilkens pronounced the name in the French fashion.

'Jean?' mused Roberts. 'As in John?'

'I expect so, sir,' agreed Wilkens. 'Anyway, they just managed to get him out of the camp before he was torn apart.'

The sergeant placed his empty mug back on the table.

'A few days later the Germans circulated a leaflet in English in the camp. It repeated exactly what the weedy character had said. Said we ought to save England from the Bolshevik threat and enlist in this British Legion which would fight side by side with the Nazis.'

'I don't suppose you managed to smuggle a copy out of the camp?'

'Didn't realise it was that important, sir,' the sergeant shrugged. 'Most of the paper came in useful, anyway.'

Roberts frowned, not understanding.

'Useful?'

'Well, sir, there was a bit of a shortage of lavatory paper in the camp.'

29

'Oh,' Roberts found himself smiling. 'Yes, I suppose that was the best use for it. Tell me one more thing, sergeant. Did you see any other attempts at recruitment for such a unit during your time as a POW?'

'Not in my experience, sir. But I have heard from prisoners that similar incidents happened at other camps.'

'Do you know if there has been a response to such appeals?'

'There have been rumours, sir. A few young kids and some hard cases. I can't say for sure.'

Roberts stood up abruptly and extended his hand.

'Thank you, Sergeant. What you have told me has been most interesting. You will remember you are bound by the Official Secrets Act not to mention this interview to anyone else. Understood?'

The sergeant stood up awkwardly and nodded.

As he turned for the door Roberts called: 'And congratulations on your escape.'

For a few moments Roberts concerned himself with making notes in the buff folder. Then, gathering his papers together, he left his office and traversed an anonymous dingy corridor to an unmarked door on which he tapped before entering. A pretty ATS corporal smiled up from her desk.

'Good morning, Gladys, is the boss in?' God, he thought, they get younger every day, or is it that I'm getting older? The girl reached for the intercom on her desk. 'Colonel Roberts is here, sir.'

A Scots voice boomed from the adjoining room. 'Send him in! Send him in!'

Roberts walked across to the far side of the room and opened another anonymous-looking door.

The office beyond was totally unlike the bare workrooms of the rest of the building. Although the same bland green paint covered the walls, they were also adorned with pictures. There was a row of filing cabinets, several easy chairs and a couch and a large oak desk strewn with papers. There was even a carpet on the floor.

Brigadier Ewart Kylie, head of the German Department, scowled from behind the desk. He was a fiery-haired Scotsman, a former professor of German literature from Edinburgh

University who had been the country's leading authority on sixteenth century German literature. Now Kylie held a unique position in Military Intelligence. As the head of a section dealing with Germany itself, he was answerable only to a few people in the War Office. He had direct access to the Prime Minister himself, and was called to give regular briefings to the premier on conditions within enemy territory.

'What can I do for you, Austin?' Kylie never articulated when he could get away with a deep-throated growl.

Roberts closed the door behind him and sprawled in the rare comfort of an armchair. He had known his commanding officer too long to stand on military formality.

'I think we are on to something pretty hot,' he said.

Kylie threw down his pen and sat back, eyes narrowing under bushy brows. He was a short, stocky man, with a white skin splattered with freckles, and twinkling green eyes. He placed his fingers together in the manner of a supplicant and stared at his subordinate with mock annoyance.

'Must you use those confounded Americanisms, Austin?' he protested. 'What is this "hot" something you have?'

Roberts grinned.

'I believe the Germans have succeeded in recruiting a unit from British POWs and that this unit is fighting on the Eastern Front against the Soviet Union.'

Kylie's jaw dropped a fraction. 'Christ!' he breathed.

Satisfied with the reaction, Roberts tapped the folder on his knees. 'From time to time we have had word about the activities of certain British Fascists who are now resident in Germany – former members of Mosley's British Union of Fascists and its various splinter groups.'

'Mostly a collection of mentally retarded morons who would be far better off in a psychiatric hospital,' interrupted Kylie.

'There are a few dangerous exceptions,' pointed out Roberts.

Kylie grimaced. 'You're referring to Amery's son, I suppose?'

'He may be a young man with problems,' replied Roberts, 'but because he is who he is, he could be a serious liability.'

John Amery was an embarrassment to the British Government. He was the son of Leo Amery, Secretary of State for India and Burma. He was the problem child of the family, spoilt

31

and selfish, a playboy with political pretensions. Following bankruptcy proceedings in 1936, John Amery had left the country for Spain and joined Franco's Fascists. In 1939 he appeared in France as a member of the French Fascist Cagoulards. He was reported living in Savoy with his French mistress. In 1942 he had appeared in Berlin and broadcast to England in November, pleading for the English to unite with the Nazis to fight Communism. Not long afterwards it was learnt that Amery's mistress had died, choking to death in her own vomit after a heavy drinking session, with Amery lying senseless at her side. Soon he was living with another French woman, Michèle Thomas from Bergerac. And he was now lecturing and writing in support of his Fascist ideology and pleading for British volunteers to fight against Soviet Russia.

'He's a sad young man,' agreed Kylie, 'but I can't agree that he is dangerous, Austin. Anyone with any intelligence listening to his half-baked propaganda would simply feel sick.'

'Anyone with intelligence,' repeated Roberts softly. 'Just recently we have been getting reports that appeals have been made to POWs. I have a report that in April last year Amery appeared at an internment camp in St Denis in France. This morning I interviewed an escaped POW from Kaisersteinbuch who placed Amery there last October. The news is that there are some people joining Amery.'

'There are always a few bad eggs,' conceded Kylie.

'Last night I was handed a folder from our Russian Department.'

'Well?'

'As you know, last month the Soviets broke out of the Zhitomir- Korosten sector, advancing on the Polish border.'

'I read the newspapers, Austin,' Kylie sighed.

'During the fighting between German troops and units of Rokossovsky's 49th Army, at a village called Serov, the Russians came across a dead soldier in a Waffen-SS uniform.'

Roberts dug into his folder and handed across some photographs.

'I think you will be interested by the uniform.'

Kylie's eyes grew round. '*Britisches Freikorps?*' The wording in Gothic characters on the armband of the dead man's jacket was unmistakable.

'What's more, the Soviets have sent us a copy of the man's *Soldbuch*, which identifies him as Private 3rd Class Edward Small. Born in London, 17 March, 1924.'

Kylie dragged his gaze away from the photographs. 'Can we get some information on Edward Small. Is there such a person or is this a German plant?'

''Fraid not, sir. I ran a check. Edward Small was indeed born in Whitechapel on 17 March, 1924. When he was fifteen he joined the Merchant Navy. In November 1942, he was working on the SS *Gresham* on the North African run. The *Gresham* was torpedoed off Gibraltar with a loss of 23 men. The Red Cross subsequently reported that Edward Small was listed among the survivors and had been transferred to an internment camp at . . . St Denis.' Roberts paused to emphasise the significance of the information.

Kylie heaved a sigh. He let his eyes return to the photograph of the dead youth in German uniform. 'Poor bastard,' he muttered. 'Poor stupid bastard.'

Roberts waited for a moment and then said: 'The Russians are worried, sir, worried and downright suspicious. They are demanding answers to questions about the size and purpose of this British Free Corps.'

'Well, they're not alone, laddie,' grunted Kylie. 'I apologise. Amery is dangerous if he has managed to bring this off for his Nazi masters. How many poor dupes has he succeeded in winning over? How strong are they? Do they have any real significance outside of the propaganda value? Are they a real fighting force?'

'Even if they are not a fighting unit,' interrupted Roberts, 'as a propaganda weapon they could do us incalculable harm.'

'Aye, you're right. Our alliance with the Soviet Union is tenuous at best. This could split it wide apart.'

He beat a rapid tattoo on his desk with his fingertips before seeming to come to a decision.

'Austin, I want you to drop everything and work full-time on this project. I want to know everything there is to know about the British Free Corps — strength, names of members, organisers, function, headquarters, and so on. Everything. And I want the information as soon as dammit! I must have all the details before Churchill starts bawling.'

Roberts gathered up his photographs and papers. 'It's going to be a hard slog, and might take time.'

'Damn it, Austin!' swore Kylie. 'Time is what you don't have.'

Chapter Four

Every morning except Sundays, at precisely 7.00 a.m. – not a minute sooner nor later – the figure of Karl Wielen left the wrought-iron portals of the Hildesheim *Postamt* with his sack of mail, pushing an old, very rusty bicycle. He was elderly – beyond military age – but he wore his postman's uniform as if it were that of a general. His black boots were polished to a mirror-like sheen; the dark-blue jacket and trousers were creased to razor sharpness, while on his breast hung the black, white and red ribbon of an Iron Cross (Second Class) won in the filth and slime of a Flanders trench in 1917. Karl Wielen carried himself with the stiff upright posture of an old soldier, his peaked cap precisely angled on his iron-grey hair. He sported a beautifully waxed iron-grey Kaiser Wilhelm moustache, whose points curled almost to the corners of his dead, blue eyes.

He was not the only postman in the town of Hildesheim, but he was certainly the best known. Everyone knew and greeted him. They looked upon him as a character. The bolder would call him Uncle Wilhelm in honour of his moustache. They knew little about him except that he was an eccentric; he lived on his own and did not seem to have any family. Only Frau Ostman, who was the landlady of the tenement house in which he occupied an attic room, knew that old Kurt Wielen had been a widower since 1938 and that he had once had a daughter who was rumoured to have run away to Hamburg. But old Karl

34

Wielen never talked about his wife nor daughter. Indeed, Karl Wielen never talked about himself at all.

That late February morning, in spite of the cold and the threat of rain in the moody sky, Karl Wielen left the *Postamt* as usual with his sack of mail. Outside, in the main square, he mounted his ancient bicycle and turned passed the *Rathaus* – the town hall – its fifteenth-century red-brick edifice decorated with frescoes illustrating the history of the old town. He rattled his way over the cobbled thoroughfare turning up by the sixteenth century *Wedekindhaus* which was now the Reichsbank. Irregular streets narrowed as the old buildings pressed closely in on them, some of the upper storeys of the houses overhanging the street with richly engraved wooden façades. Hildesheim still had its medieval ramparts, now converted into promenades for the townspeople. It was one of those old-world German towns, which vied in beauty with its more famous neighbour, Hamlin, just twenty kilometres to the west.

Hildesheim had once been an episcopal Catholic see in the Prussian province of Hanover, lying at the northern foot of the breathtaking Harz Mountains, along the right bank of the river Innerste, eighteen miles south-east of the beautiful old city of Hanover itself. It was, despite its old worldliness and charm, the centre of considerable industry. Once farming machinery had been produced there, now tanks, armoured cars and anti-aircraft weapons poured out of its suburban factories. Several times in recent weeks British and American planes had bombed the town. Several historic buildings, such as the *Knockenhauseramthaus,* headquarters of the medieval guild of butchers which had been lovingly restored after fire damage in 1884, had been hit. Even the old Carthusian monastery had received a number of hits from incendiaries intended for the nearby railway yards – for the town lay on the main line from Berlin via Magdelburge to Cologne.

At precisely 8.10 a.m., having passed the Georgstift School for the Daughters of State Servants, old Karl Wielen halted his bicycle before the tall spires of the church of St Michael. The edifice was mainly twelfth century, but it was said to have been built under the patronage of St Bernward, bishop of Hildesheim in 1022 AD, a painter and metal-worker, and patron of the arts

35

said to have been responsible for the great bronze doors, the cross, columns and candlesticks of the ancient church.

Looking around carefully, Karl Wielen climbed the steps into the church, pushed open the door and entered. The place was dark and musty. Catholic services were rare these days. Karl Wielen crossed to a dark corner by a column, knelt and crossed himself. He muttered a prayer, genuflected again and climbed slowly to his feet. Outside the church he remounted his bicycle and rode on. This was Karl Wielen's special area of the town; the roads where he was responsible for delivering the mail. He cycled around the narrow streets and turnings, criss-crossing on his tracks until the mail in his satchel became lighter; until he finally had only one more call to make – a call he had purposely saved until last. The biggest bundle of mail was always reserved for the old monastery building of St Michael's.

The monastery had not been used as a religious house since 1826 when the *Burgomeister* of Hildesheim had bought it on behalf of the town and converted into a lunatic asylum. So it had remained until 1942 when the mentally afflicted in the Reich had been more or less eliminated.

There was no room for the mentally ill or retarded in the Thousand-Year Reich. The old, grey stone buildings of the monastery had then become a hospital for the SS. But, by the end of the year, the place had been taken over by the SS *Todt* Organisation. SS *Reichsführer* Heinrich Himmler had ordered the systematic collection of historic treasures and artefacts from the various occupied countries. They were to be gathered, collected and studied by the *Todt* Organisation whose special headquarters, known as the *Haus Germanien,* were situated in Hanover. The monastery at Hildesheim was then requisitioned as a centre for 'maintaining and intensifying the political, economic and cultural bonds between the Reich and the other Nordic nations'. Members of the *Todt* Organisation, secretaries and various people from SS volunteer units from Norway, Denmark and Holland were quartered there. So far as Karl Wielen understood, little of importance went on at the old monastery except study and lectures on aspects of Nordic culture.

Then a few days ago he heard that a strange, rather undisciplined bunch of SS men had arrived at Hildesheim railway station to be met and collected in trucks and transported to the monastery. Something strange seemed to be going on there.

The sentry at the gate of the monastery knew the old postman well and waved him into the inner courtyard where the guardhouse was situated. A bored SS *Raumführer,* his uniform jacket unbuttoned, sat smoking and listening to the radio within the small wooden hut that had been erected in the cobbled yard. He glanced up as Karl Wielen heaved the sack of mail onto the table.

'Good morning, *Herr Postbote.*'

'Good morning,' replied the old man, returning the greeting of the NCO. 'Not too many letters today.'

The guard commander glanced at them briefly.

'A cup of coffee, *Herr Postbote?* It's cold today.'

Karl Wielen thanked the man who handed him a steaming cup of coffee across the table.

'Yours must be a tough job, *Herr Postbote.* Out in all weathers.'

'One does what one can for the Fatherland in times of peril,' replied the old man unctuously.

The SS *Raumführer* did not succeed in hiding his smile.

There was a movement at the door of the guardhouse behind the old man. A young man in a field grey Waffen–SS uniform hesitated on the doorstep.

'Yes?' snapped the guard commander.

'I was told to have my pass checked here before leaving the barracks,' the man replied in terrible German. He handed a piece of paper to the SS *Raumführer,* who glanced at it and nodded.

Karl Wielen turned to examine the newcomer. He was about twenty, with dark hair and blotchy skin. A little weak-looking, was Wielen's impression. It was then that the old man caught sight of the badge flashes on the man's left sleeve, the shield with the British Union Jack and the words *Britisches Freikorps.* Karl Wielen's eyes widened.

'Is the SS recruiting from our enemies now?' he asked wonderingly, when the young man had departed.

The SS *Raumführer* sniffed with disapproval. 'They arrived

last week. English pigs! Still, they are supposed to be a special SS unit who have enlisted to fight for the Reich.'

'But Englishmen!' protested Wielen. 'How can Englishmen fight for the Reich when we are at war with England?'

The man took out a cigarette and lit it. 'They've volunteered to fight the Russians not their own countrymen.'

'And their officers are Englishmen?'

The SS *Raumführer* shook his head. 'The commanding officer is a captain from the SS Viking Division. The unit is nothing to do with our *Todt* Organisation. They come under the Waffen –SS. All the NCOs are English though – well, their senior NCO considers himself a German because he had a German mother. But he was born and raised in London. They're an odd lot. We will have to learn to live with them, I suppose.'

Karl Wielen finished his coffee, thanked the SS *Raumführer* for his hospitality, and cycled off, his impassive face hiding a confusion of thoughts.

At 10.30 a.m. he was able to cycle back to his room on the Freidrichstrasse. He left his bicycle by the railings outside the tall tenement building and let himself into the darkened hallway with his latchkey.

Frau Ostman, the landlady, was sweeping the hallway. They exchanged deferential greetings. The old man climbed the stairs to his single attic room. By the time he had negotiated the six flights, he felt a little chesty. He was getting old – too old, perhaps? Or maybe it was simply the cold. Yes, that was it. It was a cold day. There was plenty of life in him yet.

He unlocked his door, entered the room and carefully re-locked the door behind him. He crossed to the gas fire. It lit with a spluttering sound and he stood a few moments to warm his freezing hands before it. Then he went to a cupboard, brought out a bottle of Schnapps and poured himself a small glass. He drained it with one gulp, stood for a moment looking at the empty glass and then sighed. He placed the Schnapps bottle back in the cupboard and neatly deposited the glass into the sink.

He glanced at his watch. It was nearly 11.00 a.m.

At the back of the attic was a chest of drawers on which was an old photograph showing a plump, blonde-haired young girl.

38

She was laughing gaily at the camera. Old Karl Wielen gazed at it a moment, his eyes watery. His lip quivered.

'For you, darling Paula. I do it for you.'

He suddenly drew himself up and walked to the fitted wardrobe beside his bed. He opened it and, reaching in, he pulled two hidden bolts. There was a click and the wardrobe swung slightly as if on hinges like a door. Karl Wielen pulled it forward so that it came away from the wall and revealed a small entrance to a hidden room beyond. He crawled through. Beyond was no more than a recess in the attic. He felt in the darkness for a light switch.

There was just a wooden box, covered in sacks, against one wall. Wielen removed the sacks and lifted the lid of the box. Inside was a powerful radio transmitter and receiver. With the ease of an expert, the old man manipulated the instrument, the batteries and aerial, and then his fingers hovered over the transmission key. A stream of morse poured from his accustomed hand.

'*Der Pfeifer* calling *Der Kaninchen*...The piper calling the rabbit . . . The piper calling the rabbit . . .'

He paused and waited.

Just over four hundred miles away in London another hand was answering.

'This is the rabbit receiving the piper. Begin your message.'

It was only two days after Lieutenant-Colonel Austin Roberts had been charged by Brigadier Kylie to gather information about the unit designated the British Free Corps that he received news of its base, strength and who commanded it.

There was one question which remained to be answered – the most important question. What use were the Germans going to make of the British Free Corps?

The fate of the unit was being decided in the village of Berchtesgaden in the Bavarian Alps. To be more accurate, in a house called Berghof, which lay just outside the village on the slopes of the Obersalzberg, with a breathtaking view across the rugged mountain range which bordered Bavaria and Austria. Two men sat in one of the rooms at Berghof discussing the potential of the British Free Corps. The room itself was

39

furnished in Bavarian peasant style – comfortable but not lavish, panelled with white satinwood, with enamelled miniatures, assorted landscape paintings, and National Socialist Party emblems and flags as decorations. The heating in the room was provided by a massive stove, tiled in green, which rose nearly to the ceiling.

Adolf Hitler, *Führer* of the German Reich, was in an expansive mood. It was a good day. He sat back smiling and joking as he nibbled at a plate of plain biscuits and sipped a cup of his specially prepared tea made from apple peelings.

Seated across the room from him was a small, sharp-featured man with a club foot. Paul Josef Goebbels was *Reichsminister* for Propaganda and Commissar for Total War Effort. Since it appeared the *Führer* was in good spirits, he was just beginning to relax. Having asked after Magda and the children, the *Führer* had been most solicitous about Goebbels' own health, adding that only the divine intervention of the Almighty had saved his trusty minister for future service to the Fatherland. In that, Goebbels could agree. He was still shaken by his narrow escape from death during an Allied bombing raid on Berlin a few days before on the evening of 15 February. He had been entertaining some generals and government officials at the Hotel Bristol when, a little after 9.00 p.m., the air-raid warning sounded. Leaving his companions, most of them having been lulled by good food and wine, he had driven rapidly away from the hotel to his private shelter off the Unter den Linden. What turned out to be the heaviest raid mounted by the RAF on Berlin, lasted from 9.15 p.m. to 9.45 p.m. When it was over the Hotel Bristol had been totally demolished and 1,000 residents and staff were missing. They were still digging bodies out even now.

The *Führer* helped him relax by being charming and amusing as only he could be – on occasion. He was half-way through a monologue on the genius of Putzi Hansfstängle's Bavarian music, which, next to Wagner, was the music the Führer most enjoyed, when he broke off.

'You have seen the report on the recruitment of the British Free Corps?'

'Indeed,' Goebbels nodded.

'Recruitment, I am told, is proceeding slowly. Only one

hundred are expected in Hildesheim by the end of the week. It is a small enough number. Amery promised that thousands would flock to join his legion.'

Goebbels coughed nervously. 'The English are a stubborn people . . .'

Hitler waved a dismissive hand. 'It is of no account, though. One hundred men will be enough.'

The *Reichsminister* frowned. 'Enough, my *Führer?* Enough for what?'

The *Führer* leant forward and scratched behind the ears of the Alsatian dog which lay at his feet. The dog growled contentedly.

'April 20 is my birthday,' he said affably.

Goebbels wondered whether the *Führer* was changing the subject again.

'I plan to celebrate my fifty-fifth birthday at Wolfsschanze.'

Privately Goebbels wondered whether the *Führer*'s secret military headquarters at Rastenburg, deep in the evergreen forests of East Prussia, would still be safe from the swift advances of the Red Army. He made no comment.

'My usual bodyguard will not be needed on that day.'

Goebbels looked astonished. 'The *SS Leibstandarte* Adolf Hitler Regiment has always been your personal guard . . .'

The *Führer* motioned him to silence.

'No, my dear Josef. On April 20 I shall be guarded by members of the British Free Corps.' He started to chuckle softly.

The Alsatian looked round at its master and let out a whine of curiosity.

For a few moments the *Reichsminister* gazed at his *Führer* in amazement. Then he too joined in the laughter.

'But that is a stroke of genius, my *Führer*! Genius! I should have expected no less. My God! What a blow for Churchill! What a blow for the tenuous alliance between the British and the Soviets! Englishmen guarding the *Führer* of the Third Reich! We must ensure that the newspapers are there in full force. The propaganda effect of this will be tremendous . . .'

Hitler nodded smiling. 'I will leave all the details to you, Josef. Particularly ensure that all the neutral countries are well represented. I want the reporters to be able to speak freely with the Englishmen so that they may be assured that they are not Germans, nor any other nationality, dressed up. I have no doubt that when it is seen that I, the *Führer,* trust the British Free Corps to guard my person, then the thousand that Amery promised me will flock to join our crusade against the Jewish Communist menace in the east.'

'It is a brilliant plan, my *Führer,*' agreed Goebbels. 'The ramifications will be tremendous . . .'

He paused. The *Führer* was not listening. There was a faraway expression on his face.

The *Reichsminister* rose.

'With your permission, my *Führer*. I will start organising the details.'

Adolf Hitler, deep in thought, did not see him go.

A week later, Otto Schroder, a minor clerk in the Reich Ministry for Propaganda, cycled slowly down the Kurfurstendamm, once Berlin's most fashionable shopping centre. In front of the deformed skeleton of the Kaiser Wilhelm Memorial Church he halted and, leaving his bicycle against the kerb, went to a newspaper kiosk to buy a packet of cigarettes and a copy of the *Berliner Boersenzeitung*. He glanced up at the old clock on the church purely out of habit and grinned ruefully. The hands on the charred clock face had stopped at 7.30 exactly – they had been that way since the previous November when one thousand acres of the city had been devastated during a single Allied air-raid.

Otto Schroder climbed back on his bicycle and headed for the Berlin Zoo which lay at the head of the Kurfurstendamm. It was now a pitiful wreckage. Most of its buildings were destroyed or severely damaged. The aquarium had been completely obliterated, as well as many of the animal cages. Schroder cycled round the rubble-strewn *Zoologischer Garten* to the Tiergarten, once a famous 630-acre park, now a sprawl of craters, bomb debris, partially demolished embassy buildings and resembling a battlefield more than a city park. The once great natural forest of luxurious trees were now a moonscape of burnt and charred stumps.

Otto Schroder chose his bench carefully, one of the few

remaining public benches along the Tiergartenstrasse, about a hundred yards away from the Swedish Embassy. Here he parked his bicycle, took a packet of sandwiches and sat down to read his newspaper. After a while a tall, fair-haired man stopped by the bench and also sat down, lighting a foul-smelling pipe. A few moments passed. Otto Schroder lay down his newspaper, which he carefully folded and set about finishing his sandwiches. The pipe-smoking individual turned and pointed to the newspaper.

'Would you mind if I had a look?' he asked.

Otto Schroder shrugged. 'The news is always the same.'

'Ah, but the news from Belgrade is very interesting.'

Otto Schroder smiled, perhaps a little tightly. 'Well, I have finished with it,' he said, standing up and mounting his bicycle.

The fair-haired man watched him cycle off along the road in the direction of the Wilhelmstrasse. Then he picked up the newspaper and spent a few moments studying its front page. After a quick glance around, he too stood up, pushed the newspaper into his pocket and began to walk hurriedly towards the Swedish Embassy building across the street.

Three days later Lieutenant-Colonel Austin Roberts knew the use to which the British Free Corps would be put.

Chapter Five

The plan did not come to Austin Roberts as a sudden flash of inspiration. It started as a vague idea, matured and evolved over several days. Even when he thought he had worked the matter out fully, he waited and pondered on every angle. Finally he went to the War Office Personnel Department in Curzon Street and spent all day Saturday and Sunday checking their files until he discovered one particular file. On Sunday evening he composed a report, typing it himself and heading it *Most*

Secret. First thing on Monday, 28 February, Roberts laid the file on the desk of his commanding officer, Brigadier Kylie.

'You're crazy!' was Kylie's snap verdict.

'Perhaps,' replied Roberts unperturbed, 'but it could be a means of bringing the war to an immediate end, saving the lives of tens of thousands – and, if it doesn't succeed entirely, it might at least discredit the British Free Corps and sabotage Goebbels' propaganda coup.'

Kylie sprawled back in his leather-upholstered chair and chewed thoughtfully at the end of a pencil. 'What you are suggesting is that we infiltrate a British agent into the Nazi British Free Corps, a man who would then devise a means of assassinating Hitler while the Free Corps are guarding him during his birthday celebrations on April 20?'

Roberts nodded.

'Supposing,' grimaced Kylie, 'just supposing we could infiltrate such a man into the Free Corps – and we have just under two months to do it – the mission would be absolutely suicidal.'

Roberts coughed uncomfortably. 'Not absolutely, sir. It would be up to the man's ingenuity. I agree, however, that the chances of our man making a get-away after his attempt are certainly low. He would have to accept the risk.'

'You would never get anyone to volunteer for the mission,' replied Kylie.

A ghost of a smile hovered around Roberts's mouth. 'I have someone in mind, sir. It's in the report.'

Kylie drew his brows together. 'You've thought this out pretty carefully, haven't you?'

'Yes, sir.' Roberts spoke with an assurance which momentarily irritated Kylie. He jabbed savagely at the intercom. 'Gladys, bring in some coffee and sandwiches, there's a love.'

He returned the switch to neutral and reached across for the file which Roberts held. 'I'm not promising, Austin,' he said slowly. 'Let's run through the details and see what you've come up with. If it sounds feasible then it would have to get clearance from Churchill himself. No one else could approve it. And Churchill will be a tough bird to convince.'

Roberts grimaced. 'I think he'll be convinced.'

Kylie's eyes narrowed. 'Then begin by convincing me, laddie.'

He let the file lie on his desk and stared at Roberts pointedly.

'Very well. Let's start by a brief outline of the plan. Objective, personnel and method. Firstly, objective. On April 20 Hitler will score a tremendous propaganda victory by parading as his personal bodyguard a group of die-hard British Fascists and social misfits, recruited into a military unit. Apart from the obvious ramifications, it will cause tremendous damage to our alliance with the Soviet Union, who are already suspicious of our intentions, believing that we might form a new alliance with Germany against them. Our objective is to discredit this group. It might also be a unique opportunity to get rid of the kingpin of the Nazi regime.'

Gladys came in with the coffee. Roberts paused awkwardly and waited until she left.

'The assassination of Adolf Hitler would shorten the war if not end it.'

Kylie tapped at his desk with a pencil. 'That, laddie, is a hypothesis. Can you substantiate it?'

'You've seen the reports, sir. The latest was Sir Heathcote Grey's assessment. We have had several meetings with German anti-Nazis and all are convinced that the Nazi regime would crumble once Hitler is eliminated.'

'Wishful thinking?'

Roberts shook his head. 'No. Although our intelligence reports lead us to believe that Hitler is partially insane, he exudes some weird fascination like . . .' he frowned trying to think of an analogy. 'Hitler is a queen ant with all his worker and soldier ants running around him. Once the queen is killed they are without purpose.'

Kylie snorted. 'It's not a very good simile, laddie, but I think I see what you mean.'

'Well, with the Nazis in disarray, the anti-Nazi groups could seize power, establish a government which would then sue for peace.'

Kylie grimaced encouragingly.

'Personnel? We need one man with certain qualifications: a man who feels he has not much to lose by undertaking the mission; a man who has confidence enough in himself to believe that he could bring such a mission to a successful conclusion.

45

However,' Roberts's mouth drooped a little, 'the man would have to be expendable.'

Roberts paused and when Kylie made no comment he continued.

'Method: the entire plan will depend on the ability of our man to improvise as the situation changes. Initially he would have to present himself to the German authorities, preferably on the Continent, as a deserter who wants to work for the Reich.'

'That alone will be difficult,' interposed Kylie. 'What makes you think the Germans would fall over themselves to rush him off to the British Free Corps?'

'It would be up to our man to tell his story well enough, and be manipulative enough, to get himself sent to join the British Free Corps before April 20. After our man is despatched to Germany, everything will be up to his capability, ingenuity and imagination. There will be no way in which we will be able to assist him. He will be entirely on his own.'

'What you are saying, Austin, is that everything will depend on this man?'

Roberts leant forward and tapped the file. 'I suggest you read my report, sir.'

'I still say you are crazy,' said Kylie, picking up the buff folder.

It was fifteen minutes before he spoke again.

'Crazy . . .' he muttered, 'but . . .'

He suddenly reached forward and took up a pen, dipping it in a pot of red ink. Over the folder he scrawled something and handed it back to Roberts. Roberts glanced at it. Kylie had written: *Operation Hagen: for immediate action.*

Roberts felt a twinge of excitement. 'You'll take it to Churchill?'

'No one else must know of this. All I hope is that you are right in your assessment of this man Collins. I can't say I like the sound of him from your report, but he certainly fits the plan.'

'We aren't supposed to like him, sir. Providing he carries out the job, we can think what we damned well like about him.'

Kylie grunted and reached out for the folder again. 'All right,

Austin. When I go to see the Prime Minister, I want you on hand.'

Roberts rose to his feet and turned towards the door. Just before he opened it, he paused and frowned at Kylie. 'Just one thing, sir. Why have you named the plan Operation Hagen?'

Kylie grinned abruptly. 'I thought you knew your Wagner's Ring Cycle, Austin? By all accounts, Hitler believes himself to be the handsome, tall blond Nordic hero Siegfrid. Well, Siegfrid was slain by Hagen.'

Charlie Collins grunted in pain as the staff sergeant's boot caught him on the thigh.

'Pick it up! Pick it up you bastard!' he heard the man scream above him.

On his hands and knees on the cell floor Charlie Collins grabbed at the spilled contents of his breakfast tray. It was not the first time that Staff Sergeant Murdoch of the Military Provost Staff Corps had performed this trick, had entered Collins's cell for morning inspection and found something to knock over so that he could put the prisoner on report. Murdoch was a sadistic little bastard, a tough-looking, red-faced Geordie. He stood over Collins, prison stick under his arm, uniform spotless and carefully creased, his peaked cap making him look taller than his five foot two inches. He grinned down at Collins viciously.

'This cell is disgusting! Disgusting! You're a pig, Collins. A pig! You and me will have to have a little talk about this down at the punishment block. Stand still, Brodie!'

Collins's cell-mate, Mick Brodie, a six-foot tall Dubliner, made a move to help Collins up. The staff's voice stayed him. He looked down at Collins with an imperceptible gesture of resignation.

Collins grabbed the tin mug, plate and fork and returned them to the tray, then placed the tray back on the table from which Murdoch had knocked it. Painfully he rose to his feet and regained his position of attention, thumbs pressed against the rough khaki trousers of his prison regulation uniform.

Murdoch pressed his sweaty face close to Collins's.

'You'll not last out your sentence here, you bloody coward!' His voice was soft and evil. 'D'you hear me?'

Collins focused his eyes on the man's MPSC cap badge and inwardly sighed. 'I hear you. Staff,' he said woodenly.

This was his fourth month in the Military Detention Barracks at Reed Hall Camp. Colchester. It seemed a lifetime and he still had eleven years and eight months to serve. Murdoch was right, He would never survive. Murdoch would see to that. The bastard had marked him out for a special case. The Military Detention Barracks was full of thieves, deserters, those who had gone Absent Without Leave for a variety of reasons, and those who had committed various breaches of military discipline punishable by varying sentences of confinement. Collins was the only prisoner convicted of mutiny – mutiny in the face of the enemy. He had originally been sentenced to death.

The memory of the hot, white brick building of the École Normale in Constantine. North Africa, swam into his mind. It was hot, unbelievably hot for an early November day, even in Africa. Tuesday, 2 November, 1943. The date burned itself in his memory. There had been five military judges seated at a long table. A lieutenant-colonel had been the senior presiding officer. They had marched him in and started reading a long indictment. Only towards the end of fifteen minutes of the officer's nasal treble did the realisation hit Collins that he was being sentenced to death by firing squad. Had he anything to say?

'I am no coward,' his voice was full of bitterness. 'It was the men who were betrayed by bloody supercilious officers . . .'

They forced him to march out before he had finished. They marched him down to the black, stifling cells beneath the old schoolhouse. There he waited for the officer to come with the blindfold, to lead him out to the baking concrete exercise-yard where six men with rifles would be waiting. The call never came. Instead, fourteen days after being sentenced, a young lieutenant came into his cell and started to read the indictment and the court-martial findings. It was a twenty-page document, he remembered.

'I've heard it all before,' Collins interrupted.

The young lieutenant looked shocked.

'Prisoner will speak only in answer to the officer's questions!' screamed a staff sergeant, face purple with outrage.

'I can only be hanged once,' retorted Collins.

The young lieutenant shook his head. 'If you would allow me to finish reading this,' he waved the papers at Collins, 'you will learn that your death sentence has been commuted. You are sentenced to twelve years' penal servitude . . . but the sentence will be suspended if you join another front-line unit and volunteer for hazardous duty. Naturally, you will loose your rank of sergeant and all back pay and privileges.'

The officer paused.

'Well, Collins, what do you have to say?'

'Answer the officer, Collins!' screamed the staff sergeant.

Collins stared for a moment and then chuckled. 'Stuff it!'

The lieutenant's face dropped.

'What?' The staff sergeant sounded as if he were exploding.

'I said, stuff it! I was not guilty of mutiny. The ones who should be punished are the officers who betrayed the men and misled them. If I accept this new sentence and volunteer for another unit, I would be admitting that I was guilty. Stuff your suspended sentence!'

Collins closed his eyes and gave an inward groan as the scene swam before him. Three, no, four months ago. A lifetime. How he wished that he had that choice now. He'd sooner be crawling around in the slime of some Italian field getting shot at than being cooped up in an icy cold cell with a sadistic little warder . . .

The butt end of the swagger stick caught Collins sharply in the stomach.

He gave an involuntary grunt of pain and nearly doubled up. Staff Sergeant Murdoch's voice was still soft.

'Stand up straight, Collins! Up straight when I talk to you!'

Painfully, Collins drew himself up.

'You were day-dreaming, Collins. Day-dreaming! Can't have that, you bloody little coward! Dumb insolence! Failure to obey an order! Oh my, we'll have to have you up before the assistant commandant, 'pon my word, we will. Cheer up, Collins. You've only just started here. Another few years and you'll be loving it . . . if you're still alive.' Staff Sergeant Murdoch chuckled as he turned and marched out of the cell.

Collins repressed an urge to hurl himself on the man, grab

him by the throat and throttle the life out of him. He swayed forward a fraction. Mick Brodie reached out a hand to check him.

'Jesus, man,' hissed the Irishman, ''tisn't worth it.'

Collins nodded. The Irishman was right. He had to wait for the right opportunity. Not now. Later. He was not going to last the full twelve years; he knew that. But if he was going to be pushed under by the likes of Murdoch then he was going to make sure that Murdoch went with him. He would bide his time.

Churchill leant back in his leather-upholstered swivel chair, his eyes closed, hands placed together, fingertip to fingertip. To Roberts he looked like a praying cherub. A cherub in a dark-blue, three-piece suit, a heavy gold watch-chain across his waistcoat, and a white spotted blue bow-tie almost hidden by his heavy jowls. He chewed on his cigar lugubriously, in a curious rhythmic motion.

Four men sat in the small, dark oak-panelled study at Number 10 Downing Street: the Prime Minister looking more like a caricature of himself than Roberts had expected; Kylie; Roberts; and the bespectacled Secretary of the War Cabinet, Sir Edward Bridges. Roberts knew Bridges to be possessed of an astute mind. The son of former poet laureate Robert Bridges, Sir Edward was one of Churchill's ablest advisors. There was an oppressive silence in the room, broken by the hollow ticking of a grandfather clock in the corner. Nothing had been said since the Prime Minister had closed the file marked *Operation Hagen*.

Roberts felt an overpowering desire to fidget.

'Gentlemen,' Churchill suddenly opened his eyes and Roberts found himself staring into those wide, bright eyes and felt like a rabbit before a snake. 'Gentlemen, I must confess that the news you bring me about this British Free Corps is abhorrent. Even if this unit does consist only of a few riff-raff, it will do our cause great harm. I repeat, great harm. I find myself entirely in agreement with Colonel Robert's estimate as to the consequences if Goebbels' plan is allowed to reach a successful conclusion.'

The Prime Minister took his cigar from his mouth and laid it carefully in the ashtray.

'Let me be frank, gentlemen. We are having a hard time of it. General Alexander's army in Italy has ground to a halt, blocked by the Gustav-Cassino Line. General Lucas's Sixth Corps landing on the beaches of Anzio, which was designed to get around the Gustav-Cassino Line and secure Rome, has been less than successful. At the moment the Sixth Corps are pinned down on their beach-head, confronted by four Nazi divisions.'

He shifted uneasily in his chair.

'We have lost nearly seven thousand men at Anzio in the last few weeks. The Germans have made a skilful defence in Italy. We have to admit it. As for the other fronts, we are still menaced by U-boats in the Atlantic, Arctic and Mediterranean sea lanes. The Germans seem to have developed an air tube called a 'Schnorkel', which allows their submarines to remain under the surface for longer periods by supplying air to their diesel engines while submerged. Though we have entered on a heavy bombing strategy, Germany is still producing war material at an increasing rate. Her industrial production is still potent and the *Luftwaffe* has improved its defence capabilities. Germany can still call on a slave labour force the like of which has not been seen since ancient Rome. On the first of this month that damnable French traitor Laval announced that all Frenchmen between sixteen and sixty-five and all French women between eighteen and forty-five are to be conscripted for work in Germany.'

He pulled a face.

'This morning I had an audience with His Majesty. The King was very perturbed at the continuing German air-raids. I could offer no reassurance. This month in London alone we have lost 961 civilians killed as a result of enemy air-raids, with another 1,712 seriously injured. Those are the heaviest civilian casualty figures since May 1941.'

Churchill picked up his cigar and relit it.

'The war is still far from a decisive end gentlemen. We are only just beginning to go on the offensive. At this time we have one million American troops on this island who, along with our boys and other Allied contingents, are waiting for the invasion of Europe. I promised Stalin and Roosevelt in December that

51

the invasion of Europe would take place in May. Time is short. Millions of lives may still be lost. I would do anything to bring this conflict to a swift victorious conclusion.'

He gazed directly at Kylie. 'If you please, Brigadier, explain the reasoning behind your plan more fully.'

Kylie shifted his weight and leant forward. 'We believe that this is a feasible plan, sir. One that has a strong possibility of success. Even if the prime objective fails it would at least discredit the British Free Corps and put a stop to the grandiose schemes of the traitor Amery.'

Churchill sighed deeply. 'Ah, yes, Amery.' His voice lowered as if he were speaking to himself. 'Poor Leo. He wanted the War Office. He was the best man for the job. Yet when I formed the Coalition Government I had to turn him down and give him the India and Burma Office. We both knew why. His son has broken Leo Amery's heart. Poor Leo, poor Bryddie, too.'

Sir Edward spoke for the first time. 'At least Leo's second son, Julian, is distinguishing himself in the forces, Winston. He'll make a fine politician one of these days.'

There was an awkward silence. Churchill glanced up, became aware of their gaze and grunted. 'Sorry, gentlemen. Let's get back to the business in hand. If Hitler were eliminated, you are relying exclusively on opposition to the Nazis within Germany. Does such resistance exist? I will admit, Kylie, from the reports of your department in recent years, I am prepared to accept that certain individual, highly placed officers in the German armed forces are disaffected.'

'That is so, sir,' agreed Kylie. 'You recall that last year Admiral Wilhelm Canaris, chief of the *Abwehr*, made contact with us to discover what the terms of an eventual peace treaty would be between the Western Allies and a Germany free of Hitler.'

Churchill nodded.

'I told Canaris then, and I tell any German dissidents now, that we must have an unconditional surrender.'

'And now Canaris has been removed from his position,' Roberts could not help interrupting. 'The function of the *Abwehr* has been absorbed by the *Reichssicherheitshauptamt*, Himmler's Reich Central Security Office. Canaris has been given some empty title at the Office for Commercial and Economic Warfare, where he can do no harm. Had he received encouragement, he might have been a key man in the formation of an anti-Nazi coup. Now he has no power.'

Churchill swung round on Roberts and smiled crookedly. 'Are you telling me what my policies should be, young man?'

'No, sir,' Roberts said lamely. 'But it just seems to me . . .'

Churchill waved him to silence.

'Foreign Minister Eden is inclined to dismiss all ideas about a German resistance as pie-in-the-sky. I must confess that I find the idea of the anti-Nazis being strong enough to overthrow Hitler as somewhat remote. Hitler appears to hold a unique place in the minds of the German people. All the evidence indicates that as the road the Third Reich has chosen to follow becomes more difficult, he is able to rouse his people to stouter efforts.'

The Prime Minister paused and glanced back at the folder before him.

'The proposal for assassination has come up before. Each time my advisors have argued against it, feeling that it would be undesirable from our point of view because it would make a martyr of Hitler and strengthen the fanaticism of the German people.'

'I disagree . . .' Roberts coloured, embarrassed by his outburst.

The Prime Minister turned his bright eyes on him. 'Go on. You'd better have your say.'

'Sir, while Hitler is alive there will be no surrender of Germany. He has made it clear on many occasions. He has said that he will never allow a capitulation. If Germany were to be destroyed, he has promised to drag the world down into the flames with it. He will fight as long as he is alive with any weapon he can get hold of. Our reports indicate that once he is convinced that he cannot win, he will probably lead his troops in battle in order to achieve his heroic fantasy of immortality. From our point of view, that end would be more dangerously romantic and more of the stuff that martyrs are made of.

'Being a psychopath we know that immortality is one of his dominant motives. If he doesn't die in battle he will stage some form of dramatic suicide to bind his people to him, to that

53

Siegfrid image he is fond of. It will be done with Hitler's usual flare for the theatrical and it might establish his legend so firmly in the minds of the German people that it could take generations to counteract it. If Hitler is killed now, the Nazis will crumble. Germany will sue for peace. We could shorten the war by at least a year and save countless lives.'

As Roberts paused, Kylie came to his support. 'I must say, sir, I am in agreement with Colonel Roberts. Hitler will certainly see Germany destroyed stone by stone before he surrenders. Every statement he has made, public and private, is an endorsement of this attitude. He has ordered that no city be left standing in Germany to fall into the hands of the Allies except as a heap of rubble. It will be a long war of attrition.

'We have a unique opportunity to circumvent this. I think Colonel Roberts's plan is workable.'

Churchill gazed directly at Roberts. 'And you believe this man Collins is capable of accomplishing such a task?'

'Yes.'

'But Collins is serving twelve years' penal servitude for cowardice in the field,' Sir Edward Bridges pointed out, making his second contribution to the conversation.

'There were mitigating circumstances,' Kylie said. 'In time of war those circumstances had to be ignored by the court martial. In time of peace there might have been an enquiry as to the conduct of the officers in charge.'

'Explain, Brigadier,' invited Churchill.

'Collins was one of those who took part in the Salerno Mutiny last year.'

'Refresh my memory on the details,' the Prime Minister said.

'The mutiny occured in September among men of the 50th Tyne-Tees Division and the 51st Highland Division. The divisions were part of Montgomery's 8th Army. I might emphasise this point, sir, because it is important to recall that General Montgomery is very ardent about unit and regimental loyalty.'

The Prime Minister inclined his head but said nothing.

'Men of these two divisions had been resting at a Transit Camp in Tripoli, awaiting return to their divisions. The order came for them to embark and the officers in charge told them that they were rejoining their units. Instead, sir, the ships were ordered to Salerno in Sicily to reinforce General Alexander's 5th Army. At no stage were the men informed of their real destination until they arrived on the Salerno beach-head. Then they were abruptly told they had been transferred to other units. Three hundred of them sat down on the beach and refused to move.

'The men told the officers that they were perfectly willing to fight, but under their own officers and in their own units. Sir Richard McCreery addressed them and told them the seriousness of their conduct. The Mutiny Act was read to them. In the end, 192 men refused to obey orders. They were shipped back to North Africa and court-martialled. One hundred and ninety-one men were found guilty. The private soldiers were sentenced to seven years' penal servitude, the corporals to ten years', and the sergeants were sentenced to death. The death sentences on the sergeants were commuted to twelve years' penal servitude, suspended if they were willing to volunteer for hazardous duty in front-line units. Only one sergeant refused.'

'Your man Collins?'

'Exactly so, Prime Minister. Collins believed himself to be in the right. Nothing makes a man more obstinate than a conviction that he is right when all around him disagree. He claimed that the mutiny was a protest at bad officering.'

Churchill chewed at his cigar. 'It was a damned mutiny whatever the reason,' he observed, 'and mutiny in time of war is a serious business.'

He paused a moment and then sighed. 'Tell me, what makes you think Collins would volunteer for this mission when he did not volunteer for hazardous service four months ago?'

Kylie pulled a wry face. 'I think four months in a Military Detention Barracks may have helped him reflect on his attitude. Colchester is hardly a rest camp.'

Churchill snorted and turned to Sir Edward Bridges with raised eyebrows. The Secretary to the War Cabinet nodded slightly.

'Very well, gentlemen.' The sudden decisiveness of the Prime Minister startled them. 'Go ahead. Hitler has thrown down a gauntlet which we must take up. I want the Free Corps discredited and if you can hand me a Hitler-free Germany to deal with, I shall not complain.'

He rose to his feet, a pugnacious figure, hands on hips, his chin thrust aggressively forward. They rose with him.

'I want action on this,' he said, handing Kylie the folder. Then he suddenly smiled. 'Are you aware of the date, gentlemen? This is Tuesday, 29 February.'

Roberts had forgotten it was a leap year.

'They say that 29 February does not count. From this moment, you are on your own. Operation Hagen is not official. There will be no minutes or record of this meeting, nor of our discussion. Do I make myself clear? I have already forgotten our conversation. It did not take place.'

Chapter Six

The next morning at 6.00 a.m. Roberts climbed into his battered pre-war Austin and, leaving his Maida Vale house, he turned north to join the North Circular and pick up the road to Colchester. It was a cold, blustery March morning and not yet light. Roberts reminded himself that it was the first of the month. He pulled a face. 'White rabbits,' he muttered aloud. 'By God, we'll be needing them!'

'Are you awake, Mick?' demanded Collins, shivering in spite of the two prison regulation blankets in which he lay cocooned on the hard bunk of his unheated cell.

Mick Brodie grunted in the darkness on the other side of the cell.

'Sure, and how can any man sleep in this cold?'

'Got a gasper then?'

There was a scrabbling noise and something landed on the blankets near his hand. Collins reached out and felt the cigarette packet. It contained one cigarette.

'That your last, Mick?'

'God look down on me, but I'm not that stupid,' replied the Irishman.

Collins searched for matches and lit up.

'You're a bloody stupid man, Mick,' he said, exhaling the smoke.

'I've been called worse,' agreed Brodie affably. 'But what makes you think so?'

'Ireland is neutral in this war, isn't it? So what are you doing here?'

'The Provost Marshal tells me that I'm here for maliciously wounding a Military Policeman. I wouldn't know. I was drunk at the time.'

'No, you idiot,' grunted Collins. 'What are you doing serving in the British Army if your country is neutral?'

'Oh,' the man paused. 'Well, Dev's neutrality may be a fine thing but it doesn't supply jobs in Clondalkin, does it?'

'What?'

'Clondalkin, where I was born and bred. Now the British Army offers you a bit of security, doesn't it?'

Collins grunted.

'I still say it's stupid, volunteering to fight someone else's war. God, if I were Irish . . .'

'You'd what?' prompted Brodie, with a cynical laugh. 'You'd be starving to death in a nice neutral Dublin slum, eh?'

'Well, this isn't my idea of an easy life, Mick.'

'You'll get used to it. I've done twelve months here. The first twelve months are the worst.'

'You know as well as I do that I won't last twelve months. Not the way that bastard Murdoch keeps after me.'

'Murdoch? Aye, the poor wee mannikin. He has a particular beef about you. He's probably upset because you were the things he can't be.'

'What do you mean?' Collins was interested.

'You were a sergeant. You won a Distinguished Conduct Medal and a Military Medal. Then you threw it all up and were sent down for cowardice in the face of the enemy.'

'Mutiny,' corrected Collins.

'Whatever,' agreed Brodie. 'Murdoch is going to take it out of you for that. When the novelty wears off he'll let you alone.'

Collins shook his head in the darkness.

'Murdoch isn't going to let me last a few months. Look what happened to Forester, poor bastard. He died in the hospital wing a week ago. Pneumonia, my eye! He was kicked to death by Murdoch and his cronies because he was a bloody homosexual. Then there was that man Aitkins. He hung himself in his cell not long after I arrived. Murdoch was after him. I tell you, Mick, I'm not going down the same path. Either I'm going over the wall or I'm getting Murdoch before he gets me.'

'Whist, man!' There was concern in Brodie's voice.

'Straight, Mick. If I could find a way out of this prison, I'd be away.'

He heard Brodie turn on his mattress.

'You wouldn't get far. Where could you go?'

Collins sighed and stubbed his cigarette out on the floor by his bedside.

'I'd try for a neutral country, I suppose. Spain . . . why not Ireland? Yes, Ireland.'

Brodie laughed.

'Now don't let the British propaganda fool you. Old Dev might be keeping Ireland neutral, but it's a biased neutrality. Allied pilots who get shot down in the Twenty-Six Counties can slip over the border while everyone looks the other way. The bloody Germans wind up in the Curragh internment camp. If a British Army deserter even made it to Ireland, the *Gardai* would round him up and send him back to Churchill with gift-wrapping.'

Brodie fell quiet.

'Yet,' he said after a while, 'yet if you could get the right papers. If you had an Irish travel document, a passport . . .'

Collins turned and stared in his direction. 'Yes?' he prompted.

'Well, it might work. You could claim you were of Irish parents, born and brought up in England, but a citizen of the Free State nonetheless. You don't even have to change your name – Collins, why, you could be a relative of the Big Fella, Michael Collins himself.'

'Whoever he is,' replied Collins.

'You're a terrible ignorant man,' said Brodie in the darkness.

'Anyway,' Collins pressed him, 'where would I get such papers? I couldn't walk into the Irish Embassy, or wherever, and demand a passport. They wouldn't accept my word.'

There was a pause before Brodie spoke.

'Are you serious, you're not fooling? You really are going to try to get out of here?'

'You watch me,' replied Collins fervently.

Brodie's voice was quietly serious. 'Then listen to me. Do you know London?'

'I've lived there.'

'London's the place to make for. A big anonymous city,' observed Brodie. 'Head for Willesden Lane in Kilburn. That's north . . .'

'I know it,' interrupted Collins.

'There's a pub on the corner of Willesden Lane and Kilburn High Street. Just past the pub is a newsagents' shop. Go in there and ask for Murphy. Say, Cousin Connie from Ballymurphy sent you. Got that? Cousin Connie from Ballymurphy. It will cost you a few quid but you'll get a travel document to get to Ireland.'

Collins frowned. 'Who's Murphy?'

Brodie made a whistling sound through his teeth. 'Now that you shouldn't be asking. Let's say that he's a man with connections, if you know what I mean. And don't ask me how I know. And for the sake of the Holy Virgin, don't ever say it was Mick Brodie who told you.'

Collins nodded in the darkness.

'Cousin Connie from Ballymurphy,' he whispered softly. 'I'll remember that, Mick.'

'Yeah, but you have a little problem first . . . getting out of . . .'

There came a rattle at the cell door. The light flashed on with blinding intensity. 'Up! Up! Up!' screamed a voice.

Staff Sergeant Murdoch stood framed in the doorway watching with a smile as Collins and Brodie tumbled from their bunks.

'Prison Regulation 672,' he smiled. 'Inspection of cells.'

Collins fought to control his temper. There had been too

many spot inspections of his cell. No one else's cell was turned over as many times as his.

Murdoch crossed to Collins' bunk, his glittering eyes swept over it and alighted with grim satisfaction on the butt of the cigarette which Collins had just stubbed out in the darkness on the floor. He let out a long, slow sigh.

'What is that, Collins?' he asked softly.

Collins moaned inwardly.

'Do you hear me, Collins?'

'Yes, Staff,' he replied.

'Well?'

'It's a cigarette butt, Staff.'

'Prison Regulation 714: item, prisoners may not smoke in their bunks; item, prisoners may not deface prison property; item, prisoners found guilty of such breaches of regulations shall serve a minimum of forty-eight hours in solitary confinement.'

Murdoch chuckled softly. 'Right, Collins.' There was an almost endearing quality to his voice. 'We are going to have a nice quiet talk together down in the punishment block. Get your things – double quick!'

Roberts sat at ease in the assistant commandant's chair and pulled thoughtfully at his pipe. The assistant commandant, Major Beeston, had vacated his office to Roberts after he had read swiftly through the letter of authorisation which Roberts had handed him. Beeston had paled visibly on seeing the headed note paper from Combined Operations Headquarters, 1a Richmond Terrace, Whitehall. He had positively fawned when he saw Lord Louis Mountbatten's signature at the foot of the letter.

Beeston was an elderly, officious little man, a career soldier with little ability who had been passed over several times for promotion. Eventually he had transferred to the Military Provost Staff Corps, the smallest corps in the British Army. He had thought promotion in a small corps would come easier; he was wrong. He hated his job, hated his staff, and hated the prisoners. He preferred to leave everything to his RSM. He had positively backed from his office before Roberts at the sight of the authorisation papers.

There was a tap at the door.

Roberts removed his pipe and called: 'Come!'

The prisoner and escort marched in, quick time, and came to a noisy halt to the scream of the perspiring staff sergeant in charge.

'Prisoner 878549, Collins, Charles, sah!' screamed the staff sergeant.

Roberts found himself wondering whether the wooden floor had been splintered by the crashing of their boots.

'Very good, Sergeant,' he said softly. 'Dismiss the escort. You may go.'

'Sir?'

Roberts glanced up at the tone of astonishment in the staff sergeant's voice. He found he disliked the man intensely; a pudgy-faced individual with a pencil moustache.

'Thank you, Sergeant, you and the escort may fall out,' repeated Roberts. It was then he glanced at the prisoner.

Charlie Collins was about thirty years old, with a broad, well-set face and a strong jaw, curly brown hair and eyes that were probably light brown. He could not be sure because they were puffy and swollen. Blood trickled from a gash along one eyebrow and oozed from the corner of his mouth.

'What the hell happened?' Roberts snapped in surprise.

'Accident, sir,' replied the staff sergeant. 'Prisoner fell down the stairs. Now then, Collins, tell the officer.'

Roberts made an impatient gesture. 'What's your name, Sergeant?'

'Murdoch, sir.'

'Well, Sergeant Murdoch, do not take me for a fool!' His voice was cold, angry. 'Take this man out, get him cleaned up and return him here without an escort. Do I make myself clear?'

'Sir!'

'At once!'

'Sir!'

Controlling his anger, Roberts watched the prisoner and escort wheel out of the room. It took him some time to calm down. Ten minutes went by before there was a tap at the door. This time Roberts opened it. Staff Sergeant Murdoch, the prisoner and escort stood outside.

'I thought I told you to dismiss the escort?' growled Roberts.

Murdoch smiled with self-satisfaction. 'Prison Regulation 347, sir: prisoners must be escorted at all times.'

Roberts realised that the bloody man was challenging him. Probably too used to getting his own way with Beeston. There was a smirk on the staff sergeant's face. 'I gave you an order, Sergeant.'

'I can only obey such an order from the commandant or his assistant, sir.'

Roberts gazed at the man for a moment. 'Very well, Staff Sergeant,' he said evenly. 'Come in.'

Frowning, Murdoch followed him into the office and watched him pick up a telephone.

'Give me Major Beeston,' he snapped into the instrument. 'This is Colonel Roberts.'

Beeston came on the line almost immediately. His voice was worried and breathless. 'Everything all right, sir?'

'No, it bloody well isn't. I have here a Staff Sergeant Murdoch who prefers not to obey orders. Now I want you to tell him that he is in no position to refuse an order given by me. I further want you to instruct him that he is guilty of gross insubordination and that you will be relieving him of all duties pending a disciplinary hearing. Do I make myself clear?'

For a moment Beeston spluttered. Behind Roberts, Staff Sergeant Murdoch looked absolutely stunned.

'There must be some misunderstanding. Murdoch is a good man, first rate . . .' Beeston was saying.

Roberts interrupted him. 'I may well be contemplating a more serious charge of ill-treatment of prisoners. Is that also understood?'

He turned and shoved the telephone receiver at Murdoch. The staff sergeant placed it cautiously to his ear and listened white-faced. When he put it down, Roberts smiled grimly.

'Get out of here, Sergeant,' he said softly. 'And send Collins in as you go.'

Staff Sergeant Murdoch turned to the door.

'Murdoch!' snapped Roberts.

The man turned. He was still dazed.

'Aren't you forgetting something?'

The staff sergeant hesitated, then drew himself up and executed a brisk salute.

A moment later Collins entered the room.

Roberts re-seated himself behind the desk and gestured to the vacant chair before it. The marks of Collins's accident still showed plainly, although the blood had been cleared up. Roberts tossed a packet of Players across the table and a box of matches.

'How do you feel?'

Collins grimaced. 'I'll survive.' He lit up and exhaled with a deep sighing noise.

Roberts examined him for a while. He liked what he saw in the rugged, almost ugly-featured face of the man. There was an intelligence, a quick wit. The reports showed that Collins was a man with the ability to improvise.

'You've had a rough time.'

It was a statement. Collins merely shrugged. Roberts waited a moment and then went on.

'You are a Yorkshire man, born in Bridlington, I believe?'

'It's in my records,' grunted Collins.

Roberts let himself smile. 'Indulge me a little and the time will pass more quickly.'

'I'm not too worried about that. I have quite a lot of time to spare.'

There was no humour in his voice.

'Quite so,' acceded Roberts. 'You enlisted in the Army in 1938 and qualified as a German interpreter. You spent a year in Germany working in Hamburg and then did an Army crash course in the language. However, you asked for a transfer to an active service unit in January 1940, and were sent to France. At Dunkirk you won a Military Medal. You became a weapons instructor and joined the 50th Tyne-Tees Division and served in the 8th Army during the North Africa campaign, where you won the Distinguished Service Medal. You became a sergeant and last year turned down a commission.'

Collins stared at him coldly. 'I was then found guilty of mutiny at Salerno and am now serving twelve years' penal servitude,' he said bitterly. 'And that is the end of my military career.'

'As you said, Collins, it's all in the record.'

'So what's this about?'

Roberts reached for his pipe.

'Don't you ever call anyone "sir" these days?' he asked mildly.

'So what is this about, *sir*?' repeated Collins.

'Indulge me a little further, Collins. You were born in Bridlington but you grew up mainly with an uncle and aunt in West Hartlepool. Is that right?'

Collins hesitated. 'My dad was drowned when I was nine. He was a fisherman. My mum died not long afterwards. Yes, I grew up in West Hartlepool.'

'Not many jobs there in the early 1930s – those were the days of the hunger marches on London. You moved to London after you left school. You showed quite a lot of promise at school. They wanted you to stay on, perhaps go to university.'

'That's a rich man's game,' replied Collins. 'University for a poor working-class lad? Get away out of that!'

'So you moved to London looking for a job?'

'Where's this leading?'

'A little more patience. You were unemployed in London for some time. Then you joined Oswald Mosley's British Union of Fascists.'

Collins eyes widened. 'So that's it?' he breathed. 'Are you trying to say that I'm an active Fascist now? Is that it? Are you trying . . .'

Roberts held up a hand. 'I'm not saying anything. I just want to make sure that I have the facts right. You joined the BUF?'

'Lots of people did,' replied Collins. 'Thousands of people. Mosley offered us easy answers to our problems at that time. People always want easy answers.'

'You contributed a few articles to the BUF official journals – *Action* and *The Blackshirt*?' pressed Roberts.

'Yes. I was about twenty-one or two at the time.'

'Then in late 1936, just after Hitler re-occupied the Rhineland, you went to Germany, to Hamburg.'

'It was an exchange visit between members of the German National Socialist Party and the BUF,' explained Collins. 'When I arrived in Hamburg, I took a job in the docks and worked there for nearly a year.'

'And learnt passable German?'

'Enough to get by. One had to.'

'Then you returned to England? You left the BUF?'

'I'd had enough of Mosley by that time. For a short time I joined the British National Socialist League, a breakaway group formed by William Joyce, and helped to distribute Joyce's magazine *The Helmsman*. Then I got tired of Fascism altogether. I began to realise what was really going on in Germany, Italy and Spain.'

'And you joined the Army?'

'There was bound to be a war soon. Anyway, it was hard to get a job in civvy street.'

Roberts paused and flicked through the file. He knew Collins's record off by heart. There was really no need to ask the questions, but he wanted to build the man up slowly.

'So now you are serving twelve years'?'

Collins eyed the colonel narrowly. He said nothing.

'And you still claim Salerno was the fault of bad officers?'

'For what it's worth – yes.'

'You were given a choice back in November: serve the sentence in full or volunteer for hazardous duty. Tell me, Collins, if you still had that choice what would you do?'

A sudden curiosity seized Collins. What was this colonel getting at?

'There wouldn't be a choice,' he said bitterly. 'Screws like Murdoch will ensure that I don't last out my sentence. And hazardous service usually means suicide missions with the commandos. Still, on reflection, it would be better to have a fighting chance outside than being cooped up in here.'

Roberts nodded slowly. He got to his feet and walked to the door, opened it and peered into the corridor. Then he turned back.

'Can we speak in German?' he asked, breaking into the language.

Collins frowned. 'Very well.'

'I have a proposition for you.'

Speaking slowly and carefully, Roberts began to outline Operation Hagen. Collins did not say a word throughout Roberts's recital.

'If you volunteered for this job, Collins, you would naturally be completely pardoned, reinstated with your rank and full remission of pay and privileges.'

Roberts paused. For some time he and Collins gazed directly into each other's eyes.

'You're mad,' said Collins, reaching for a cigarette and lighting it.

'Probably,' admitted Roberts.

'You're really serious?'

'Never more so.'

'It's crazy, ridiculous!'

'No more crazy than a lot of things being done in this war.'

'It's also suicidal.'

'That depends on the ability of the man undertaking the mission and his capability as an improviser and extemporiser.'

Collins stared hard. 'By God! You *are* serious.'

Roberts nodded. 'Well?'

'What made you pick on me, Colonel?'

'You're the perfect choice. There would be no need to invent a cover story for you. Your membership of the British Union of Fascists and the fact that you have been sentenced to twelve years' detention would make you an ideal candidate for the British Free Corps.'

'You make the whole thing sound easy.'

'The best plans are those that require a minimum of invention.'

'But surely more experienced agents would be better?'

'There's no one with your qualifications, your background and knowledge as a weapons instructor.'

Collins grimaced. 'You really expect me to be able to find a way of assassinating Hitler?'

Roberts nodded.

'You are out of your mind and so is anyone else who believes in this cock-eyed idea.'

There was another silence. Collins toyed with his cigarette and then stubbed it out in the ash tray savagely.

'I'll go,' he said abruptly.

Roberts fought to control his feeling of excited elation. 'Why?' he forced himself to say. 'Why, if you feel that it is such a crazy idea?'

Collins gave a wry grimace. 'I'll go because I want to get out of here. I'll go because I haven't anything else to do.'

Roberts broke into a crooked smile. 'Well done, Collins . . .'

Collins groaned. 'Spare me that shit. Don't give me lectures about king and country. I don't have a choice. Anyway, what makes you think you can trust me? What if I simply went as far as a neutral country and put my feet up for the rest of the war?'

Roberts chuckled softly. 'As you say, Collins, you don't have a choice. I think we understand each other?'

Collins nodded morosely. 'Yes, I bet you've thought out all the angles.'

'That's right. Now, all we have to do is arrange your escape from military custody. You will be taken under guard to London tonight. In the morning you will be brought to my office for a final briefing. On the return journey you will be allowed to elude your guards and arrangements will be made for you to stow away on a neutral ship for Sweden. From there you'll have to make your own way to Germany. I suggest via the German embassy in Stockholm. Then everything is in your hands. It will be up to you.'

Collins stood up and shrugged. 'You'd better keep Murdoch off my back until this evening,' he said. 'I fancy that little sod is thinking up something nice to repay himself for what you did to him.'

'Don't worry about Murdoch,' replied Roberts. 'I'll see you in London tomorrow.'

Collins flung up his hand in a casual salute, it was a mock gesture.

Roberts watched him leave with a sigh. It was all very well reading about someone on paper, assessing their character from official reports. Meeting them in the flesh was something else. He had certainly not misjudged Collins's intelligence. What worried him was the degree of Collins's anarchism. He should have known that no man who was fully incorporated into the ethos of the Army would have taken part in a mutiny. Collins was certainly not a 'yes, sir' and 'no, sir' soldier. He made up his own mind about things and went his own way. Wasn't that exactly the sort of man Roberts needed for the job? Exactly.

But it did not stop a feeling of unease growing in Roberts's mind. Roberts had worked everything out like a chess game, but it was hard to manipulate the pieces when one had a maverick on one's hands. Collins was a maverick. He hoped that he was not making a mistake.

Chapter Seven

The train had been delayed several times on its journey from Colchester. There was an air-raid alert at Chelmsford which proved groundless. It was not until 2.00 p.m. on Thursday, 2 March, that the train reached the outskirts of London. It had been an exhausting journey. A sergeant and corporal of the Military Police had collected Collins from Reed Hall Camp after supper, handcuffed him and taken him by truck to St Botolph's Station. Collins grinned at the poster which greeted them at the station entrance: *Is your journey really necessary*? Ignoring the antagonistic glances of the crowds, both civil and military, who thronged the station, he had been escorted to a third-class compartment with a sticker *Reserved for War Department Use*. The sergeant had pulled down the blinds and sprawled in a corner seat, unbuckling his webbing and taking off his battledress jacket. The corporal gestured to Collins's handcuffs.

'Wot abaht these, Sarge?' he demanded in an aggrieved Cockney voice.

The sergeant sneezed abruptly and fished for a handkerchief.

'Bloody cold,' he muttered. 'I should have reported sick. Lock his hands in front of him.'

Collins sighed. 'Have a heart,' he said. 'What happens when I want to go to the lavatory?'

'Just sing out, sunshine, and I'll take you myself,' smirked the sergeant.

The corporal took out a key from his battledress pocket and undid the cuffs, relocking them with Collins's hands in front of his body. Then the man sat back in a corner and drew out a dog-eared Edgar Wallace paperback and immersed himself in it.

Collins slumped in the third corner seat and glanced at the sergeant, who had deposited his jacket, cap and equipment on the luggage rack, and was preparing to sleep.

'Let's have a look at your newspaper, Sarge,' asked Collins.

The sergeant grimaced, took the newspaper he had bought at the station kiosk and threw it across. Collins eagerly scanned the pages. He hadn't seen a newspaper for months. There was not much that interested him. The Allied advance in Italy had been halted and the Germans were attacking the Anzio beachhead with heavy artillery. German tanks were preparing for a thrust designed to drive the British and Americans back into the sea. Things were not looking good. The main news, however, was the Soviet successes on the Eastern Front. In the north, they had ploughed through Estonia and cut off Germany's ally Finland. The newspaper gave the terms for a Finnish surrender and speculated on whether Finland would accept them or try to fight on. If Finland made a separate peace with the Allies, it would be a bitter blow for Hitler.

The train eventually started half an hour behind schedule and moved towards London with incredible slowness. The alert at Chelmsford delayed them a full hour-and-a-half. There seemed to be more delays every few miles. Just past Romford and into the eastern suburbs of London, they were delayed yet again. Abruptly the lights went out and the sergeant woke from his snoozing with a jerk. He leant across to the window, pulled the black-out blind and peered out.

'Another bloody alert,' he muttered.

The wail of the sirens signified the first alert London had had during the hours of midnight to dawn since 22 February. A group of enemy raiders had been spotted crossing the Kent coastline, making towards the capital. Night-fighter squadrons were scrambled, but the engagements which occured did not deflect the main German bomber force from dropping low over the silver ribbon of the Thames and following the moonlit path to the city's eastern suburbs. The anti-aircraft barrage started, spasmodically at first and then growing in intensity. Searchlights pierced the night sky with their brilliant white fingers. The aircraft dived low, red flares were dropped by the pathfinders, and then came the bombs, exploding across the city with streaks of red, white, orange and yellow. Most of the bombs fell on the outskirts and soon the raiders were turning for France. The barrage died away, the searchlights went out one by one. Soon the all-clear sounded.

The sergeant sat looking up at the sky.

Outside, they could see the flickering light of several fires which marked the spots where the raiders' bombs had fallen. The eerie glow caused the sergeant's face to assume a satanic quality.

'Welcome to London,' he sneered. 'Wel—'

The whistling scream was not familiar, but some inner sense made them all throw themselves onto the floor of the compartment. The world suddenly exploded in a cacophony of sound and a blurr of vivid colours. Collins had a dim recollection of struggling against a terrific weight. Then everything went black.

When he came to, he was lying on his back, hands still cuffed, with part of the shattered compartment seat across his chest. Around him was thick acrid smoke which caused him to cough and feel sick. He could hardly see a foot in front of him. Then the smoke began to clear a little. The compartment no longer existed. It was a mess of twisted metal and broken wood. The flames from some nearby fire shot up in the night, lighting the scene like some illustration of Dante's *Inferno*. Collins became aware of distant noises. A soft wailing cry. A chorus of moans like the voices of the damned. A shrill scream. Shouting. A police whistle shrilling the air. He succeeded in pushing the seat from his chest and struggling into a sitting position. Next to him, the corporal was sitting with his head on his chest.

'Hey,' called Collins, 'for Chrissake help me out of this.'

The man did not reply.

Collins peered at him closely and cursed.

The eyes of the Military Policeman were wide and staring. A twisted, jagged piece of metal protruded from his chest. Around it was a dark wet stain.

Collins glanced round. There was no sign of the sergeant at all. The window by which the man had been sitting had shattered

70

into a million silver fragments and its frame was twisted into a grotesque shape. Only the luggage rack, still bearing the sergeant's cap, battledress and webbing, his MP's holster and pistol, remained to mark the place where he had been.

The shouting came nearer.

Collins did not know what motivated him at that moment – perhaps some inner impulse for survival. He scrambled to his knees beside the dead Military Policeman and, fumbling awkwardly, rummaged in the man's battledress pocket. The key to the handcuffs was easy to extract. It took a moment to unlock the cuffs. A moment more to tug off his military prison regulation fatigues blouse. Then he took the sergeant's jacket from the rack, slipped it on. It was not a perfect fit. The hat was a little on the small side. He slipped on the holster belt and webbing, feeling the weight of the pistol inside. A check of the jacket pockets revealed an identity card, travel warrants and a buff envelope with War Department markings and some money.

Collins felt no feeling of abhorrence nor of regret; just a curious, pulsating exhilaration.

Then he was scrambling out of the wreckage into a weird fantasy world.

The train was lit by a number of fiercely burning fires. Three entire carriages lay on their sides, twisted and mangled beyond recognition. Wreckage was strewn across the tracks. People were moving to and fro like sleepwalkers. Voices blended into a terrifying pandemonium.

He leapt from the side of the train onto the track and collided abruptly with an elderly Air Raid Precaution warden.

'Watch where you are leaping, young feller,' growled the old man indignantly, swinging a flashlight on him.

For a moment Collins was blinded by the light.

Then the ARP man spoke more kindly. 'Are you all right, Sergeant? Not hurt?'

'No, not hurt. What happened?'

He was confused, still trying to adjust to the bedlam around him.

'Bloody Jerry,' replied the ARP man. 'One of them was either very lucky or very clever. He let loose a stick of bombs and blew away most of these sidings. The train received a couple of direct hits.'

'Where are we?'

'Stratford Marsh Sidings not far out of Liverpool Street Station. I expect Jerry was going for the gas works over there at Bromley-by-Bow.'

The man grunted and turned away.

Collins remained still for a moment as people bustled around him. He began to edge away, away from the milling people, the clanging of approaching fire engines and the wail of a police siren. He walked slowly back along the railway tracks until he was swallowed up by the darkness. Then he began to clamber up the embankment. He reached the top with some difficulty but succeeded in hoisting himself over the stone parapet wall into the dark London street. He stood hesitantly, realising that it was cold. He tried to draw the sergeant's jacket more snugly around him, turned and set off at an easy pace along the street.

It was dawn when he reached the gates of a park. There were few people about – some railwaymen and a few civilians hurrying off to work. Outside the gates of the park was a kiosk selling tea to the early-morning risers. Collins sauntered across. A woman of indeterminable age, head wrapped in a scarf, wearing a siren-suit, with a cigarette in the corner of her mouth, grunted: 'Yes, love?'

Collins asked for a cup of tea and something to eat. He chose an apparently ancient cheese sandwich as the lesser evil of the choice offered him.

'Can you tell me where I am, miss?' asked Collins as he handed over the four pennies demanded.

The woman glanced at him suspiciously, but decided that he didn't look like the German parachutist the posters warned about.

'I was caught in the raid this morning and lost my bearings a bit.' explained Collins.

'Victoria Park,' she said.

'How's that?'

The woman removed her cigarette.

'This is Victoria Park, South Hackney.'

'Oh.' He only vaguely knew where Hackney was. He turned

72

and made for a bench near the park gates. He swiftly demolished his sandwich and began to sip his tea. As he was so doing he decided to take another look at the sergeant's effects. The buff-coloured envelope was a written order telling the sergeant to take his prisoner, Collins, C. Number 878549 to Kensington Palace Gardens and report to a Lieutenant-Colonel Roberts in Room 279. Collins stared at the paper for some while memorising the telephone number on the letterhead. Then he tore the paper into shreds and crumpled them into a ball, which he deposited in a litter bin.

What next? Yesterday he would have had no hesitation.

He started to feel automatically for a cigarette. The sergeant's jacket contained none. Still, he had some money. He walked back to the kiosk and asked for another cup of tea and a packet of cigarettes. 'We are only allowed to sell V-Brand to soldiers,' sniffed the woman.

Collins groaned. V-Brand were a cheap cigarette manufactured in India for the troops. For some time soldiers had been complaining that they were unsmokable and the Government had been promising to withdraw them.

'Better than nothing,' he grunted, handing over the money.

He was thinking that he would never have another opportunity like this. The perfect escape. But now what? 'Cousin Connie from Ballymurphy'. The line suddenly went through his mind. He smiled softly.

'How do I get to the nearest tube, love?' he asked the woman in the kiosk.

'The underground? The nearest is at Bethnal Green. It's quite a walk. You won't get a bus this early.'

'Which way?'

'Walk down this road, Victoria Park Road, turn left and down to Cambridge Heath and you'll come to the station.'

Collins acknowledged her directions with a wave of his hand.

Roberts sat at his desk, his face taut. He had just arrived at his office and found a hard-faced captain of the Military Police waiting for him. With him was a bemused-looking man in the remnants of military khaki, his face was cut and bruised and one arm was wreathed in bandages and held in a sling before him. The captain saluted and presented an identity card.

'Colonel Roberts? My name is Ashcroft. This is Sergeant Grant from Colchester.'

Roberts tensed.

'Yes?' He forced himself to sit back, his hands spread, palm downwards, on his desk.

'Sergeant Grant and Corporal Fenner were transporting a prisoner named Collins to London for an interview with you. Is that correct, sir?'

Roberts inclined his head.

'You probably know that London had a raid last night, sir. The train from Colchester was hit.'

Roberts's mouth tightened.

'And?'

'Corporal Fenner was among the eighteen fatal casualties. Sergeant Grant was wounded. I'm afraid there is no sign of your prisoner.'

Roberts did not relax. 'Can you be more explicit?'

The captain shrugged. 'They are still working on clearing the wreckage sir, but it seems the authorities are confident that all the bodies have been recovered and all the injured accounted for. When the bombs hit, Sergeant Grant reports that your man was cuffed. The handcuffs were found near Corporal Fenner's body. So far we have not been able to recover Sergeant Grant's jacket, cap, pistol and papers.'

Roberts groaned inwardly. 'You are saying that the prisoner, Collins, has done a bunk?'

'That's about the size of it, sir,' agreed the captain. 'He will be posted as a deserter and his description circulated to the local police. He won't get far, sir.'

'The best laid schemes o' mice and men . . .' Roberts hadn't realised that he had spoken aloud.

'I beg your pardon, sir?'

Roberts shook his head.

'One more thing, may I ask why Military Intelligence wanted to interview him, sir? Is it anything which might assist our tracing him?'

'I'm not at liberty to say, Captain,' Roberts shrugged. 'Off the record, though, it was a routine matter.'

Long after the captain and his woebegone sergeant had left, Roberts sat swearing softly to himself. Collins had obviously decided that his immediate freedom was a better option than the offer made by Roberts. Damn it! It meant that 'Operation Hagen' would have to be aborted.

The walk to Bethnal Green tube station had taken Collins some time. He had been thinking a lot. The inventory of the sergeant's jacket had brought to light £2 19s 6½d; he also had the sergeant's service revolver, spare ammunition and military passes. That was hardly enough to start a new life on. And he was going to be conspicuous walking round in an MP's uniform. By the time he reached the station foyer he had made a decision. It was not a new decision, just a confirmation of an old one. He found a telephone, inserted two pennies and dialled the number memorised from the letterhead. When a voice answered, Collins asked for Colonel Roberts in Room 279. The voice politely enquired his name. Collins paused and then smiled broadly.

'The name is Hagen.'

Roberts's voice came over the line within moments. 'Where are you?' he demanded.

'It doesn't matter, Colonel. I'm afraid your plan has been pre-empted. Instead of losing the MPs after your briefing, I've lost them now. Anyway, are we still in business?'

There was a pause. 'Yes. We will have to meet and discuss matters.'

'No,' Collins's voice was sharp, 'You said extemporisation was the key to success. The plan is already moving. We've just missed out a stage, that's all.'

'You're not prepared,' protested Roberts.

'I know enough.'

'You need contacts, money, enough to get you out of the country . . .'

'If I'm that well prepared, our friends will be suspicious,' replied Collins. 'Leave everything to me.'

'This is an open line. Can you ring me back in one hour on a number I shall give you? Don't write it down. Memorise it.'

'Go ahead.'

Collins repeated the number and hung up.

Roberts put down the telephone thoughtfully. He still did not trust Collins entirely. But Collins was right. His escape from the Military Police could not have been stage-managed more perfectly. If Collins was caught or surrendered now, then the entire operation would be placed in jeopardy. German intelligence would laugh themselves sick if they found out that Collins had escaped, given himself up and then escaped again to defect to Germany. The plan was already running. Extemporisation. Without improvisation, the plan would fail.

He glanced at his watch. He had to move quickly.

He could not interfere with the Military Police and civilian authorities in trying to recapture Collins. Indeed, it was an important part of the plan that they should make the effort. He hoped Collins would not slip up and get caught.

He rose and walked briskly along the corridor to Brigadier Kylie's office. He was tingling with excitement now. 'Operation Hagen' was on.

Chapter Eight

Collins made his telephone call one hour later from Kilburn Underground Station.

'Do you recall where the Free Corps is based from our talk yesterday?' asked Roberts. When Collins answered in the affirmative, he went on: 'Good. There is no need for me to repeat the name of the town. I am giving you a contact there should you need help. On no account write it down. Just commit it to memory. Can you do that?'

'Go ahead.'

'If you need help, call at the *Postamt* – the post office – and ask for Uncle Wilhelm. You are to say that you have a message from his daughter, Paula, in Hamburg. Your name is Otto. Got that?'

Collins repeated it.

'Is there anything we can do for you now?' asked Roberts.

'No.'

'You are on your own from here on.'

'I know that.'

'Good luck.'

Collins replaced the receiver and felt an almost frightening sensation of utter isolation. He was not fully sure as to why he was volunteering to go through with this insane job. He was certainly no patriot. Patriotism was all right so long as it did not conflict with his personal interests. When he was willing to give the matter thought, he felt it was as simple and as mercenary as the fact that it suited his long-term ambition. Collins had an ambition, which had been his motivating force since joining the Army. It was to save enough money to emigrate to Australia and start a new life, perhaps in the sheep-farming business. Ever since he joined up in 1938 he had been saving as much of his pay as he could afford towards the fulfilment of that ambition. He wanted to survive, even more so now. But going through with Roberts's crazy scheme was his only way of redemption, of salvaging his Army career so that he could leave, when the war was over, with his Army pay intact.

He turned into Kilburn High Street and walked briskly along to the junction with Willesden Lane. He was beginning to feel conspicuous in his ill-fitting Military Police jacket, cap and his cumbersome side-arm. Even the soldiers mingling past in the crowd gave him suspicious glances. But then Military Police did not endear themselves to the rest of the service.

He spotted the large Victorian pub at once and soon came upon the dingy newsagents' shop a little further on.

An old lady in hair curlers was serving behind the counter. He waited until her customer, a little boy purchasing a comic, had left the shop.

'Good morning,' he smiled. She made some inarticulate noise in response, so he pressed on: 'Is Mr Murphy around?'

The old woman's eyes narrowed. 'Murphy is it? Which

Murphy would that be now?' There was no mistaking the Irish accent in her slightly high-pitched voice.

'Murphy who has a Cousin Connie in Ballymurphy,' Collins replied. 'I have a message from her.'

The old woman's face showed no expression. She examined Collins intently before turning to the parlour door behind the counter.

'Tá fear airm anseo, a Pheadair!' she called.

Collins realised the old woman was speaking in Irish.

'Cad é sin?' wheezed a heavy voice and a red-faced man of middle age, running to fat, came to the door and examined Collins with bright, staring blue eyes.

'What is it?' he repeated, seeing Collins did not understand.

'Cousin Connie from Ballymurphy sent me.'

The man frowned, bit his lip. Suspicion showed on his face.

The old woman began to speak to him rapidly in Irish until the man turned and hissed at her: *'Go socair leat! Rachaidh díom nó déanfad é.'*

The woman shut up.

The man gestured Collins into the parlour. 'Come inside.'

'Are you Murphy?' asked Collins.

'Mise fear agat,' nodded the red-faced man. 'I'm your man. What's this about Cousin Connie?'

He turned and pulled a baize curtain across the open door between the small parlour and the shop beyond. Collins gestured, indicating the old woman in the shop.

'Can I speak freely?'

'You can,' Murphy assured him gravely, lowering his bulk into an old thread-bare armchair.

'I heard from one of the, er, the boys . . . that you would be able to help me.'

Murphy's face creased into a smile.

'Now I'm a helpful sort of person, but why would I be helping you?'

Collins paused, looking straight into the man's eyes. His scrutiny was returned without falter.

'I was a sergeant in the British Army. I was serving twelve years for mutiny. Last night I was being brought under escort to London. There was an air raid and a bomb hit the train before we got to Liverpool Street. In the mess I managed to grab a battledress off one of the guards and came here. I'm on the run.'

Murphy's expression of amusement did not change. 'And didn't your guard object?' he asked softly.

'He wasn't in a position to,' replied Collins. 'He was dead.'

Murphy's only reaction was a soft exhalation. 'And why would you come here? You're an Englishman, aren't you?'

Collins shrugged. 'I was sharing a cell with an Irishman who told me that if I ever got over the wall you might be able to fix me up with some papers.'

'What sort of papers?'

'An Irish identification card so that I could get to Ireland, a neutral country, and sit the war out.'

Murphy beat a tattoo on the side of his chair with his fingers, his bright blue eyes never leaving Collins's face.

'What's your name?' he asked.

'Collins. Charles Collins.'

'Number?'

'Prison number 878549.'

'What prison?'

'Reed Hall, Colchester.'

The man moved his head as if considering. 'The news about the train was on the wireless an hour ago,' he mused. 'You wait here. I'll have to check your story.'

Murphy levered his bulk out of the chair and left.

A full hour passed before he returned. Collins tried to control his nervous agitation, but he wondered how far he could trust this big impassive Irishman. Murphy re-seated himself and gazed thoughtfully at Collins before he spoke.

'The civil and military police are searching for you. It seems your story checks out.'

Collins blinked, wondering how the man could have found out so soon. 'So you want to get to Ireland?'

Collins nodded eagerly. 'I need some civvies, an identity card and a ticket to get me to Dublin.'

Murphy leant back in his armchair with his soft smile. 'And how much can you offer for that service?'

Collins bit his lip.

'I only have a few pounds on me. I stole it from the MP.'

Murphy raised his eyebrows and hooted with cynical laughter. '*Dia linn!* That's not going to get you far, boy.'

Collins thought rapidly. 'You can also have this uniform, the identity cards, the pistol, holster and ammunition. They ought to be worth something to someone in your line.'

Murphy said nothing but pointed towards the pistol and held out his hand.

Collins handed the gun over.

Murphy examined it almost with a fondness. He looked back at Collins and held out his hand again. Collins handed over the sergeant's military pass and identification papers.

'Ay,' Murphy said, almost to himself, 'these we can use.' He sat for a few moments deep in thought, then he looked up, his face wreathed in a smile.

'You're in luck, Charlie Collins. We'll do a swap. We'll supply you with a civilian suit, identification and arrange a nice passage to Dublin in return for these. But the passage you will have to work as a crewman on an Irish boat.'

Collins stilled his sudden elation.

Murphy got up and told Collins to follow him. He led the way up the stairs to an attic room. It was sparsely furnished – just a bed, dressing table and a couple of wooden chairs.

'Make yourself comfortable here for a while. The bathroom is at the foot of the stairs on the next floor. I'll be back when I can.'

After Murphy had gone Collins sat down on the bed and realised how tired he was. He had not slept properly for a couple of days. He lay back, feeling the comfort of a soft bed for the first time in years. He closed his eyes and was asleep immediately.

Collins awoke to find the old woman standing by his bedside holding a cup of tea.

'What's the time?' he demanded.

'Three o'clock in the afternoon, near enough,' grunted the woman.

Collins swung his legs off the bed, took the tea and began to gulp it.

'Has Murphy arrived back yet?'

The old woman sniffed. 'He's just come in. You wait here.'

It was not long before the rotund Irishman came in. He carried a battered suitcase which he set down on a chair.

'You're a lucky man, Collins,' he said. He pulled some papers from his pocket. 'Here's your new identity card.'

Collins took it. It was a small pale-green card marked in Irish and English characters: *Carta Sitheantais* – Identity Card. It was made out to the name of Pat Collins of Mount Sion Road, Drumcondra, Dublin. The photograph was blurred and hazy and could have been Collins or a hundred men of his build and age. His occupation was given as 'merchant seaman'. Murphy handed over another, smaller card.

'This is your Seaman's Union membership card, also made out to Pat Collins. This', he produced another card, 'is a pass into the Royal Victoria Docks. You'll see the papers show that you arrived in London on the Irish coaster, SS *Grainne,* two days ago. This paper shows that you have now signed on the SS *Ard Rí,* which is tied up at the Royal Victoria Docks and sails at midnight tonight. The first mate, Hennessy is expecting you.'

Collins was staggered at the efficiency of the corpulent Murphy. He had not believed such thoroughness could exist in what Mick Brodie had euphemistically called 'the organisation'. As if reading his thoughts, Murphy handed him a few more items.

'This is some padding, just in case. A couple of letters to Pat Collins, one from his mother, another from his girlfriend; an Irish ration book, not used since 28 February when the SS *Grainne* left from Cork. A copy of *Dublin Opinion* and fifteen shillings in Irish money.'

He jerked his hand at the suitcase.

'There's some civvies in there for you – socks, canvas shoes, trousers, two shirts and a jersey. I hope they fit. There's also a duffel coat.'

Collins had to admit that Murphy had a good eye for size. The clothes were not a perfect fit, but they certainly were better than the MP's jacket. While he was changing, Murphy sat rolling a cigarette.

'Don't you think you ought to throw away those identity discs,' he asked.

Collins hesitated, glancing down at his army dog-tags. 'I'll keep them,' he said. 'Sentimental reasons.'

He realised that he would need them if he was to convince the Germans.

'Your funeral,' observed Murphy. 'Do you have a good memory?'

'Yes.'

'Then I'll give you an address in Dublin to remember. Go there only if you need help desperately. Tell them I sent you. We can always do with the services of a trained military man in the organisation, if you understand me.'

Collins committed to memory the address Murphy gave him.

The Irishman gathered up the discarded uniform and pistol, and bundled them into the wardrobe. He had taken out the papers and stacked them neatly on one side. Now he removed the English money and handed it to Collins.

'You'll need this to get down to the Royal Victoria Docks. The docks are in the East End at Silvertown.'

He stood and let his critical eyes wander over Collins's appearance.

'You could pass for a Dublin bowsie,' he admitted, 'but I would try to lose that harsh English accent. You're supposed to be an Irishman, though you can use the excuse that you were brought up over here. God knows, there are plenty in the same boat. Still, it's better not to be noticed in the first place. Try to adopt an American drawl. Sure, some English don't know the difference.'

'I'll try.'

'Good. Can you find your way to Silvertown?'

'Yes.'

'And when you get there?'

'Go the the Royal Victoria Docks. Report to Hennessy, first mate on the . . . the . . .'

'The *Ard Rí.*'

'The *Ard Rí,*' repeated Collins. 'What does that mean?'

'The High King. You not knowing Irish might present a problem. An Irishman will spot you as English for sure. With an Englishman you could probably get away with gabbling any nonsense. They wouldn't know about the difference between Irish and Urdu. You'll have to be careful about that.'

Collins nodded.

'Right then, Collins, *beannacht Dé leat* – good luck. You should be in Dublin in ten days.'

Collins jaw dropped. 'Ten days?' He frowned.

'Sure, the *Ard Rí* is sailing tonight for Dublin via Lisbon.'

Chapter Nine

On the morning of Sunday, 6 March, the *Ard Rí* reached Lisbon and tied up alongside the Avenida Ribeira das Naus quay, near the Campo das Cebolas. She had made the journey in surprisingly good time for her age and the weather conditions. The ship was really a converted coaster of 823 tons, a utilitarian ship that was no more than a metal box with one boiler and engines aft, and a thick, high funnel rising from a grubby engine casing which also housed two full-time engineers and a small galley where a solitary cook-steward did his best to prepare meals for a ravenous crew. From the for'ard part of the casing to the short forecastle head, the steel deck was broken only by the superstructure of the bridge house, mounted on a little block of cabins and a small chart room. The *Ard Rí* was once a Newcastle coaster, 195 feet in length, with a cargo hold for'ard and one aft. On this trip she was running in ballast, ready to pick up a cargo in Lisbon.

Collins had not enjoyed close confinement with her Irish crew. Only the red-haired, boisterous first mate, Hennessy, knew for sure that Collins was a counterfeit Irish sailor and so went out of his way to ease the tension of the passage. Hennessy was a strange man. From the conversations Collins had with him he learnt that he had worked in 'the organisation' since the first flush of teenage political idealism; the idealism was still there but was tempered with cynicism born of political reality. He admitted that he had been part of the IRA contingent which had gone to Spain to fight for the Republic against Franco's Fascist Falange. He had been an officer in the International Lincoln Brigade. Returning to Ireland on the fall of the Republic, he had become a merchant seaman. Now and again the organisation asked him to arrange travel, usually for Irishmen who found it difficult to move about by more conventional methods.

Collins had presented him with a problem. He was certainly not an Irishman, nor did he know much about Ireland. Hennessy was obviously intrigued as to who Collins actually was, but while he led the conversation near the subject, he never asked outright. Anyway, Murphy had guaranteed that Collins was 'all right'. So Hennessy tried to help Collins, who had obviously never been on a ship before, by picking out easy jobs for him, so that his lack of seamanship would not be remarked on. Collins tried to keep his conversation to a minimum, but the other members of the crew of the *Ard Rí* were more open in their inquisitiveness than Hennessy. They joked about his English accent although he tried to deflect their more serious questions with the story of being English-born of Irish parents. Judging by their suspicious looks, it was obviously not a convincing performance.

One thing that was favourable was that at least he did not have to run the gauntlet of being interviewed by Flynn, master of the *Ard Rí,* who had been confined to his bunk since London with a bout of bronchitis. According to Hennessy, Flynn was one of the old school of sea captains, honest and no nonsense. If Collins had been unable to satisfy him as to his *bona fides,* Flynn would have put him off the ship. Collins hoped that Flynn's indisposition would continue. He had, however, already made up his mind to jump ship at Lisbon. Portugal was neutral enough and he could as easily make contact with the German embassy there as in Dublin.

The last day on board had been agony. As the ship began to cross the Bay of Biscay the weather turned bad; the vessel began to roll in heavy seas, with squalls blowing from the north. The crew had to fight hard to keep the old steel hulk on course. Eventually the storm blew itself out after they had weathered

Rias Gallegos and began to run down the Portugese coastline past Pontevedra. Finally, the rusting old ship rounded into the river Tagus, between the twin lighthouses at Deiras and Burgio.

Hennessy approached Collins as he stood at the rail gazing at the white expanse of buildings in the Portugese capital.

'Got a fag?' the first mate asked.

Collins pulled a pack from his pocket.

'We'll be here a couple of days picking up our cargo,' Hennessy volunteered as he lit up. 'Then we'll be heading straight for Dublin.'

'Any chance of stretching my legs ashore?' asked Collins.

Hennessy gave him a curious look. It was as if he had some intuition of what was passing through Collins's mind.

'We start loading tomorrow, so it would be best if you go now. Be back on board at nine o'clock.'

'Thanks,' Collins hesitated. 'Can you let me have some Portugese money?'

Hennessy sighed and thrust a hand into his pocket.

'Give me a ten-bob note,' he said handing over a collection of silver coins. He took the note, turned and strode back to the wheel house. For a moment Collins remained where he was, gazing at the opaque blue sky above the city. It looked so tranquil in the lukewarm March sun. It was hard to imagine that a war was raging elsewhere in the world. He gave a quick glance around the *Ard Rí*, turned and walked down the gangway.

Roberts looked up with surprise as Brigadier Kylie entered his office. It was unusual for Kylie to pay him a visit.

'Morning, Austin. Have you a drink hidden around here?'

Roberts rose, went to his filing cabinet and extracted a half-filled bottle of whisky and two glasses.

'Good show!' muttered Kylie. 'Four pounds and sixteen shillings a bottle nowadays. Daylight robbery.'

He waited while Roberts filled a glass and handed it to him.

Kylie sipped at it appreciatively.

'Fancy a flutter on the fight?'

Roberts frowned.

'The fight?'

'I thought you were a boxing man,' replied Kylie. 'The fight between Freddie Mills and the Canadian heavyweight, Al Delaney. I see it's been announced for next month.'

Roberts tried to turn his thoughts away from the war. 'And who are you putting odds on?'

'Mills, of course.'

'I would have thought you'd be backing Delaney after the way Mills beat your Scottish middleweight, Gilroy.'

'Aye, well, my Scots' pride did suffer but I admit Mills was the better man.'

He paused. Roberts sensed he had just been making conversation.

'Any news about Hagen?'

So that was it.

'No. I don't expect we'll hear from him until the job has been completed – one way or the other.'

'How do we know that he's doing anything more than simply lying low in London?'

'We don't,' said Roberts. 'That's the way this thing has to work. It's like blindfolding yourself and throwing a stone in the direction of a target, just hoping you hit it.'

'It's a hell of a way to fight a war.'

Roberts grimaced but made no reply. Kylie drained his glass and strode towards the door.

'Let me know if you do hear,' he said as he left.

Roberts too was wondering where Charlie Collins had got to. Was he still in London or making his way to a neutral port?

At that moment Collins was sauntering along the crowded Rua Aurea towards the Prace dos Restauradores in search of the German embassy.

At the main square he sighed. It was tiring walking around a strange city where he could not make himself understood. On an impulse he entered a bar and ordered a coffee – at least the word *café* was international. The coffee was strong, hot and black. He sipped it slowly.

'Speak English?' he suddenly asked the long-faced proprietor who was washing cups behind the counter.

The man looked at him with a frown.

86

'Little,' he replied slowly, almost distorting the word beyond recognition.

'Where is the German embassy?'

'What?'

'German embassy,' repeated Collins slowly. 'Where?' He made a gesture of looking.

The man shrugged. 'Wait, please. I find information.'

He ducked behind a beaded curtain at the back of the bar. After a few moments, Collins could hear his voice mumbling. A few more moments passed before the man reappeared.

'You wait,' he said with a lop-sided smile.

Collins sighed with impatience. Clearly the man had misunderstood. He drained his coffee and stood up. The man waved his hands in agitation.

'No. Wait. Soon come.'

Collins shook his head and turned towards the door. It suddenly opened and two uniformed Portugese policemen entered to bar his way. 'Papers please,' the elder of the two said in English. Collins noticed that the young one's hand rested lightly on the flap of his gun holster. He handed over his seaman's identity card. The policeman stared at it.

'English?'

Collins shook his head violently. 'No. Irish.'

The policeman looked puzzled. 'Please?'

'Irish seaman.'

The young man peered over his colleague's shoulder at the pass and they exchanged a few rapid words, with the proprietor of the bar joining in.

'Look,' interrupted Collins, feeling the situation was getting out of hand. 'I don't want to create a problem. Just tell me where the German embassy is and I'll be on my way.'

'Ah, embassy?' A look of comprehension spread over the elder policeman's face. He smiled and handed back the identity card. 'We take you to embassy. You come, please.'

With a feeling of relief, Collins followed them outside. They had a police car parked there, and the elder man motioned Collins to get into the back. Things were looking up. A free ride to the German embassy in a police car. Collins smiled his thanks.

The two policemen climbed into the front, the younger one

driving, and the car surged forward with a protesting squeal. Driving at a rapid pace, it was not long before they skidded through a gateway of a large building and halted in the court-yard. The elder policeman turned and smiled.

'This embassy.'

Collins grinned with relief. It had occured to him that the policemen might have been taking him to the station where he would have had to do a lot of explaining.

A tall, fair-haired civilian came down the steps of the building and bent down to speak with the elderly policeman. He had hard, angular features and a disdainful expression. His eyes were blue and cold. The stereotype German, Collins thought as he climbed out. A rapid conversation in Portugese took place. Then the fair-haired man moved away, the elderly policeman waved at Collins. With a crash of gears, the police car moved off.

Collins turned towards the man.

'Could you take me to your military attaché?' he asked in German.

'Certainly,' replied the man in the same language. There was a faint smile on his features. 'For what reason?'

'I would like to discuss with him the possibility of working for Germany.'

'Now that would be difficult, old boy,' the man's voice slipped into an English drawl. 'You see, those police wallahs thought you wanted the British embassy.'

Collins stared in disbelief at the fair-haired man. But there was no mistaking the hard glint in the man's eyes, nor the small snub-nosed automatic he held in his hand.

'All right, old boy,' the voice was harsh. 'Up the steps – quickly now!'

Weak with mortification, Collins obeyed.

They passed through a deserted hallway, along a corridor and into a small, darkened room. Shutters at the window stopped the light. Collins could make out a desk and a few chairs. The man crossed to the desk and switched on the desk lamp. He made no move to open the shutters nor did the aim of his automatic waver as he reached out to pick up a telephone on the desk.

'Ask Major Kenny to join me,' he said into the mouthpiece.

Turning to Collins, he motioned him to sit in the chair before the desk, then perched on the edge of the desk, one leg swinging and gazed thoughtfully at Collins.

'Well now, chummy,' he drawled, 'We've had some rum coves show up here but you take the biscuit.'

Collins tried to gather his scattered thoughts. 'I am an Irish citizen,' he said. 'You cannot hold me here by force.'

The fair-haired man pursed his lips cynically. 'You claim to be Irish? With an accent like that?'

'I spent most of my youth in England, like thousands of other Irish people.'

'Really? Then you'll have some identification, won't you?'

Collins handed over his papers. The man glanced at them, still keeping his automatic pointed in Collins's direction. As he examined them Collins heard the door open behind him. Someone entered and stood just behind his chair.

'Ah, Kenny,' smiled his captor, 'this gentleman mistook us for the German embassy. Wants to work for the Germans. Claims he is an Irishman, a citizen of a neutral country.'

There was no mistaking Kenny's Irish accent. 'Bloody republican, eh?'

The tall man smiled softly.

'Perhaps. I think his Irish citizenship is in doubt.'

'*An bhfuil Gaelige agat?*' demanded Kenny.

Collins hesitated.

'*Labhraim amach!*' snapped Kenny.

Collins could see no way out. 'I don't speak Irish. I was brought up mainly in England,' he said. 'I told your colleague that.'

'Oh, but you live in Ireland now?' asked the fair-haired man.

'I'm a seaman. I don't often get home. But you'll see from my papers that I live in Drumcondra.'

'Drumcondra, is it?' came Kenny's voice. 'You'll know Dublin well then? Whose statue is it on top of the pillar in O'Connell Street?'

Collins's bluff had been called.

'Come on man,' went on Kenny. 'Who is the *Taoiseach* of

89

Ireland? What party is in government? What colours are the Dublin trams painted? Name the Six Counties?'

The questions were shot at him with merciless persistence.

'I have been away for some time,' Collins tried desperately for a way out.

'All of eight days, according to your papers,' smiled the fair-haired man. 'Come on Collins, or whatever your name is, pull the other one.'

'He's no more Irish than Oliver Cromwell was,' sneered the man behind him. 'Who are you?'

'My name is Collins. I am an Irish citizen. You've no right to hold me,' Collins doggedly maintained.

'You can kiss my royal Irish arse,' replied Kenny.

The fair-haired man chuckled softly. 'You are the victim of what is termed "a fair cop", my friend. Now, there are two ways of finding out what you're up to. The easy way or the hard way, I don't mind. We have plenty of time, my loquacious Lothario.'

'I've told you who I am,' insisted Collins stubbornly.

'Righto!' The fair-haired man shrugged. 'We can easily check out your papers. Take him below, Kenny, let him cool his heels for a while.'

Resignedly, Collins allowed himself to be prodded by Kenny's pistol out of the room, down a corridor to a circular stairway which led down into the cellars of the embassy building.

'Here we are,' grunted Kenny, halting before a small cell-like room. 'You can make yourself comfortable in here.'

Obeying the motion of Kenny's pistol, Collins took two steps into the room. His captor swung the metal-studded door shut behind him. There was a clang of a bolt being driven home. In the utter darkness Collins started to swear softly to himself, overwhelmed by a terrible feeling of frustration and anger at his amazing, colossal stupidity.

The façade of 8 Prinz Albrecht Strasse, in Berlin, was little different from the imposing frontages of the other public buildings in that street and the nearby Wilhelmstrasse. Like the other buildings, it was pitted by shrapnel now and some of its windows were broken. The only difference between number 8 and the other buildings was the swastika flags which bedecked it and the black-uniformed *Schutzstaffel* SS guards who stood at the entrance like grim statues.

On the second floor of the building, in a luxurious office, a slight, narrow-shouldered man with a wispy moustache sat before a gigantic desk. His steel-rimmed spectacles perched on a face which had high Mongoloid cheekbones, a receding chin and sparse hair. His flesh was flabby, the skin livid, almost the colour of bee's wax.

Reichsführer Heinrich Himmler was the most feared man in Germany – head of the SS and lord of the Gestapo.

Seated in the chair opposite him was an elderly, thin man, clad in the uniform of a major of the Waffen–SS. He was in his early sixties, and his six-foot frame was bowed in a slight stoop, noticeable even as he slouched in his chair.

'Well,' Himmler asked softly, 'what do you think, Stranders? Will the *Britisches Freikorps* be up to it?'

Sturmbannführer Vivian Stranders stretched uneasily.

'You are an Englishman,' pressed Himmler. 'Your opinion is of value.'

Stranders raised his pale eyes to stare at the glinting gaze of the *Reichsführer*. 'I am a German,' he replied in annoyance. 'I was granted full nationality in 1934.'

Vivian Stranders was a complex personality. He had been born into a comfortably middle–class English family. His father had been professor at London's famous Guildhall School of Music. After graduating from London University, he had married and moved to Germany in 1903 where he became a teacher. Returning to England, he had taught at a variety of schools. Following a divorce, he had married for a second time in 1910. On the outbreak of the war in 1914 he had been sent to the Western Front as a gunnery officer in the Royal Artillery, later transferring to the Royal Flying Corps and ending the war as a captain posted to Germany as military interpreter to the Reparations Commission.

On demobilisation he settled in Dusseldorf, becoming involved in the German aircraft industry and also working for German intelligence. In December 1926 he was arrested, tried and sentenced by the French for spying. On returning to Germany he became a journalist, writing articles, lecturing and, in

1929, publishing a book on espionage. He had been an early convert to the National Socialist Party, who welcomed him to their ranks despite his British nationality. Three months after Hitler came to power, Stranders was rewarded with German citizenship and the post of professor of English at Bonn University.

With the coming of war in 1939, Stranders joined the Waffen –SS and reached the rank of *Sturmbannführer*. His initial job was liaison officer for the England Committee of the German Foreign Office. Now he had been given the task of organising the British Free Corps, recruited from dissidents and prisoners of war.

'Your opinion is of value,' pressed Himmler.

Stranders plucked at his lower lip thoughtfully. 'If the *Führer* and *Reichsminister* Goebbels want a propaganda show, then I think the British Free Corps can be made ready. But God help us if the *Führer* is serious about using them as a fighting unit like the Flemish, Dutch or French SS units. The British Free Corps number less than one hundred half-wits, social misfits and a few hardened fanatics who live in cloud-cuckoo-land.'

Himmler made a whistling sound through his teeth. 'What is wanted, so I understand, is a unit of Englishmen who will provide a symbolic bodyguard for the *Führer* on his birthday. They must be English so that when the world's press are invited to see this, the *Führer* can allow them to speak with any member of the unit to establish their *bona fides*. We therefore need some men among them who will give the press some good National Socialist replies to their questions, who will convince the press that there are many among the English who support the ideals of National Socialism and the struggle against the Bolshevik tyranny.'

Stranders looked thoughtful. 'There are some among the Free Corps who are articulate – not many. Most are frightened, ignorant sheep.'

'Then we must step up recruiting. I want nothing to go wrong with the *Führer's* plans. You must make another search of the camps for the right sort of recruits.'

Stranders heaved his tall frame out of the chair. 'Very well, *Herr Reichsführer*. It shall be done.'

Himmler waved his dismissal.

As Stranders left the room, a spasm of pain crossed the *Reichsführer's* face. He reached out for the telephone and asked for his secretary.

'Is Doctor Kersten at Hartzwalde?' he grunted. 'Tell him I need him. Tell him to come quickly.'

Felix Kersten was not really a doctor. He was a masseur. An Estonian turned Finnish citizen whose clientele ranged among the wealthy and influential of Europe, he had, since March 1939, been the only man whom Himmler allowed to treat his flaccid, pain-racked body. As the *Reichsführer* replaced the telephone, another spasm contorted his face. Then he pulled himself together. It would not be good to let anyone see that he, lord of life and death for millions of Europeans, was something less than a superman. He reached for the folder on his desk, marked with the title *Britisches Freikorps*, stared at it for a moment, and then tossed it into his out-tray with an expression of distaste.

Chapter Ten

Hauptman Werner Elberfeld put down the telephone with a perplexed expression. He brushed his hair away from his forehead and stared across the room at the dark, thin-faced man who stood by the ornate fireplace.

'That was my contact at the British Embassy,' he said. 'Something is up.'

The thin-faced man gazed back. He was in his mid thirties. His sallow skin contrasted with the blueness of his chin, indicating his need to shave at least twice a day. His thin lips appeared as vivid lines. His eyes were black, so black they seemed to have no pupils and stared without expression. In contrast to Elberfeld, dressed immaculately in his army captain's uniform, the thin-faced man wore a dark-brown civilian suit and a soft-brimmed black hat that sat well back on his head.

Elberfeld was reminded of a character from a bad American gangster movie. In other circumstances, he would have smiled at the man's theatrical appearance, but one did not smile at a member of the *Geheime Staatspolizei.* Especially a man known to be as close to Ernst Kaltenbrunner, chief of the Gestapo, as Rudi Behrens was. Elberfeld also had to remind himself that while he was a captain in the *Wehrmacht,* Behrens carried the SS rank of *Standartenführer,* a full colonel. Elberfeld knew that when Reinhard Heydrich, former head of the Gestapo, had been killed in Prague in 1942 by Czech partisans, Kaltenbrunner had taken over, bringing with him Rudi Behrens to purge the Gestapo of any that might oppose the new commander, who was answerable only to Himmler.

Elberfeld was nervous as Behrens turned those black expressionless eyes on him.

Elberfeld was the Lisbon embassy's intelligence officer, until recently an officer in Division II of the *Abwehr.* But the *Abwehr* had fallen into disfavour with Hitler. Its chief, Admiral Wilhelm Canaris, had been removed from office on 18 February and the function of the organisation had been transferred to the Reich Central Security Office. Himmler's SS security service, the *Sicherheitsdienst* or SD, were beginning to take over all functions of the *Abwehr* staff. Elberfeld knew that Behrens had been sent to Lisbon to check up on him and his small intelligence staff. He knew he should do nothing to bring himself into any antagonistic position. Elberfeld was a loyal enough citizen of the Reich, but sometimes, especially nowadays, that was not enough.

'Something is up at the British embassy,' he repeated.

'Explain,' the word was drawled in a soft Swabian accent.

'I have a contact who works in the domestic staff section of the British embassy,' explained Elberfeld. 'Apparently the British are holding a man prisoner in the embassy. He was brought in this morning by the Portugese police. It seems he is an Irishman whom the British suspect of being an agent.'

Behrens raised an eyebrow. 'Do we know anything about this Irishman?'

'I have instructed my contact to find out all he can.'

'Then there is no more to be done.'

Elberfeld nodded. Behrens walked across the room to gaze out of the window onto the broad stretch of the Avenida da Liberdade, with its beautiful white façades and green borders stretching away to the famous Parque Eduardo VII.

'A beautiful city, this Lisbon,' he said. 'It is so peaceful here compared with Berlin. Yes, I shall be sorry to leave.'

Elberfeld tried to keep the hope out of his voice. 'You are leaving us, *Herr Standartenführer*?'

Behrens nodded.

'Yes, early in the morning. I shall take the opportunity of the flight back to Berlin with the *Luftwaffe*.'

The previous Tuesday the *Luftwaffe* had been allowed to fly in a Dornier DO 17 Z-2 to facilitate an exchange of prisoners-of-war between the Reich and the Americans. That Sunday morning the last American POW had arrived in Lisbon and the two wounded Germans, whom the Americans were exchanging, were to be allowed on the aircraft for a special flight back to Germany in the morning. The humanitarian gesture had been milked for all it was worth by both sides, with Portugal's dictator, Doctor Salazar, basking in the reflected glory of the exchange. Behrens had flown into Lisbon on this 'mercy mission' and Elberfeld was now considerably relieved that he was preparing to depart so soon.

'Yes,' said Behrens. 'I have finished here. My most difficult task has been complete.'

Elberfeld gazed at him silently.

'Buying presents for my wife and son,' went on Behrens as if the question which passed through Elberfeld's mind had been asked aloud.

Elberfeld frowned. Was this grim-faced man laughing at him? It seemed incongruous that a Gestapo man should be a dutiful husband and father.

'Well,' Elberfeld said with forced brightness. 'perhaps you will allow me to invite you to dinner this evening. There is a superb restaurant on the Rua da Rosa and I would be delighted to have your company.'

Behrens turned his expressionless eyes on Elberfeld.

'Delighted,' he said.

Elberfeld tried to repress a shiver. There was a soft inflection in Behrens's voice which made his acceptance sound more like an ironic question.

Collins had been waiting two hours in the cell-like room of the embassy cellar. He had ceased to curse himself for his stupidity. Instead he had worked up a frustrated anger. The cell brought on a claustrophobia born of his days at Reed Hall and the feeling made him determined to escape. Things were going to be more difficult for him if he did succeed because he would have no identification papers. His hand strayed to his army dog-tags, hanging round his neck under his shirt. He broke out into a sweat. If the British intelligence officers found those, then the game would be up. Of course, he could tell them the truth, get them to telephone Roberts in London, but that would mean that the mission was over. No; he had to escape under his own steam.

It was easier than he expected.

Sometime later, how long he did not know, the door was unbolted and Kenny came in. Collins's body had become tense like a coiled steel spring. It was all reaction. He flung himself on the startled officer, hands grasping his throat before the man had a chance to cry out. His knee came up to the solar plexis, crippling the man. The major doubled in agony. Collins smashed his fist against the man's temple and he dropped to the floor without a murmur.

Collins uncoiled from his crouching position and stood listening. He could hear nothing. He moved to the door. He had to get out fast, and the only way he knew was the way he had been brought in.

He found his way to the spiral stairway and up to the ground floor. Then he was moving along the corridor. The door to the room in which he had been questioned was slightly ajar. He froze as he heard a sound from within. Then the nasal drawl of the fair-haired man came to his ears. The man was speaking on the telephone.

'Yes, yes,' he was saying. 'No idea except that we are sure the man is not who he claims to be. At the moment his story does bear up. He did arrive on the *Ard Rí* this morning but he signed on in London. His papers say he arrived in London on the *Grainne* from Dublin. We are waiting a double-check from London.'

Collins took a deep breath and walked softly be the door, along the corridor, through another door and into the hallway.

A man was sitting at the reception desk. He looked up with a frown. There were a couple of groups of people in the hall. They took no notice of Collins as he hurried towards the main doors.

'Hey!' the man at the reception desk called. 'Sir, you have to sign out!'

Collins ignored him, pushing through the doors and out into the late afternoon sunshine. Behind him he could hear shouting. He paused on the top step and glanced into the courtyard. No one was about. Against a pillar, at the bottom of the steps, a pile of bicycles were stacked. Running swiftly down, he seized one, leapt on it and began to pedal furiously out of the gates and into the roadway.

It was only after he had been going some time that he became aware of the shouts from other cyclists and the honking of an occasional car-horn. To his horror he realised that he was cycling on the left-hand side of the road. He turned swiftly off the main boulevard and switched to the right side of the road.

Hauptman Werner Elberfeld smiled broadly as he replaced the telephone.

'It seems that we might have to delay our dinner.'

Behrens turned to look at him.

'It seems that our Irishman has succeeded in escaping from the British Embassy and leaving my opposite number, Major Kenny, in a rather deplorable condition. The British embassy doctor has had to be called in for the poor fellow.'

Behrens's mouth puckered. 'And where is the Irishman now?'

'He was last seen cycling towards the Palacio da Independencia.'

'H'mm . . . is there any way we can have him picked up?'

'Not overtly, *Herr Standartenführer*. But I have a feeling that he will find his way to us sooner or later.'

'What makes you say that, *Herr Hauptman*?'

Elberfeld shrugged. 'Where else would he go?'

Collins halted before a dingy café in a small side-street. He propped his bicycle against the wall and entered. There were two or three people inside having an afternoon coffee or drink. Collins demanded a *café*, handed over a coin and peered round.

'Telephone?' he asked, thanking God for another international word.

The man behind the bar said something and jerked his thumb towards the back of the café. Collins moved in that direction, spying a telephone and a dog-eared book beside it. With a feeling of relief he picked it up and peered through the pages. As he was unused to Portugese, it took him some time before he found what he was looking for: the address and number of the German embassy. Now all he had to do was find out where the address was. He finished his coffee and went out.

For a while he cycled about aimlessly before coming on a main boulevard. At a junction he looked round for street-name placards. With a gasp he realised he was in luck; the name of this main thoroughfare was the very one in which the German embassy was situated. But which way?

He turned and decided to head along with the gentle flow of late Sunday afternoon traffic.

There was no mistaking the building; an imposing edifice with a giant red-and-black swastika flag moving idly on the flagpole on top of the building. Above the magnificent marble-columned portico was a shield with the swastika emblem. It was on the opposite side of the boulevard to Collins and he was about to make his way across to the main gate when something stayed him.

A black Riley saloon car was parked a little way from the gate. Four men were seated inside the car. In the back, leaning forward just at that moment to speak to the driver and thus exposing himself to Collins's view, was the fair-haired man from the British embassy.

Feeling a cold tension in his body, Collins forced himself to cycle on for a while, not daring to glance over his shoulder, wondering whether he had been spotted.

Jesus! He was making all the worst mistakes of some crass bungling amateur. Of course the British would realise that he would make straight for the German embassy. Of course they would try to intercept him.

He halted by a newspaper kiosk and glanced back.

The traffic flowed normally. There was no sign of any pursuit.

Getting into the German embassy was going to be difficult – more difficult than getting out of the British embassy.

He glanced at his watch. It would be getting dark soon. Already there was a pale tinge to the eastern sky which was a prelude to dusk. Darkness would make things easier, but not much. The main avenue was a busy one and would probably be well lit at night. This was a neutral city and there was no such thing as a black-out.

The German embassy would most likely have a back entrance, but the British would probably have that covered as well as the front. The embassy building itself lay back in a spacious garden, surrounded by high walls. On each side were other such buildings. He did not know whether they were private or government buildings. If he could get into the grounds of one of the adjoining buildings, he might be able to slip over the wall into the embassy without having to go through the gates covered by the British agents.

He suddenly became aware of a Portuguese policeman staring at him.

He fumbled in his pocket for his cigarettes, lit one up, turned and smiled to the policeman and pedalled slowly away. The policeman automatically smiled back, though he stared after Collins for a few moments before he returned to his beat. Collins chuckled to himself. The smiling technique was very effective when someone was suspicious.

He cycled around until it was dark before approaching the embassy from the rear. The street contained several parked cars. Collins's eyes narrowed as he tried to guess which one contained the British agents. He propped up his bicycle against the wall of a house about two hundred yards from the embassy back-gate and began to stroll nonchalantly towards it.

When he was about a hundred yards away, he saw two men get out of a car nearby and stare at him. They turned abruptly, apparently taking no further notice of him. He saw a flicker of flame as they lit cigarettes, hunching their shoulders. He knew they had spotted him.

Collins now reached the wrought-iron gates of the villa which stood next to the embassy building. He halted. They were closed and padlocked. Damn it! He would have to scramble over and trust he was faster than the men waiting for him down the road. Then he saw the smaller gate set into the wrought-iron frame. He couldn't see any lock on it. Taking his courage in both hands, he turned, grasped the handle and pushed.

It opened.

Then he was running across the dark lawns of the villa, running towards the high wall which separated it from the German embassy. He thought he heard someone shout but he increased his speed, heading towards a shadowy bush-like tree which filled the air with the sweet aroma of bay. It grew in the shadow of the wall. He grabbed at it and heaved himself upwards, using it as a step to fling himself at the top of the wall, wincing in pain as his grasping hands came into contact with the broken glass on top of the wall. He shut his mind to the sudden pain, pulled himself up and rolled over the wall, falling heavily into the flower-beds on the other side.

He scrambled to his hands and knees in the soft, damp earth.

A beam of light blinded him.

'*Hände hoch!*' snapped a voice.

He was aware of a figure in uniform pointing a pistol at him.

'I want to see . . .' he began in English, then changed to German. 'I want to see your military attaché. It is most important.'

The figure made a motion with his pistol. 'Come,' he said, indicating the black building behind him.

Aching and feeling the cuts tingling in his hands, Collins rose and walked ahead of the man.

He was prodded through a doorway, through a darkened room, up a flight of stairs and into a large room with an ornate fireplace above which a life-size portrait of the German *Führer* glowered down at him.

A thin, sallow-faced man in a brown suit stood before the fire, hands behind his back. On the couch, seated in a relaxed position, was a young man in a *Wehrmacht* officer's uniform. He smiled and rose to his feet.

'You may go,' he said to the man who had conducted Collins to the room.

'*Jawohl,* Herr *Hauptmann,*' snapped the man.

Still smiling, the German officer regarded Collins, shaking his head gently.

'Welcome, Mr Collins,' he suddenly said in excellent English. 'We have been expecting you.'

Chapter Eleven

Collins stared at the man with open mouth.

The *Wehrmacht* captain chuckled. 'You must not be so surprised, Mr Collins,' he explained. 'We have an excellent intelligence service.'

His English was good; there was a touch of Oxford about it.

Collins's mind was in turmoil. Did the Germans know everything? How had they . . . ?

The sallow-faced man coughed. 'Let's not play games, Elberfeld,' he snapped in German. 'Let's find out who this Irishman is and why the British were holding him.'

He obviously thought that Collins spoke no German.

Collins let out an inner sigh of relief. They did not know much after all. He saw the captain, Elberfeld, turn with a frown of annoyance.

'Very well, Herr *Standartenführer.*' He turned back to Collins. 'Why did the British arrest you?'

'I was looking for the German embassy,' said Collins. 'The Portuguese police took me to the British embassy by mistake.'

'Why were you looking for the German embassy?'

'I wanted to offer my services to the German Reich,' replied Collins.

Elberfeld raised an eyebrow. 'What makes you think that the Reich requires the services of an Irish sailor?'

Collins waited a moment and then he said slowly.

'I am not Irish. My name is Charles Collins. I am . . . I was . . . a sergeant in the British Army. I am English. I want to volunteer to serve the Reich.'

Elberfeld did not attempt to conceal his surprise. He turned and swiftly relayed this information in German to Behrens.

The Gestapo man's lips compressed. 'Can he prove what he says?'

Collins, without waiting for a translation, drew out his Army identity tags and held them towards Behrens.

Elberfeld's eyes widened. 'You speak German?'

'A little. I picked it up in '37 when I was on an exchange visit between members of the British Union of Fascists and the National Socialist Party.'

'You were a member of the British Union of Fascists?' queried Elberfeld.

Collins nodded, glancing at Behrens who was examining the dog-tags.

'In themselves, these mean nothing,' the Gestapo man said finally. 'Let's hear your story, Collins. I warn you, be truthful. If you are a British plant, we shall find out.'

'I can't see the British going to these lengths, *Herr Standartenführer*,' said Elberfeld. 'I can't see Major Kenny allowing himself to be put in hospital to support such a plot.'

'The British are well known for playing such games,' replied Behrens coldly. 'Sit down, Collins. Tell us your story.'

When people asked him about his daughter, Paula, old Karl Wielen usually told them that she had run away to Hamburg before the war and he had later heard that she had died in the bombing. It was not so. Paula Wielen had initially left home to study for a teacher's diploma at Hanover. Like her parents, Paula was a strict Catholic. She had become a member of the organisation *Aktion*. The movement was proscribed and its president, Doctor Erich Klausener, who earned his living as a permanent under-secretary at the Ministry of Transport, was shot dead by SS men on the 'Night of the Long Knives', on 1 July

1934. Paula Wielen, along with many other Catholic opponents of Hitler, was arrested by the Gestapo in the subsequent purge which raged through German society. All Communists, socialists, trade unionists, Jews, Catholics and Protestants who did not fully subscribe to the ideas of the new Nazi state were rounded up. Political parties had been banned, trade unions were suppressed and the press censored. Over 200,000 Germans disappeared within the first few years of the new regime. Paula Wielen was among those 200,000.

Later, old Karl Wielen, thanking God his wife Heidi had not lived to see Hitler's hell on earth, discovered that the Nazis had set up 'labour camps' on the Hanover moors; camps which were swiftly succeeded by concentration camps where the anti-Nazis were systematically eliminated. Paula had been transferred to a new camp at Neuengamme, near Hamburg. It was in Neuengamme that she celebrated her twenty-fifth birthday and on that day was told to remain behind after the morning *appell* parade was dismissed. A thin-faced female guard escorted her to a corner of the camp where a ditch was being dug. She was told to halt. Puzzled, she turned. The last thing she saw was a tall, handsome SS guard holding a machine pistol. Paula Wielen was one of the 987 German Catholics who were executed in 1939 in concentration camps.

Karl Wielen learnt the news through his priest. The priest had known someone who had been in the camp at the time. The man had been released after serving a sentence for fraternisation with a Jewish woman.

For a long time old Karl Wielen had kept his grief to himself, building up a terrible hatred. He had been a good Catholic. Now he found himself no longer attending mass nor going regularly to church. True, he went to church now and again; he would sneak into a corner after services were over and pray quietly. But his prayers were for revenge. His heart was too full of hate to pray for anything else.

It was in 1941 that he met a Jesuit priest named Olbricht. For some reason a friendship grew between the dour, grief-stricken postman and the intellectual Jesuit. Olbricht was a member of the Kreisau Circle, a heterogenous group of anti-Nazis, men from many walks of life who gathered around Count Helmuth

James von Moltke, the great-great nephew of the field marshal who led the Prussian Army to victory over France in 1870. The name of the Kreisau Circle was taken from the Moltke estate in Silesia. Lutheran pastors, Jesuit priests, socialists, trade unionists, liberals, intellectuals, former diplomats and others gathered to discuss ways and means of overthrowing the dictatorship of Adolf Hitler. Mostly, they were talkers, ineffectual as real opposition.

Father Olbricht was different. He was an activist. His frequent visits to the Vatican detoured through Switzerland, to Berne, where he had contacts with the British and Americans. His commitment to fighting Hitler was total. He recruited his own circle of a dozen anti-Nazis, people who did not just talk but acted. In Karl Wielen he found a man with a mission of vengeance against the Nazis. Returning from one of his regular trips to Berne, Olbricht brought Wielen a package – a radio-transmitter. He taught the old postman how to use it; taught him how to report to London useful military information which the group supplied him with. Under the code name 'the Piper' Wielen became one of Brigadier Kylie's best informants.

The Olbricht group remained intact even when the Jesuit priest was arrested by the Gestapo while crossing the Swiss-German border with contraband. He was taken to Gestapo headquarters in Freiburg, questioned and executed. Father Olbricht, in spite of the refined methods of interrogation of Kaltenbrunner's men, revealed nothing. The Olbricht group continued its work.

Sitting in his secret little attic room, Wielen tuned in to London to listen for any instructions. Usually there were none. That evening however, as he sat drinking his ersatz coffee, his call sign came through. Excitedly Wielen acknowledged.

'Piper, this is Rabbit. Otto may call. He has a message from Paula in Hamburg.'

Wielen's face went white as he keyed his acknowledgement.

Months ago it had been arranged with Father Olbricht that if any agent wanted direct personal contact, they would go to the *Postamt* and ask for Uncle Wilhelm, the nickname by which he was known to his fellow workers. To identify themselves, the person would say that he was Otto and had a message from Wielen's daughter, Paula, in Hamburg.

As old Karl Wielen sat keying his acknowledgement, he wondered who Otto might be.

Standartenführer Behrens stretched back in his chair and drew deeply on his cigarette. He examined Collins from under half lowered lids. The Englishman had been talking for half an hour.

'An interesting story, Collins,' Behrens said slowly. 'You realise that we can check it?'

Collins shrugged indifferently. 'You can check it all you want. I have nothing to hide.'

Elberfeld smiled reassuringly. 'Of course not. But you will understand that we cannot take such an amazing story on face value.'

'I understand. But you'll find it checks out.'

Behrens stubbed out his cigarette. 'And you wish to work for the Reich? Very commendable,' he said drily. 'Why, if you feel this way about the Reich, did you drop out of the British Union of Fascists in 1938? You claim that you have never ceased to believe in Fascism, is this not so?'

Collins was ready for the question. He decided to follow Roberts's advice and stick entirely to the truth. 'I began to feel that Mosley was not fit to be our leader. Many of us felt that at the time. William Joyce, for one. When he left Mosley and founded his British National Socialist League, I joined it. I used to work on his magazine *The Helmsman*.'

Behrens raised an eyebrow. 'You know Joyce?'

He had met Joyce at the offices of *The Helmsman*.

'Joyce works for Radio Concordia in Berlin,' said Elberfeld. 'You will have the opportunity of meeting your old friend if you go there.'

Behrens rose from his chair, glancing at his watch. 'That is precisely what will happen,' he said. 'Collins will accompany me to Berlin tomorrow morning.'

Collins was startled by the swiftness of the decision. He had expected to spend some time in Lisbon while the Germans made up their minds about him.

Behrens spoke to Elberfeld. 'I suggest you get on to the

Tirpitz Ufer and ask your headquarters to run checks on this man's story. In the meantime I will take him into my custody until we reach Berlin. And you'd better have a *Wehrpass* made out for him.'

'A military pass, *Herr Standartenführer?*'

'Yes, this man is now under military custody until he gets to Berlin.'

'Very well, *Herr Standartenführer.*'

Behrens gazed at Collins with his dark expressionless eyes. 'So, Collins, by midday tomorrow you will be in Berlin and by that time I would imagine that we shall know if you have been telling us the truth about yourself. If not . . .'

'You will find out that I am who I say I am,' replied Collins confidently.

'That will be good – for you,' smiled Behrens.

Collins stood up. 'When do we leave?'

It was Elberfeld who replied. 'Not until five o'clock tomorrow morning. You will spend the night here in protective custody. The British will still be smarting about your escape.'

'In that case, can I have a meal and a bath? My hands are pretty painful from trying to get over your wall.'

'Of course,' smiled Elberfeld. He rang a buzzer on the table and a uniformed guard entered. The *Wehrmacht* captain issued rapid instructions to him.

'Good night, Collins,' he said. 'Have a pleasant meal.'

After he had left the room, Elberfeld turned to Behrens. 'He seems genuine enough.'

'Perhaps,' replied Behrens gruffly. 'It is true that there are a number of British traitors who have volunteered to work for the Reich. I have met some of them.' He frowned thoughtfully.

'But what, *Herr Standartenführer?*' prompted Elberfeld.

'This man Collins does not seem to be one of their sort. He does not strike me as the sort of man who would change sides so easily. Call it an instinct. I don't like him.'

'Well, I shall get onto *Abwehr* head . . . to headquarters,' Elberfeld corrected himself. 'I'll see what they have to come up with. We might even know before morning.'

'And save a passage to Berlin,' Behrens smiled grimly. 'After you have made your call, *Herr Hauptman,* I suggest that you take me for that dinner you promised me. It has been a long day.'

Chapter Twelve

The *Luftwaffe* navigator, a grotesque figure in his leather, fur-lined flying jacket and cap clambered back to where Collins and Behrens were sitting in their uncomfortable bucket seats amidships of the Dornier.

It had been a little after 4.00 a.m. when the aircraft had taken off from Lisbon. There had been some abrupt change of schedule and an embassy car had rushed them to the airport just after 3.00 a.m. Collins had a strange sensation of familiarity when he saw the aircraft. He recognised if from old Spanish Civil War newsreels, for the Dornier had first been bloodied in Hitler's Condor Legion, used for bombing Basque towns. Now it had been stripped of its main armaments and converted from bomber to hospital ship. Where the bombs were normally stored, two stretchers had been placed for the badly wounded German ex-prisoners. There was a *Luftwaffe* doctor in attendance. The only other passengers were Collins and Behrens.

The aircraft had flown across Franco's Spain towards Vichy France, crossing the border south of Toulouse. At Toulouse the Dornier circled and put down at the military airfield of Blagnat. The Dornier had a maximum range of 795 miles but it was obvious that her five-man crew were flying her within strict safety margins. The next leg of the journey was from Toulouse to Munich. The aircraft was refuelled again at Munich-Oberwiesenfeld airfield. It took off again as soon as refuelling was complete.

It was close to one o'clock when the navigator came back and gestured downwards. He leant close and shouted: 'Berlin!'

Behrens turned. 'We shall soon be landing at Tempelhof airfield. We shall go directly to headquarters. We shall have confirmation of your story waiting for us – confirmation or . . . ?' He raised his voice in a question.

Collins scowled. He had taken an intense dislike to Behrens. Nevertheless, he knew Behrens was not a man to deceive or to cross.

'You'll find my story checks out,' he said. 'I have told you the truth.'

'The truth is relative, they say,' returned Behrens. 'One man's truth is another man's lie. It is like history. One nation's truth is another nation's propaganda. Is it not so?'

'You're a philosopher, *Herr Standartenführer*.'

'Merely a realist.'

The Dornier started to circle, losing height. Within a few minutes it had squealed to a halt on the concrete tarmac, its engines slowed and stopped.

The injured Germans were taken from the aircraft first. A group of cameramen and reporters had gathered to record their arrival. Through the window Collins could see a group of civilians waving small Swastika flags. There were uniformed policemen and military personnel. The exchange of prisoners was also being played up in the Reich.

'Come, Collins.' Behrens was making his way to the exit door at the rear of the aircraft.

Outside stood a man in a belted raincoat and soft felt hat. His hands were thrust deep in his pockets. He gazed at Collins for a moment. Collins had an impression of parchment skin, high Slavic cheekbones a thin cruel mouth, and cold grey eyes. The man was moving forward to greet Behrens.

'Welcome home, *Herr Standartenführer*.'

'Hello, Manfred. You've come to meet me?'

The man called Manfred nodded and glanced curiously at Collins. 'Yes, *Herr Standartenführer*. I've brought a car. Is this the Englishman?'

Behrens nodded. 'This is Collins. Collins this is my assistant, Deputy *Kommissar* Manfred Reinecke.'

Reinecke made no acknowledgement of the introduction. He just stared at Collins and then turned away. 'I'll get the car,' he said.

An airport official came up, hovering nervously and mumbling something about formalities. When Behrens presented a card the man visibly paled and then glanced at Collins.

'And this gentleman is with you, *Herr Standartenführer*?'

'He is,' replied Behrens. 'Collins, show him your *Wehrpass*.'

Collins dug into his pocket for the military pass which the Lisbon embassy had given him. The official waved it to one side.

'If you are travelling with the *Geheime Staatspolizei,* then I am sure all is in order,' he said.

Behrens fixed the man coldly. 'Whether you believe things are in order or not, it is your duty to examine this man's pass.'

'At once, *Herr Standartenführer,*' the man gurgled unhappily.

Collins watched him with amused sympathy as, with trembling hands, he took the pass looked at it, jaw dropping slightly as he read it.

'You are an Englishman?' he gasped.

Collins smiled. 'Working for the Reich.'

'That is yet to be decided,' Behrens said softly.

The official bit his lip. 'You vouch for this man, *Herr Standartenführer*?'

'He is travelling in my custody,' replied Behrens.

As the official turned away, Reinecke drove up in a low-slung black Horche saloon. He climbed out and opened the back door for Behrens. Collins climbed in after the *Standartenführer*. Reinecke slipped back into the driver's seat and the car glided almost silently across the airport tarmac.

Beside him, Behrens pulled out a pack of cigarettes, placed one in his mouth, hesitated and then offered one to Collins. Collins took it and accepted a light from Behrens.

The car moved slowly through the gates of the airfield, was checked through a military checkpoint and then turned north towards Berlin city-centre.

They had not gone far when the banshee wail of air-raid sirens rose from the city.

Reinecke glanced at his watch. 'One o'clock exactly,' he said. 'They are early today, *Herr Standartenführer*. Shall we pull in?'

'Yes, Manfred. Have things been bad while I have been away?'

The Gestapo *Kommissar* shrugged. 'There has been a lull

these last few days but mainly it has been the Americans by day and the British by night.'

Along the street people were hurrying this way and that, obviously racing to their respective shelters. But there were no signs of panic and few signs of bomb damage along the street.

Reinecke pulled into the kerb-side under a group of trees, and switched off the engine. 'Shall we find a public shelter, *Herr Standartenführer*?'

'No. It may be a false alarm. We'll sit it out for a while.'

A uniformed policeman, apparently acting as air-raid warden, came hurrying to the car, but backed away when Reinecke showed a pass. He turned, shepherding people before him.

For about fifteen minutes they waited. The street was deserted now. The only movement was a stray dog.

'Here they come,' said Reinecke.

A heavy droning came to their ears. The deep rhythmic roar of aero engines high above. Collins squinted out of the window. Ah, he could see them now, really high up. My God! There were hundreds of them.

'Flying Fortresses!' he whispered, recognising the silhouettes.

'Americans,' agreed Behrens. 'If the raid is a daylight one, you can be fairly sure it is the Americans.'

They could hear the explosions now. The high-pitched whistle of falling metal, the earth-shaking crump of the explosion. Smoke was tailing into tall columns high above the city.

'Look, there is the *Luftwaffe!*' cried Reinecke, pointing as small specks appeared in the sky, edging closer to the large outlines of the bombers. The smaller specks began to dart and twist about, seeming now and again to be joined by lines of sparkling white and red. The noise was incredible.

'It might be best if we left the car, *Herr Standartenführer*,' observed Reinecke nervously.

Behrens climbed out and they followed. He strolled casually, as if oblivious to the bedlam around him, across the pavement and entered a café. Whatever else Behrens was, admitted Collins, he had nerves. The café was deserted. Behrens seated himself on a bar stool.

'This will do until the American swine have left.'

Collins stood at the door gazing up at the sky above. Almost directly above them a black cross-shape was twisting and diving, turning and zooming in a desperate effort to escape the black clouds of shells exploding around him. Then a tremendous flash lit the sky. Collins nearly said 'Poor devil!' out loud.

The anti-aircraft guns were thundering all around with a deafening cacophony.

Then they heard the whine of bombs and explosions. The first one was some way away. The second one seemed nearer. The third was nearer still. It took that time to register in Collins's mind that the bomber was following the line of the roadway outside and that the next bomb would be coming directly at them. Whether he threw himself on the floor first, or whether they all threw themselves down together was a matter for debate. Collins found himself nestling under a table, fingers in his ears and mouth open. There was a tremendous whoosh, sort of a thin whistle, like tyres skidding on a smooth road. The ground heaved like a ship in a gale. The noise was incredible. The room was filled with smoke and brickdust and shattered glass.

After what seemed an eternity Collins heaved himself to his knees and gazed around. He fully expected the building to have been demolished. But the bomb had struck a building on the opposite side of the road. Coughing and spluttering, Collins staggered over some rubble and out onto the street. Behrens and Reinecke followed him.

The noise of the guns, the drone of aircraft and the rocking explosions continued. To this was added the crash of tumbling masonry and the crackle and roar of flames. People were running towards the half-demolished house, tearing at the rubble with their hands. For a moment Collins thought he was back in London in '41 so similar was the scene before him. The only difference was in the language and the uniforms.

He stood unsure of what to do.

'Welcome to Berlin, Herr Collins.'

He turned to find Behrens smiling crookedly at him.

A policeman came running down the road. 'Take cover, take cover! Don't you know the raid is not over yet?'

Behrens produced his identity card. The policeman halted and saluted.

'Will we be able to get to the city centre?' asked the Gestapo man.

'No, *Herr Standartenführer*. Not at the moment. This is the heaviest raid yet. They have bombed Friedrichstrasse, Potsdammerplatz and the Tiergarten. I am told that the Underground stations at Friedrichstrasse and at Dreigleisech have been totally destroyed and there is another wave of bombers coming in any time now.'

Behrens bit his lip and waved a dismissal at the man.

They heard before they saw the second wave of bombers, even more numerous than the first, passing high above them. Behrens squinted up and swore softly.

'They are heading towards the Daimler Benz works in Genfhagen.'

Suddenly a great ball of flame descended out of the sky with a shrieking roar of an express train. The explosion must have been a mile away but they felt the impact from where they stood.

'I think one of the Americans must have crashed,' ventured Reinecke.

Collins was staring around him in stupefaction. He wondered how long the Berliners could hold out against such raids. Then he shrugged as the thought occured to him: Londoners had stood up to it.

It was a long time before the thin wail of the all-clear sounded and they climbed back into the car. One side-window had been smashed, the windscreen was cracked in one corner, and the car was generally pitted and scored by flying metal and masonry. They moved gently forward amidst the rubble-strewn streets. To Collins it seemed as if the whole of Berlin was a mass of flames and smoke. Wide areas were cut off from supplies; broken water mains flooded streets; here and there gas ominously hissed from twisted and broken pipes causing further fire hazards. One street they passed was a weird fiery wasteland in which a twisted, jagged, flaming wreckage of a Flying Fortress lay, having demolished almost all the nearby buildings in its fall.

Reinecke made slow progress, but finally, after constant detours, he reached Prinz Albrecht Strasse and slid to a halt before number 8. It stood untouched amidst the flames and

112

carnage, its giant red swastika flags grotesquely bright in the light of the dancing flames from nearby buildings. It stood like a rock in the inferno – like a forbidding gateway to hell.

Collins threw a last glance towards the carnage outside, before he followed Behrens into the building.

It was not an auspicious arrival.

Chapter Thirteen

Roberts arrived at his office at the usual time, asked Doris to fetch his tea, and sat in his customary morning contemplation before he turned and began to go through the various reports and paperwork which made up the major part of his job. It was a report forwarded by the Military Police which caught his eye, an incident report from the military attaché at Lisbon. Roberts read it with a broad grin.

He left his office and hurried along the corridor to Brigadier Kylie.

Kylie looked up with a frown. 'And what makes you so damned boisterous this morning, laddie?' he grumbled. 'You're grinning away like a damned Cheshire cat.'

'Hagen, sir,' replied Roberts. 'He's made it to Berlin.' He handed over the report.

'This must be our man,' muttered Kylie, as he read it. 'The coincidence would be too great . . .'

Roberts nodded. 'Look at the description. It's our man all right.'

Kylie reached into a side-cupboard and fished out a bottle of Glenfiddich. 'I think this calls for a wee dram by way of celebration,' he said, pouring two glasses. 'To Hagen, wherever he is!'

At that precise moment Charles Collins was gazing at the heavy jowls of *Oberstgruppenführer* Ernst Kaltenbrunner, head of the

Geheime Staatspolizei, and answerable only to Heinrich Himmler and the *Führer* as controller of the repressive organisations of the Third Reich. Behrens was lounging against the marble fireplace in the room. It seemed a favourite stance of the *Standartenführer.* Reinecke, divested of his American gangster-style raincoat, stood deferentially by the door.

Kaltenbrunner had been silent for some time as he read a file. Finally he looked up.

'So, Sergeant Collins. You have been the cause of much radio traffic between here and our friends in London.'

Collins stirred uneasily.

'Yes,' went on the general, 'we have, as the Americans say, checked you out pretty thoroughly. Your story is supported by our investigation.'

Collins tried to hide his elation. 'I am pleased that you encountered no problems.'

'None at all,' assured the head of the Gestapo. 'Our intelligence system is second to none. We have even had a report from your erstwhile friend Mr Murphy.'

Collins started. 'You *are* thorough,' he admitted.

'Exceptionally so,' Kaltenbrunner assured him blandly. 'We have even found Herr Kroger in Hamburg. Thank God he was a survivor of the criminal terror-bombing of the RAF.'

Kroger? Collins tried hard to recall the name. 'Hans Kroger?'

Kaltenbrunner smiled 'So? You remember him? He remembers you. He was party secretary at the time you were living in Hamburg. He was one of the organisers of the exchange visit between the party and your British Union of Fascists. Herr Kroger was most helpful. He referred us to copies of the Hamburg party journal which recorded the arrival of the British visitors. The journal carried photographs of all the members of the British delegation. May I say that the war has not changed you, Sergeant Collins?'

Kaltenbrunner sat back and smiled softly at the astonishment on Collins's face. 'Our thoroughness surprises you, does it not? Good. There is only one other point to check . . .'

He signalled to Reinecke at the door.

Collins tensed as Reinecke turned and opened it.

114

Someone came in. Collins wondered whether he should stand up and greet the new arrival.

'Good morning, *Herr Oberstgruppenführer,*' the voice spoke a nasal and tortured German. 'I hope this business will not take long. I have to be at the studio very shortly . . .'

Collins recognised the voice; indeed, half the population of Britain would have done so. They called the man Lord Haw Haw. Collins recognised him from before the war. He forced a smile, stood and turned round.

The man who had entered was small. His hair was mouse-coloured and grew thinly, particularly above the ears. His nose was slightly mis-shapen, oddly angled, with a narrow bridge and pointed nostrils. His eyes were dark blue, like shiny pebbles. His eyebrows were thick and irregular. His neck was elongated on narrow sloping shoulders. His body was flimsy, but his arms were short and thick. He had a deep scar running across his right cheek from his ear to the corner of his mouth, which was extremely small. His movements were jerky.

William Joyce had not changed much since Collins had last seen him in the offices of *The Helmsman,* the party journal of his British National Socialist League.

Joyce gazed at Collins, frowning as if trying to dredge up some memory.

'Do you recognise this man, *Herr* Joyce?' asked Kaltenbrunner.

'I have met him before, a long time ago,' Joyce muttered. 'I think he worked for my National Socialist League.'

'Does the name Collins help?'

Joyce's face cleared. 'That's it. Collins. He was a member of the League and before that of the British Union of Fascists.'

Kaltenbrunner grunted in satisfaction.

Collins took Joyce's limp hand.

'Have you come to work with us, Collins? Help overthrow Bolshevism?'

'I have come to volunteer my services to the Reich,' affirmed Collins.

'Excellent. There are several openings with Radio Concordia.'

Kaltenbrunner interrupted. 'Thank you for coming in, *Herr* Joyce. We just needed a positive identification.'

115

'A pleasure, *Herr Oberstgruppenführer*,' Joyce bowed in a jerky fashion. It had obviously been a dismissal and Joyce took it as such, leaving the room hurriedly.

Kaltenbrunner waved Collins to be seated again.

'A formality, you understand. Photographs are good but eye-witnesses are even better. We can now be sure that you are, indeed, Charles Collins.'

He shuffled the papers on his desk.

'I will forward your file to the good Doctor Freidrich Hansen who is chairman of the England Committee at the Foreign Office. You will be able to discuss your future employment with the Reich directly with him. *Standartenführer* Behrens here will take you to the Hotel Adler and see that you have a comfortable room. For the next few days, until Doctor Hansen discusses matters with you, you are a guest of the Reich.'

Behrens guided Collins out of Kaltenbrunner's office as the thick-set Gestapo chief bent over his papers, apparently taking no further notice of him.

Outside Behrens stared curiously at him. 'You are a strange man, Collins,' he said. 'You do not appear to be the sort of man who would be a turncoat.'

Reinecke, standing behind Behrens, said nothing.

Collins glared angrily at them. 'Turncoat is an abusive word, *Herr Standartenführer*. Also, it is a strange word for you to employ. Is it to be sneered at as a turncoat that I have come to Berlin? I and many other Englishmen are now recognising the morass into which Churchill's war-mongering has led us. Churchill has blinded himself to the terrible threat which world Jewry and Bolshevism pose to us. He is betraying the interests of my country in leading it in a futile war against the Third Reich, whereas we should be allies against the Bolshevik threat.'

Collins tried hard to keep his face straight. He thought his speech pretty good.

'Surely you do not deny that threat, *Herr Standartenführer*? Surely you believe that England has been misled and that the salvation of our Nordic Civilisation rests on Germany and England joining as allies against Jewish Bolshevism? Why, the *Führer* himself has said as much. You do not disagree with the *Führer*, do you?'

Collins could read nothing from Behrens's black expression-less eyes. The man's thin lips parted, showing his teeth in a mirthless smile.

'You are a clever man, Collins. Perhaps too clever. Time will tell.'

Chapter Fourteen

Countess Helga von Haensel turned over on the bed and gazed at the young man who lay by her side.

'Give me a cigarette, please,' she said languidly.

The dark-haired man, in his late twenties, reached to the bedside table and picked up a silver cigarette case, took out two cigarettes, and lit them with a matching silver lighter. He exhaled with a sigh and passed one of them over to the girl.

'It's dangerous for you to go to Sweden again, Helga,' *Freiherr* Helmuth von Fegeleinn said. 'The Gestapo are getting nervous about travellers to neutral countries.'

The girl drew herself up on the pillows and pouted. 'As a secretary in the Foreign Office I don't suffer the same restrictions as everyone else.'

'Sooner or later they will find out that you are not travelling purely on Foreign Office business. Look what happened to Olbricht.'

'It was different with Father Olbricht,' the girl replied.

'I worry for you, Helga.'

Helga von Haensel was a girl with a strong personality. While she felt a deep emotional attachment to Helmuth von Fegeleinn she knew he was a weak person. Before the war he had been an indolent playboy. His family had owned a large farming estate in Silesia, next to the estate of the von Haensels. Both families were monarchist, aristocratic and wealthy. Von Fegeleinn, how-ever, was not interested in politics. He wanted to pursue the 'good life'. His world was rudely shattered shortly after his

117

twentieth birthday when, on 16 March 1935, Hitler ordered the reintroduction of compulsory military service. Von Fegeleinn had decided to volunteer for the *Luftwaffe* as an administration officer. Exploiting family connections, he had managed to get an appointment as adjutant to a *Luftwaffe* general in Berlin. The early years of the war had been comfortable. His connections allowed him to rise swiftly through the ranks of Göring's air force until his present appointment as *Oberstleutnant* in the planning department, with his own office in the Air Ministry building in the Wilhemstrasse. In fact, von Fegeleinn's office window looked out into the Prinz Albrecht Strasse towards the headquarters of Himmler's SS.

He had grown up with Helga von Haensel. They had hunted together, attended the same balls and ski-ing holidays. He had seen her turn from a skinny, gawky teenager into a highly attractive and vivacious young woman. She had seen him change from a pimply-faced youth to a lean, handsome young man. One thing that didn't change was his weakness of character; he needed people to guide him, to make decisions for him. How he survived in his job was simply due to the fact that he relayed orders and did not originate them.

It had been six months ago that von Fegeleinn had started sleeping with Helga von Haensel. The girl felt a curious and overpowering animal attraction towards him. Sexually, they were extremely compatible. They had the same background, but on certain levels – intellectually – they were poles apart. While von Fegeleinn hated the way in which Germany had changed under National Socialism, he did not have the foresight nor the courage to think of changing it. Helga von Haensel did. She had already become one of the Kreisau Circle of anti-Nazis and allowed herself to be recruited to Father Olbricht's group. Her unique position as secretary to Doctor Hansen, chairman of the England Committee of the Foreign Office, allowed her fairly unrestricted travel. In this manner she had been able to establish contact with many anti-Nazi groups throughout German. It was, in fact, due to her that proposals for a liaison committee between all the groups had been accepted and, since January of that year, the first tentative secret meetings of a united resistance council had met.

She had been sleeping with von Fegeleinn a month when she recruited him to Father Olbricht's group. He was scared, unwilling at first, but eventually he accepted the situation – too weak to stand up to her enthusiasm. At first he had thought the group was simply a political discussion group; later, he discovered they were engaged in printing and distributing anti-Nazi propaganda from secret printing presses.

Helga von Haensel let him think that this was all the group were engaged in. While she loved von Fegeleinn, she doubted his reliability.

When Father Olbricht was caught and executed by the Gestapo, it had been Helga von Haensel who had taken over as head of the group. Only she had any idea of the full extent of the potential German resistance movement. She had acted twice now as the *envoi-extraordinaire* between the resistance council and the Allies. The main stumbling block between the resistance council acting as a cohesive force against the Nazi regime was the Allies' demand for total surrender and the division of Germany between the Allied powers. Had the Allied powers held out any hope of treating with an anti-Nazi government that might oppose the Soviets, now massing for the thrust across Poland, then the opposition would have been a strong one. But the insistence on total surrender and occupation made the resistance leaders hesitate, arguing among themselves and vacillating, hoping that the British and Americans might change their minds.

It was left to isolated groups to organise attempts on the life of the demonic *Führer*. There had been half a dozen such attempts between September 1943 and January 1944 alone. In January, *Generalleutnant Freiherr* Henning von Tresckow had organised an attempt in which three young officers volunteered to model new military overcoats for the *Führer* with bombs hidden in their pockets. The plan was that as the *Führer* stood near them they would detonate their bombs, killing themselves and the *Führer* with them. The modelling session was cancelled. A similar attempt on 20 February, organised by *Oberst* Josef Hoffman, also failed. Hitler was a difficult man to kill. The *Führer* knew well that he was a potential target, and he lived an irregular life to counter such attempts. He once told his friends: 'I quite understand why ninety per cent of the historic assassinations have been successful. The only preventive measure one can take is to live irregularly – to walk, to drive, and to travel at irregular times and unexpectedly . . . As far as possible, whenever I go anywhere by car, I go off unexpectedly and without warning the police.' Hitler's method of combatting assassination had certainly worked. Count Klaus von Stauffenberg, a professional army officer and member of the resistance council, had made four attempts so far. Luck was always on the *Führer*'s side – luck and the weapon of inconsistency. Few people knew the *Führer*'s timetable. At any given time he was rarely where people expected him to be. In addition, the *Führer* hardly moved without a bullet-proof vest and a three-and-a-half pound, laminated steel plate in his military cap. It was also known that he always carried a revolver and was a first-class marksman. His personal bodyguard consisted of highly trained sharpshooters.

As Helga von Haensel lay against the silk pillowcase, smoking her cigarette, it was hard to guess that thoughts of assassination and bloodshed were being conjured up behind her attractive blue eyes. It was time for the resistance council to stop vacillating and organise themselves properly, not leave affairs to individuals.

Von Fegeleinn stubbed out his cigarette and smiled down at her.

'I can wangle some leave soon, darling,' he said abruptly. 'How about going down to Austria, away from Berlin and the bombing, and going up into the mountains for some ski-ing?'

The girl looked at him and frowned. 'How can you make such a suggestion with things the way they are?'

Von Fegeleinn pouted like a naughty schoolboy being scolded by his mother. 'Honestly, Helga, I am worried about you . . . about us. I think . . .'

Helga von Haensel gave an exasperated sigh and stubbed out her cigarette with a jerk of annoyance. 'Don't think, Helmuth. I'm thinking for both of us.'

She turned and switched on the radio. There was a burst of martial music and then the announcer reminded listeners that it was Heroes' Day for the Reich.

She laughed sourly. 'Heroes' Day!' She snapped off the radio and turned back to the sulky von Fegeleinn.

'Come on, Helmuth,' she said with a grimace. 'Make love to me. Make me forget this damned war for a few moments.'

In his room in the Hotel Adler, Collins lay on his bed smoking and listening to the radio. Grand Admiral Karl Doenitz was making a speech in honour of Heroes' Day. It was full of the usual sentiments which Collins had been hearing in speeches made by Nazi leaders. The Admiral called for the unity of the German people in the 'pitiless struggle for the existence or annihilation of the nation'. At the end of the speech there was a pause and then a grave-voiced announcer thanked the Grand Admiral, who had insisted on making the broadcast even though, a few hours before he was due on the air, news had reached him of the death of his son, naval officer *Leutnant* Doenitz, who had been killed in the Atlantic. There was another pause before a recording of the Horst Wessel song was played.

Collins bit his lip and switched it off.

He was wondering how much longer he was going to be confined to the hotel. Since arriving in Berlin the only trips he had been allowed to make outside the hotel room were the almost twice-daily moves to the hotel's air-raid shelter in the cellars. Since 7 March, mass daylight bombing had been a daily occurrence in Berlin. The *Berliner Boersenzeitung,* the only reading material he could get, commented:

'During the last weeks, the air offensive against Germany has reached dynamic proportions, dominating all other types of warfare.

'The Allies' air strategy is closely connected with the coming invasion and, therefore, they consider the Continent as a fortress which must be heavily bombarded before the actual attack commences. Furthermore, the Allied air offensive is aimed to destroy the *Luftwaffe.*'

The RAF and the US 8th Air Force were certainly sending their aircraft over in strength, thousands at a time. Collins had never seen anything like it. On March 7, the German authorities claimed to have shot down 140 Allied bombers during the one

121

daylight raid on Berlin. And it was not just Berlin that was taking the brunt of the aerial offensive. Throughout early March, Stuttgart, Frankfurt, Essen and Nuremburg were all systematically bombed. Aircraft factories at Leipzig, Regensburg and Augsberg too were bombed day and night. The Reich was reeling from the attacks.

Collins was reaching out for another cigarette when there was a sharp tap at the door. He swung himself off the bed to open it.

A tall man, elderly and slightly stooping, stood in the passageway. He wore an SS *Sturmbannführer*'s uniform and carried a worn leather briefcase.

'Sergeant Collins?'

Collins frowned at the drawling English accent.

'Can I come in? I'm Vivian Stranders.'

Collins stood aside and let the man in. He took off his cap, threw it on the bed and, dumping his briefcase on the floor, sprawled in a chair.

'You're English,' said Collins as he shut the door and crossed to sit on the bed.

'German by naturalisation in '34,' smiled Stranders. He glanced around the hotel room.

'Are you comfortable here?'

'It's all right, but I am bored with inaction,' Collins replied.

Stranders reached for his briefcase and extracted a file. 'I have your file here from SD headquarters. Kaltenbrunner's office did a thorough job checking on you.'

Collins waited silently.

'You've volunteered to work for the Reich?'

'Yes.'

'Why?'

Collins gestured to the file. 'It must be in there.'

Stranders smiled thinly. 'Suppose you tell me.'

'I was court-martialled. I didn't want to serve twelve years, so I escaped and came here.'

'As simple as that?' queried Stranders. 'You are just a British Army deserter?'

Collins shrugged. 'What else am I?'

'By your record you were a damned good NCO. I notice that

122

you are not claiming political ideology has prompted your desertion.'

'It wouldn't be true.'

'But, on the other hand, you were a member of the British Fascists and you did tell my colleague Behrens that you had, er, "seen the light" and wished to take part in the great struggle against Bolshevik barbarianism.'

Collins grimaced. 'I believe that stuff,' he admitted. 'But I can't say it was my main motivation. I wouldn't have fought in the British Army for these past four years if I were a dedicated Fascist, would I?'

Stranders chuckled. 'I like your candour, Collins. I get sick of men like Joyce, Amery and Baillie-Stewart all bleating away about their faith in Fascism. Let's not pretend: we are all out for what we can get, what is expedient for our own comfort. The question I ask myself is – what do you want?'

Collins reached for a cigarette. 'I just want a simple job, something I can do.'

'Propaganda broadcasting?'

'I've been a professional soldier for the past five years, since I joined the Army in 1938. I'm not qualified to do much else. I wouldn't feel right broadcasting.'

'What could you do then?'

'Couldn't you get me a job in the military line? Training recruits or something?'

Stranders suddenly smiled broadly. Without saying anything he reached into his briefcase and took out a leaflet. He handed it to Collins. Collins read:

'As a result of repeated applications from British subjects from all parts of the world wishing to take part in the common European struggle against Bolshevism, authorisation has recently been given for the creation of a British volunteer unit.

The British Free Corps publishes herewith the following short statement of the aims and principles of the unit.

1. The British Free Corps is a thoroughly British volunteer unit conceived and created by British subjects from all parts of the Empire who have taken up arms and pledged

their lives in the common European struggle against Soviet Russia.

2. The British Free Corps condemns the war with Germany and the sacrifice of British blood in the interests of Jewry and international finance and regards this conflict as a fundamental betrayal of the British people and British imperial interests.

3. The British Free Corps desires the establishment of peace in Europe, the development of close friendly relations between England and Germany, and the encouragement of mutual understanding and collaboration between the two great Germanic peoples.

4. The British Free Corps will neither make war against Britain nor the British Crown, nor support any action or policy detrimental to the interests of the British people.

Published by the British Free Corps

'The Corps urgently needs good NCOs,' Stranders said quietly. 'They need training instructors. Would the job appeal to you?'

The excitement in Collins's face was not exactly forced. 'Yes, it would.'

'You'd volunteer for the unit?'

'Yes.'

Stranders grunted in satisfaction. '*Reichsführer* Heinrich Himmler has appointed me in charge of recruitment. I am glad I reached you before Hansen of the England Committee. He would have tried to enlist you for the propaganda department. You'll be much more use as a training instructor of the British Free Corps.'

'It sounds exactly the sort of job that would make me happy,' agreed Collins.

Stranders rose to his feet.

'Very well, Collins, I shall be in touch within a day or two. We'll transfer you to the corps' headquarters.'

Collins watched him go with a tingling feeling of excitement. Surely it couldn't be as easy as that?

124

Chapter Fifteen

Rudi Behrens sat at his desk in his office in the Prinz Albrecht Strasse, his feet balanced on the corner of it, reading a pamphlet. He took long drags on his cigarette as his expressionless eyes glanced over the paragraphs which exhorted the German people to express their anger at the anarchy into which they had been led by the National Socialists. *Let us put an end to the present state of things, so that we can again begin from the beginning. Things could not become worse.*

'Treacherous swine!' muttered Behrens.

Across the far side of the desk, Manfred Reinecke nodded morosely. 'These illegal pamphlets are being circulated all over Berlin and in many of the provincial towns *Herr Standartenführer*,' he said. 'The whole thing is carefully organised.'

Behrens stubbed out his cigarette. 'There is no way of tracking down the printing press?'

Reinecke shook his head. 'I have had a long talk with the *Kriminalpolizei* who undertook the initial investigation. They got absolutely nowhere.' Reinecke grinned. 'That's probably why General Nebe decided to hand the whole case over to the Gestapo.'

General Nebe was head of Kripo, the *Kriminalpolizei*.

'So what do we know?' pressed Behrens.

'We know that there are various dissident groups throughout the Reich,' Reinecke said. 'So far, they have been small groups – intellectuals, communists, trade unionists and other riff-raff. Until now there has been no co-ordination among them. They have been isolated. The production of these pamphlets, however, indicates a certain amount of cohesion, especially when it comes to distribution.'

Behrens slung the pamphlet on his desk and glanced at his assistant. 'So?'

'General Nebe is sure that the pamphlets are being produced by the Allies and smuggled into the country. I think they are being printed within the Reich.'

The telephone interrupted them with a jangle.

'*Herr Standartenführer? Frau* Behrens is on the line.'

There was a few moments before Inge Behrens was put through. Her voice sounded breathless, a little hesitant.

'Rudi?'

'Is anything wrong, Inge?'

'It's Jo-Jo.'

Jo-Jo was their pet name for their ten-month-old baby, Joachim.

'What's wrong?'

'That awful cough he had last night. It's got worse. I took him to the doctor. He suggests giving him honey in hot water. Rudi, where can we get honey from?'

Behrens thought a moment.

'Don't worry, Inge,' he said reassuringly. 'I'll come home lunch-time and bring some honey with me.'

'Can you really do that, Rudi?' her voice was suddenly happy.

'Don't worry.'

'Poor little Jo-Jo. He's so prone to infection.'

'Don't worry. I'll be home soon.'

After he had put the telephone down, Behrens sat still for a few moments thinking. Then he glanced at Reinecke.

'Come, Manfred. Let's go down to the Geisler Strasse in Kreuzberg and see our old friend there.'

Reinecke raised a questioning eyebrow.

At a house in the Geisler Strasse there lived a black-marketeer whom the Gestapo employed as an informer, as well as using his services to supply their wants from time to time.

'You think he might know something about the seditious pamphlets?' asked Reinecke.

'I think he might know where I can buy some honey,' replied Behrens gravely.

Collins was bored. It was two days since Stranders had visited him and he was bored. Nothing had happened. True, he was not wanting anything. Cigarettes and alcohol were freely supplied and he had been able to get some reading material – copies of the magazine *Das Reich*. But he was wondering whether he was going to be incarcerated in the Hotel Adler for ever.

The woman who knocked softly on his hotel-room door came as a surprise. She was tall, pale blonde and very attractive. He could not make up his mind whether her eyes were blue or grey. She wore a neat pale-blue suit, a matching overcoat, and she carried a small briefcase.

'Good morning, Mr Collins,' she said in neat, precise English. 'I am Countess von Haensel. I am secretary to Doctor Hansen of the England Committee of the Foreign Office.'

Collins felt gauche and awkward. It had been a long time since he had been near an attractive woman. She sat primly in the same chair that Stranders had sprawled in, opened her case and took out a file.

'I am told that you have volunteered to work for the Reich, Mr Collins?'

Collins said nothing.

'*Sturmbannführer* Stranders has visited you?'

'Yes.'

It was an unnecessary question. It must all be down in the girl's file.

'And we understand that you have volunteered to join the SS unit known as the *Britisches Freikorps*.'

'Yes.'

'Well, there is little need for our department to trouble you, Mr Collins. We just have to make sure that you volunteered to join the unit of your own volition, your own free will, and that you have not been pressurised by any one.'

'No,' smiled Collins. 'I have joined of my own free will.'

'You would not be prepared to accept a civilian appointment in the Ministry of Propaganda? Perhaps a position with Radio Concordia under your old comrade, Mr Joyce?'

Collins shook his head.

'Training the men in the British Free Corps is something I know and can do.'

Helga von Haensel closed her file and replaced it in her case. 'That is all I need to know,' she said, rising.

'When will I be sent to the unit?' pressed Collins.

She suddenly looked at him for the first time. Until then she had been distant, avoided looking at him. What she saw made her frown.

'As soon as the papers have been approved from the Prinz Albrecht Strasse,' she said, dropping her eyes.

At the door she paused and turned back to him. 'Tell me, Mr Collins . . . I am interested. What makes you a traitor to your country?'

Collins was taken aback. 'Surely it is in the file?' he said.

She shrugged, gazing at him with a look which melded curiosity and hostility. 'Doesn't it worry you that most of your countrymen regard you as a traitor?'

Collins gazed back at the enigmatic young woman. 'In the eyes of your countrymen, however, I am a patriot, pursuing a true internationalism. Traitor is such a relative term. If men and women fail in their plans to overthrow a government and change their country, then they are called "traitors". If they succeed, then they are acclaimed as heroes and statesmen.'

The girl stared at him for a moment before leaving. The curious look on her face bothered Collins for a long time afterwards.

Behrens had his apartment in the suburb of Wilmersdorf, an area which, so far, had escaped most of the chaos and destruction of the bombing raids. A typical piece of Berlin humour had been painted up in the bomb-blackened wastelands of the central districts: *The Wilmersdorfers are last to reach their coffins.* Behrens's apartment was a comfortable, well-furnished, three rooms, bathroom and kitchen on the second floor of a new apartment block.

He let himself into the apartment just before mid-day. At once his wife Ingeborg hurried in from the kitchen.

She was a mousey-haired, dowdy young woman who, was possessed of a well-shaped body and a capacity for sensual love-making belied by her heavy facial features. She was a peasant girl from the same village in which Behrens had grown up. Behrens's father had also been a peasant farm-worker, on one of the great Swabian estates owned by a nobleman army general. Behrens, a bare-foot, ragged-arsed farmboy, had not been noticed by the inhabitants of the great *Schloss* which dominated the estate. As he grew up, he saw the appalling conditions endured by those around him, and decided that he would not live as his father had done, and his father's father. Rudi Behrens would improve his lot. He took a job in the village as a butcher's delivery boy. He bought his first pair of shoes the week before he attended his first National Socialist Party meeting. He was a ready candidate to enlist in the *Sturmabteilung,* the SA stormtroopers. Maintaining order at meetings, or running riot on the streets and beating up the opposition appealed to the young Behrens. He came to the notice of certain prominent local party officials.

When the SA fell into disfavour with the *Führer* and was replaced by the SS, Behrens was one of the first to transfer his allegiance, eventually transferring again to the *Geheime Staatspolizei,* where he came to the notice of Ernst Kaltenbrunner. The former bare-foot delivery boy was good at his job. It was a job that he never discussed with his wife, nor did his wife ever display any curiosity about it. She simply accepted that he was a policeman, brought in a good wage and had a secure position.

'Jo-Jo's cough is really bad, Rudi,' she said, hurrying to take his coat and pecking him absently on the cheek.

Behrens could hear the plaintive wail of the infant in the bedroom. With a grin and the air of a conjurer taking a rabbit out of a hat, Behrens produced a small jar of honey from his pocket. Inge's eyes lit up.

'Oh, Rudi! I knew I could rely on you. Wait a minute, let me mix this up for Jo-Jo and then I'll get your lunch.'

She hurried into the bedroom while Behrens relaxed on the settee and picked up a newspaper. It was their regular daily, the National Socialist *Volkischer Beobachter.* He thumbed through it idly. The editorials were full of the fact that the Irish Free State had refused to withdraw its embassies and legations from the Axis countries in spite of severe pressure from Britain and America. Now Britain had decided to suspend all travel across the Irish Channel, while the Americans were talking about economic sanctions. A loose page fell out, no, not a loose page – a leaflet.

Behrens reached down and picked it up from where it had

fallen on the floor. He wondered whether it was some advertisement. He scanned it and his eyes widened in disbelief. *An appeal to the German people not to be misled as to the real issues of the war...*

He closed his mouth in a grim line. 'Inge!'

She came to the living room door at once, frowning at the tone in his voice.

'Inge, where did you buy this newspaper?'

She pursed her lips in thought.

'The usual place, I suppose. Yes, the kiosk on the corner of the street. I bought it on my way up, when I came back from the doctor.'

'You didn't leave the newspaper anywhere, put it down so that someone could slip something inside?'

'No. Slip what inside, Rudi?'

'A damned treacherous piece of subversion, that's what,' muttered Behrens. 'I must go and talk with the kiosk owner.'

'But lunch is ready,' protested his wife.

Behrens hesitated. 'All right. The kiosk owner will keep. I'll see him after lunch.' He smiled at her. 'How's Jo-Jo now?'

'He likes the honey and warm water. I'll give him some more later.' She looked over her shoulder. 'Bless him, he's sleeping now. I'll get the lunch.'

Behrens nodded absently and turned his attention back to the leaflet.

Chapter Sixteen

Hauptsturmführer Gerhard Gottschalk had not wanted to join the SS; in fact he had not wanted to join the armed forces at all. At the time of the reintroduction of enforced military service, in 1935, Gottschalk had been approaching forty years of age; he was overweight and slightly asthmatic. He was over age and generally unfit for service, and was therefore not bothered by the new law. He continued his job as schoolmaster of a small Bavarian village school until November 1939. That was when two men had arrived from Berlin. Gottschalk, it seemed, had one qualification which had made it impossible to continue his anonymous way of life. He had a degree in English and had spent many holidays in England, supplementing his income in the late 1920s by translating English books into German for a Berlin publishing house.

It was with some bewilderment that Gerhard Gottschalk was transformed from a Bavarian back-water schoolmaster into an SS officer, leaving his homely wife and two daughters in the picturesque mountain village while he went to work in Berlin.

The job was easier than he had at first imagined. It consisted mainly of translation work. He was so good at it that he was soon promoted to head of his section. In December 1943, he had been made a captain and the following month had received orders to report to Hildesheim where he was to be commanding officer of a small unit of the Waffen-SS, called the *Britisches Freikorps*. Before he left Berlin, the pudgy-faced captain had been called into the office of SS *Sturmbannführer* Stranders, a man with a strange accent he could not place. The *Sturmbann-führer* had told him that the new unit had the wholehearted approval of the *Führer* and consisted mainly of ex-POWs who wished to join the Germans in the common European struggle against the Soviets. Stranders had assured him that there were many such Britishers.

Then Stranders had called a young man into the office; a pale-faced youth with sunken eyes and an exhausted expression. Gottschalk could detect in him the dregs of some animal charm and vitality, a degenerated handsomeness, in spite of his nervous, jerky movements. He spoke to Gottschalk about his vision – the vision of a British Legion fighting with the Reich against the Bolshevik menace. He spoke of thousands of his countrymen who would flock to join the Legion of St George, as he called it. The time was coming when he would head a British government-in-exile on the Channel Islands, until the ultimate German victory over his misguided fellow countrymen, dominated by the contemptible warmonger Churchill. Gottschalk listened without comment. Finally, the young man departed.

Sturmbannführer Stranders simply grimaced. When Gottschalk pressed him, he said that the man was an English ally, the son of a British Cabinet minister with important connections.

The young man's vision of a British legion was a fantasy. When Gerhard Gottschalk arrived in Hildesheim he was bitterly disappointed. The *Britisches Freikorps* was no more than a bunch of forty or so rowdy children. They were hardly a military unit. They were controlled by six of their number who seemed to have appointed themselves NCOs. Like children who had been promised sweets by a stranger and followed that stranger into unfamiliar country, they were bewildered, frightened and sad creatures who had tried to escape from the harsh realities of prison camp life by volunteering for the unit on the promise of better treatment, food and general conditions. There were, of course, some hard cases among them, men who would sell their allegiance for the price of a cigarette. There were a few – very few – fanatical Fascists, men such as Sergeant Francis McLardy. According to his file, he had been a prominent member of the British Union of Fascists. He had enlisted and been captured in 1940. Sent to a POW camp in Poland, he had volunteered to join the SS to 'take part in the struggle against Bolshevism'. The SS had accepted the offer and brought him to the British Free Corps. McLardy still believed all the half-baked theories drummed into him as a member of Oswald Mosley's Blackshirt organisation.

They were an odd bunch, these British, Gottschalk reflected. His main job was to increase recruitment and instil some military discipline. To that end he had asked Stranders to send him more qualified NCOs. Of the few NCOs he had, Gottschalk found that he could only trust one – the unit's senior NCO or *Hauptscharführer*, Tom Cooper. Cooper was a dependable, unquestioning soldier. In fact, he ought not to have been a member of the *Britisches Freikorps* at all. He considered himself completely German. But Tom Cooper was, in fact, a Londoner born and bred. His father was English and his mother was German. It had been the mother who was the dominant influence in young Cooper's life. She had raised her son to think of himself as a German. In his youth, Cooper had joined the British Union of Fascists and was proud of the fact that he had taken part in the attacks on East End Jews. Just before the outbreak of the war his mother had taken him to her home in Germany, where he had become a teacher. When war came, he had joined the Waffen-SS believing himself to be completely German. When he was told that had his father been German, this would have decided his nationality, Cooper had promptly naturalised himself. That had been in 1943. As a soldier in the SS Adolf Hitler Division he had become just another average, unthinking soldier. When his division had been pulled back for a rest, the meticulous files of the SS were sifted and he was transferred to the British Free Corps. Cooper hated being associated with the Corps, but orders were orders. He accepted the position of senior NCO with resignation.

But without Cooper, Gottschalk found it difficult to control the unit. In January there had been near disaster when Cooper had escorted six members of the Corps to the Eastern Front. Headquarters had come up with the idea that if members of the Corps saw what conditions were like in Russia, it would help them in convincing their fellow countrymen to enlist when they visited the POW camps. The British Free Corps party had in the event become cut off by the rapid Soviet advance, and two of its members had been reported missing, believed dead. Cooper and the others had only just managed to withdraw safely.

Gerhard Gottschalk sighed deeply in his unhappiness. He wished he were back behind his comfortable desk in Berlin. At least he had no decisions to take then. Better still, he wished he were back teaching at the school in his village.

He opened the file before him. Sergeant Charles Collins, sentenced to twelve years' penal servitude for mutiny, escaped from a military detention barracks, had reached Germany and volunteered to join the corps.

Gottschalk leant back in his chair and gazed at the man standing quietly at ease before his desk. The rotund little captain saw no hint of weakness in the firm set of Collins's jaw, the steadiness of his eyes, the strong mouth. There was no slackness there, as there was with many other members of the Corps.

Gottschalk let his eyes drop back to the file.

Collins watched him with hidden amusement. That morning

a uniformed SS man had arrived at the Hotel Adler and told Collins to get ready for an immediate journey. The journey by train had been slow and tedious, with frequent stops for air-raid alarms. Eventually they had arrived at Hildesheim and reported at a converted jumble of buildings which reminded Collins of ecclesiastical architecture. It was later he learned that it had been an old monastery.

'An impressive record, Collins,' the little captain said, looking up from the file, 'two decorations for bravery. I need good NCOs. The men here are not what I would call first-class soldiers. There are few here I would trust to carry out the simplest military duty. Most of your compatriots are more concerned with leading an easy life. They drink, fraternise with the local women, and are not susceptible to discipline.'

Collins said nothing during the pause that followed.

'You realise the aims and principles of this unit?'

'I believe so, *Herr Hauptsturmführer*,' said Collins quietly.

'This is the vanguard of a great movement. You and your comrades will be fighting with the best of Europe's youth to preserve European civilisation and your common cultural heritage from the menace of Jewish Communism. What the warmonger Churchill does not recognise is the fact that Europe includes England. Should the Soviets overcome Germany and the other countries of Europe, nothing on this earth would save the Continent from Communism. England would inevitably succumb. The conflict between England and Germany is racial suicide. We have a common enemy to face. Germany and England should stand shoulder to shoulder.'

Collins smiled at the man's pathetic naivety. 'I believe that too,' he nodded.

'*Sturmbannführer* Stranders says that your prime motive is not a political one.'

'That is true,' agreed Collins. 'But I need to do something and I don't have to be a political fanatic to be a drill sergeant in your unit.'

Gottschalk grimaced. He certainly needed a good drill sergeant and Collins's record showed him to be competent.

'Last week I received an order to increase drill-training and discipline. I have been ordered, heaven knows why, to make this unit into a first-class drill unit. The unit must be able to parade with the same military precision for which your Guards regiments are famous. Can you do that?'

Collins shrugged. 'Any group of men can be taught to drill and march. It requires no intelligence.'

'Good,' Gottschalk closed the file. 'I am placing you on the strength of this unit, Collins. As from today, 14 March, you will receive one mark per day in payment. In addition, you will draw ten marks on the tenth, twentieth and thirtieth days of each month. The additional payment is an SS supplement. Passes are not too difficult to acquire. Make your applications to me. You will be given the non-commissioned rank of section leader, SS *Raumführer*. It will be your task to give the men close-order drill and weld them into a cohesive military unit. Is that clear?'

As Collins nodded, the little captain pressed a buzzer on his desk.

The man who entered was young, tall and blond. He wore his uniform as if it had been tailor-made for him. He halted before the *Hauptsturmführer*'s desk and threw out his hand in the Nazi salute.

'This is Sergeant Collins,' said Gottschalk. 'He will be *Raumführer* Collins from now and will be in charge of drill. Collins, this is *Hauptscharführer* Cooper, our senior NCO.'

Cooper remained at attention, only his blue eyes flickered towards Collins to examine him.

'See that Collins is fitted with a uniform.'

'At once, *Herr Hauptsturmführer*,' snapped Cooper.

Gottschalk gazed up at Collins and suddenly smiled. 'Welcome to the British Free Corps, Collins.'

Brigadier Kylie sat rather ill at ease on the edge of his chair in the Prime Minister's small study. The Prime Minister had just lit one of his cigars and was sitting back in his swivel chair as if meditating on a complex problem.

'I'd say another year if we are lucky, Kylie,' he said at last. 'The war will drag on for another year and the casualties will be appalling, especially when we invade Europe.'

Kylie nodded agreement. He had no comfort to offer the

Prime Minister during his regular weekly briefing on the situation in Germany.

'Hitler has just appointed Field Marshal Rommel as commander of Army Group B, in the west. The appointment was made in January, but we have only just learnt about it.'

'Army Group B?'

'The main force with which the Germans will meet our invasion troops on the beach-heads.'

Churchill removed his cigar and grimaced. 'Of all Hitler's generals, Rommel is the most gifted and astute. That sounds like bad news for us.'

'Perhaps, sir. But we have reports that opposition to Hitler is growing stronger and . . .'

'Those reports have been arriving on my desk ever since I came to this office,' interrupted the Prime Minister. 'It seems that all German generals do is whine and complain about the Austrian corporal who leads them. They are like a lot of recalcitrant schoolboys. They try to bargain. Will we negotiate if they get rid of Hitler? In other words, they will not act until we promise them the moon. That is not resistance, that's finding alternative butter for their bread.'

Kylie smiled. 'It may soon be out of their hands, sir.'

Churchill nodded thoughtfully. 'Hagen?'

'Yes sir.'

'Not that I know anything about it,' smiled the Prime Minister, 'but how is your man faring?'

'Our last report was that he was in Berlin. Certain German agents over here, whom we know and use to feed information to the German High Command, were ferreting round for details about Hagen a few days ago. Naturally, we did not stand in their way.'

The Prime Minister sighed. 'So you believe Hagen is still in the running?'

'Yes sir.'

There was a tap on the door and one of the Prime Minister's secretaries entered. 'Excuse me, Mister Prime Minister, may I draw your attention to the time?'

Churchill glanced at the clock and sighed. 'Very well.'

The secretary left, and Churchill shrugged apologetically.

'That was a diplomatic way of reminding me that His Majesty is coming to dine with me here tonight,' he explained. 'I have to get ready.'

Kylie stood up and collected his papers. 'I presume our war aim is still the same, sir? Unconditional surrender?'

'What makes you ask, Brigadier?'

'We have had another plea from the German dissidents. This time they're asking, if Hitler was ousted and a more democratic government were established in Germany, would we then help them to turn back Soviet advances in the east, rather than let eastern Europe fall to the Communists?'

Churchill chewed on his cigar. 'The Soviets are our allies.'

'Expedient allies, sir.'

Churchill gazed at Kylie for a moment and then his mouth softened into a smile. 'While Hitler and his Nazis thugs are in power, our war aim is absolutely clear: unconditional surrender. If, for example, your man Hagen were to be successful, the situation would undoubtedly change. We'll just have to wait and see, won't we? Good night, Brigadier.'

Brigadier Kylie saluted politely and left the room.

Chapter Seventeen

The week had passed in an atmosphere of total unreality. Within a day of joining the British Free Corps, Collins had been fitted with a field grey Waffen-SS uniform and the insignia of a *Raumführer*. His quarters consisted of a small cell-like room. Apparently all the NCOs in the unit had their own rooms, while the other ranks slept in a large dormitory dominated by a huge portrait of the Duke of Windsor. They were a poor lot; not one was really cut out to be a soldier. Neither did the NCOs impress Collins. Only Cooper's behaviour seemed reasonable, because he believed himself to be a German and that it was to Germany he owed his allegiance. He apparently felt, and behaved as if he were, superior to the others in the unit.

McLardy, for example, was a bore. He was always enthusing about his half-baked ideas on race, his anti-communism, and the fact that he believed Hitler to be the saviour of the Western world. Within half an hour of meeting him, Collins had been pressed with a copy of Amery's book *England Faces Europe*. Out of curiosity Collins thumbed through it to see what the founder of the British Free Corps had to say. It was a childish farrago of such stupidity that Collins wondered how even the most fanatical Fascist could stomach it. According to Amery, 'Hebrew interior colonisation of the United Kingdom has reduced a former great democracy to a vested dictatorship', while 'Roosevelt's Jewish bankers financed the Bolshevik Revolution of 1917'.

Whereas McLardy was a bore, Collins found Lance-Corporal Roy Courlander to be a man of ambition, living in a dream world. He envisaged himself as *Brigadeführer,* commanding officer of the Corps, which would rise to become several thousand strong. Courlander was a New Zealander who had volunteered in order to escape the hardship of his POW camp. He had fantasies of his own importance. He told Collins that soon a provisional British government would be established in the Channel Islands with John Amery as its head and Lance-Corporal Courlander as commander-in-chief of its armed forces.

One NCO for whom Collins felt a contemptuous sorrow was Warrant Officer Raymond Hughes, a naive Welshman. He had been an air-gunner in the RAF, was shot down, and volunteered to show the Germans how to improve their air defence of Berlin. He had then gone on to broadcast propaganda, being trained in radio technique by Margaret Joyce, wife of William Joyce. He was no good at it, but for a while was allowed to broadcast in Welsh, with a religious theme running through his tirade of anti-English and anti-Jewish nonsense.

The rest were of a similar stamp. Private Ewan Martin of the Canadian Scottish Regiment had promoted himself to NCO rank. He had joined the Corps by way of being an informer in his POW camp and having to be transferred for his own safety. He had given the Germans details about escape attempts, secret radios, and had even volunteered information about the Dieppe landings.

Corporal Frank Maton of the Royal Artillery and Private Hugh Cowie of the Gordon Highlands, who made up the hierarchy of the Corps, were not interested in war or politics. They were weak, indolent men, simply out to make life for themselves as easy as possible.

Collins tried to avoid them, and settled down to concentrate his efforts on drilling the men. No arms nor weapons of any sort were allowed to be handled by the Corps, so the emphasis was on parade-ground drills. Discipline and drilling, according to Cooper, had been tightened up by Gottschalk during the past week. Immediately before breakfast, at eight o'clock, the unit was on parade and an inspection was carried out. It was Cooper who usually conducted the inspection and reported to Gottschalk. After breakfast Collins was allowed to drill the men for two hours. Then the unit formed up and marched to the Hildesheim swimming pool or to the municipal sports fields for physical training. Gottschalk told Collins that he wanted the men toughened up, as they had become flabby after months of inaction. Collins did his best, but he could not help thinking that they would not last long in front-line conditions.

After the mid-day meal there came lectures on Fascist philosophy by McLardy and his disciples. Courlander also gave lectures on techniques for recruitment. Gottschalk was preparing some members of the unit to make tours of POW and internment camps. Collins fervently prayed that he would not have to become involved in such visits.

There was friction among the members of the Corps. Collins found himself observing with amusement the conflict between the ardent Nazis, led by McLardy, and those who didn't give a damn about anything other than their own comfort. McLardy often organised political meetings, at which he would harangue everyone in sight on the virtues of the German *Führer*. There were members of the Corps who objected to being subjected to Nazi propaganda twenty-four hours a day, but one former BUF member in the Corps went so far as to hang a swastika flag over his bed, with a large photograph of Hitler, before which he would kneel in an attitude of prayer each evening.

McLardy complained to Gottschalk frequently about the lack of political motivation in the Corps. The indolent members of the Corps asked Gottschalk to remove the British Nazis from their midst. Friction only subsided when Collins got them on the parade ground.

The days passed quickly. Collins found himself worrying. So far there had been no indication that the intelligence which Roberts had received was correct. No one mentioned anything about the *Führer*'s birthday. It was on Saturday, 25 March, after he had spent eleven days at Hildesheim, that Collins began to get nervous. What if the Germans had changed their minds? What if Roberts had been wrongly informed? What then? He had already made up his mind that he must go south, escape across the Swiss border. But if Roberts was right and the Corps was going to be used as a birthday honour guard on 20 April, then it was time he made some preparations.

The barracks at Hildesheim contained no armaments, certainly there were no explosives nor detonators. Where was he to get them? Even if he managed to get some, it would not be wise to hide them in the barracks. He had already become aware that the informer, Martin, had searched his room on two occasions, probably reporting to Gottschalk. No, Collins could not risk hiding explosives in his room. The first thing to do, of course, was find out whether he could, in fact, get explosives at all.

That was why a visit to 'Uncle Wilhelm' was now necessary. He decided that it was time to get Gottschalk to give him a pass, wander down to the Hildesheim *Postamt* and see if he could make contact.

The *Führer* was in a mood for reminiscing as he relaxed in his study at Berghof. It was a small study on the first floor: a bare, almost bleak room, with a little desk, a few books and, on the wall, a picture of the *Führer* addressing a political rally. The *Führer* liked the room. It was where he had once entertained Neville Chamberlain and assured the British premier that he had no intention of starting a war; that there would certainly be 'peace in our time'. Now he sat lounging in his chair to one side of the tall Bavarian stove which threw its warmth into the small room while, outside, the freezing rain could be heard splattering on the roof.

Seated on the other side of the stove was the *Führer*'s mistress, Eva Braun, more diplomatically referred to as the *Führer*'s 'dearest companion'. Seated opposite them was Josef Goebbels and his wife, Magda. They had enjoyed a pleasant luncheon and now they sat recalling the early days of the Party, the struggling rise to power.

'I never really wanted a war with England,' the *Führer* said with a characteristically abrupt change of subject. 'It is only Churchill who stands in my way. I have always had the deepest respect and admiration for the English. Why,' his face grimaced in silent laughter, 'didn't my own brother marry an Englishwoman?'

Eva raised a curious eye and glanced briefly at Josef and Magda Goebbels. They looked a little shocked. The *Führer* made it a rule never to mention his family and then it was only his sister, Angela, who was acknowledged, certainly not his brother, Alois, who ran a restaurant in Berlin, and who had married in London, in 1910, a woman called Bridget Dowling. No one present dared to point out to the *Führer* that his erstwhile sister-in-law had, in fact, been an Irish woman. Certainly the child of that marriage, William Patrick Hitler, had been born and raised in England. Alois Hitler had deserted his wife in 1914 and it was not until the 1920s that 'Willie' Hitler had arrived in Germany looking for his father, intrigued by the fact that he bore the same name as the rising new political leader. As a stop to the persistent young man, the *Führer*, on becoming Chancellor, had secured his English nephew a job in the Berlin Reichskreditbank. Now no one spoke of Willie Hitler, not since the young man had fled Germany just before the war and began to earn his living by writing and lecturing about his famous uncle. Mention of Willie Hitler usually brought on a paroxysm of rage from the *Führer*.

Josef and Magda Goebbels exchanged nervous glances, but Hitler was smiling gently.

Eva bit her lip, trying to suppress her annoyance. She hoped that Adolf would not mention his friendship with that Mitford woman. She felt a jealous rage as the memory of the young

English aristocrat came to mind. The girl had positively simpered like a pet dog around her beloved Adolf. Thank God he had seen the danger signs. After the girl's suicide attempt, the best thing had been to arrange a passage back to England through Switzerland. Ironically, it was Eva who had had to oversee the transference of the girl across the border.

'The English are stubborn,' Goebbels was volunteering. 'They can't see that their only choice is to make a deal with us or allow themselves to be over-run by the Soviets.'

The *Führer* made a dismissive gesture. 'The English and Americans will come to their senses. They will have to come to an agreement with us or go under to the Muscovite barbarians. They will come to their senses, of that I am assured. The English are an intelligent people.'

'Isn't Winifrid Wagner English?' Eva pouted thoughtfully. She liked to make an intelligent contribution to the *Führer*'s conversations.

Hitler smiled benignly at her. 'She is a good friend. But it is true she was born and raised in a place called Kent.'

Winifrid Wagner had married Siegfrid, the son of the composer, and not only become fiercely German but a staunch supporter of the New Order. Strangely, another of Wagner's children had also married an English citizen. His daughter Eva had married Houston Stewart Chamberlain, the Portsmouth-born son of an English admiral. He had settled in Germany when he was twenty-seven and written several books on German philosophy and culture. He had become a naturalised citizen in 1916 and was awarded an Iron Cross by the Kaiser. Hitler had acknowledged his book *Foundations of the Twentieth Century* to be the gospel of National Socialism. A few years before his death in 1927, Chamberlain had hailed Hitler as ordained by God to lead the German people. The *Führer* still remembered that meeting in Bayreuth with the frail, fanatical old Englishman. He smiled in his reminiscences.

'Yes, one could say we owe the English much. My birthday will be a fitting tribute to them. Is everything going well in that respect, Josef?'

'I believe so, my *Führer*,' Goebbels assured him.

The *Führer* leant back in his chair, and closed his eyes in satisfaction. He was well content – for the moment.

Chapter Eighteen

Collins entered the cold, blue veined marble hall of the Hildesheim *Postamt* and looked around. There were several people queuing at the counters, waiting to be served by officious-looking men seated on the other side of the high grille counter. To one side of the large hall there was a door marked *Staff Only*. Collins walked across and opened it. Beyond was a large sorting room; several postmen stood at a long table parcelling up bundles of letters and cards.

An elderly man turned and glanced at him. 'Lost your way, soldier?' he asked. There was no animosity in his voice.

'I'm looking for Uncle Wilhelm,' replied Collins.

The old man grimaced and turned. 'Anyone seen old man Wielen?' he shouted at his colleagues.

Collins made a mental note of the name.

'Try over at the café. He'll probably be having lunch,' called one of the men.

'Which café?' asked Collins.

'The *Küchenshabe* across the street.'

Collins waved his thanks and, leaving the tall *Postamt* building, he crossed the cobbled thoroughfare to a small café. It was not crowded and he had little difficulty in spotting the old man in the postman's uniform, and sporting the Kaiser Wilhelm moustache, seated by himself, eating a bowl of soup. Collins slipped into the vacant seat in front of the old man.

'Uncle Wilhelm?'

Karl Wielen raised watery blue eyes to stare nervously at the man in the Waffen-SS uniform.

A waiter hovered near by.

'Beer, please,' Collins said. Then he turned his gaze back to the old man.

'I think you are expecting me. My name is Otto. I have a message from your daughter Paula in Hamburg.'

The old man jerked perceptibly, spilling soup from his spoon. He glanced quickly round. 'What is it you want?' he hissed.

Collins sat back with a smile. 'Take it easy, uncle. You look like a stage conspirator.'

The old man made an effort to pull himself together. 'What is it?' he repeated less tensely than before.

'I need a contact,' replied Collins.

The waiter came up with a glass of beer and demanded payment. Collins gave the man a few coins.

'A contact?' asked Karl Wielen, after the waiter had gone. He gazed at Collins with narrowed eyes. 'What sort of contact?'

'I want someone who can supply me with military equipment. Explosives. Detonators.'

Wielen gave a soundless whistle.

'I can't supply you with anything like that.'

'But you know who can?' Collins pressed him.

'I will have to pass you on to someone else,' Wielen said after a long pause. He was frowning at Collins's uniform. 'You come from the old monastery, don't you? Are you English?'

'That's right,' Collins admitted.

Karl Wielen struggled with his thoughts and then shrugged in an acceptance of an incomprehensible situation. 'Can you travel to Hanover?'

'I have a pass until midnight tonight.'

'Good. Do you know the city?'

Collins shook his head.

'Well, don't take the mainline train to Hanover. There is an electric train system which also runs from the *Bahnhof*. It's just one line which goes between here and Hanover . . . a ten-or fifteen-minute run, that's all. When you get out at the station go to Leinestrasse, which runs along the embankment of the river there. Can you remember that?'

Collins nodded an affirmative.

'Off the Leinestrasse is a small side-street called Calenburgerstrasse. There you will find a night-club called *Der Ausleger*.'

'The Outrigger?' repeated Collins.

'That's it. Go there. They have a cabaret. You will see a singer called Else-Else. Tell her that you have been sent by Uncle Wilhelm. The message is: Paula is . . .' the old man had a sudden catch in his throat. 'Paula is alive. She will know what to do.'

Collins finished his beer. 'Thanks.'

'It is all I can do for you,' muttered the old postman. 'Good luck.'

The cellar was lit by candles which flickered and spluttered in the draughts which permeated the old brick walls. Around them were empty wine-racks, criss-crossed with cobwebs – few people could afford wine nowadays. Ten men and two women sat at a long trestle table on which the candles had been placed. With the exception of one man and the two women, everyone was in uniform; none of them was under the rank of *Oberst*. At the head of the table sat an elderly *Generalfeldmarschall*.

'Well,' he said solemnly, gazing around at them, 'the cards have been dealt. It is now up to us to play them as best we can.'

A colonel seated at the far end of the table beat an irritating tattoo on the edge of the trestle with a pencil. He had one eye, no right hand and his left hand had only the thumb, index and middle finger left. Klaus Philip Schenk, Count von Stauffenberg, gazed aggressively at Countess Helga von Haensel. 'Are you sure that you put our case plainly to the representative of the British Government?' he said belligerently. 'Are you sure that the Allies' refusal to negotiate is final?'

Helga von Haensel inclined her head. 'The British made their attitude clear, Count,' she said slowly and with deliberation. 'Only unconditional surrender is acceptable.'

Von Stauffenberg looked furious. 'Have they no conception of what is happening in Europe?' he demanded.

The *Generalfeldmarschall* sighed deeply and held up a pacifying hand. 'Countess von Haensel has done her best. We must accept that the Allies are not interested in Germany. It has come to our attention that there is now a plan in existence. The basis of the plan was apparently worked out last year.'

The gathering looked at the old man attentively.

145

'The Allies are going to adopt a partition of Germany – Britain, America and Russia at the moment, although the so-called Free French are demanding a share. We have learnt that the first steps towards defining their policy were taken in October last year at a conference in Moscow. It has already been agreed among the Allies that after the war the Soviet Union will be given control of forty per cent of Germany, thirty-six per cent of our population and thirty-three per cent of our product resources.'

There was a long silence.

'Are you saying, *Herr Generalfeldmarschall,* that there is no alternative to the devastation of our country but to support Hitler?'

The question came from the civilian.

The *Generalfeldmarschall* shook his head.

'No. What I am saying is that it becomes even more imperative to elimate Hitler. More imperative that Germany has a new government which will offer immediate negotiations to Britain and America. The British and Americans will not give the Soviets anything that they do not have to. I am sure that once Hitler and the Nazis are gone they would be prepared to negotiate with us.'

Von Stauffenberg nodded eagerly. 'Our principal task is to get rid of the maniac who has led our country into this mess.'

'But what if Britain and America still insist on total surrender?' demanded a dour-faced *Generalleutnant.*

'Nonsense!' replied another officer. 'Our troops can hold the Soviets back on the Polish and Rumanian borders for a time while we negotiate with the West. I am sure the *Generalfeldmarschall* is right. We can reach an understanding. The only person who stands in the way is Hitler. Eliminate him and the Allies will negotiate. Do you think the Allies want to see the Soviets dominating a large section of Europe. Of course not.'

Helga von Haensel cleared her throat. 'I wish I had such optimism. Whatever their ideological differences, I think the British and Americans are quite determined to allow the Soviets into Eastern Europe.'

'I disagree,' replied the *Generalfeldmarschall* wearily. 'I think they would help us in defence of our eastern borders once we return to a democratic government.'

There was a silence.

'We must take a vote,' prompted the civilian.

'Very well,' agreed the *Generalfeldmarschall*. 'Each one of you here represents groups opposed to the National Socialists. You are here to represent the interests of your groups. We must reach a policy decision. Do we go forward with all seriousness in our plan to assassinate Hitler, establish a new government and seek negotiations with Britain and America?'

It was the grey-haired woman who posed the question. 'Is there an alternative, *Herr Generalfeldmarschall*?'

'The alternative . . .' the *Generalfeldmarschall* paused and shrugged. 'The alternative is that Germany must fight to the death to support the Nazis as the only alternative to preventing the division and occupation of our country.'

Von Stauffenberg gave a bark of ironic laughter. 'Then there is no alternative, *Herr Generalfeldmarschall*.'

The old general gazed around at the circle of faces in the flickering candlelight. 'You are all agreed then? Shall we go forward with our plans to assassinate Adolf Hitler?'

A ragged chorus rang out hollowly in the shadow-filled cellar. 'Agreed!'

Inge Behrens let herself into the apartment carrying Jo-Jo in her arms and stopped in surprise.

'Rudi!' she exclaimed. 'I didn't know that you would be back for lunch.'

Behrens was relaxing on the settee, smoking and listening to the radio. He glanced up with a grimace. 'I have to be out this evening, perhaps all night, so I came back this afternoon to get some rest.'

Inge lifted the baby into a small wooden playpen and made clucking noises at him. 'There now, darling,' she cooed, 'you play with your toys like the beautiful baby you are. Daddy is going to get some rest, so you play nice and quietly.'

Baby Jo-Jo squealed and grunted.

Inge turned back to her husband with a smile. 'He likes that

147

toy you brought back from Lisbon,' she said. 'Shall I make you some coffee?'

Behrens nodded. 'I wish I had thought to bring back a supply of real coffee so that we wouldn't have to put up with this ersatz rubbish.'

Inge began to busy herself in the kitchen. 'Must you go out tonight?' she called.

'Yes.'

'It gets lonely without you, Rudi,' she sighed. 'It is so frightening, especially during the bombing.'

She brought the coffee to the couch and sat down beside him.

'Yes,' he agreed, 'things are not good in Berlin these days. In fact, only today I was thinking that we might move out of the city. Not far, just a little way. I can get an apartment at Mittenwalde or, if you wanted, I know a house that is free at Teuntz, just by the lake.'

Inge stared at him with wide eyes. 'An entire house? But I thought all movement was restricted?'

Behrens smiled deprecatingly. 'Your husband has a position of some importance. I can arrange the move if I want to.'

Inge closed her eyes and sighed. 'Teuntz is such a lovely little village. An entire house by the lake? I'd much rather go there than Mittenwalde. How did you know that there was a house available there?'

'Oh . . . I have contacts,' replied Behrens. Inge wouldn't understand if he told her. That morning he had signed the Gestapo requisition order for the small house at Teuntz himself. Its previous owners no longer had a use for it. They were, at the moment, *en route* to new accommodation near the village of Bergen – a camp called Belsen. They were Jewish. Behrens wondered how many more Jews were still living as Germans within the Reich. Their ability to survive was amazing.

'Rudi, you are not listening.'

He dragged his thoughts back to Inge.

'I was able to buy some fresh meat for tonight. I'll cook it before you leave.'

He smiled at her as she nestled up to him. She was, in many ways, like a child. She did not really understand what it was to be the wife of someone of his position. Sometimes, not often, he wished she was a little more intelligent, able to appreciate his place in society, within the New Order. But then . . .

He turned towards her and let his hand slide up her skirt to rest on the warmth of her thigh above her stocking.

She reached forward and kissed him hungrily. Then she drew back and smiled coquettishly. 'You'd better go to bed now, Rudi, and get your rest for tonight.'

'I'll go to bed, Inge,' replied Behrens, as she knew he would, 'but you'll come with me.'

She laughed and shivered with pleasurable anticipation.

As Behrens led her into the bedroom she remembered to give a quick glance to where Jo-Jo was playing, absorbed in his toys. Inge Behrens was a conscientious mother.

Chapter Nineteen

Hanover was an old-world town of castles, churches, museums and palaces which rose in an untidy heap on a sandy but fertile plain where the rivers Leina and Ihme joined. It was a beautiful old town but, unfortunately for its beauty, it was also where the main rail crossing from Berlin to Cologne and from Hamburg to Frankfurt-on-Maine was situated. The railway crossing attracted the attention of the Allied bombers. In addition, in the sprawling suburbs, factories for chemicals, india rubber, machine construction and munitions also made Hanover an important military target. Hanover, which was proud of being the first German town to have gas lighting in the streets, had long been among the prominent industrial and commercial centres of the country and therefore had to suffer the consequences of the Allied economic bombing strategy.

Collins alighted at the terminus station in Ernst August Platz and sauntered with his fellow passengers out into the square, pausing by the bronze statue of the old Prussian monarch, who looked down disapprovingly on the chaos of the New Order.

The irregularly built houses reminded Collins of Hildesheim as they clustered around the Markt Kirche, a red-brick fourteenth-century church with its high steeple rising to 310 feet – the highest structure in the city. So far, the beautiful stained-glass windows had survived the ravages of the bombing. Collins walked across the market square before the medieval town hall, and through the old quarter – the once-quaint Bohemian area – known as the Calenberger quarter. Following the old postman's instructions, it was fairly easy to find the Calenbergerstrasse.

The door of the night-club was open. The place was deserted apart from an old woman scrubbing the floor. 'We're closed!' she snapped, catching sight of Collins on the threshold. 'Come back later.'

'What time does the cabaret start?' asked Collins innocently.

'Not until eight o'clock. Come back later.'

Collins turned and left. It was just after four o'clock. He had four hours to kill. He began by wandering around the historic city. There was plenty to see. There was the Guelph Palace, most modern of all the great palaces, which had never been occupied by the royal family but had been a technical high school since 1875. There was the *Herrenhausen,* summer palace of former Hanoverian kings, with its extensive gardens, open-air theatre and museum, approached by a mile-long avenue through artificial orange groves; all was silent and closed now. There was the seventeenth-century Royal Palace Schloss with its great portals, handsome quadrangle and chapel, which contained relics of Henry the Lion, brought from Palestine where he had perished in the crusades. Hanover – with its monuments to the composers Liszt, Eilenriede and Marscher, and the philosophers Schiller and Liebnitz – was a city which awed Collins a little.

After a time of aimless wandering, he returned to the station and found a small café for a meal. There were nearly two hours left before he could return to the night-club, so he found a cinema. The film that was showing was Leni Riefenstahl's *The Triumph of Will,* a documentation of the great melodramatic opera of the Nuremburg Rally. Collins watched it with a curious detachment. When he was younger he had been enthused by

150

Oswald Mosley's pale imitation at London's Olympia. Now the drama meant nothing to him. He saw it for what it was – a great stage-managed pantomime, a contrived hallucination, with blinding searchlights, stamping boots thundering on cobblestones, the bells of the Nuremburg churches pealing as bands of marching musicians blared National Socialist marches. The focus of the pageantry to which the camera always came back was the face of Adolf Hitler standing below a great towering eagle with outspread wings, its talons resting on a naked sword. It was only now that Collins realised that the eagle and sword had been constructed to form the shape of a cross. Below it the animated form of the *Führer* worked himself into a passion – the Messiah of the New Order!

It was an odd contrast to the serene beauty of Hanover.

Collins left the cinema feeling a strange nausea, wondering why, as a young man, he had responded to such emotionalism.

When he arrived at *Der Ausleger* the place was fairly crowded. It was full of uniformed men from all branches of the German forces; and the women, mostly young, were all heavily made up and clad in an assortment of pre-war gowns and dresses. Many of the dresses had been painfully patched or altered to fit. As he entered, a three-piece band was playing while couples smooched across the floor to popular dance tunes. He fought his way through the crowd to the bar.

'Beer, please.'

The barman scowled at him. 'No beer. Only wine or schnapps.'

'A schnapps, then.'

The price was ridiculous but Collins paid without protest.

He felt a tug on his arm and turned back to the smoke-filled room. A woman was smiling at him with an expression she probably considered one of allurement. The badly applied, thick red lipstick, the rouge and eyeshadow made her look obscenely comic. Her figure was too thin to hold any physical attraction. He realised, with surprise, that she was no more than a girl, not even that – a child. She could hardly have been fifteen or sixteen.

'Like some company, soldier?' she said, her features twisting in what was probably a smile under the caked make-up.

151

'Some other time,' replied Collins. 'I'm waiting for Else-Else. Is she on soon?' He gestured inquiringly towards the small stage.

The girl grimaced grotesquely. 'That stuck-up bitch! She doesn't go with soldiers. You'll be out of luck. Best settle for me.'

'I'm a friend,' said Collins. 'I've a message from her uncle.'

'Oh,' the girl regarded him with a speculative expression. 'In that case, when you've seen her come and look me up. Greta's the name. I'll be around.' She turned and walked away, attempting to sway her figure like a vamp in a bad movie.

The band ceased playing and the dancers returned to their tables or the bar. A sweaty master of ceremonies, in shirt sleeves, came on, made a few bad jokes and then introduced the next act. It was the one Collins had been waiting for.

'Here she is, ladies and gentlemen, the sweetheart of the 10th Prussian Army Corps . . . Else-Else!'

The curtain suddenly swept aside to reveal a single chair by a badly painted backdrop of a wall and a lamp-post. Seated casually on the chair was a girl. Under the black tammy she wore, her hair was a riot of close golden curls. The face was delicately shaped and her expression was slightly wistful. The eyes were wide and blue, with an air of innocence. It was difficult to tell with the distortions of the lighting, but her lips seemed naturally red, the mouth dimpled and sensual. Her reclining figure, though clad in a man's belted raincoat, seemed slight and well proportioned – the legs were certainly finely shaped. She could not have been more than twenty-five. Perhaps it was the haunted melancholy of her expression, perhaps it was just natural beauty which made Collins swallow hard.

Her voice, when she began to sing, was soft, almost husky. The song was an old favourite from the Great War – *Lilli Marlene*.

The applause was thunderous.

Several love songs followed, all of them sad, before the curtain swished to, accompanied by a frenzy of clapping.

Collins finished his drink and moved across the stage as the three-piece band started up with a selection of lively dance tunes. He pushed his way between the curtains. The sweaty-faced master of ceremonies barred the way.

'We don't allow customers back here, soldier,' he grunted.

'I want to see *Fraulein* Else.'

The man leered. 'You and a couple of thousand other soldiers. The girls you want are in the café.'

Collins kept his temper. 'You don't understand. I am a friend.'

'That's what they all say.'

'I have a message from her uncle.'

'What?'

The voice made him turn, and he found himself gazing into the anxious blue eyes of the girl he had come to see.

'*Fraulein* Else,' Collins smiled reassuringly. 'I have come from Hildesheim with a message from your Uncle Wilhelm.'

The girl was tense. 'Is . . . is everything all right?' she stammered.

Collins glanced sideways at the master of ceremonies who was staring with unconcealed curiosity. 'Yes. Paula is alive,' replied Collins.

The girl gave a shuddering sigh, and her taut face relaxed a little.

'I have finished for the evening,' she said, her eyes sweeping over his uniform in undisguised curiosity. 'Perhaps we could go for a coffee and you can tell me what Uncle Wilhelm has to say?'

The master of ceremonies interrupted. 'Are you sure everything is all right, Else?' he demanded.

'Perfectly, *Herr* Probst. This gentleman has come with a message from my uncle.'

She turned to Collins. 'I will join you outside. I need a moment to get ready.'

Collins smiled, turned and forced his way back across the crowded night-club floor and emerged in the cold evening air. It was a welcome change after the stifling smoky atmosphere of the club. He fumbled for a cigarette. In close proximity, Else-Else was as attractive as on stage. He realised that he was fascinated by her wistful melancholy.

It was a moment before she came hurrying out of the night-club, her golden hair tumbling loosely about her shoulders. She was still clad in the man's belted raincoat which seemed to

153

enhance her attractiveness. Her voice was soft and breathless. 'Sorry to keep you waiting. I had to collect my money.'

He fell in step beside her.

'There is a café not far from here. We can talk there,' she suggested.

'I hope I did not frighten you,' he said awkwardly.

In the darkness he saw her shoulders rise and fall. 'It is of no matter,' she replied. 'Everyone is frightened these days.'

There was a pause.

'You are not German. I cannot place your accent.'

'I am English.'

She halted in mid-stride and turned to gaze at him. 'English?'

'I am in the *Britisches Freikorps*. It is a Waffen-SS unit. We are stationed in Hildesheim.'

'There are Englishmen in the SS?' her voice was disbelieving.

Collins turned and gestured to the other side of the road where a railing skirted the embankment of the Leine. 'Let's go across and look at the river for a moment,' he urged. 'We can talk there. There is no one about.'

Hesitantly, she followed.

'Let me be straight with you, Else,' he said, lowering his voice. 'I am a British agent. I was sent by London to infiltrate a group of treacherous Englishmen who have been recruited into the SS.'

She said nothing. He could not see her expression in the darkness.

'I am shortly to carry out a job to discredit this unit. I shall need some help – some materials which are difficult to come by. I was given the name of Uncle Wilhelm in Hildesheim. He passed me on to you.'

The girl was silent. For a long time they both leant on the iron railings gazing into the blackness of the river below them.

'I understand,' the girl said slowly.

'Are you in a position to help me?'

'What materials do you need?'

'Military explosives and detonators.'

There was another pause.

'I have a contact who would help. When will you need these . . . materials?'

Collins threw the stub of his cigarette into the water. 'At the end of this month. I would probably only be able to give you twenty-four hours' notice, perhaps less.'

'Very well. I'd better give you an alternative method of contacting me. I do not work in the club all the time.'

Collins smiled. 'Fine. Now let's find this café and have a coffee.'

When Inge Behrens answered the buzz at the apartment door, Manfred Reinecke was lounging against the door-post with a lopsided grin on his Slavic features.

Inge gasped slightly. 'You! I thought you were out with Rudi tonight.'

Reinecke shook his head. 'Sometimes the *Standartenführer* likes to do things by himself,' he smiled. 'Well, aren't you going to let me in?'

Frowning, she stood to one side and let him enter. Reinecke sauntered in, removed his overcoat and threw it down on a chair.

Hesitantly, Inge shut the door and stood with her back to it, watching as he walked with assurance towards the drinks cabinet and poured himself a whisky.

'The *Standartenführer* always keeps a good stock,' he said with an appreciative smack of his lips.

'What do you want, Manfred?' Inge Behrens said a little fearfully.

Reinecke grinned broadly. 'While the *Standartenführer* was in Lisbon you had no need to ask such a question,' he said, dropping into the settee.

Inge shivered slightly and closed her eyes. 'He might come back at any moment,' she protested.

Reinecke shook his head. 'He is off chasing subversives in Potsdam. He won't be back until much later.'

'It's too dangerous.' There was no strength to her objection.

Reinecke knew that the protest was only an empty gesture, Ingeborg Behrens was a simple woman. A good mother, yes; a good wife, perhaps. Behrens did not show her enough affection, was too distant in his treatment of her, too autocratic. She was a simple woman who needed affection, even false affection.

155

And, dowdy as nature had made her, nature had also compensated by giving her an exacting sexual appetite with which to repay affection. He had found that out while Behrens was in Lisbon. True he had made the first overtures and been astonished by her demanding sensuality. It was with grim satisfaction that Reinecke reflected that his job had its compensations, and having an affair with *Standartenführer* Behrens's wife was a throughly enjoyable part of his work.

'Get me some coffee, Inge.'

Inge Behrens nodded nervously and went into the kitchen.

Reinecke's eyes narrowed and swept round the room to the small bureau in which Behrens kept his private papers. He silently rose from the settee and crossed to it. He smiled as he thought that Behrens must be very trustful of his wife; the key was in the bureau lock. It took a moment to extract Behrens's notebook and skim through the latest entries.

'Do you want something to eat?' called Inge from the kitchen.

Reinecke glanced up and swiftly replaced the notebook.

'No,' he replied, as he re-locked the door of the bureau.

Inge appeared in the doorway as he was moving back to the settee. Reinecke turned and moved towards her, encircling her well-shaped body in his arms, feeling its animal vitality respond eagerly to his embrace.

'I've missed you these last few days,' he whispered, bringing his mouth harshly onto hers.

She made a feeble attempt to turn aside his kiss. 'No, we shouldn't . . . not now he's back.'

Reinecke chuckled. 'It was all right when he was in Lisbon. It must still be all right now that he's in Potsdam.'

'No, Manfred. Rudi's my husband. We . . . we are moving into the country and . . .' She made a half-hearted attempt to push his hand from her breast. 'No . . .'

He stopped her protest with another kiss, moving his hand round to tug at the zip-fastener on the back of her dress.

In spite of her protest she moved the warmth of her body against his, firing him with urgent desire. He pulled and guided her to the settee.

'Don't wake Jo-Jo,' she murmured, allowing his hands to move beneath her dress.

Reinecke smiled; it was a pleasure to spy upon *Standarten-führer* Behrens.

Seated in the café, Collins stared in the dim light at the girl called Else-Else. There were only two other people in the place, seated at the far end.

The attractive night-club singer returned his scrutiny with a frown. 'What is wrong?' she asked abruptly.

'I was wondering what an attractive girl like you was doing involved in this sort of work?'

She pouted. 'Compared with what is happening in the occupied countries, it is not much that we do.'

'Nevertheless, it takes courage to work in opposition to the Nazis.'

She gave a swift glance around, hesitating before replying.

'There is little courage in talking, sometimes distributing leaflets and making reports to send to the Allies. The occupied countries demonstrate more courage.'

Collins offered her a cigarette. 'How did you come to be mixed up in this?'

She exhaled softly. 'I knew a man once. He was a beautiful man. I do not mean that in the physical sense. He was simply a truly good and caring person. He believed that all men were created equal and should have equal opportunities in life. He believed that moral rights stood above the law. He was a lecturer at the technical college, and I was a student in his class. One day, in the middle of the class, they came and took him away. We heard that he had been executed. He was a Communist. I am not a Communist. I don't have the idealism. I don't really know what I believe, although I know what it is I should fight against. Does that make sense?'

Collins nodded awkwardly. 'I think I understand,' he said.

They sat silently a while. Then he spoke again: 'My name is Collins, Charles Collins.'

She frowned as she tried to pronounce the Christian name.

'Call me Karl, if you like.'

'Very well, Karl' she said obediently.

There was a moment of mutual understanding between them, some sort of empathy which did not need words. In a sudden flash of intuition, he knew the reason for her haunted sadness, and she knew the depth of his loneliness.

'Damn!' he said, glancing at the wall clock above the café bar. 'I'll have to get the train back to Hildesheim. The last one leaves in half an hour.'

'I'll walk back to the station with you. My apartment is not far from there.'

They walked for a while in comfortable silence through the blacked-out streets, enjoying the strangely familiar sense of well-being each of them derived from the other.

'Is your name really Else-Else?' he suddenly asked as they were crossing the cobbles of the Ernst August Platz.

She chuckled warmly. It was the first time she had laughed since he had met her. 'No! That's the name I sing under. My name is Lottie, Lottie Geis.'

Collins swung round and held out his hand gravely. 'I am pleased to meet you Lottie Geis.'

'I also, Karl.'

At the station he was reluctant to leave her. 'If I can get another pass next weekend, may I come up to Hanover? Perhaps we could spend a day together?'

She smiled faintly. 'That would be nice, Karl. You will probably know by then what materials you want.'

With a start he realised that he had almost forgotten. 'Yes,' he grinned apologetically. 'I suppose so. Where will I find you?'

She gave him her address and he memorised it.

'Perhaps I can get a pass for next Sunday.'

He would have to continue his daily drills at Hildesheim during the week.

'Next Sunday will be fine,' she held out her hand. 'Give my regards to Uncle Wilhelm.'

Collins smiled and turned through the barrier among the crowds of uniformed personnel pushing their way onto the electric train for Hildesheim. He went with a light step, experiencing a strangely happy sensation, and all the way back to the barracks, he meditated on the beautifully wistful face of Lottie Geis.

Chapter Twenty

Helga von Haensel smiled warmly as her maid showed the visitor into her drawing-room. He was a balding, middle-aged *Generaloberst* of the *Wehrmacht*. She did not rise from the couch on which she was sitting but raised her hand. The *Generaloberst* bowed low and brushed it with his lips.

'I trust I find you well, Countess?'

'Very well, *Herr General*,' she smiled, indicating a chair opposite and ordering her maid to bring a whisky-and-soda. They exchanged pleasantries until the maid returned, gave the general the drink and returned to the kitchen.

'Can we talk?' the general asked.

'Certainly,' replied the countess. 'Anna is trustworthy.'

'*Generalfeldmarschall* Rommel is with us.'

The girl's mouth opened in surprise. 'Rommel?'

The general nodded vigorously. 'With Rommel on our side, the Allies are bound to pay attention to us.'

He took out a silver cigarette-case from which he extracted a cheroot, looking at the girl in interrogation. She nodded and asked: 'How was Rommel convinced?'

The general lit his cheroot and blew smoke into the air. 'The *Generalfeldmarschall* has been worried about the deterioration of the political situation within the Reich for some time,' he replied. 'At the end of last month he confessed his fears to his friend, Karl Stroelin.' Doctor Karl Stroelin was not only the *Oberburgermeister* of Stuttgart but a friend of the anti-Nazi opposition. 'We asked the good doctor to have further discussions with the *Generalfeldmarschall*. Apparently Rommel was in favour of senior army officers arresting Hitler and forcing him to announce his abdication of power over the radio.'

The girl grimaced in disgust as the general went on.

'We have arranged things so that General Hans Speidel will be appointed Rommel's chief-of-staff. He will be our contact.'

Speidel was one of the leading anti-Nazi generals, a man of unusual talent. He had received a *summa cum laude* doctorate from the University of Tuebingen in 1925.

'So Rommel now approves the assassination attempt?'

The general shrugged slightly. 'So far, the *Generalfeldmarschall* opposes the assassination of the *Führer*, not on moral grounds, but for practical reasons. He argues that to kill the *Führer* would make a martyr of him. He wants Hitler to be arrested by the *Wehrmacht* and taken before a German court to be tried for crimes against the German people and the people of the occupied countries.'

Helga von Haensel laughed shortly. 'What does the *Generalfeldmarschall* think the SS, Gestapo and the sychophants of the Nazi Party are going to be doing while Hitler is being arrested and tried? Are they going to go on holiday?'

'Rommel believes that he is the only person who could prevent a civil war in Germany by lending his name to the operation. He believes he could control the SS and Gestapo and prevent any rescue attempt.'

'I know he is acclaimed our greatest general, he is certainly our most popular, but I fear his egocentricity is dangerous,' said the countess slowly. 'I can't help wondering about his conversion. Before he became popular, he was regarded as an opportunist who courted the *Führer*'s favour. It appears to me that he is deserting him only because he now realises that the war will be lost.'

The general shook his head sadly. 'You are hard on the *Generalfeldmarschall*, Countess.'

'Life, during the last few years, has taught me to be hard.'

The general rose to his feet. 'There are some papers which we want delivered to our representative in Hamburg,' he said, reaching into his tunic and drawing out an envelope. 'The attempt must be made very soon now . . . with, or without, the *Generalfeldmarschall*'s approval.'

Helga von Haensel took the envelope and smiled tightly. 'I shall do as you wish, *Herr Generaloberst*.'

The man sighed. 'With Rommel on our side, we have a far

better chance of making the British and Americans negotiate seriously with us once Hitler is removed. They don't want a Bolshevik empire in Europe.'

'In the meantime, we must keep the Communist resistance groups from realising our intention,' smiled the countess cynically. 'I understand that, *Herr Generaloberst*. But remember that a large section of our active support comes from the Communists and trade unionists.'

The general chuckled. 'My dear Countess, I do not have to tell you what to say to them. Tell them we are all set to overthrow Fascism and we shall do so with their help. We do not have to be explicit about the degree of support we expect from the British and Americans to help keep out the Soviets.'

Helga von Haensel placed the envelope on the seat beside her. 'I shall start for Hamburg tomorrow.'

The general bowed over her hand once more. 'We must be vigilant, Countess. Things are working towards a climax for the Reich.'

'Right . . . Wheel!' The harsh parade-ground tones of Charles Collins echoed against the stone walls of the former monastery as he drilled his squad of men. As they turned in obedience to his commands, he nodded to himself with satisfaction. They would do – they would do for the Germans but not for him. The men were still too ragged; they were not co-ordinated enough. They did not move as a single entity. But it would take an expert to see that, and *Haupsturmführer* Gerhard Gottschalk was no expert. So, they would do.

The last week had been a curious one of mixed thoughts and emotions for Collins. Since returning from Hanover he had hardly been able to concentrate on the job. He kept thinking about Lottie Geis, kept seeing her sad, wistful, haunted face. It was almost impossible to turn to the task of drilling his bunch of social misfits into some passable military order, much less to think about his real mission in Germany.

He dismissed his squad and lit a cigarette.

McLardy, the fanatical Fascist, was lounging by the door. 'You're doing a great job, Collins,' he called sarcastically.

Collins struggled to keep his temper. He disliked McLardy

intensely. The man was pitiful. When he held his classes in an effort to explain Fascist ideology to his fellows, he could only repeat things parrot fashion from books or propaganda pamphlets; he lacked any power of conceptual thought to argue matters out in logical fashion. He was a profoundly unintelligent man who was emotionally attracted to Fascism because it promised to satisfy his unsophisticated aspirations.

'Better than lounging about doing nothing,' replied Collins evenly.

McLardy grinned with what was almost a sneer. 'Our job is to teach the great tenents of National Socialism. We ain't in the British Army now.'

Collins laughed shortly. 'No, you poor boob! You're in the German Army and I can't see them suffering indiscipline any more than the British Army.'

He brushed past McLardy and made his way to his room. As he flung himself down on his bed he found that all he could think about was the forthcoming Sunday and his trip to Hanover. He felt he was living in a dream world, a peculiar disturbing nightmare. Hanover was reality; the haunting serenity of Lottie Geis.

Behrens signed the document and sighed deeply. 'That does it,' he said to the officer from Gestapo Requisitions.

'Indeed, *Herr Standartenführer*,' replied the balding man, blotting the paper and slipping it into a folder. 'The property of the Jew at Teuntz is yours.'

'Good. I'll be able to move in before the Easter weekend. My wife will like that.'

'A beautiful spot, *Herr Standartenführer*, if I may say so,' commented the man. 'But then these Jews always found the best spots, while we had to live in hovels.'

'Those days are in the past,' Behrens assured him, gravely.

The officer saluted respectfully, picked up his papers and left.

Behrens watched him go with satisfaction. He was certainly moving up in the world. What price now for the bare-footed butcher's delivery boy? He shook his head, as if to dispel the image he had suddenly conjured from his past. Thank God for the *Führer* and the Nazi revolution. The old order was swept

162

away; the days of the languid aristocrats who had led Germany to near destruction were past, and gone too were the raucous advocates of Jewish Bolshevism. He smiled down at the slip of paper which gave him possession of the beautiful little cottage on the lakeside at Teuntz. Inge would love the place, he was sure of it.

There was a deferential tap on his door.

'Come!'

Manfred Reinecke entered.

'Yes, Manfred?'

Reinecke tossed a leaflet on Behrens's desk.

'Another leaflet has appeared, *Herr Standartenführer*. That's the third leaflet they've issued during the last few weeks. I think they are building up towards something.'

Behrens frowned. 'You say "they"; are you so certain that all these leaflets emanate from the one place? General Nebe is absolutely convinced that they are printed by the Allies and smuggled into the country.'

Reinecke tapped the leaflet with a forefinger. 'Look at the letters *P, G,H* and *O*. With your permission?'

He reached across the desk and picked up a magnifying glass. 'Look at the outlines of those letters. Note the indentations on each of the pamphlets. They are the same. They were printed on the same machines.'

'How was the latest one distributed?'

'The leaflets were slipped through the letter-boxes of certain houses in the Pankow suburb of the city last night.'

'And no one saw or heard anything, I suppose?'

Reinecke shrugged.

'Well, now,' nodded Behrens, as he gazed at the pamphlet, 'I am sure we will be able to achieve some success by working on the distribution lines of the *Volkischer Beobachter*. Somewhere along the line, someone slipped pamphlets into the newspaper. We should be able to find out exactly where and then . . . then we will have these traitors!'

Lottie Geis had been thinking about Charles Collins for the past week. She had somehow found it impossible to erase him from her mind. She could not understand why. She had never thought about another man ever since . . . since they had come for Anton. She shivered slightly as she realised that it was difficult to visualise clearly the features of Anton's face. It was easier to recall the craggy, almost ugly face of the Englishman.

She had never mentioned Anton to anybody before. She wondered why she had mentioned him to Collins. True, she had not told Collins the full story about Anton, but she had seen from his gaze that he knew and understood. Anton had been her lover. How could the Englishman have realised that, simply by her brief mention of him? No one had ever been close enough to her to be able to read her thoughts like that; not even Anton. She shivered slightly. She had never compared Anton unfavourably with anyone before.

In August 1937, soon after her eighteenth birthday, Lottie Geis had gone with her parents to the Olympic Games in Berlin. Her father was a bank clerk and her mother had been a fairly ordinary Hanoverian housewife. They were an average middle-class family who had usually voted for one of the liberal political parties. In Berlin, Lottie's mind had rebelled at the great stage-managed spectacle which the Reich had rigged up for the world. It was then that she realised that she hated the cynical manipulation of the people by the National Socialist machine.

Not long after the invasion of Austria, in the March of the following year, Lottie had started a course in textile design at the technical college in Hanover. One of the classes which she attended, a class on the history of design, was given by a Sudeten German named Anton Basche. Aged thirty-five, divorced, and highly political, Anton Basche had taken up his teaching job at Hanover only the year previously.

Lottie Geis had fallen in love with him, and tutor and pupil began a tempestuous affair which lasted through the summer of 1938. It was Lottie Geis's first and only love affair.

On 1 October, 1938, the German troops entered the Sudetenland and by 14 March 1939 the swastika emblem was flying over the parliamentary buildings in Prague. The secret files of the Czech police were taken over by the Gestapo. Among the files was one devoted to Anton Basche. However, it was not until November 1939 that the Gestapo acted on the information.

On 8 November, the *Führer* had attended the annual meeting of National Socialist Party workers at the *Bürgerbraukeller* in Munich. After a half-hour tirade against Britain, Hitler and *Reichsführer* Himmler abruptly left the hall. Twelve minutes later a bomb, hidden behind the speakers' platform, exploded, killing seven persons and wounding sixty-three. The attempted assassination enabled Himmler to begin a purge of suspected 'enemies of the Reich'.

Among those arrested was Anton Basche who had been an active member of the Communist Party in the Sudetenland. He was arrested in the middle of a class.

Lottie Geis would have run to him, attempted to stay his captors, but he had already told her she must not involve herself if they came to take him – it might endanger the lives of others. Red-eyed, but outwardly cold and calm she watched her lover being marched off.

A few days later it was announced that the traitor Basche had been executed. In December the technical school was closed and all the able-bodied young men were drafted into the armed forces. The female students were urged to go home and bear children for the Fatherland.

For months Lottie Geis sat at home. Her parents were worried and frightened by her monosyllabic utterances and her lack of interest in life. But Lottie survived, taking a variety of jobs to earn a living. She resumed the apparent normality of a mechanical existence. When in 1942, both her parents were killed in a train crash, she found that she had exhausted herself emotionally. She could not feel the same shock she had experienced over the death of Anton Basche. Her matter-of-fact acceptance of her parents' death worried those who knew her.

She might never have found a reason for living again, truly living, rather than simply existing, had she not met Father Olbricht. They met at the house of an old technical-college classmate and within a month he had enlisted her into his group, giving her a reason to live. Father Olbricht was wise enough to know that sometimes hatred can be a more powerful stimulant than love. He unashamedly worked on the great hatred which he recognised was stored within the girl. He used it to motivate her and, for the first time in years, Lottie Geis suddenly became alive, and all her energies were directed towards avenging the death of Anton Basche.

Work was scarce, especially now, and she had learnt to support herself by singing. She had a good voice and found reasonable work in a Hanover night-club. She had moved into a cheap apartment near the Ernst August Platz. She was attractive and had been propositioned several times but Lottie Geis had never welcomed the attentions of men. As far as love was concerned she had remained emotionally dead since Anton Basche's death. No one could ever replace Anton.

Why, then, during the last week had she been thinking of the Englishman? She shook her head in bewilderment. It was that moment of complete knowledge that had passed between them, the fact that he had understood so much from her brief reference to Anton, the fact that he knew, and she had felt his sympathy and desire to be of help. She had felt him reach out from his loneliness to feel sorrow for her. Logically it was ridiculous. She wondered whether she had glamorised him because he was a British agent. She was rational and intelligent enough to hope not. Emotions were difficult to understand.

All she knew was that she was looking forward to seeing Charles Collins again.

Chapter Twenty-One

It was late when Helga von Haensel arrived back at her apartment in the select Berlin suburb of Gatow, overlooking the Havel River, opposite the broad green stretch of Grunewald Park. Helmuth von Fegeleinn was waiting for her, sitting nervously on the couch pretending to listen to a gramophone record. The girl smiled at him as she entered.

'Miss me?' she said lightly.

Von Fegeleinn grimaced wryly at her flippancy. 'I'm always worried for you when you go away,' he replied seriously.

She shrugged off-handedly. 'I'm starving. The journey from Hamburg was terrible.'

She was about to ask where Anna was but suddenly realised it was her maid's day off.

'How was Hamburg?'

'I don't know,' she said, moving into the kitchen. 'No one's allowed into the city centre these days.'

Von Fegeleinn could hear the rattle of crockery as the girl busied herself. In a moment she returned with a plate of sandwiches and some beer.

'I was trying to get in to see our contact in the city but was turned back. The SS have a military cordon around the entire centre. Apparently the *Reich Komissar* for Dwellings has forbidden all travel into Hamburg unless it be of an essential military nature. They say that things are difficult. I heard from one old woman who survived the bombing that there are eight hundred thousand homeless in the ruins, and no one knows what to do with them. Someone told me that they are in an angry mood and have even attacked uniformed Party men.'

Von Fegeleinn watched her attack her food with relish.

'It's dangerous for you to make these trips, Helga. It's getting more dangerous all the time.'

'Everywhere in Germany is dangerous now. What with the Allied bombing, no one is safe.'

'I didn't mean that, Helga.'

'I know perfectly well what you meant,' she repled irritably.

Von Fegeleinn pouted like a sullen schoolboy. 'I don't like the way you treat me, Helga. I don't like being bossed about.'

Helga Von Haensel smiled broadly. It amused her when he became indignant. She blew him a kiss. 'If I don't tell you what to do now and then, Helmuth, you'd be lost, you poor lamb.'

Von Fegeleinn bit his lip in annoyance. 'This business is not a game, Helga. If the Gestapo ever became suspicious of you, do you realise what would happen?'

The girl calmly returned his gaze. 'I know perfectly well.'

'Well, then,' von Fegeleinn said, 'surely you realise that it is time to start looking after your own interests?'

She shook her head slowly. 'My own interests? Personal interests no longer matter, Helmuth. There are no other interests of importance now but the survival of Germany and the freedom of the German people from tyranny, whether an internal tyranny or an external one.'

She paused, sighed and patted the couch beside her. 'Come and sit down, Helmuth. Relax. You are worrying for nothing.'

Reluctantly, von Fegeleinn sat down.

'If it wasn't for you, Helga . . .'

Helga von Haensel leant forward and kissed his ear. 'If it wasn't for me you would be a good little Nazi and not say anything,' she finished mockingly.

She wondered what it was that attracted her to him. He had all the failings that she thought would have made her detest the man. He was cowardly, weak, vacillating, unable to do anything without being pushed. In peace-time, in another era, he would have been the perfect country gentleman with no greater problem than what horse to ride to hounds, or what wine to choose for dinner. He was a hopeless displaced anachronism. Yet it was some peculiar animal attraction that fascinated her. That was it, he was a magnificent animal; no more, no less.

'You know damned well I hate the Nazis,' he protested. 'And I love you.'

'And desire me?'

'Of course I do, damn it! You have desires too.'

She raised her face to his and chuckled softly. 'Yes. I have desires too.'

Von Fegeleinn stared at her a moment in perplexity and then dragged her towards him, burying his face in the white of her neck. 'If it wasn't for you . . .' he whispered savagely as she sighed softly against him.

Sunday 2 April, began with a warm spring sun shining from a blue sky in which only a few clouds scudded like drifting cottonwool. Charlie Collins rose with a feeling of elation, of excited anticipation. The new uniforms for the *Britisches Freikorps* had arrived the day before and were issued to each man; two sets of uniform, a greatcoat and a ski-type hat with a death's-head badge in front and an eagle perched on a swastika on the left-hand side. Collins wondered whether the new issue of immaculate uniforms might have something to do with Roberts's report that the Free Corps were to form the *Führer*'s birthday honour guard. No announcement was made, however. Collins dressed in the new uniform and reported to *Hauptsturmführer* Gottschalk's office.

The pudgy-faced captain looked up as he entered. 'Ah, Collins. You have come for your pass?'

'Yes, *Herr Hauptsturmführer*.'

'That is all I ever seem to do for this unit – sign pass after pass. I do not refer to you, please understand, when I say that most members of this Corps would be living in the brothels in Hildesheim, if they could. All they seem to be interested in is drinking and women.' The little man wrinkled up his face in disgust. 'Sometimes, Collins, I wonder why the *Reichsführer* is prepared to allow this collection of riff-raff to exist? Surely you would be better employed in the propaganda department in Berlin? You are wasting your time with these half-wits!'

Collins smiled gently. 'If I am, *Herr Hauptsturmführer*, then so are you.'

Gottschalk sighed deeply. 'For me, it is different. Orders are orders. Why don't you apply for a transfer, Collins? I would endorse it. You are too valuable to be buried here.'

'Thank you, *Herr Hauptsturmführer*. The situation suits me well enough for the moment.'

'Well,' Gottschalk signed the pass with a flourish, 'at least I know you will return on time and not be incapably drunk. Where are you off to?'

'To Hanover.'

'A beautiful city,' Gottschalk nodded solemnly. 'Before the war it was a great centre for English students. Enjoy yourself.'

Collins caught the electric train to the station in Ernst August Platz and then made his way to Lottie Geis's address. He was admitted to the tenement by a suspicious and dour-faced old lady who made him wait in the hallway while she climbed the stairs to Lottie Geis's second-floor apartment. The girl, flushed and breathless, soon appeared and urged him to come up. Collins passed the old woman with a smile, but she sniffed sourly.

'Don't mind *Frau* Bebe,' the girl grinned, as she showed Collins into her apartment. 'The old dear thinks she is my guardian.'

'She did look at me very suspiciously.'

'That's because she is not used to seeing gentlemen calling here . . .'

The girl broke off with a flush of embarrassment. 'Can I get you a coffee?'

Collins nodded, removed his greatcoat and cap, and dropped into a chair. The girl's apartment was a single bed-sitting room with a self-contained bathroom and toilet. It was decidely a woman's room. There were all the neat little feminine touches which made it look lived in – potted plants and shrubs, framed photographs and knick-knacks. It was a warm, comfortable room.

The girl bent over a solitary gas-ring by the fireplace and set a pan of water to boil. Soon the harsh smell of ersatz coffee drifted up into the room.

There was an awkward silence between them.

'Is everything all right?' It was the girl who finally spoke.

'All right?' Collins frowned. Then he smiled. 'Oh yes. No problem.'

'Do you know yet when you will require the materials?' ·

'Not yet. I don't really want to pick them up until I have to. It's dangerous to have unauthorised explosives in barracks. The later I leave it, the better, for it gives me a greater margin of safety.'

She nodded, not really understanding.

It seemed, however, that the awkwardness was over; they were no longer strangers. The hours sped by as they became engrossed in talking. Lottie began to tell him about Anton. She had never really talked about Anton before, not even to her parents. Now she found herself telling Collins the whole story, and how, later, she had met Father Olbricht and become involved with the resistance movement. In turn, Collins found himself telling her about his early life; his youthful acceptance of Fascism as an easy answer to his anger and frustration at being unemployed in the years of the depression. He told her about the security which the Army had given him; about his ambition to become a sheep-farmer in Australia. How his principles had caused him to take part in the mutiny at Salerno and how he had been asked to come to Germany. He omitted the objective of the job, simply saying he had been asked to infiltrate the British Free Corps.

It was Collins who suddenly realised that it had grown dark outside. 'It's too late for that walk around Hanover,' he said. 'but the least I can do is buy you dinner.'

'I hope there'll be another time for that walk, Karl,' smiled the girl.

He helped her on with her coat. Both of them felt at ease, as if they had known each other for many years.

'Do you know somewhere?'

'There's a little place within walking distance.'

In a quiet café which served plain German food, they continued to talk about themselves. Collins admitted he had known many women but had never really had a close relationship with one. In turn, she told him that she had never had a relationship before nor since her affair with Anton Basche. The conversation ended only when Collins caught sight of the clock on the wall of the café.

'The last train to Hildesheim is in half an hour.'

He paid the bill and they walked towards the station. It seemed natural for the girl to take his arm.

'I haven't enjoyed myself so much in years, Karl,' she confessed happily. 'It is so lonely, *has* been so lonely. I feel that I've suddenly come alive again.'

He nodded happily. 'I'm glad, Lottie. I've enjoyed myself too.'

At the barrier she smiled. 'Will you come next Sunday?' she asked.

'I would like to very much. Can I reach you by phone?'

Lottie shook her head. '*Frau* Bebe is not on the telephone and it would be best to avoid the night-club. Telephone calls are listened into these days.'

'Then I'll come next Sunday.'

'That is good. It is Easter Sunday. I'll cook dinner for us.'

Collins bent and kissed her hand. 'Until next Sunday, Lottie.'

On the crowded train back to Hildesheim, Collins realised with concern that he had fallen in love with Lottie Geis.

Chapter Twenty-Two

Oberstgruppenführer Ernst Kaltenbrunner raised his head from contemplation of the papers on his desk and gestured to Rudi Behrens to sit down.

'I hear that you have settled into your new house at Teuntz,' the Gestapo chief said.

'Yes. We moved on Monday so that we could be settled in before the Easter weekend.'

'Excellent. It is a nice house? A pleasant view?'

Behrens nodded, wondering why Kaltenbrunner was interested.

'General Nebe informs me that Kripo has handed you their file on the subversive literature which is circulating in Berlin?'

Behrens drew out a cigarette and lit it. 'That's right, *Herr Oberstgruppenführer.*'

'Himmler is adamant that these subversives must be wiped out. Are you having any success?'

'We are working on several leads at the moment.'

Kaltenbrunner frowned. 'You have not tracked down the press yet?'

Behrens shook his head.

'We must have some action after that deplorable case last week,' snapped the Gestapo chief. 'I refer to the leaflet which was actually distributed in the party newspaper *Voelkischer Beohachter.* It made us a laughing stock.'

Behrens smiled grimly. 'It could well be that our treacherous friends have made a mistake in using that method of distribution.'

'Yes?' Kaltenbrunner looked hopeful.

'We were able to trace the sales points of most of the newspapers which contained the pamphlets. We have questioned the

172

owners of the kiosks to find out where they got their supplies from.'

'You believe the leaflets were put in the newspapers before they reached the kiosks which sold them?'

'Yes, *Herr Oberstgruppenführer.*'

'Very well, Behrens. I leave the matter to you. But remember that the *Reichsführer* is impatient to see some results to this enquiry. The defeatists and Bolsheviks are damned clever. We must not fail to stamp out the vermin in our midst if we are to stamp out the external enemies.'

Behrens rose. 'I will have some results very soon, I can promise that.'

'Excellent. Let me know as soon as you have something so that I can inform the *Reichsführer.*'

The sweaty-faced printer grunted in satisfaction, reached for a switch and shut down the monotonous 'clackity-clack' of the small press. Taking a screwdriver, he carefully unlocked the two type-plates and placed them in a box. He grinned across the cellar room to Countess Helga von Haensel.

'Another batch finished.'

Helga von Haensel gave a wan smile, reached forward and picked up one of the leaflets. '*To the German People,*' she read aloud. '*It is time to stop this madness, this senseless destruction and turn back to the road of sanity.*'

The old man standing at her shoulder smiled softly. 'What it lacks in literary style it makes up for in rhetoric,' he said.

Professor Faupel had once been the holder of the chair of philosophy at Berlin University. It was both his philosophy and his religion that made Professor Faupel, at the age of seventy-one, an enemy of the state. He was a Jew who, for the last eight years, had been living under an assumed identity in Berlin. He had been born and raised in Berlin; his father and mother, his grandfather and grandmother had been Berliners. Professor Faupel refused to be told that he was not a German by a little upstart Austrian.

'All right,' said the Countess, 'we'll pack them up and Helmuth can take them to the distributor.'

173

The old professor sighed. 'Sometimes I wonder whether writing these leaflets achieves anything.'

'If it makes even one person start questioning, start thinking about what is going on, then it achieves something.'

Professor Faupel shrugged. 'Sometimes I wonder,' he repeated.

Helmuth von Fegeleinn coughed. 'Where am I to take these, Helga?' he asked nervously.

'To our man on the *Volkischer Beobachter*.'

Faupel frowned. 'We used him last week. Isn't that chancing things?'

Helga von Haensel shook her head. 'We can still get away with one more distribution in the same manner.'

'We mustn't underestimate the efficiency of the Gestapo,' warned Faupel.

'Don't worry, *Herr Professor,*' smiled the girl. She turned to von Fegeleinn. 'You are to take the package of pamphlets to 31 Lichtenberg Strasse.'

Von Fegeleinn frowned. 'That's in Weissensee. It's going to take me half an hour to get there.' There was a note of peevishness in his voice.

'Then the sooner you start out, the sooner you will return,' replied the girl.

He stared at her for a moment. He wasn't sure whether she was mocking him. Well, he couldn't help but be anxious. All these risks just to distribute a few badly printed leaflets. It was madness.

'I'll telephone to let our man know that you are on the way,' the girl said, as they carried the package out to von Fegeleinn's car.

Back in the house she picked up the telephone, thankful that the lines were still open to Weissensee, the eastern suburb of Berlin. The Allied bombing had created havoc with a major portion of the telephone system.

A nervous voice answered.

'Hello, Carl,' said the girl. 'I have a present from Uncle Wilhelm. It is coming over by special messenger now.'

There was a hesitation.

'Very well,' said the voice.

Helga von Haensel put down the telephone and gave a sigh of relief.

Carl Henseler replaced the telephone receiver and turned to face the dark-featured man who sat across the room watching him.

'Well?' snapped the man.

Henseler glanced to where his wife and young son sat at the table, faces deathly pale. Another man, with Slavic features, clad in a belted raincoat, stood at the door.

'Don't play for time, Henseler,' advised Rudi Behrens. 'You don't have it.'

Carl Henseler, delivery man for the *Volkischer Beobachter*, let his shoulders sag. 'It was them, *Herr Standartenführer*. They are delivering more leaflets now.'

Behrens grinned in fierce triumph. 'So? We have our rats in a trap, eh?'

'It would seem so,' nodded Reinecke from the door.

'You are a fool, Henseler! A treacherous fool! You have forfeited everything, except a nice long stay in prison for you and all your family.' He reached forward and stubbed out his cigarette. 'In the meantime, we will wait for your friends. Your wife will make us coffee while we wait.'

Frau Henseler cast a frightened glance at her husband, as if seeking his permission.

'Get it!' shouted Behrens. 'Your scum of a husband doesn't give orders now!'

The woman jerked up in agitation and scurried out into the kitchen.

The little boy started to sob softly.

Carl Henseler stood head bowed, shoulders bent, a defeated man.

Chapter Twenty-Three

Helga von Haensel let herself into her apartment and went to the window. It was a clear evening. The moon was already up in a cloudless sky. It reflected on the broad blue-black ribbon of the Havel River and flickered its silver light on the leaves of the conifers in the Grunewald Park. She shivered slightly. The clear night would mean that the British would be over Berlin later. She drew the black-out curtains across the windows and turned on a low table lamp. She felt suddenly lonely. Anna had taken a week off to go home to Oberkirche because her mother had died. Helmuth would be at least another hour making his way across Berlin and back.

She tried to shrug away the feeling of loneliness. There was time for a shower before Helmuth returned. She went into the bedroom and turned on the wireless and began to undress. The news, as usual, was full of optimism in spite of its being bad. The announcer was sneeringly reporting that Radio Moscow claimed the Red Army was already pushing forward from the Ukraine and making exploratory sorties across the river Pruth into Rumania. Soviet Foreign Minister Vyacheslav Molotov had issued a warning to King Michael of Rumania and his Government to end its alliance with Germany or suffer the consequences. Soviet General Zhukov was driving a wedge along the northern border of the Pruth, while his fellow commander, Konev, had taken the town of Jasi on the lower reaches of the river. This was plainly false, claimed the announcer. General Freissner's Army Group South, with its Rumanian allies, were counter-attacking Soviet advances and repulsing them. Parts of the Ukraine and the Crimea were still held by the valiant forces of the Reich.

The girl switched off the radio with an exasperated sigh and entered the bathroom. For nearly ten minutes she luxuriated in the warm water. She climbed out and dried herself then put on the silk wrap she had bought in Paris in the easy days of peace. Helmuth would be back soon. She hoped he would hurry.

Gerhard Gottschalk sat at his desk, his eyes on the paper before him. He took off his glasses, rubbed the bridge of his nose in a strangely agitated gesture and then looked up. The NCOs of the *Britisches Freikorps* stood uncomfortably before his desk.

'Gentlemen,' he began hesitantly as if unsure of how to proceed. 'Gentlemen, I must tell you that the Corps is confined to barracks over this weekend.'

As usual it was McLardy who voiced the first protest. 'But it's Easter. The boys will want to go into town for a few jars.'

Gottschalk strained to catch his idiomatic English.

For once Collins agreed with McLardy's protest, but not for the same reasons. He was thinking about Lottie Geis.

Gottschalk spread his hands in a vague apology. 'I am aware that it is Easter. However, I have received instructions from SS High Command. The unit will be confined to barracks until further notice. An SS general will be coming from Berlin to inspect the unit and address them on Tuesday morning. In the meantime, the unit is to continue its drills and make sure all its uniforms and equipment are clean and smart.'

Collins felt a tingling excitement. So Roberts was correctly informed after all . . . at least that's what it sounded like. The unit was being prepared to become the birthday honour guard for the *Führer*. The SS general from Berlin would probably be coming to brief them. Damn it! Had he left it too late to get the explosives he needed?

'I cannot give you any details, but I can warn you,' Gottschalk said slowly. 'Apparently, headquarters has a special task for you to perform which will be a singular honour. You must be a credit to your unit.'

'What task, *Herr Hauptsturmführer*?' asked Collins.

'I cannot tell you, Collins. You must wait until the arrival of the SS general,' said Gottschalk apologetically.

Collins bit his lip. He did not know which concerned him more – the fact that he would miss seeing Lottie Geis or the fact that he might be unable to obtain the materials he would need if Roberts's information was correct.

'You look worried, Collins,' sneered McLardy, as they left Gottschalk's office. 'Scared they're gonna send us to the Russian Front, eh?'

'Get lost, McLardy,' Collins was irritated. 'Go and read *Mein Kampf* to the sparrows.'

'You better not insult the *Führer*'s book,' began McLardy belligerently.

Collins told him explicitly what he could do with Adolf Hitler's book.

McLardy gazed at his retreating figure in open-mouthed surprise, turned and hurried after Cooper to report the matter to him.

In his office, Gerhard Gottschalk sat for a long time gazing at the '*Most Secret*' order which had come from the Prinz Albrecht Strasse. Finally, he shook his head. *Reichsführer* Heinrich Himmler must be mad, absolutely mad, to authorise this. The *Führer* must be insane to allow such a thing. Birthday honour guard, indeed! But orders were orders. Orders were made to be obeyed and not to be questioned. All the same, he wondered how he stood as commanding officer of the unit if anything went wrong.

Helga von Haensel woke to the sound of the door of her apartment being opened. She yawned. She must have fallen asleep on the couch. The girl blinked and gazed at the clock on the mantelshelf. She frowned suddenly. It was four hours since she had had her shower.

'Helmuth?' she called. 'Where the devil have you been?' She stopped short, growing cold with fear.

A dark man with a heavy jowl stood at the door. There was a silence while his dark expressionless eyes wandered over her body. The girl drew the sheer silk wrap around her and stood up.

'What is the meaning of this?' she demanded, as she sought to regain her composure.

The man, dressed in a dark brown suit, smiled thinly. 'Are

you Countess Helga von Haensel?' His voice was soft and menacing.

'I am.' The girl felt a strong desire to shudder under his scrutiny.

'I am *Standartenführer* Behrens of the *Geheime Staatspolizei*.'

Her knees went weak. She wanted to collapse on the couch. Instead she thrust out her chin aggressively. 'You have not explained the reason for this intrusion into my home,' she said, hoping that he wouldn't notice the quiver of fear in her voice.

Behrens made no reply. He slowly unbuttoned his overcoat, took it off and draped it over a chair. Then he strode to the fireplace, pulled out a packet of cigarettes and lit one, exhaling the smoke with studied slowness.

'Well?' she snapped.

He sat down, crossed his legs and gazed up at her with a sardonic expression. 'Well, Countess?' There was a mocking imitation in Behrens's voice.

'I have no idea who you are or what you want. Anyone can come in and say they are from the Gestapo, but . . .'

Behrens reached into an inside jacket pocket, withdrew a small card and tossed it towards her. She let it lie where it had fallen. She did not need to pick it up to know that this man was really from the *Geheime Staatspolizei*.

She struggled to retrieve the situation. 'I must warn you that I have highly placed friends . . .'

Behrens raised an eyebrow and sneered. 'They would have to be very highly placed to help you, Countess.'

Her eyes narrowed.

'This evening,' went on Behrens 'we arrested your lover, *Freiherr* Helmuth von Fegeleinn. He was a silly young man. Fancy risking his life to distribute this garbage!'

Behrens took out one of the leaflets that they had printed earlier that evening and tossed it accusingly towards the countess.

The girl tried hard to control herself. 'I cannot believe that Helmuth would . . .'

Behrens jerked his head up. 'You can stop play-acting, Countess. Your weak-minded lover has told us everything. Everything, you disloyal little cow!'

Helga von Haensel took a step backwards as if the man had

179

dealt her a physical blow. Many times in her mind she had lived this moment. It had come to so many friends of hers; it had come to Father Olbricht. She had been brave, scornful and heroic in her mind's eye. Reality was not like that at all.

Behrens was watching her with black expressionless eyes.

A sudden hard resolve went through her. If Helmuth had been weak, she must be strong. She must try to buy time for the rest of the group. She would simply pretend that she knew nothing. Not even von Fegeleinn really knew how much she was involved.

'I have no idea what you are talking about, *Herr Standartenführer,*' she said, fighting to keep her voice even. 'It is a great shock to me to learn that Helmuth was distributing subversive literature. I take your word he was. However, I can see no excuse for foul language in my presence. I find your behaviour completely boorish.'

Behrens only reaction to her attitude was to curse her stupidity. 'There is a hard way and an easy way of extracting the truth, Countess,' he said softly. 'The hard way is in a basement at Prinz Albrecht Strasse. I am sure you have heard rumours of how efficient the young men of the Gestapo are at making even the dumb talk?'

He let his eyes wander over her trembling figure clad only in a flimsy wrap. He stood up slowly. Suddenly he felt a curious overpowering desire to belittle this haughty woman, to demean her as once her kind had degraded him. The desire became coupled with a deep sexual impulse. He wanted to have this woman, to dominate her, to hurt her and humiliate her. All the frustrations of his childhood welled up in him. 'I hope, for your sake, you choose the easy way, Countess.'

He reached out a hand. She stared into his face without flinching, feeling his hand tugging at the belt of her wrap, tugging until it came loose and the wrap fell open.

'You are a very attractive woman,' he said.

She felt the flat of his hand move over her stomach and slowly travel upward to caress a breast. She stood completely still, gazing at him like a rabbit before a snake.

'I am sure you would prefer the easy way,' Behrens suddenly grinned wolfishly. It added some malignant quality to his features. 'It would be such a shame to damage such a work . . . of art.'

The palm of her hand striking him across the cheek was sudden and unexpected. The blow was not hard but its very unexpectedness caused Behrens to stagger back, hand to face.

Helga von Haensel glared at him in triumph. 'You gutter-snipe!' she hissed. 'I may have to take your peasant manners but I will not willingly submit to you.'

Behrens stared back at the venomous hatred in her eyes. For a wild moment he was a bare-foot child once more, he felt he ought to touch his cap and apologise. Then something snapped in his mind.

'Upper-class whore!' he spat. 'Get dressed. You'll soon sing a different tune in the basement of the Prinz Albrecht Strasse.'

The girl drew herself up and, with mustered dignity, she walked into her bedroom.

Behrens followed.

'Give me some privacy to get dressed,' she tried to demand. The words came out as a plea.

Behrens chuckled. 'Where you are going, Countess, you will soon learn to forget such privileges.'

Chapter Twenty-Four

Only on the Eastern Front that bright April Easter weekend of 1944 was there any considerable activity. The rest of Europe seemed to pause to catch its breath. Not so the Red Army. Following the breakthrough made by Marshal Georgi Zhukov's First Belorussian Army to Lvov on 5 April, the Soviet forces pushed on. That weekend Odessa fell, pushing the remnants of the German 17th Army back into the inhospitable Crimea. All along the front the Soviet armies rolled westward, an unending tide of machines and men eager to close on the heartland of the German Reich.

Adolf Hitler was resting in his mountain retreat at Berchtesgaden. He had spent most of the time with his military advisers discussing the deteriorating situation in the East. *Generaloberst* Alfred Jodl, his Chief of the Operations Branch OKW (*Oberkommando der Wehrmacht*), the High Command of the Armed Forces, would usually begin these discussions by outlining the military situation from the latest reports. Then the *Führer* would commence to dictate the measures he wanted taken. 'I order . . . I order . . .' would become a repetitive phrase. And if any order were questioned, the *Führer* would hammer home his decisions with a clenched fist on the table top. 'I order!'

That Easter weekend, the *Führer* summoned Josef Goebbels to the Berghof.

'The situation in Berlin is intolerable,' the *Führer* began before Goebbels could enquire after his leader's health.

Goebbels felt a sudden clenching of his stomach muscles. As *Gauleiter* of Berlin, he was responsible for the welfare of the capital.

'American planes by day, British planes by night,' went on Hitler. 'I have heard that there is a joke which is popular among Berliners.'

'A joke, my *Führer*?' Goebbels asked wonderingly. The *Führer* was not usually given to relating jokes.

Hitler nodded morosely. 'They say that there is a new method for the identification of aircraft over Berlin. If an aircraft is silver, then it is American. If it is grey, then it is British. If there are no aircraft at all, then it is the *Luftwaffe*.'

There was a silence.

Goebbels had a wild desire to laugh but he decided against it.

'I have spoken of this matter to the *Reichsmarschall*.' There was a coldness in the *Führer*'s voice. Goebbels felt a vague feeling of pity for the fat drug-addict, Hermann Göring.

'Command and I shall follow, my *Führer*,' said Goebbels stolidly.

Hitler suddenly smiled at him affectionately. 'You are the man I most count upon, Josef,' he patted the *Reichsminister*'s arm. 'I am appointing you *Stadtspresident,* the city president of Berlin. Due to the Allied bombing there has been a breakdown of fire-fighting services, looting has gone on unchecked. Severe measures must be taken against the rabble. The city is over-strained by traffic problems. There are no medical services, no gas, water nor electricity supplies in many parts. As city president you will have to rectify these matters.'

Goebbels stiffened. 'It shall be as you wish, my *Führer*.'

Hitler nodded slowly. 'I knew I could trust you, Josef.' He paused. 'What is the news concerning the *Britisches Freikorps*? I shall be leaving here in a few days for Rastenburg. Is everything prepared?'

Goebbels smiled. 'Everything is in order. A unit of the *Freikorps* will leave Hildesheim in a day or two for Wolfsschanze. They will be instructed on their duties there before your arrival. We shall have a dress rehearsal on 18 April and on 20 April the press will be brought by special train. Particular emphasis has been placed on getting the Swedish, Swiss, Portuguese, Spanish and Turks along, also the neutral South Americans, such as Argentina.'

'Argentina?' the *Führer* sniffed. 'I am told this new Argentine President, General Farrell, is too much in favour of the Allies. Farrell is an English name, is it not?'

'Irish, my *Führer*,' corrected Goebbels gently.

'The same thing,' dismissed Hitler. 'We cannot trust Argentina.'

'No, my *Führer*,' Goebbels agreed obediently. He paused and then as Hitler said nothing further he added: 'It will be a magnificent propaganda coup, my *Führer*. Only the mind of a genius such as yourself could have thought of it.'

The *Führer* smiled, suddenly lost in his dreams of victory.

In London, Austin Roberts was also thinking about the *Führer*'s birthday. He had to suppress his growing anxiety about Operation Hagen because he had promised to take his wife, Maude, to the Good Friday performance of Handel's *Messiah* at the Albert Hall. It was actually their first evening out since the war started. Roberts would have far rather sat worrying about Collins in his office than amidst the wartime utilitarianism of the Victorian concert hall. The performance was first class and did take his mind off matters a little: Doctor Malcolm Sargeant conducted the Royal Choral Society and the solo parts were sung by Isobel Baillie, Kathleen Ferrier, Heddle Nash and Robert Easton. But his enjoyment was transitory. He could not escape the fact that 20 April was only a matter of days away.

It was a curious weekend for most people; the first lighthearted holiday since the war started. The weather was bright, but there was a ban on travel to coastal resorts, most of which were packed with over two million troops awaiting the day which Churchill had promised Stalin would be coming shortly – the invasion of Europe. Undaunted by the restrictions, however, the British public either stayed in their back gardens, holding local parties, while some – more adventurous – headed for the parks. London's riverside haunts at Richmond and Hampton Court were packed. Hampstead Heath was athrong with holiday-makers attending the traditional annual fair, while in Avenham Park, in Preston, the ancient egg-rolling ceremony was revived. One newspaper estimated that ten thousand people had bicycled to Windsor to see the historic town and castle. The more conscientious among the public saw the holiday as one which should be devoted to working on their allotments. 'Dig for Victory' was still the exhortation of the day, but the mood was optimistic. Even the BBC entered into the spirit of things with the publication of their *Year Book for 1944* in which they forecast that everyone would be able to afford a television set after the war.

But for others the war continued. King George of Greece left London on Easter Monday for Cairo to deal in person with an anti-monarchist mutiny in his Government-in-Exile. The Allied Expeditionary Air Force headquarters in London announced that some of the biggest air raids of the war had been undertaken against the Reich and would continue. Even as the official spokesman began to brief press correspondents, RAF aircraft were taking off in the biggest British air raid of the war to date.

Mostly, however, it was an odd lull – the calm before the storm. Even President Roosevelt decided to leave the White House that weekend for a two-week vacation 'somewhere in the country'. As well as his personal physician, the President was also accompanied by his Chief of Staff, Admiral Leahy, who had been ambassador to Vichy France during the earlier period of American neutrality.

184

For Lottie Geis it was the unhappiest weekend she had spent since Anton Basche had died.

She had been so eagerly looking forward to Collins's visit, like a schoolgirl on her first date. She knew it was ridiculous, but she found she had no control over her feelings. She had cooked a special meal, concocted from a few black-market purchases. She did her hair and put on an old but serviceable pre-war dress; a dress she had not worn since her last night out with Anton. She spent hours altering it to fit. When Sunday came and went and Collins did not show up, she felt an overwhelming black despair. Throughout the day she ran the entire gamut of emotions: anger at herself for being so vulnerable; anger at Collins; fear of what might have happened to him; despair, loneliness and longing. Above all she was left with loneliness and longing. By the evening of Monday she felt a dull ache, a resignation and an acceptance that she had no right to expect happiness in such a world, at such a time.

The meal went cold and untouched, and only frugality born of wartime exigency made her force some of it down her the following day.

On the morning of Tuesday, 11 April, just after ten o'clock, a black Mercedes-Benz saloon, with four motorcyclist outriders, drew up in the courtyard of St Michael's Monastery. The duty guard stamped to ramrod attention as an SS *Brigadeführer* climbed out. The general was young, in his mid thirties, and fastidiously groomed. Walter Schellenberg had been made a colonel at the age of thirty and at thirty-four had risen to be Germany's youngest general. He was in charge of counter-espionage and took his orders directly from Heinrich Himmler. His black SS uniform glittered with decorations. At his side hovered a nervous *Obersturmführer* with thick-rimmed spectacles and a bulky briefcase.

Hauptsturmführer Gerhard Gottschalk came smartly down the steps into the courtyard and saluted the general. Schellenberg returned the salute half-heartedly.

'I want the *Britisches Freikorps* volunteers to parade in the gymnasium at eleven hundred hours. I shall address them briefly,' he snapped.

185

'Very well, *Herr Brigadeführer*,' replied Gottschalk. He tried to sound efficient, but he was nervous and his words were spoken in jerky fashion. He turned and ushered Schellenberg and his aide towards his office, snapping orders at Cooper, whom he motioned forward. Inside his office, he provided schnapps and glasses for his visitors.

'Is the *Reichsführer* serious about this birthday honour guard business, *Herr Brigadeführer*?' he asked.

Schellenberg eyed him coldly. 'The *Reichsführer* is always serious about his plans, Gottschalk.'

The pudgy-faced little captain swallowed nervously. 'I . . . I meant no disrespect . . .' he let his voice trail off under the scrutiny of the young SS general.

Schellenberg motioned to his aide who unbuckled the fastenings of his briefcase and handed his commander some files. 'Now . . . we have a complement of fifty men from this unit. Is that so?'

Gottschalk nodded. 'There are a few men away conducting recruitment tours of the POW camps, but our strength at this time is six NCOs and forty-five other ranks.'

'H'mmm. The NCOs are trustworthy?'

'*Hauptscharführer* Cooper, our senior NCO, is excellent and already has a fine record serving on the Eastern Front with the SS Adolf Hitler Division,' Gottschalk said eagerly.

Schellenberg flicked through the files. 'Yes, yes,' he sounded a little impatient. 'And this man – Collins?'

'A solid man, *Herr Brigadeführer*. A good drill instructor. He has worked wonders with the discipline of the corps.'

'The NCOs can be relied on? Can the men pass muster? They must have all the appearance of first-class professional soldiers.'

'I can assure you of that, *Herr Brigadeführer*.'

'There can be no room for doubt. It is the *Führer* that they have been chosen to guard and the eyes of the world will be on these men.'

'I will guarantee that they will acquit themselves well,' nodded Gottschalk in his eagerness to please this dour SS general.

'That is good. Very good.' The ghost of a smile played around the young man's thin lips. 'I will pass on your assurances to the *Reichsführer*. I am sure he will be delighted.'

The members of the British Free Corps paraded in the converted gymnasium. The unit was divided into five squads of men with an NCO as their section-leader and with Cooper in overall command as their sergeant-major. SS *Brigadeführer* Schellenberg nodded approvingly as he let his eyes wander down their serried ranks. They certainly looked like soldiers. They stood at ramrod attention, and had marched into the room in perfect precision. Ceremonial soldiers did not make combat troops, but then all the *Reichsführer* wanted was a group of ceremonial soldiers. Schellenberg inspected the men carefully before he spoke.

'Pioneers! Allies! The Reich, the world, expects great things of you.'

Collins was surprised to hear faultless English from the young German general.

'As a result of repeated applications from British subjects, the *Führer* himself gave the authorisation to form this British volunteer unit. You men are the pioneers of the unit. You have taken up arms and pledged your lives in the common struggle for the survival of Western civilisation against the ravages of Soviet despotism. You have been far-sighted enough to condemn Churchill's war with Germany and the sacrifice of British blood in the interests of Jewry and international finance. I have no need to remind you that this is a fundamental betrayal of the British people and British interests. We all desire the establishment of peace in Europe, the development of friendly relations between England and Germany and the encouragement of mutual understanding and collaboration between our two great Germanic peoples.'

Schellenberg paused.

'Pioneers of the British Free Corps, those sentiments are applauded not only by the German people but by their *Führer*, Adolf Hitler! When history is written, your names will be inscribed on a roll of honour as having been the first to take the historic step towards bringing about such a state of affairs, the first to recognise the true enemies of civilisation.'

Schellenberg paused again and looked slowly at their ranks. 'The twentieth of April is a special day for us; a significant day for the Reich. It is the birthday of our *Führer*. In honour of that day, in honour of the far-sighted volunteers of the British Free Corps, the *Führer* has decreed that his own personal bodyguard will be stood down on that day and a special birthday honour guard shall be formed by the men of the British Free Corps.'

A murmur broke out among them. Cooper snapped an order to bring them to silent attention again.

'I knew you pioneers would recognise this great honour,' smiled Schellenberg. 'The *Führer* shows his respect and confidence in you. In two days from now, on Thursday, you will be taken to Hanover to board a train for Rastenburg . . .' The *Brigadeführer* broke off with a frown. It was a momentary hesitation, but Collins was quick to notice it. He had obviously revealed something which he should not have mentioned.

'You will be transported to the *Führer*'s field headquarters and there shall be instructed in your duties before 20 April.'

Collins made a mental note to check where Rastenburg was. Two days, however, was not much time to get things organised. His pulse was beating quickly now. Roberts had been right. He hoped that Gottschalk would not continue to confine the men to barracks. He needed to get to Hanover and pick up the explosives.

'Pioneers of the British Free Corps,' Schellenberg was saying, 'I salute you.' This he did in punctilious Nazi fashion with a click of his heels and a half bow. Then he turned, with his aide and Gottschalk trailing in his wake, and left the hall.

Cooper dismissed the men and they fell into groups talking excitedly among themselves. Collins had to pretend astonishment at the news, but as soon as he was able, he made his way to Gottschalk's office. The little captain had just finished bowing his distinguished visitor out and was sitting mopping the sweat from his flushed face. He looked up with a frown.

'I am busy at the moment, Collins. What is it?'

'Are we still confined to barracks, *Herr Hauptsturmführer*?' Collins enquired innocently. 'It will be very strenuous over these next few days and I could do with a day's relaxation in town.'

'My God! Is this all you Britishers think about? Passes, passes, passes!'

'But we were confined to barracks over the Easter weekend,

188

Herr Hauptsturmführer and I have only asked you for passes twice,' said Collins.

Gottschalk shook his head resignedly. 'Very well,' he said, 'you may have twenty-four hours, if you must. I would do this for no one else.'

From Gottschalk's office, Collins made his way to the stores office. The German orderly there glanced up with a frown of disapproval.

'I want to have a look at a gazeteer of Germany.'

'We don't have one,' retorted the man with a scowl.

'Any idea where I can get one?' pressed Collins.

'Try the library in Hildesheim.'

Collins had no difficulty finding the old *Bibliothek* building. The old woman at the desk gazed nervously at his Waffen-SS uniform.

'Can I help you, soldier?'

'Do you have a gazeteer of Germany?'

She pursed her lips in thought.

'There's only a 1927 edition. It should be at the end of that shelf over there.'

'That will do excellently,' Collins assured her.

He flipped the pages until he found Rastenburg, a moderate-sized town in East Prussia, whose population at the time of the last census before the book was published was 11,889. It lay on a flat, sandy plain on the river Guber, 64 miles south-east of Konigsberg and on the main rail route to Prosken. It was an old town built round a medieval fortress erected by the Teutonic knights. In pre-war days it was the centre for the manufacture of farm machinery, flour, sugar, oil and beer. On the map the book fortunately included, Collins noticed the town was surrounded by a vast expanse of pine forest. Rastenburg. Was this, then, the place where Adolf Hitler had his secret field headquarters?

Chapter Twenty-Five

'Karl!' Lottie Geis's heart beat rapidly as she opened the door of her apartment and saw Collins standing there. She felt a wild impulse to throw herself into the arms of the Englishman. Instead she drew her brows together and said: 'I waited for you on Sunday.'

'We were confined to barracks,' he said awkwardly. 'I'm sorry, Lottie, but there was no way I could contact you.'

The lonely anguish she had felt over the last two days evaporated. At least he was here. She stood aside and motioned him in.

'Are you hungry?'

He shook his head: 'No, but I'll have coffee if you have some.'

He removed his greatcoat, took off his hat and unbuckled his belt.

'Why were you confined to barracks?' she asked, as she bent over the gas-ring. 'Is it serious?'

'We are being moved out in two days' time. It is now that I shall need the materials which I asked for, Lottie. Within a few days I shall either have succeeded in the job I have been sent to do, or I will have failed.'

Her eyes were serious as she turned to him.

'So soon?' she whispered.

'I'm afraid so.'

'Can you tell me now what this job is exactly?'

'It is too dangerous for you to know.'

She pursed her lips. 'You said you needed explosives and detonators?'

'Yes'.

'Wait here, Karl. I must go and make a telephone call in the café down the street.'

Collins watched her go, reflecting on the way the sunlight

190

glinted in her hair, causing it to sparkle and flicker like golden fire. There was a lingering odour of her perfume, soft and gentle in the air. He sighed deeply. For the first time since he had decided to take on this job, he began to feel serious doubts. The girl served to remind him that life should be lived and enjoyed; life should not be about subterfuge deceit, lying, killing and all that was anti-life. He wished he was not in love with Lottie Geis. He would have no qualms about his job then.

She returned shortly. 'I have spoken to my contact, Karl,' she said seriously. 'We are to meet him in one hour at the monument to Count von Alten in the gardens near the victory column in Waterloo Platz.'

'Is he trustworthy?' was Collins's first question.

The girl nodded soberly. 'Very trustworthy, Karl. Come, let's walk there.'

Outside, in the sunshine of the pleasant April day, Lottie Geis tucked her arm under Collins's arm and the two of them strolled across the city like any normal young couple in the springtime of their days. Only the uniforms and the occasional bombsite, the rhythmic stamp of marching feet and the wail of sirens on some official car, brought them momentarily back to reality. For a time Collins was oblivious to it all, feeling only the warmth and friendship of the girl on his arm. They strolled through the irregularly built, narrow streets, past the old-fashioned gabled houses of yesteryear, along the banks of the sedately flowing Leine.

From the old town they turned south towards the newer quarter, built during the days of Kaiser Wilhelm, along the banks of the river Ihme where it joined the Leine. Waterloo Platz stood on the banks of the Ihme and was dominated by a high column, rising 150 feet, which celebrated the victory over Napoleon Bonaparte in 1815. The names of the young men of Hanover who gave their lives at Waterloo, fighting side by side with their English allies, were engraved on the column. Collins shook his head remembering another victory column in London celebrating the same battle. War was such an insanity.

Across the platz was an open garden with a rotunda. The philosopher Leibnitz scowled at passers-by from a memorial marble bust, while not far off stood Hanover's memorial to

191

General von Alten who had commanded the city's troops at Waterloo.

Lottie glanced at her watch. 'We are on time,' she murmured. They halted before the statue and pretended to be interested in the inscription.

Out of the corner of his eye, Collins saw a' *Wehrmacht* officer entering the gates of the gardens. He paused and looked in their direction. Then he strolled nonchalantly towards them as if he had all the time in the world. As he drew level, he pretended to suddenly recognise Lottie.

'It is *Fraulein* Geis, isn't it? Do you remember me? I met you at *Der Ausleger...*' The man was a good actor.

Lottie rose to the occasion. 'Of course,' she smiled, extending her hand, over which the officer bowed. 'It is *Herr Major* von Krancke.' She turned to Collins. 'Karl, this is Baron von Krancke. *Herr Major,* this is my friend . . . Karl.'

The major saluted in military style, his eyes widening as he gazed at Collins's military insignia. 'So?' he breathed. 'I have heard of your unit. I was sure it was a piece of propaganda. But it does exist?'

Collins returned his salute. 'It does, *Herr Major,*' he replied softly.

For a moment the two men gazed at each other, trying to assess each other's strengths and weaknesses. Collins found himself gazing into intelligent grey eyes, set in a handsome face with a strong jawline.

Von Krancke gestured to a coffee stall across the other side of the gardens which was almost deserted. 'Perhaps I may buy you coffee?' he suggested.

They walked slowly towards the stall which had a few tables and chairs clustered around it. The major talked inconsequentially about the weather and the night-clubs of Hanover, and how he had admired Lottie's singing. He sat them at a table and went to get the coffee. He returned, apologetically, with some watery beer.

'I regret, even the ersatz coffee is on ration,' he smiled.

They sipped at the beer silently for a moment. Then von Krancke sat back and gazed thoughtfully at Collins. 'Lottie tells me that you require help.'

'I need a small quantity of military explosives,' Collins said.

The *Wehrmacht* major raised his eyebrows a fraction. 'For what purpose?'

Collins grimaced. 'I can't tell you that.'

'Then how can I trust you?'

'There is no way I can make you trust me,' replied Collins. 'All I can say is that I have a job to do – a job to further our common cause.'

Von Krancke hesitated. He was a professional soldier, and an aristocrat descended from a Swabian noble family. He had been raised in a monarchistic tradition with due reverence to Church, country, culture and good manners. Like his forebears before him, he had become an officer cadet in a cavalry regiment, and his life had become devoted to his horses, art, literature, music and good food. His idyll was brutally shattered when Hitler came to power. The National Socialists stood for everything he abhorred. He had joined the Wednesday Club, an anti-Nazi group formed by General Ludwig Beck, a former chief of general staff. The Wednesday Club consisted of high-minded intellectuals, but von Krancke was something more, which was why he had become a member of Father Olbricht's group. He had survived so far because he was a good judge of men; he had an instinct for whom to trust and whom not to trust. For a long while he stared hard at Collins and the Englishman returned his scrutiny.

'Exactly how much explosive and what sort?' he asked finally.

'About two pounds,' said Collins. 'Hexite would be best because it gives off no fumes and is therefore difficult to trace. I also want a small timing device and detonator.'

Von Krancke bit his lip thoughtfully. 'When do you need this?'

'Within twenty-four hours.'

'I would not be able to get it before tomorrow morning. Where can I deliver it?'

Collins hesitated and glanced at Lottie.

'Bring it to my apartment,' the girl said.

'That's dangerous,' von Krancke frowned.

'We are all in danger,' shrugged the girl.

'Very well,' von Krancke stood up. 'I will see you tomorrow morning.'

He bowed low over Lottie's hand: 'A pleasure to see you again, *gnädige Fraulein*.' He saluted Collins, turned and walked swiftly from the gardens.

Lottie was looking at Collins with a worried expression.

'You will be careful, Karl.'

Collins smiled softly at her. 'I'm selfish enough to look out for myself, Lottie. But now I'd better find a place to stay until tomorrow. If I go back to barracks, I might not get back. My pass is a twenty-four-hour one so it would be best if I stay in Hanover until our *Wehrmacht* friend makes his delivery.'

'There are only military hostels and small hotels in which everyone's papers are constantly checked.' She hesitated and then added quickly: 'You can stay at my place. It would be no trouble.'

'That would be fine,' Collins replied, sensing her awkwardness. 'That way I can avoid any problems.'

She nodded with a smile: 'Well, then we have a whole afternoon before us. What shall we do?'

Collins felt a sudden surprise. It was true. There was nothing to do, nothing to worry about until the next day. 'I'll leave it up to you,' he said. 'What would you like to do?'

'Let's go to the cinema.'

'The cinema?'

'Yes. I haven't been to see a film in a long, long time.'

They found a cinema just off the market square, behind the red-bricked medieval *Rathaus*. The place was full, mostly with men in uniform and a few women. The programme was varied. First came a newsreel showing how the Germans were apparently winning the war in Italy; a similar item about the Eastern Front called forth some mocking laughter from a group of soldiers in the front row. They were young men, so it seemed, until you looked at their eyes; then they seemed incredibly old, as if they had lived several lifetimes. Most of them wore the 'Winter War' ribbon and between them they carried an assortment of silver wound badges, tank destruction badges and Iron Crosses. They hooted and howled as the commentator talked about the glorious advances on the Eastern Front.

Two black-uniformed SS men told them to shut up. There was a heated exchange but the men fell silent. By which time the newsreel had switched to the war being waged by the Japanese in the Pacific. Then there was an item about the heroic sacrifice *Reichsmarschall* Göring's nephew, Waldimar von Essen, who had been killed by Albanian guerillas. He was to be accorded a state funeral. After the newsreel came an incomprehensible comedy starring the German comedian Heinz Rühmann and his beautiful actress wife, Bertha Feiler. It was crude slapstick, but Collins sat back and chuckled. Finally there came an old horror movie made in the 1920s starring Conrad Veidt. Lottie enjoyed it, screaming in the appropriate places and clutching at Collins's hand in the darkness, afterwards making no attempt to withdraw it and nestling against his shoulder for the rest of the film.

Collins had a feeling of regret when the lights went up. It had been comfortable in the darkness of the cinema, with the flickering silver fantasy being enacted before his eyes, and with the girl warmly resting against him, her soft hand tight in his. For a brief period he had escaped the terror and destruction of the war the chaotic frenzy of their world. It was with a feeling of regret that he emerged into the early evening. A fine drizzle had started but not enough to dissuade them from walking back to Lottie's apartment.

No sooner had they left the dingy comfort of the cinema foyer than a light flashed over them and a harsh voice rang out.

'*Ausweis, bitte!*' Two uniformed SD men emerged from the shadowy gloom of a doorway.

'Your papers, please,' one of them repeated.

Collins proferred his *Soldbuch*.

The SD man, his face anonymous in the gloom, gasped as he looked at it. 'You are English?' he was unable to keep the astonishment out of his voice.

'Yes. *Raumführer* Collins of the *Britisches Freikorps*,' he replied. 'We are stationed at Hildesheim.'

'I will have to check this,' the man said.

'There is a telephone in the cinema foyer,' Collins said gruffly. There was only one way to deal with these types and that was to give them orders. 'Telephone the Waffen-SS barracks at St Michael's Monastery, Hildesheim. Asked for *Hauptsturmführer* Gottschalk.'

'Certainly, *Herr Raumführer*,' spluttered the man, turning and hurrying back to the cinema. The second SD man said nothing. Collins noticed that his hands rested lightly on his gun. Within minutes the first SD man came hurrying back.

'*Alles ist verruckt!*' He handed back the *Soldbuch* and saluted.

Collins thanked the man and, taking Lottie by the elbow, turned away. He realised that in the SD man's surprise, Lottie's identification had not been checked. It was just as well. After April 20 the fewer leads he left for the Gestapo to follow, the better.

However, the incident had broken the spell and brought both of them back to reality. As if to underscore the point, the nerve-jangling wail of an air-raid siren suddenly sounded. Lottie gripped his hand hard and he was aware of the sharp intake of her breath.

'There is a public shelter up ahead.'

People had begun to run this way and that, as the siren's warning shriek grew louder. Along the street stood an elderly uniformed policeman who was ushering people through the entrance of a church. Collins and Lottie followed the pushing crowd through the great wooden doors, across the tiled entrance and down cold stone steps into the crypt which had been converted into an air-raid shelter. Hundreds of people were pressed among the tombs. A solitary electric light bulb bathed the place in its weak and eerie glow.

Collins had an uncanny feeling of familiarity. It was as if he was back in London during the mind-shattering year of 1941 when the realities of civilian bombing had finally come home to people; when the experiences of the Spanish people were visited upon the towns of Britain. War was no longer a game enacted by two armies on some far-away battlefield; patriotism was no longer an indulgence which could be pursued in comfort and safety. War was a brutal part of everyday life.

He gazed at the tense, nervous faces around him. Children, old men, women, young soldiers on leave who, because of the uniforms they wore, were acting out the role of braggadocio, boasting false courage. Collins had seen their sort several times before; young, frightened men who had to perform collectively because they felt it was expected of them.

He and Lottie found a corner seat and settled down.

Collins found himself next to an old man who appeared to be with his daughter, a haggard woman of middle age. The old man seemed oblivious of the tension in his surroundings.

'It'll be the Tommies again,' he suddenly confided in Collins.

'I expect so,' Collins replied.

The old man snorted. 'Herrenhausen Castle, the Wagenheim Palace, the Kreuzkirche . . . they've all gone now. Where will it end, eh?'

Collins shrugged non-committally.

'Why should the Allies bomb them?' the old man went on plaintively. 'They are not military targets.' He gazed at Collins and suddenly frowned. 'But you are not a German. I can tell by your accent.'

Collins felt a wild desire to tell the old man the truth. Instead he smiled and said: 'No, I am an *Auslands Deutscher*.' It was easier to pretend to be a German from overseas. He knew that people did not make fine distinctions during bombing raids. He had once seen a German pilot, having baled out over London, nearly torn apart by an enraged crowd near Victoria Station.

'You are in the SS,' the old man said, almost accusingly.

'I'm in a *Liebesgaben* unit,' lied Collins. The *Liebesgaben* was the German welfare supplies centre, the equivalent of the British NAAFI.

The first explosion was far away and muffled. It was followed by others in rapid succession. Lottie clung tightly to his hand. The soldiers were singing now, one of them had a good voice and started to sing some old pre-war songs. Then they all burst into a strident chorus of the *Preussens Glorie* march.

The old man looked at them and spat.

'I was in the last war,' he turned to Collins again. 'That *was* a war. This is just mass murder, because of the whims of an upstart Austrian corporal . . .'

'Father!' the woman with a pinched face hissed sharply. 'This man is in the SS.'

The old man was unrepentant. 'It's true. He's not even German. He's a damned Austrian. He only became a naturalised German the year he became Chancellor. Did you know that?'

'Father, be quiet!'

Collins turned and patted the agitated old man's arm.

'I would heed what your daughter says, my friend,' he said softly. 'It is not good to speak your mind these days.'

The sound of bombing grew nearer.

Collins gave Lottie a smile of encouragement in the gloom. She tried to return his smile, but anxiety and fear showed clearly in her face.

The whole crypt seemed to shake and brick dust showered down on them. The light flickered, went out and came back on again.

'That was close!' called out someone.

Another voice from the direction of the stairs of the crypt shouted: 'There's been a direct hit on the Johanniskirche.'

Beside him the old man grunted. 'Bombing churches! For why? What good does it do?'

The soldiers began to sing the Horst Wessel Song.

The old man spat again and muttered: 'Bloody Austrian corporal.'

There was a terrific explosion. No warning at all before the light went out and mortar dust fell in a great stifling cloud. People started to cry out in fear and pain as the floor of the crypt rocked back and forth. Collins heard the rumble of falling masonry. The noise seemed to last for an eternity. He thought the crypt was caving in. Then the rumble stopped. Around him he could hear people crying and coughing in the poisonous brick-dust-filled air.

He suddenly realised he was no longer holding Lottie's hand. He cried her name in panic. In the noise and confusion his voice did not carry. Frenziedly he started to fumble for his matches and then stopped. If there were any broken gas mains in the vicinity, it would be a stupid thing to do.

'All right everyone,' came a voice from the direction of the stairway. It was calm and sounded as if it expected to be obeyed. 'There is no fire. There is no need to panic. Take your time and follow the direction of my torch in orderly fashion.' The beam of an electric torch stabbed across the crypt.

In spite of the call for calm, people began to surge forward, pushing, tugging, pulling, shoving. Collins found himself swept forward in the midst of a tide of frightened humanity. He tried to turn and shout for Lottie, but the tide carried him relentlessly towards the steps. Anger and fear seized him, and he too began to push and strike out, trying to get back to where he had last seen the girl. It was no use. He was carried up the stairs and into the church.

The vaulted roof of the church no longer existed. He could see the pale night sky and see the beams of searchlights sweeping frantically across the heavens. Here and there the sky was dotted with livid pin-points of light, tracers seared in orange arcs in pursuit of the white searchlights.

Somehow he managed to retain his footing until he was outside the building. He peered at the milling crowd trying to spot Lottie, calling her name in vain. For the first time in his life he experienced a feeling of utter loneliness and despair. It welled from somewhere deep within him. He felt a frustrated anger such as he had never known before. He found himself crying and waving his fist in impotent rage at the war planes overhead.

'*Englisches schweinhund!*' muttered a voice behind him. The elderly policeman who was acting as air-raid warden patted his shoulder. '*Britisches terrorfliegers.*' He spat and passed on.

The words heightened Collins's sense of bewilderment, confusing him totally. His alienation and sense of loneliness weighed heavily on him. Collins looked about him in a daze.

The old man who had sat beside him in the crypt wandered by, his face bloody, his clothes torn. 'Dead,' he was muttering. 'Bertha's dead. Why? What good does it do? Churches, women . . . all . . .'

A rescue worker came forward and led the old man off.

Collins fought to get a hold of himself, fumbled in his pocket and took out a cigarette and matches.

Bodies were being brought out on stretchers. He caught one of the bearers by the arm. 'Are there many dead?' he demanded.

The man nodded. 'Very many.'

'Where are you taking them?' The stretcher-bearer gestured across the road with his chin.

With a feeling a black despair, Collins followed the bearers and their grisly burden towards the ranks of bodies being deposited on the pavement opposite the church.

A soft voice penetrated his befuddled mind as he was

summoning up the courage to gaze on the faces of the corpses.
'Karl! Karl! Oh thank God!'

He spun round, his mouth working but only inarticulate sounds came forth.

She stood in the roadway hardly recognisable in her torn dress and coating of mortar dust. Curiously, the thought registered inconsequentially in his mind, she was still clutching her handbag. 'Lottie!' He took a couple of steps forward and caught her in his arms.

'Oh my God! My God!' he found himself repeating over and over again. The tears stood out in his eyes. He kissed her harshly, demandingly.

'It's all right, Karl,' she murmured, when he allowed her to draw breath. 'It's all right. I'm fine.'

In the distance the reassuring notes of the all-clear sounded.

Chapter Twenty-Six

It was dawn when Collins awoke and found Lottie lying beside him, head propped on her hand and turned slightly towards him. He could not see her features but knew instantly that she was awake and watching him.

'What is it?' he asked anxiously.

The girl sighed. 'I am just being foolish, Karl. I wish that we could stay here until the war is over.'

He eased himself up in bed, reached out for a cigarette and lit it. As he exhaled the smoke, the girl nestled up to him and lay her cheek on his chest.

'One day the war will be over. One day it will be just a few pages in school history books. And one day people will start living again.'

She did not reply.

'If I survive . . .' he felt her shiver slightly and repeated, 'If I survive, I am going to Australia. Would you come with me?'

'We live in an insane world, Karl,' she said, after a long pause. 'No one has the right to expect any happiness nor plan for the future.'

'The only way to survive the insanity is to plan for the future,' he said. 'I intend to survive.'

'This job of yours . . .' There was anxiety in her voice. 'Is it really that important? Important enough to get killed for?'

'I don't aim to get killed,' he assured her.

'Can't you tell me about it?'

'The less you know, the better for you.'

'But I might be able to help.'

'All you need know is that my unit is being posted to a place called Rastenburg. It is in East Prussia. On or before next Thursday my job will have been accomplished, successfully or otherwise. After that I shall make my way to a neutral country . . . will you come with me?'

She turned her head to his. 'You don't have to ask me.'

'I want you to come. It is too dangerous for you to continue living here.'

'You might stand a better chance of travelling on your own.'

He shook his head. 'When I lost you in the air raid, I nearly went mad; I don't want to lose you again.'

'If you want me, I'll come,' she said softly.

He bent to kiss her. For a while they lay together in an easy, comfortable silence.

'Did you say you were going to Rastenburg in East Prussia?'

He frowned. 'Do you know it?'

'I was born near there and lived there until I went to high school. That was when my parents moved to Hanover. I still have an aunt and a cousin who live on a farm near Korschen – that's a few kilometres from Rastenburg.'

She sat up abruptly, excitement in her voice. 'I could get Major von Krancke to get me a travel permit to visit my aunt and meet you at Korschen when your job is done.'

Collins shook his head. 'No, Lottie. I don't want you involved.'

But Lottie was insistent. 'That's silly. I am involved, and, besides, you might need someone fairly close. I couldn't get to

Rastenburg, but Korschen is the next best place. You might need a place to hide.'

Collins bit his lip. The girl was making sense. He certainly had no plans to commit suicide – especially not now. The assassination attempt would have to be carried out in such a way that it allowed him time to escape. But escape to where? An old farmhouse not too far away, somewhere to hide when all hell broke loose – it was the perfect solution.

'Anyway', Karl,' Lottie was saying, 'it would be far easier to get from Rastenburg to Konigsberg or Danzig, and find a way of getting across to Sweden, than to try and return through Hanover and south to Switzerland or Spain.'

Collins nodded and stubbed out his cigarette. 'You said your aunt and cousin live on the farm. Will it be safe?'

Lottie nodded. 'Perfectly safe. It's a small farm on the outskirts of the town, near the river Guber. I know those woods like the back of my hand. Do you want me to write down the address and directions?'

'No, just tell me. I'll memorise the directions. Are you sure that von Krancke can get you a travel permit?'

'Oh yes, that's one of his jobs.'

Collins smiled. 'Then I will join you at your aunt's farm either Wednesday or Thursday at the latest.'

'And then Sweden?'

'Then Sweden,' he affirmed. He bent forward and kissed her demandingly. 'I love you, Lottie,' he whispered.

'Please do, Karl,' she replied softly. 'I need your love very much.'

They were having coffee when Major von Krancke arrived.

'It was difficult,' said the *Wehrmacht* major as he settled himself into a chair and opened his briefcase. 'Supplies are short, but there was confusion after the raid last night. Some of the ordnance records were detroyed by a hit on the barracks.'

'We were in the Kreuzkirche when it was hit,' replied Lottie.

Von Krancke pursed his lips. 'You were lucky. There were sixty-one dead in that area. The Allies are stepping up their raids.'

He turned his attention back to his briefcase and took out a package wrapped in newspaper. Unwrapping it, he produced a substance which resembled a slab of brown wax some six inches square by two-and-a-half inches thick. Collins picked it up and turned it over in his hands with a smile of approval.

'Hexite,' von Krancke said grimly. 'Plastic explosive.'

Lottie shuddered nervously.

'It's perfectly harmless,' Collins said reassuringly. He sniffed at it. There was no discernable odour. 'Excellent. I should be able to disguise this in my equipment. What about detonators?'

Von Krancke looked uncomfortable. 'That was the problem. I have been less fortunate there. No detonators were available from our stores . . .' He held up his hand pacifyingly as Collins gestured in exasperation. 'I have already contacted a friend at the ordnance depot in Hildesheim. He can get a detonator.'

'How do I pick it up?' demanded Collins.

'The detonator will be passed to another member of our group. It will be delivered to the postbox at 20 Viktoriastrasse. Do you know it?'

'It's just by St Michael's.'

'Good. It will be delivered at six o'clock this evening. At six-fifteen you will go to the postbox. You will find the door open. Reach inside and remove the detonator which will be in a small brown parcel. Make sure no one observes you.'

Von Krancke rebuckled the straps on his briefcase.

'Can you get me a travel permit to visit my aunt in Korschen?' asked Lottie.

The *Wehrmacht* major frowned. 'Korschen in East Prussia? It's a long journey and the Allies are concentrating their raids on rail routes and crossings.'

'It's important,' pressed the girl.

Von Krancke sighed and nodded. 'When do you wish to go?'

'As soon as possible.'

'This afternoon?'

Lottie glanced at Collins and then shrugged. 'Why not? I can be ready.'

Von Krancke smiled. 'In that case, I will have the permit ready for you at two o'clock if you call by my office. I can also provide you with an escort for part of the way. *Leutnant* Neidenberg, of my staff, is travelling to Danzig to take up a new assignment. It might save trouble if you went with him.'

'That will be perfect,' agreed Lottie.

Von Krancke turned to Collins and held out his hand.

'Good luck, my friend,' he said. 'Remember, 20 Viktoria-strasse. The postbox.'

With a gesture midway between a wave and a salute, the dapper *Wehrmacht* major was gone.

The black Horsche saloon car, with its silver swastika emblem, was travelling swiftly westward along the *Autobahn* which connected Berlin to Hanover. It was a great white ribbon of road that was once Adolf Hitler's great pride and the symbol of the rising Reich. On the back seat, *Standartenführer* Rudi Behrens gazed out moodily as the countryside flew by. On his lap was a briefcase. In the driver's seat, relaxed at the wheel, Manfred Reinecke whistled tunelessly.

Behrens moved forward. 'When you take the turn-off to Hanover, go straight on to Hildesheim.'

'Gestapo headquarters?'

'Yes.'

'Very well, *Herr Standartenführer*,' replied Reinecke.

Behrens leant back in his seat again and let his eyes travel to the briefcase in his lap. Inside, among the files, was the confession of *Oberstleutnant Freiherr* von Fegeleinn; a confession signed two hours ago in the baron's cell in Wing B of the star-shaped Lehrterstrasse Prison of Berlin. Behrens smiled thinly. He still had a mental vision of the man on his hands and knees, face stained with blood, crying and pleading for his life. Behrens glanced at his wristwatch. Well, by now *Oberstleutnant Freiherr* von Fegeleinn would be dead. The Reich had no use for treacherous swine like him. Before the *Führer* came to power, pompous weaklings like von Fegeleinn would have spat on ex-butcher's boy like Behrens. Behrens would have had to touch his cap as von Fegeleinn passed by. People like that, like von Fegeleinn and that bitch Helga von Haensel, still thought they were superior to the people – the people as personified by the *Führer* and the Party. They plotted and planned and boasted, but they were weak.

Behrens had made von Fegeleinn talk without too much effort. It was his job to make people talk and he was efficient at his work. He had no compunction about it. Why should he care about the suffering of a few traitors? Behrens was a servant of his *Führer,* Adolf Hitler, head of the German people, and he had no regrets for what he did. Last night the Allies had dropped two thousand tons of bombs on Berlin, killing and maiming he did not know how many men, women and children. If the Allies considered mass murder a legitimate act of war, why should he care for the suffering of such scum as von Fegeleinn and Helga von Haensel?

He stirred uncomfortably. Helga von Haensel had proved to be a strong-minded and stubborn bitch. He had tried all the usual methods on her. Nothing. Not a word. It was only on the direct orders of Kaltenbrunner that the interrogation of the woman had been stopped. The Gestapo chief was apparently trying to curry favour with some of her highly placed friends who had protested at her arrest. Dying in the basement of 8 Prinz Albrecht Strasse was not for her. Well, von Fegeleinn had given them enough information to make a number of arrests. That was why Behrens was going to Hildesheim. 'If any of us were in trouble,' ran a sentence in von Fegeleinn's confession, 'we were to contact a man in Hildesheim. Someone called Uncle Wilhelm in the *Postamt.'*

The trouble was that the town of Hildesheim rang another bell in Behrens's memory, but he could not quite connect what it was about Hildesheim that he should remember.

'How much longer will we be, Manfred?' he snapped.

Manfred Reinecke glanced at his superior in the driving mirror. Behrens could not see the grin of derision on the man's lips.

'Probably an hour, *Herr Standartenführer,'* he replied.

Behrens sighed and reached into his pocket for a cigarette.

Old Kark Wielen left the 4th *Gruppe's* Ordnance Depot in the suburb of Maritzberg, just behind the eleventh-century abbey, at a little after five o'clock. He had just delivered some mail there, after which he collected a bag of soldiers' mail for the *Postamt.* He had exchanged his customary greeting with the guard commander and had been turning to leave when a young *leutnant* hurried down the steps and pressed something into his hands.

'I nearly missed you, *Herr Postbote*,' he said. 'A gift for my girlfriend in Berlin. It's her birthday tomorrow.'

Behind the young *Leutnant's* back, the guard commander winked crudely at old Karl Wielen.

The postman tooked the package, nodded, and cycled away. A few yards from the depot, he stopped and, making sure no one was about, he looked at the package. Pencilled instructions were written on a slip of paper attached to it. He tore the instructions into shreds and then pressed the package to the bottom of his satchel before cycling on.

The traffic around the city centre was busy. There were a lot of people about, taking advantage of the good April weather to make a descent on the shops in search of whatever bargains they could find. The old postman cycled across the cobbled streets. Parts of the *Rathaus,* the Knockenhauer Court and several old and valuable houses were now yawning bombsites. It was sad, and for what? Who was really responsible? The Allies? He remembered how the people of Hildesheim had cheered and applauded when Göring's *Luftwaffe* had devasted London, Coventry and Birmingham. Well, tit for tat, eh? He turned his bicycle into the square which led to Viktoriastrasse where the instructions directed him. It was a few minutes before six o'clock now. Plenty of time.

A girl was crossing the street just ahead of him. He slowed his bicycle. The girl was tall, a willowy blonde-haired girl . . . just like Paula. In fact, she was so like Paula that . . . Old Karl Wielen's heart quickened. It was impossible. No, it could not be. But . . . he turned his head as he passed by to examine her more closely.

The blare of the car horn made him swerve wildly. Too late! Karl Wielen's bicycle smashed into the side of an Army vehicle, sending the old postman sprawling on the sharp cobbles, his satchel flying in one direction, his crumpled bicycle in another, while he tumbled painfully in the road. People began shouting all around him. He glanced up, dazed. 'Paula!' he muttered.

A ring of people were gazing down in sympathy, including the willowy blonde girl. He groaned. It was not Paula. What a fool he was.

Willing hands helped him rise to his feet and steady him.

The driver of the Army vehicle, a sour-faced *Feldwebel* was shouting incomprehensively at him, calling him all kinds of animal.

A uniformed policeman moved in to pacify the man and finally the crowds began to drift away.

'Are you all right, *Herr Postbote?*' asked the policeman.

'Just a graze,' old Karl Wielen said, gazing ruefully at his bicycle. 'But my cycle . . .' The front wheel was twisted and buckled. Then a panic seized the old man. ' . . . and my satchel? Where is my satchel?'

'Is this it?' A florid-faced man in civilian clothes moved forward. He was holding the satchel in his hand. It had split open and its contents had obviously spilled out. The man carried several letters stained with mud. On top of them was a little packet . . . the packet the *Leutnant* had given him and which had burst open, revealing its contents.

Old Karl Wielen made a move to take them, but the florid-faced man held them back. 'I repeat, is this your satchel, *Herr Postbote?*' he demanded.

'Yes.'

'I am *Kriminalkommissar* Wulff of the Kripo,' said the man. 'Do you know what is in this package, *Herr Postbote?*'

Wielen had been in the Great War and understood the principles of detonators only too well.

'This is an explosives detonator, *Herr Postbote*,' went on the policeman. 'How does it happen to be in an unmarked, unaddressed box in your satchel?'

'I do not know,' bluffed Karl Wielen. 'I collect mail and I deliver it.'

'So? And where would you have delivered this?'

'If there is no address on it, it is returned to the *Postamt*.'

'Where did you get it? From what point did you collect it?'

Wielen shrugged. 'I have no idea.'

The Kripo *Kommissar* signalled to the uniformed policeman.

'Perhaps the *Herr Postbote* will accompany us down to headquarters where his memory might be refreshed?' he said softly.

The uniformed policeman took old Karl Wielen by the arm and pushed him firmly forward, while the Kripo man trailed in their wake carrying the satchel.

Chapter Twenty-Seven

Kurt Ludecke was an assistant *Kommissar* of the *Geheime Staatspolizei* in Hildesheim. It was not an important post. Hardly anything happened in the quiet, old-fashioned backwater. In many ways Kurt Ludecke thought he had been hard done by. He had applied for a transfer to a larger town, but his application had been turned down by the Prinz Albrecht Strasse people. However, Ludecke was young, zealous and determined to be a success.

He had just finished yawning over a boring report concerning a local postman, a well-known figure called Uncle Wilhelm Wielen. Ludecke wondered why the matter had been referred to him. The old man had been found carrying an unmarked package containing an explosives detonator. So far as Ludecke was concerned the Kripo officer who had arrested the old man had been a little too enthusiastic. Wielen could have picked it up anywhere in the normal course of his job.

He sighed and reached for a pen to sign the old man's release order. It was senseless keeping the old postman in custody on suspicion of being an enemy saboteur. He smiled to himself at the very idea.

His office door opened and a dark, gaunt man in civilian clothes came in followed closely by another man with Slavic features. Before Ludecke could voice his annoyance, the first man shoved an identification card in front of him.

'I am *Standartenführer* Behrens from Berlin,' he announced.

Ludecke climbed nervously to his feet. 'What can I do to be of service to you?'

Behrens dropped into a chair before Ludecke's desk, 'I want some local manpower to track down a little group of traitors and saboteurs. I have to start by making an enquiry at the local *Postamt* for someone who calls himself Uncle Wilhelm.'

208

Ludecke's eyes widened in amazement. 'Did you say Uncle Wilhelm, *Herr Standartenführer?*' he gasped.

Behrens grunted an affirmative. He was irritated by the slow smile he saw spread across Ludecke's face.

Ludecke noticed the beginning of a scowl and hastily composed his features. 'I beg to report *Herr Standartenführer*, that the man known as Uncle Wilhelm is now in custody. He was arrested after being found in possession of a detonator. I have the report here,' he pushed the file across to Behrens. 'I was just going to question him when you arrived.'

Behrens gazed at Ludecke with his dark expressionless eyes and then reached for the file. He read it carefully.

'There can be no question that this is the man known at the Hildesheim *Postamt* as Uncle Wilhelm?'

Ludecke nodded.

'Has his home been searched?'

'I was about . . .'

Behrens did not let the man finish.

'My assistant Reinecke will take some of your men and search Wielen's apartment.'

Manfred Reinecke sighed softly: 'At once, *Herr Standartenführer,*' he said. 'Will you arrange it, Ludecke?'

The assistant *Kommissar* reached for the telephone. 'At once,' he echoed.

In an attic room at London's Kensington Palace Gardens, a room lined with radio equipment, an operator bent over his receiver-transmitter with a worried expression. The Army captain in charge of the communications room came to stand at the operator's shoulder.

'Trouble?' he asked.

'I'm not sure, sir,' replied the operator. 'Someone tried to get through on the Piper's frequency a moment ago.'

The captain frowned. 'Try his call sign.'

The man tapped his key: 'Rabbit calling Piper. Rabbit calling Piper.'

He paused. There was a moment and then the equipment started to buzz. The captain smiled. 'That's all right,' he muttered.

The operator still had a worried expression. He was tapping out something else. His expression grew more intense as he listened to the reply.

'There's an alien hand on the Piper's key, sir,' he reported.

It was an expression meaning that the sender of the morse signal was not the man who was supposed to send the message. A good operator could tell the difference between individual keying. It was like handwriting.

'Did you ask for identification?' demanded the captain.

'Yes sir. The sender just keeps asking what our message is.'

The captain whistled softly. 'The Piper? That's Hildesheim, isn't it? Break all contact. I'll report that Hildesheim has been blown.'

Brigadier Kylie put down the internal telephone and glanced up at Roberts with a worried frown.

'Communications report that our man at Hildesheim has been taken. There was an alien hand on his key tonight.'

Roberts bit his lip.

'Damn it!' he muttered. 'That's Wielen.'

'Wasn't Wielen the contact you gave Collins?'

Roberts nodded.

'Will this throw a spanner in the works?' demanded Kylie.

'I hope not. Let's hope that Collins did not need to make contact with Wielen.'

Behrens watched as Ludecke brought old Karl Wielen into the room. The postman stared around bewilderedly.

'Sit down, *Herr Postbote*,' smiled Behrens.

Ludecke almost pushed the old man into a chair opposite the desk behind which Behrens had seated himself.

'You are in a lot of trouble, *Herr Postbote*,' Behrens said evenly.

Wielen made no reply.

Manfred Reinecke, leaning against a wall to one side of the room said softly: 'We have found your radio, Piper.'

Wielen could not disguise the jerk of his head.

'You do not protest, *Herr Postbote*,' said Behrens, lighting a cigarette. 'You do not say: "I have no radio". You are a sensible man.'

Wielen sighed deeply. So it was finished. He had played his part and now he could do no more except refuse to betray his comrades.

Behrens was leaning forward. 'A friend of yours named von Fegeleinn told us that if he wanted help, all he had to do was ask at the Hildesheim *Postamt* for Uncle Wilhelm. Unfortunately, your friend is no longer with us, Uncle Wilhelm.'

Wielen remained silent.

Behrens sat back and sighed deeply. 'Conversationally, I can see that we are a bore to each other, *Herr Postbote*. Because you are a swine and a traitor, you are going to die. But you have a choice. A clean quick bullet or . . .' he paused. 'There is a new method which is favoured by the *Reichsführer* for your sort of traitor. It consists of beheading while the victim is looking upwards as the axe descends. Or there is an even better method: slow strangulation with piano wire.'

Wielen stared stiffly ahead of him.

'The choice is yours, Wielen. If you prefer the clean, quick bullet, then I suggest that you tell me the names of your accomplices, your contacts and what information you pass to the enemies of the Reich on your radio.'

'I have nothing to say,' the old man licked his lips and spoke slowly. 'Nothing, except the hope that God may forgive you.'

Behrens sat back with a frown.

Wielen became aware of the man who had led him into the room and who was now standing by his chair. Wielen glanced sideways at him. He was a tall, fair-haired young man who looked very healthy and fresh. Wielen wondered if he had just come from a bath. He smelt faintly of eau-de-Cologne.

'A last chance, *Herr Postbote*,' Behrens was saying. 'Tell us what we want to know.'

Wielen remained rigidly silent.

Ludecke turned and gripped Karl Wielen's right wrist in a vice-like grip; it was so hard that the old man gasped. Then Ludecke caught Wielen's little finger. It happened so quickly, so smoothly, that Wielen did not know what he was doing until there was a sharp crack and the pain shot up his arm. He screamed.

'You might as well tell us and save yourself a lot of trouble,' the old man heard Behrens say.

Ludecke grasped his second finger.

Old Karl Wielen heard himself screaming again. Then he was drowning in recurring waves of nausea. He shut his eyes, smelling the clean smell of soap and water and eau-de-Cologne from Ludecke's body. He tried to concentrate on some thought. He must not break now. He owed it to Paula. Paula! That was it. He owed it to his daughter.

'*Domine, exaudi orationem*...O Lord, hear my prayer,' he whispered. He opened his eyes and tried to concentrate on the expressionless face of Behrens. '*Et clamor meus ad te veniat*...and let my cry come unto thee!'

Behrens shook his head and gestured at Ludecke.

Before the Gestapo interrogator had reached Wielen's forefinger, the old man had fainted.

Behrens sighed with impatience.

Manfred Reinecke, still leaning against the wall, pulled out a packet of cigarettes and lit one. 'The old man is stubborn,' he said.

Ludecke went to a washbasin in the corner of the room and returned with a wet towel. He had soon brought Wielen back to conciousness. 'Wake up, *Herr Postbote*,' he said softly. 'We still have much to discuss.'

The room swam into focus for Wielen and the terrible throbbing pain of his hand caused him to whimper in agony.

'Paula!' groaned the old man.

'What's that?' Behrens leant forward eagerly.

'Who is Paula?' repeated Ludecke, shaking him. 'Is that your contact?'

Wielen tried to collect his pain-racked thoughts. The name of his daughter on the lips of the leering Gestapo man gave him a sudden frenzy of strength.

'My Lord and my God,' he suddenly shouted, 'from this moment I accept at Thy hands, with resignation and cheerfulness, the kind of death it may please Thee to send me, with all its pains and anguish.'

To their surprise the old man abruptly leapt from his chair and was running towards the window.

He did not reach it.

The bullet fired from the pistol of Manfred Reinecke caught him just below the left shoulder blade and passed through his heart. Karl Wielen spun round and collapsed onto the carpet. He lay still, his arms outstretched in the manner of a supplicant.

Behrens rose slowly from his desk and walked over. It took him a moment to ascertain that there was no pulse beat. He glanced angrily up at Reinecke who was nonchalantly holstering his pistol.

'There was no need for that! We could have stopped him and made him talk. All you have given him is what he wanted.'

Reinecke shrugged. 'The man was a religious fanatic, *Herr Standartenführer*,' he said. 'They are stubborn.'

Behrens stood up and glanced at Ludecke. 'Get it out of here,' he said, gesturing at the body.

Chapter Twenty-Eight

Some fifty miles north of Berlin lies a group of lakes which, during the 1920s and '30s, were a rendezvous for the rich and idle of Berlin. They came to the shores of the lakes by car and caravan, by motorcycle and bicycle, to spend the weekend during the hot summers; to extend their pale bodies in the sun; to swim; to indulge in large quantities of food and drink; to play and have fun. One of these stretches of water was called Furstenburg, yet Furstenburg was not as popular as its neighbouring lakes. It was a little too swampy; too dank and gaseous.

It was to this lake that the black saloon car bearing Countess Helga von Haensel travelled on the morning of Thursday, 13 April. But the bland-faced young men who sat on either side of the young countess in the back of the car were not escorting her to the lakeside for a treat, for a weekend of pleasure. They were taking her to Furstenburg for another purpose.

Not far away from the lake of Furstenburg, in 1939, a special camp had been built for women prisoners of the Reich. It had been designed to contain a maximum of six thousand internees. By train, by cattle truck, by lorry and on foot, came a never-ending queue of women. They shuffled through its gate in tens of thousands. Forty thousand women were eventually crowded behind its barbed wire fences. The majority who shuffled in found only one exit; via a new brick building placed neatly between the camp's main perimeter fence and the lake itself. It had a tall chimney and constantly belched black smoke.

The camp was called Ravensbrück.

The chief wardress, a plump, fair-haired young woman, scornfully confident, greeted the new arrival at the gate. She carried a long lashed whip in her hand and a large dog trotted at her heels.

'You are Haensel?'

Helga von Haensel tried to draw herself up before the rough-spoken woman. She knew that her face must be mis-shapen and bruised, one eye half closed. Rags wrapped her bleeding hands and feet where Behrens and his experts had been at work. Yet she tried to muster some dignity.

'I am Countess Helga von Haensel,' she replied.

The wardress sneered. 'It is not often that we get your sort in here, although we've had a few people with titles – decadent swine! In here you are called Haensel. Don't give yourself airs and graces. They'll soon be knocked out of you.' She turned on her heel with a single command: 'Come!'

Helga von Haensel tried not to shudder as the great mesh-wire gates of the camp slammed shut behind her.

Two lorries carried the men of the British Free Corps through the old arch of St Michael's Monastery and down the road to the town of Hildesheim. They skirted the suburbs and headed north to Hanover. *Hauptsturmführer* Gerhard Gottschalk, riding in the first truck, was feeling rather proud of his men. Clad in their new uniforms, they looked smart and soldier-like. They were immaculate, looking the epitomy of highly trained and well-disciplined troops.

In the second truck Collins sat morose and worried. The previous evening he had gone to the postbox at 20 Viktoriastrasse. The door was not open. He had spent an hour waiting at the mail box but there was no sign of the deliverer nor of the promised detonator. He wondered whether he should contact Uncle Wilhelm again, but there was no time. He would have to improvise. He spent a sleepless night worrying, but finally resigned himself to seeing what developed. He had been able to pack the plastic explosive in his uniform webbing, in the ammunition pouches, but it was going to be useless without a detonator.

That morning they had been awakened early to start their journey. It was a long one. From Hildesheim to Hanover they were transported by truck. At Hanover, they were entrained in a special railway carriage with SS guards in attendance, each carrying machine pistols. It was obvious that the British Free Corps was not entirely trusted. The journey was tedious and the men whiled away the hours playing cards, gambling their pay or reading. McLardy tried holding his Fascist indoctrination classes, but he did not get any enthusiastic pupils.

Collins spent most of the time in the corridor of the train, smoking and thinking. He wondered whether Lottie had already arrived at Korschen. He felt a desperate tug of loneliness as he thought about her. God! He hoped nothing would happen to her. He had never needed anyone in his life as much as he needed her now. His life seemed to make sense because of her – now he had a purpose. He wanted very much to survive this god-awful war. He occupied himself with fantasies of the future – Australia, a sheep-farm, settling down with Lottie until the war in Europe was just a dim, bad memory.

The train chattered on, from Hanover to Hamburg, by-passing the torn railway system of the former busy port. Where Hamburg had once stood was now a terrifying desert. On the night of 25 July 1943, over 20,000 citizens had died and 60,000 had been injured by Allied bombs. Eighty-five per cent of the city and its environs had been totally destroyed. It took many hours for the train to negotiate its way around the devastated city, first turning north-east towards Lubeck, then due east to Neu-brandenburg, then to Stettin on the Oder, before turning for Danzig on the Baltic coast and along the naturally sheltered coastline of East Prussia to Königsburg. Finally, the train turned south-east for Rastenburg. The journey took an infuriatingly slow two-and-a-half days, and the train steamed slowly through Rastenburg at midday on Sunday.

At the same moment, nearly a thousand miles away, Prime Minister Winston Churchill was musing on the whereabouts of Sergeant Charles Collins, and the fact that 20 April was only a few days away. As the Prime Minister sat in an ante-room of Buckingham Palace, awaiting his regular audience with the King, he cynically wondered what odds a bookmaker would give on the success of Operation Hagen.

Strangely enough, Collins was thinking the very same.

Rastenburg appeared to be a sleepy little town, picturesque amongst the great forests of conifers, dominated by an old castle and a medieval Gothic church. Snow still covered the landscape, making it seem unreal, like a picture-postcard illustration. But Collins was not interested in the scenery. His eyes took in the roads and vantage points. His life might depend on what he noticed. They must have by-passed Korschen. According to the map he had seen in the library, it lay only a few kilometres to the north.

The train was delayed just outside Rastenburg station while all the carriages except the one carrying the members of the British Free Corps were uncoupled and shunted off to a siding. Then a special engine was attached to the carriage. More uni-formed SS men joined the guards, all in full combat uniforms. The train set off slowly, pushing deeper and deeper into the pine forests where the snows lay thick on the ground, unmelted by the spring sunshine. The scene reminded Collins of some Arctic wasteland. He wondered why Hitler had chosen such a place for his field headquarters.

They came upon Wolfsschanze abruptly, without any warning at all. One moment they were pressing through a seemingly impenetrable forest and the next they had arrived at a small station whose buildings were built of pine logs. A sprawl of huts and high barbed-wire fences, with signs warning of electrical currents, lay in a clearing on the east side of the single-line track. On the western side there were several long Army barracks. It was a small town in itself.

Collins was conscious that he alone of the members of the British Free Corps knew the position of Wolfsschanze.

Now he must try to destroy the wolf in its lair.

Reinecke braked his car and switched off the engine. The small house by the lakeside at Teuntz was beautiful. He felt a moment of jealousy for Behrens. As he climbed out of the car, the door of the house opened and Inge Behrens came out, stopping short at the sight of him.

'Manfred! I thought it was Rudi.'

Reinecke showed his teeth in a mirthless smile. 'Alas, the *Standartenführer* has been called in to a special meeting with *Oberstgruppenführer* Kaltenbrunner. I decided to come in his stead. Are you going to ask me in?'

Hesitantly, she moved aside and he entered the hallway. In spite of her feeling of fear – fear of her husband – she felt excitement at the sight of Manfred Reinecke, a tingling chemical attraction.

She forced herself to shut the door and face him. 'What do you want, Manfred?'

He eyed her in amusement. Then he threw off his coat, draping it over a chair in the hallway.

'The *Standartenführer* asked me to call by to collect some papers he has left here. Do you know where he keeps them?'

She frowned, half nodding. 'You did not come to see me?'

Reinecke grinned broadly at the peevish quality in her voice. 'The purpose was to kill two birds with one stone,' he said, moving close to her and placing his arms around her waist. She stood still, making no protest.

'Where are Rudi's papers?'

She stood trembling a little as he bent down and softly brushed her lips with his. He felt her body mould itself to his.

'Get them later,' she said with a catch in her throat. Her arms came up to encircle his neck. She responded demandingly to his kiss.

Out of the corner of his eyes he caught sight of the clock on the wall; it was an ornate Swiss cuckoo-clock, executed in exquisitely bad taste. He had to get back to Berlin before Behrens missed him, but he had to examine those papers, the private file that Behrens was keeping on the German resistance movement. He had to see them. Well, there was time enough.

He brought his attention back to Inge Behrens.

Yes, there was time.

Behrens stubbed out his cigarette and gazed at the morose face of Ernst Kaltenbrunner, the chief of the Gestapo.

'I believe this group which the traitor Fegeleinn called the Olbricht Group is something more than the usual ineffectual liberal or Communist dissident group, *Herr Oberstgruppenführer,*' he said.

Kaltenbrunner was toying with a pencil. 'What gives you that idea?'

'We know there are some highly placed people within the group, as well as many nonentities. Membership ranges from officers in the *Wehrmacht,* members of the Foreign Office, to an old postman in Hildesheim who, let me point out, had radio contact with London. They are well organised.'

'I've read von Fegeleinn's confession,' sighed Kaltenbrunner. 'It was obvious that he was not the ring leader and did not really know much.'

'That bitch Haensel knows a lot.'

Kaltenbrunner shrugged. 'And she would have died rather than tell you.'

'Hildesheim!' Behrens suddenly swung round and thumped his fist into the palm of his hand.

Kaltenbrunner raised his eyebrows.

'Hildesheim!' repeated Behrens. 'I knew something has been lurking in the back of my memory all this time. That's where that Englishman, Collins, went. That is where this crazy unit called the British Free Corps is stationed.'

Kaltenbrunner laughed. 'You are not suggesting that the British Free Corps are some purposely infiltrated subversive organisation? That would be ridiculous.'

'Why not?' scowled Behrens. 'At least, why shouldn't one or more British agents be infiltrated into it?'

'With orders to do what?' The Gestapo chief was amused.

Behrens shrugged. 'I don't know . . . yet. But I don't believe in coincidences. I think I ought to go back to Hildesheim and have a talk with these so-called British crusaders against Bolshevism.'

He turned to go, but Kaltenbrunner stayed him. There was a sudden worried look on the face of the *Oberstgruppenführer*. 'You won't find them at Hildesheim any longer,' he said quietly.

Behrens turned back with a frown. 'Where are they now?'

'They have been sent to East Prussia on the special orders of *Reichsführer* Himmler, who has also left for the same destination. They have been sent to Rastenburg, to the *Führer's* field headquarters.'

Behren's jaw dropped. 'Can't that order be rescinded?' he said slowly.

Kaltenbrunner shook his head. 'It was a special wish of the *Führer*. There is no way those plans can be changed now, not unless you have something specific, apart from your dislike of the *Britisches Freikorps*.'

Behrens bit his lip before replying. 'In that case, *Herr Oberstgruppenführer*, may I request a special pass? I must get to Rastenburg immediately.'

Chapter Twenty-Nine

The *Führer* had a love–hate relationship with Wolfsschanze, his 'wolf's lair' at Rastenburg. It had been prepared for him as a secret field headquarters during the summer of 1941, during the early days of the invasion of Soviet Russia, hidden deep within the dark, brooding conifer forests of East Prussia. It was only to be a temporary headquarters, for the *Führer* confidently predicted that the Soviets would collapse within eight weeks. But as the war continued, Wolfsschanze grew like a small town, haphazard and unplanned.

A special pine-log cabin had been constructed as living

219

quarters for the *Führer,* then a concrete underground bunker had been added; a special kennel was even built for the *Führer's* wolfhound. Then another hut was erected close by where military briefings could take place. This was a multi-purpose, prefabricated building with white strawboard walls. It differed from the rest of the buildings at Wolfsschanze by being enclosed within an eighteen-inch shell of concrete to protect it against incendiary bombs. Inside was just enough space for a conference room, a battery of telephones, a cloakroom, washroom, and an entrance hall which could, if needed, be transferred into another conference room. These buildings constituted the *Lagebaracke* at Wolfsschanze, standing at the centre of a complicated system of checkpoints, guardposts and surrounding barbed-wire entanglements and minefields.

Just outside the perimeter fence of the *Lagebaracke* was another compound designated *Sperrkreis* A, a zone which was forbidden to any but the most privileged of the *Führer's* entourage. There were specially constructed quarters for the *Führer's* personal physician, Theodore Morell; *Reichsmarschall* Göring; Wilhelm Keitel, the chief of staff; Alfred Jodl, chief of operations; and others. Included in this building complex were a radio station, telephone exchange, map room, cinema, teahouse, garage, field kitchen, stores, and an air-raid shelter. This area too was surrounded by barbed wire, minefields and road blocks. The rail track from Rastenburg ran straight into this compound through the various checkpoints, so also did the small roadway.

Across the rail tracks, which formed the south-western boundary, stood the main complex of guard barracks and general quarters. Not far away was the small airfield which had been added in recent years. The outer perimeters were usually guarded by seven companies of the SS *Gross Deutschland* Division while the interior was guarded by Hitler's élite SS *Leibstandarte* Adolf Hitler Regiment.

No one liked Wolfsschanze. In summer it was unbearable. The forests were humid and threatening. The mosquitoes, breeding in the adjacent lakes and marshes, filled the air with an irritating humming. Even when gasoline was sprayed on them, they never seemed to die. In winter it was even less tolerable; buried under heavy snows and slush, the temperatures were usually freezing. In the milder days, damp grey mists clung eerily to the pines – unhealthy and choking mists. Out of the *Führer's* hearing, everyone complained – about the mosquitoes in the summer and the misery and loneliness of the damp primeval forests in the winter.

Yet, although he shared the general dislike of this depressing place, the *Führer* clung to it obstinately for months at a time. It was his special sanctuary, his refuge, an asylum where he could feel perfectly secure. It suited his character admirably, for its seclusion and silence reflected his profound alienation from the world over which he ruled. Wolfsschanze was an abstract portrait of his own disorganised mind, surrounded by barbed wire, minefields, electrified fences, yet with no real centre. The *Führer* seemed to relish its grim, spartan existence. From his lonely hut in the brooding East Prussian forest, the ruler of millions had but to whisper, and vast armies would move in response to his whims; another whisper might send ten thousand human beings to their deaths. Time seemed to stand still in Wolfsschanze; the winters were long, the springs a too brief interlude and the summers a test of endurance. The cycle of life was boringly repetitive. Only the marks on the maps indicating the progress of the war gave any suggestion that the passage of time effected any changes.

And it was to Wolfsschanze that the *Britisches Freikorps* came.

Under the curious stares of the élite SS guards, the men of the Free Corps disembarked onto the wooden platform at the gates of the main complex. Gottschalk, his face flushed and nervous, darted hither and thither, ensuring they did not disgrace themselves as they lined up to be inspected by a dour-faced *Obersturmbannführer* who scarcely acknowledged Gottschalk's presence. After they had been lined up, counted and inspected, the *Obersturmbannführer* stood back and raised his voice.

'My name is *Obersturmbannführer* Streve. I am the commandant of Wolfsschanze.'

He paused and surveyed them critically.

'You men are to be under my command for the next five days.

Today and tomorrow you will be instructed in your duties. On Tuesday there will be a complete rehearsal of the duties you will be expected to perform on Thursday, the birthday of the *Führer*. I expect loyalty, obedience and diligence. If any man fails in his duty he may expect to suffer the supreme penalty. Among the *Führer's* bodyguard, no breach of military etiquette nor discipline is tolerated. You have been chosen to serve as the birthday honour guard of Adolf Hitler. I hope you appreciate that honour.'

With a casual salute to Gottschalk, the officer turned and said a few words to an SS major who saluted punctiliously and moved across to Gottschalk.

'March your men after me, *Hauptsturmführer*,' he said. 'I will show you to your quarters.'

He led them across the railway line to the complex of long wooden barrack huts and ancillary buildings. The barrack was like any other – a miserable cold dormitory which, the SS major told them, they were to keep spotlessly clean and in good order. They were to take their meals in the barrack room, and were not to fraternise with any other personnel.

The men were dismissed, mumbling and groaning. Collins laid claim to a bed near the door under a window which gave a bleak view of the snow-shrouded forests nearby. They had barely unpacked their kit when Gottschalk came in followed by a number of orderlies with trollies bearing panikins and large metal tureens of steaming soup.

'After the midday meal,' Gottschalk said, 'you are to be conducted to the main complex which you will be guarding on the *Führer's* birthday.'

Obersturmbannführer Streve was certainly taking no chances.

After the meal, they were lined up and counted under the watchful eye of the SS major and an armed guard who then conducted them back to the station and through three closely guarded checkpoints which were the only entrances through the great tangles of electrified barbed wire. Within the inner complex Collins noticed an even smaller compound in which only a few buildings stood. It did not take him long to discover this was the *Führer's Lagebaracke,* his inner sanctum. The SS major conducted the men round the complex explaining the positions which they were to take up during the rehearsal. It fell to Collins and the eight men of his squad to guard the garage and cinema buildings situated almost opposite the entrance to the *Lagebaracke*.

Collins's mind was working rapidly as they marched back through the checkpoints. They had not been searched so far. He thanked God for that, for he still had the plastic explosive in his ammunition pouches. If an attempt was going to be made to plant the explosive, then it had to be done within the inner compound. The garage was the obvious place to hide it. Using an old watch and some wire, he had been able to construct a crude but effective timing device. But the explosive and timing device needed a detonator and that was going to be the problem.

After they were marched back to their barracks, Gottschalk told them that a practice would be held the following morning.

'What are we supposed to guard the *Führer* with?' grumbled one man. 'Our bare hands? Doesn't anyone trust us?'

Gottschalk regarded him seriously. It was certainly true that the men of the British Free Corps were not to be trusted with loaded weapons near the *Führer*. However, the *Reichsführer* had ordered complete authenticity for the scrutiny of the press, especially for the photographs which Goebbels wanted to send to the newspapers of the world.

'On the morning of the rehearsal, all NCOs will be issued with side-arms, while you men will be issued with machine pistols.'

'But we've never handled German machine pistols,' complained one man.

Gottschalk smiled. 'It is of no consequence. They will not be loaded.'

'Begging the *Herr Hauptsturmführer's* pardon,' it was Cooper who spoke somewhat morosely, 'even though the weapons are not loaded, it might be wise to allow the men some familiaris-ation with them. Weapons drill would make the men carry them correctly and smartly. It would be terrible if the *Führer* saw that his guards did not know how to handle their weapons probably.'

Gottschalk looked thoughtful. 'A good point, Cooper. I will look into the matter.'

They spent the rest of the afternoon and evening playing cards. Collins mostly lay on his bed smoking, trying to think out a scheme, but no ideas would come. Finally, he got up and made his way to the washrooms, which were situated in a separate hut across a strip of snow- and slush-covered trackway.

There were a few men in the washroom as he entered. He nodded a greeting as they stared wonderingly at him. The Germans could not, apparently, get used to the idea of the *Britisches Freikorps*. Collins went to the urinal.

From the corner of his eye he noticed a stocky *Hauptscharführer* standing at the washbasins, taking off his jacket. His side-arms, holster and webbing already hung on a hook. The jacket was placed over them. The warrant officer scowled at his face in the mirror and then turned into a toilet and slammed the door.

Collins gasped as the idea seized him. He glanced around quickly. The others seemed to have left. He reached for the warrant officer's jacket, felt for the holster underneath and unhooked it. A Walther PPK nestled there. He drew it out and slipped out the ammunition clip.

There came the sound of a chain being pulled.

Damn it! The bullets were stiff. The warrant officer did not look after his weapon very well. Collins managed to dig out two bullets from the clip before he heard the sound of a bolt being drawn back. He shoved the clip back in place, replaced the pistol in the holster and turned away, pretending to wash his hands.

The warrant officer came out, glanced at him and turned to the washbasin.

Collins sauntered out, the two bullets in his pocket. His mind began to work furiously as to how he could construct a makeshift detonator from the bullets.

Luck rather than ingenuity solved the problem.

The next morning Gottschalk and the SS major lined them up for inspection. The SS major spoke: 'I understand that you men have not handled the German MP40 machine pistol? It is essential that you should be familiar with these weapons so that you do not disgrace yourself before the *Führer*. We will have a weapons drill now.'

He turned to Gottschalk. 'I want six men to accompany me to the armoury to collect the machine pistols.'

Gottschalk nodded nervously. 'McLardy! Collins! Take four men and accompany this officer.'

They moved forward, gesturing to two men from each of their squads, and marched silently after the dour-faced SS major. There was a well-guarded concrete bunker away from the barrack complex. The SS major showed his pass and they were allowed into a well-stocked arsenal of weapons: rifles, machine-guns, mines, grenades, explosives . . . all manner of weaponry. Collins glanced around, suddenly excited. If only . . .

'Right!' snapped the SS officer to Collins. 'Tell your men to take these boxes here.' He gestured to three oblong boxes without lids. Inside were lines of machine pistols, new and freshly oiled.

Collins repeated the order. His wandering eyes had almost given up hope when he saw a stack of detonators on a nearby table.

'Come on,' McLardy was muttering. The others had already shifted their boxes and McLardy was waiting with impatience for Collins to help him lift the third.

Collins nodded, turned and pretended to trip. He fell headlong towards the table on which the detonators lay, hands outstretched as if to save himself. Several items fell under him.

'My God!' The SS major's eyes popped wide open. 'You clumsy English oaf! Don't you realise those are explosives? Pick them up and be careful.'

Collins scrambled up muttering apologies. He rose awkwardly – his awkwardness was a disguise as he palmed a detonator into his pocket. He spent a few more moments picking up the other items he had knocked flying, and then, with an apologetic shrug at McLardy, he helped lift the last box of machine pistols out of the bunker. The SS officer came behind them, still white-faced and nervous.

Collins felt elated. It was so simple.

The men of the Free Corps were given two hours' drill with the MP40s. They were allowed to strip and re-assemble them, drill with them and, in fact, do everything but put ammunition into them and fire them. The machine pistols were returned to the arsenal while the men had lunch.

That afternoon they were marched back within the inner perimeter of Wolfsschanze. This time, under Gottschalk's command, they were marched smartly to their positions in squads and each NCO became responsible for positioning his men.

'May I walk around the cinema and garage, *Herr Hauptsturmführer*, to familiarise myself with them?' Collins innocently asked Gottschalk.

The nervous little captain nodded. 'I can see that you are a professional, Collins,' he said approvingly. 'While you are doing that, I want to check McLardy's positions.'

As Gottschalk marched away, Collins turned to his men. 'I want us to do this job well,' he growled. 'I don't want any problems. I am going to check that the vantage points of this picquet are covered.'

Indifferently, they watched him go.

He walked round the cinema building, pretending to examine it carefully. It was the garage that drew him, however. Its doors stood partially open. Inside was room for several cars and a couple of black military staff cars were already parked there. At the back of the garage was a work-bench, against which a motorcycle was resting.

Collins walked to the bench. He moved quickly. He took out the explosive from his ammunition pouches, the crude timing-device and the detonator, then with a swift glance around him, he assembled them before taking an oily rag from the bench and wrapping them in it. He suddenly paused, reached in his pocket and placed the two surplus bullets in the bundle. They might come in useful. Underneath the bench was a pile of rubble. Crouching down, he cleared an area, placed the oily rag and its contents inside, and replaced the rubble.

He stood up and heaved a sigh.

'What are you doing here?'

Collins swung round startled. A German sentry stood in the doorway, his machine pistol at the ready. Collins sought to compose his features into a smile. 'I shall be commanding the guard in this section tomorrow,' he replied, trying to sound casual. 'I just wanted to inspect what I am guarding.'

'This is the garage for officers' vehicles,' replied the sentry, still suspiciously.

'So I see,' Collins said disarmingly. He turned and brushed past the sentry.

The man followed him hesitantly. 'Perhaps I should check . . . ?' began the man, a little abashed at dealing with an Englishman in the *Führer's* headquarters.

Gottschalk chose that moment to come round the corner of the building. 'Where have you been, Collins?' he demanded.

'With your permission, *Herr Hauptsturmführer,* I was checking out the area to which you assigned me.'

Gottschalk frowned and dismissed the German sentry.

'You really must be careful, Collins. Do not wander about too freely. Remember that this is the *Führer's* headquarters.'

'And we are supposed to be his guards,' Collins replied gravely.

Gottschalk shrugged. 'For display purposes only, Collins. You are an intelligent man. You must realise that this is all something of a . . . of a pantomime?'

Collins suddenly felt sorrow for the nervous little man. 'I will bear in mind what you say, *Herr Hauptsturmführer,*' he said solemnly.

That evening *Obersturmbannführer* Streve, the SS major and Gottschalk entered the barrack room and called the men to attention.

'I have to inform you that tomorrow, Tuesday, will be a big day,' began Streve without preamble. 'At precisely eleven-thirty, the *Führer* will be arriving here. So, at eleven o'clock you will be marched to your guard positions. The *Führer* is to stay at Wolfsschanze until twelve o'clock midday when he is due to go into Rastenburg to inspect our local defence forces. He will return in the afternoon and it may be that he will want to walk around and talk with you individually.'

He paused to allow them to appreciate this honour which the *Führer* might bestow on them.

'At the end of the day the *Führer* will undoubtedly inspect you. For this, you will be paraded outside the *Lagebaracke.* The band of the *Leibstandarte* Regiment will play the "Song of the Saar" while the *Führer* makes his inspection. You will then be

227

marched past the *Führer* to your barracks while the band plays the *Führer's* favourite march – the *"Badenweilermarsch"*.' Streve smiled confidently.

'Tomorrow was to be simply a rehearsal, but the *Führer* likes to be unpredictable as to his plans. So we shall call it our dress rehearsal. If it goes well, on Thursday, our *Führer's* birthday, you will be paraded under the *Führer's* eye once more. It will be a singular honour. You will go down in history as the only foreign troops to be allowed the greatest honour we can bestow – to be birthday honour guard to the *Führer* of the Third Reich.'

The commandant of Wolfsschanze saluted the dumpy Gottschalk and left with the SS major. Gottschalk gazed at them hesitantly.

'I have no need to tell you that, as your commanding officer, I am expecting you to fulfil this task with honour. The British Free Corps may be a small unit at this time, but soon, I am sure, your example will be the cause of many more of your countrymen volunteering to serve the cause.' He hesitated. 'Rest well, men. Tomorrow will be a day of great excitement.'

Gottschalk was right but not for the reasons he envisaged, thought Collins with grim satisfaction.

Chapter Thirty

It was known only to a few of his intimate circle that the *Führer* disliked flying. It was too much a reminder of his vulnerability and he hated to dwell on the concept of mortality. Nevertheless, his schedule had precluded his taking the special train to Rastenburg. At the very moment that the *Führer's* aircraft was flying over Berlin's southern suburbs, his personal train was steaming quietly out of the city's Silesia station for the journey to the quiet ice forests of East Prussia. The rumbling snake of the blue sleeping cars still bore the faded yellow lettering of *La Compagnie Internationale des Wagons-Lits et des Grandes*

Expresses Européens which was now simply designated *Der Führerzug I*.

The *Führer* was not in his best mood. It was not simply his dislike of flying, but the continuingly depressing news from the Eastern Front. Yesterday the Soviets had captured Yalta. Soviet General Fedor Tolbukhin's troops had bottled up the German 17th Army in the Crimea during the winter offensive. The main attacks on the German positions in the Crimea had commenced on 8 April. Now, Yalta having fallen, the remnants of the 17th Army had dropped back to Sevastopol, the chief city of the Crimea, where they were holding out with no hope of supplies or reinforcements. The *Führer* had just finished dictating his orders for the commander of the 17th Army to his personal adjutant *Sturmbannführer* Otto Günsche, who sat nervously beside his leader.

'Surrender is forbidden. The 17th Army will hold their positions to the last man and the last round of ammunition, and by their heroic endurance will make an unforgettable contribution towards the establishment of a defensive front and the salvation of the Western world.'

Otto Günsche was too nervous to point out that this was the same message which the *Führer* had sent to *Generalfeldmarschall* Friedrich von Paulus and the 6th Army at Stalingrad before their surrender on 3 February, 1943. Privately, Günsche wondered how long it would be before the remnants of the 17th Army decided to follow the example of von Paulus. Instead of articulating his thoughts, he cleared his throat and glanced at a piece of paper which the navigator of the aircraft had just handed him.

'My *Führer*,' he said, 'we shall be arriving at Wolfsschanze at eleven hundred hours. The inner perimeter is now guarded by men of the *Britisches Freikorps* in rehearsal for the press visit on Thursday.'

Hitler nodded morosely. 'You have an itinerary for today?'

Günsche glanced at some papers before him. 'On arrival at Wolfsschanze a military briefing has been arranged to appraise you of the latest developments in Italy and in the East. *Generalfeldmarschall* Keitel and *Generaloberst* Jodl have already arrived and will be in attendance. Also *Obergruppenführer*

Köhler has arrived from Warsaw to bring you up to date on developments there.'

'Köhler?' Hitler smiled. Köhler was one of his favourite SS generals.

'Yes, my *Führer*,' replied Günsche. 'Preliminary reports suggest he has been successful in organising a new SS division based on the Dirlewanger Penal Brigade and the Kaminski Brigade, which is recruited from former Russian prisoners-of-war.'

'Good. That is good. I can trust Köhler,' the *Führer* beamed. 'Köhler is one of the few generals who has my implicit faith.'

'After the conference, which is scheduled to end at twelve hundred hours, you are to attend a luncheon in your honour at the Rastenburg *Rathaus* with the *Burgermeister*. After luncheon there is to be an inspection of the local *Volksturm* units. We will return to Wolfsschanze at sixteen hundred hours.'

'And the *Britisches Freikorps*? They are shaping up well? Everything is prepared for Thursday?'

'*Reichsminister* Goebbels and *Reichsführer* Himmler will be in attendance on Thursday and have been in personal charge of all the details,' Günsche assured him.

The aircraft suddenly veered sharply. The *Führer* clutched wildly at the arms of his seat and swore, his face pale and trembling.

Almost at once the navigator came hurrying back. 'Forgive us, my *Führer*,' he sounded anxious, 'but enemy aircraft are reported approaching from the west. We are taking evasive action.'

The *Führer's* trembling was uncontrollable. 'Enemy aircraft?'

'Yes, my *Führer*. A large force of bombers and fighters. It looks as though they are heading for Berlin.'

They were. That morning some 2,000 aircraft of the US 8th Airforce, consisting of Flying Fortresses, accompanied by Mustangs and Lightnings, attacked Berlin in the biggest air raid of the war so far. The dark speck of the *Führer's* aircraft was ignored by the Allied pilots as it disappeared quickly towards the north-east. Even had the pilots realised who was in the aircraft, they had not the height nor speed to do much about it.

Hauptsturmführer Gerhard Gottschalk fussed along the ranks of the fifty members of the British Free Corps as they stood lined up within the main compound of Wolfsschanze. The nervous little captain worried and fretted as he tried to assure himself that the *Führer* would find no fault with the appearance of his men.

Collins stood outwardly wooden, yet within his body the adrenalin coursed, causing his face to flush slightly. Luck had certainly been with him so far. With the impending arrival of the *Führer,* the men had been carefully searched as they had been marched through the three perimeter checkpoints. Collins shuddered wondering what would have happened had the search been carried out the previous day, or if he had waited until today to smuggle the explosive and detonator into the inner compound. After each man of the Free Corps had been passed inside the inner checkpoint, each NCO was issued with a Walther PPK and an empty ammunition clip; each private soldier was issued with a German MP40 machine pistol. Then, after Gottschalk had inspected them, and the SS major had conducted a further inspection, *Obersturmbannführer* Streve arrived for a final inspection. Then they were marched to their positions.

Collins placed his eight-man squad at their posts around the garage and the cinema. The positions gave an excellent view of Hitler's *Lagebaracke* with its solitary gateway positioned almost opposite the cinema hut.

Well, this was it. He had the necessary materials, he was close to the *Führer,* but where and how could he plant the explosive? The *Britisches Freikorps* might be allowed ceremonially to guard the inner compound of Hitler's headquarters, but they were not allowed anywhere near the *Lagebaracke*. There was no way any member of the *Freikorps* would be allowed near the *Führer's* living quarters nor personal conference room. He might just as well be a million miles away.

There was a commotion at the inner checkpoint – harsh shouted commands and the blare of a car horn. Several motorcycle outriders came sweeping through, followed by a large black Mercedes car with an open top.

Collins forced himself to stiffen to attention as the cavalcade turned left into the inner compound and drove up to the

Lagebaracke gate opposite his position. He had a faint feeling of unreality, or of watching some newsreel. Sunk deep in the back seat of the car he caught a glimpse of a greying face, a face almost hidden in a military cap and uniform but distinguished by its well-known moustache. There were several other high-ranking people in the car. Collins watched with curiosity as the *Führer* of the German Reich climbed out and led his entourage through the *Lagebaracke* gate and across the compound to his conference hut.

Collins found himself thinking how small the man was, how insignificant he would be in civilian clothes.

After a moment, the motorcycle outriders sped off while the *Führer's* car began to back down the road and then turned into the garage. Collins watched the driver skilfully manoeuvre the great black machine into the building. Then the man came out, paused and casually lit a cigarette.

The idea occurred to Collins immediately. A broad smile crossed his face. Surely it was not going to be so ridiculously simple? But then the best plans were always simple.

He turned and sauntered down the pathway towards the driver, who still stood beside the garage door. The man watched him coming curiously.

'That's a fantastic machine,' Collins smiled.

'The best,' agreed the chauffeur. 'You're one of the British, aren't you?'

'*Britisches Freikorps*,' nodded Collins.

The German shook his head wonderingly. 'Are there many like you?'

'Oh, a considerable number,' Collins assured him. 'In fact, the majority of the British people really think as I do.'

The man whistled softly. 'Then there is a chance we may yet make peace with England?'

'Would you mind if I looked at your Mercedes?'

The chauffeur glanced nervously about. 'I suppose so. After all, you are supposed to be guarding it.'

Collins grinned. 'That's right.'

'Well, I don't have to report for half an hour yet. We are leaving for Rastenburg at noon. I'm off to get a coffee.'

Collins pretended to be interested in the vehicle. 'I bet it wouldn't take long to get to Rastenburg in this.'

'In these weather conditions . . . .' the driver shrugged. 'About twenty minutes at the most.' The man dropped his cigarette and crushed it with his heel into the snow. He turned and left.

Collins's mind was now in top gear. It *was* going to be simple. The perfect answer – the *Führer*'s car which had been driven into the very place where the explosive was hidden. But he had less than half an hour to plant his explosive, ensure that he had timed the detonator properly, and then try to get himself out of the compound just in case the chauffeur survived the blast and remembered his interest in the vehicle.

He glanced at his watch. Damn! It was time he made his first check of his men's positions. Gottschalk, the SS major or Streve himself might be watching. He left the garage reluctantly.

General Artur Nebe, head of the *Kriminalpolizei*, sat back with a satisfied smile and gazed at Manfred Reinecke.

'You have done an excellant job, Manfred,' he said softly, glancing back to the papers which the assistant *Komissar* of the Gestapo had placed before him. 'These lists are extremely important. Do you know where *Standartenführer* Behrens is now?'

Reinecke pursed his lips.

'I believe he left Berlin yesterday. He has gone off on some wild-goose chase to Rastenburg.'

'I see,' Nebe looked thoughtful. 'Well, I shall see to it that he is taken care of. He is a clever man and, as such, a great threat.'

Reinecke said nothing.

'I hope this assignment was not too unpleasant a task, Manfred. It is not often that we need to have a surveillance on such prominent officers of the *Geheime Staat Polizei*. And Behrens was a friend and colleague.'

'And my superior,' added Reinecke. Then he smiled, remembering the shapely body of Inge Behrens. 'But no, no it was not too unpleasant, *Herr General*.'

'That is good. Now . . . where do you go next?'

'To Konigsberg, Herr General. I have to pick up some papers at Gestapo headquarters there.'

The general rose to his feet and held out his hand. 'Good luck, Manfred. Germany needs men like you.'

Manfred Reinecke smiled thinly as he shook the general's hand.

'Thank you, *Herr General*. What I do, I do for my country.'

Collins was making his way back to the garage when the dumpy little Gottschalk stopped him.

'Is everything in order, Collins?'

In spite of its being a crisp spring morning, Gottschalk's face was red and perspiring.

'Everything is in order, *Herr Hauptsturmführer,*' replied Collins gravely.

'Good. Did you see him?'

'The *Führer*? Yes.'

Gottschalk's voice was tremulous; it held a note of awe as if he had seen a vision of some deity. 'Isn't it wonderful? To be so near to the *Führer,* to actually be in command of his body-guard?' The little man was positively drooling. 'I'm told that he will probably wish to speak to me.'

'I'm sure he will,' replied Collins. He was trying hard to control his impatience.

For a few moments, Gottschalk's face was a picture of ecstasy, as if he were imagining the scene. Then the little man drew himself together. 'I shall make another inspection within the hour. Make sure all continues to be well, Collins. It would be terrible if one of your men were found wanting.' He strode off through the snow to the next guard post.

Collins waited until he was out of sight and then looked at his watch. Damnation! It was already eleven-forty. If Hitler kept to his noon-day schedule then he had little time. He hurried to the garage and felt relief when he found it still deserted. Thank God he did not have to prepare the timing device beforehand. He went straight to the workbench and dug out the bundle in the oily rag. Everything was still there.

Working swiftly, he fixed the detonator into the hexite, and then positioned the small wrist watch, removing the glass from its face so that the hands were free. He paused and glanced at his own watch. It was 11.47. If Hitler left at noon and the

234

journey to Rastenburg took twenty minutes, he did not have much time to play with. What if Hitler were late? It would be awkward if the explosion took place within Wolfsschanze. It would be impossible to escape. The latest time for which he could safely set the timer would be 12.15 p.m. If he set it after that time, then the ridiculous situation might arise whereby Hitler's car having arrived safely in Rastenburg, could blow up after he had left it. Biting his lips, he adjusted the hands of the watch and started it, fixing the timer to the detonator.

It was 11.52 a.m.

Wiping the sweat from his brow, Collins grabbed some tape from the work-bench and some old sacking which he threw onto the garage floor. He lay on his back on the sacking and eased himself partially under the black bulk of the Mercedes and, using the tape liberally, he bound the charge into place, siting it so that it was just under the floor of the passenger compartment.

As he struggled out, dusting his uniform, he heard a crunching footfall outside. He ducked and moved swiftly across the garage, throwing himself almost headlong behind a Horsche saloon which bore *Generalfeldmarschall* Keitel's flag and insignia.

Lying there he heard the footsteps enter the garage, heard the slamming of a car door and an engine start up. Peering around the side of the Horsche, he saw the sleek black body of the Mercedes glide out of the garage.

He stood up with a deep sigh. It was now 11.55 a.m. His mind was still ticking away at a furious rate. If the *Führer* were late coming out of the conference, if the Mercedes did not clear Wolfsschanze by the time the explosive went off, if . . . He tried to still his thoughts, forcing his mind to think about something else.

The oily rag still lay on the work bench. It was then he saw the two bullets still nestling in it. Well, they had not been needed, since he had managed to find a detonator. It occurred to him that they were Walther PPK bullets and that he had a Walther PPK with an empty ammunition clip in his holster. He took out his pistol, undid the clip and inserted the two bullets into it. He replaced the pistol with a wry smile. It gave him some small comfort to know that he was not completely unarmed.

He stood at the work-bench wondering what his next move should be. A wild idea of trying to crash through the checkpoints in the Horsche saloon car came to him, but he dismissed it. Then his eyes fell on the motorcycle still propped against the work-bench. Frowning, he gave it a quick inspection. It seemed all right. It had a fairly full tank of gasoline. He would have liked to try the starter, but that was impossible. Instead, he quietly wheeled the machine out of the garage and propped it up against the garage wall.

An idea was beginning to take shape in his mind. Someone had mentioned that the *Führer's* personal physician, Doctor Theodor Morell, who had permanent living quarters at Wolfss-chanze, was arriving from Berlin sometime during the day. If the explosion did occur before the Mercedes left the complex, then he must try to leave immediately, pretending to the guards that he was being sent to the airfield to collect Doctor Morell. In the confusion, it might just work.

He glanced at his watch. A chill began to grip him. It was already 12.04 p.m., and there was no sign of the *Führer* leaving the conference hut.

Chapter Thirty-One

In the conference hut of the *Lagebaracke,* the *Führer* was poised over a map of Italy.

'I want the Gustav-Cassino line fortified,' he said tapping at the area just south of Rome. 'Mackensen's 14th Army are to attack the Allies' bridgehead at Anzio. I want them driven back into the sea in preparation for our re-taking Italy for *Il Duce*.'

Generaloberst Jodl, chief of the Operations Branch OKW, exchanged a sharp glance with *Generalfeldmarschall* Keitel, chief of the High Command.

The *Generalfeldmarschall* cleared his throat. 'My *Führer* . . .General Mackensen has already lost three-quarters of his men in the February attacks on the Anzio bridgehead.'

There was a tension in the room as they waited for Hitler to react to this questioning of his authority. Instead, the *Führer* smiled benignly. 'The answer is simple, Kesselring must reinforce him.'

Keitel hesitated, but saw Jodl making warning gestures with his eyes. The *Generalfeldmarschall* sighed. 'I will send the order, my *Führer*.'

Hitler pounded on the map with his fist.

'We can roll the Allies back into Sicily, send them reeling in Italy, and then return our troops to the Westwall in Europe before the main landings begin.'

Sturmbannführer Otto Günsche coughed politely. 'My *Führer*, you have not forgotten your luncheon with the *Burgermeister* of Rastenburg?'

Hitler's smile was genial. 'No, but I was hoping everyone else had.'

There was a polite murmur of amusement.

'The man can be incredibly boring company and the *Volkstrum* can wait until another day to meet their *Führer*.' Hitler paused and gestured vaguely at the map before him. 'And I . . . I must have more time to discuss our strategy in Italy with *Generalfeldmarschall* Keitel. I cannot spare the time.'

'Shall I telephone Rastenburg, my *Führer*?' asked Günsche.

The *Führer* paused, nibbling at his nails in contemplation. 'No, no. *Obergruppenführer* Köhler will deputise for me.'

A tall man dressed in the black uniform of an SS general clicked his heels and saluted.

Gottfried Köhler was a former bricklayer who had been an early adherent of the Party, firstly as a member of the *Sturmabteilung* or SA before transferring to the SS when membership of the SA became unfashionable. It was said the Köhler earnt favour with Hitler by betraying the leader of the SA, Ernst Roehm, during the so-called 'Night of the Long Knives'. Roehm, Hitler's early companion and friend, had been incarcerated in Stadelheim prison. Since the *Führer* did not wish to bear entire responsibility for his friend's death, he had instructed the commander of the SS unit to hand him a loaded pistol so that he could kill himself. The commander, it was said, was Köhler. Roehm had rejected the pistol, saying: 'If Adolf wants to kill me, let him do the dirty work.' Stripped bare to the waist, Roehm had stood in the centre of his cell, mocking Köhler and the SS executioners who then fired through the bars of the cell door, riddling him with bullets. After that, Köhler had been made an *Oberführer* and by 1944, after service in Poland and Russia, he had risen to the rank of SS general.

'At your command, my *Führer*,' said Köhler, coming forward.

Hitler reached forward to pat his favourite general on the arm. '*Herr Obergruppenführer*, you must now sacrifice yourself for your *Führer*,' he chuckled. 'You must suffer the tortures of having luncheon with the *Burgermeister* in my stead.'

The *Führer* looked round while the assembled men laughed a little uneasily at his joke.

'You will also make an appraisal of the local *Volksturm* units and report.'

'The *Führer* commands, I obey,' replied Köhler dutifully.

'*Herr Obergruppenführer*...'

Köhler turned back towards the *Führer*.

'You may use my car since it is waiting outside for me.'

Köhler saluted and left.

Collins was waiting nervously by the garage door. Hitler was late. It was near enough 12.15 p.m. The car certainly would not have time to clear the compound before the charge went off. He felt an overwhelming frustration, and a great sense of failure. He glanced once more at his watch. Sweating in apprehension of the explosion, he turned towards the motorcycle. His escape from the impregnable Wolfsschanze depended so much on the confusion of the guards. So much . . .

His heart quickened. The door of the conference hut had opened. Now! *Now!* A tall SS general came walking down the steps and across the compound followed by an SS captain.

Where was Hitler? Where?

The SS officers walked to the Mercedes and spoke to the

driver. Any time now! Collins glanced at his watch again. It was already past 12.15 p.m. The SS officers were climbing into the car, the driver was getting in and starting the engine.

Collins knew in that moment that he had failed. He knew that Hitler had made a typically abrupt change of plan. His one and only chance at assassination had failed.

A moment later, the Mercedes exploded with an ear-splitting roar, spewing flame and debris in all directions.

The windows of the conference hut shattered with the blast.

Sturmbannführer Günsche threw himself across the body of his *Führer* as the explosion rocked the room. Several generals were cut by the flying splinters. Jodl received a graze across his cheek, while Keitel was knocked to the floor. Pandemonium broke out. People started shouting all at once.

Collins, astride the motorcycle, kicked at the starter. It did not work. He kicked again in panic and felt a sudden elation as the motor roared into life. He manoeuvred swiftly from the garage, around the cinema and passed Jodl's living quarters to the perimeter road. Out of the corner of his eye he saw soldiers running in all directions. He swung across the twin railway tracks and roared towards the first checkpoint gate.

The guards at the checkpoint were looking towards the *Lagebaracke* from which smoke was rising from the shattered Mercedes. There was only one German NCO in command, with four members of the *Britisches Freikorps*. The German NCO was holding an MP40 as were his companions, but Collins knew there was a difference – the German's MP40 was loaded. He skidded his bike to a halt.

'The *Führer* has been badly hurt,' he gasped in German to the NCO. 'I have been sent for help.'

The German gazed at him stupidly. 'The *Führer* is hurt?' he echoed.

Collins repeated it to the bewildered men of the Free Corps, this time in English and then reverted to German.

'Yes, yes. Doctor Morell, the *Führer's* personal physician, is landing at the airfield. I have been sent to bring him swiftly. There is little time.'

The NCO stood undecided for a second, then lifted the barrier and waved him through.

Collins accelerated away with a fierce exhilaration. He wanted to shout and laugh. The first gate! So easy!

But the first gate was the easiest because there was only one SS man with his motley flock of British Free Corps men.

The second checkpoint was just a few yards away. This time there was a full complement of SS *Leibstandarte* Adolf Hitler Regiment guards. All carried loaded weapons, fingers white against the trigger guards, eyes flickering nervously towards the rising column of black smoke. Again Collins brought his bike to a halt.

'Quickly!' he yelled at the guard commander who came forward. 'The *Führer* has been injured. Badly injured! I have been sent to the airfield to get *Herr* Doctor Morell, the *Führer*'s personal physician.'

The NCO looked suspiciously at Collins. 'Where is your pass?' he demanded.

'*Dummkopf!*' Collins forced himself to yell. 'With the *Führer* lying bleeding to death, who is going to spend time writing passes? It is a matter of life and death. If the *Führer* dies because you have held me up, it may well be your death for not allowing me through.'

The man hesitated, then he shrugged. After all, the first gate had passed this man. He waved the second barrier up.

Oh, my God! Collins found himself almost crying. But the third checkpoint was still to come. Just one more barrier and then the long road through the forest to Rastenburg and then to Korschen – Korschen and Lottie, Lottie and Korschen.

Inside the conference hut Hitler was being helped to his feet by his adjutant, Günsche. The *Führer* was white-faced and trembling.

'What is it?' he whispered.

General Schmundt, Chief Adjutant to the *Führer* and Chief of the *Wehrmacht* Personnel Branch, came running into the room.

'A bomb!' he gasped. 'An assassination plot, my *Führer*.

Your car has been blown to pieces. Köhler, his adjutant and your driver . . . all dead.'

Hitler gazed at Schmundt blankly. 'A bomb?'

'A bomb, my *Führer*.'

'But who would dare? Who would dare?' His voice rose on a dangerously hysterical note.

Obersturmbannführer Streve came hurrying into the room. 'My *Führer*...what are your orders?'

The *Führer* was still shaking.

'Close off all the perimeter gates. No one is to leave nor enter. Shut down all communications until further notice. Is *Reichsführer* Himmler still in Berlin?'

Streve shook his head. 'No, my *Führer*. He is at his headquarters on Lake Maur, ready to come here tomorrow in preparation for your birthday.'

'Good. He can be here in half an hour then. Tell him I want him to take personal charge. I want the people responsible. They are to be executed before the day is over.'

Streve threw up his arm in a salute and hurried out.

The *Führer* was more composed now. He drew himself up. 'Gentlemen,' he said quietly, 'No one must know of this incident. I owe it to the German people to withhold this terrible news from them.'

He paused and looked round at the debris which littered the conference room.

'You have just witnessed the intervention of Providence. When I reflect on this, it becomes obvious to me that I am under the protection of Providence, which shields me against the time when my great task shall be accomplished. Undoubtedly it is my fate to continue what I have begun and bring my task to completion. This is not the first time that I have escaped death miraculously. I am more than ever convinced that the great cause I serve will survive present perils and that everything will be brought to a satisfactory conclusion.'

He smiled at the mixture of expressions on their faces.

'Himmler shall find out who is at the bottom of the outrage and when he does, that person's fate shall serve as a warning to others.'

Collins came to a halt before the third checkpoint. Beyond the barrier, the road curved alongside the railway track in the direction of the airfield and Rastenburg itself.

A warrant officer with a wooden expression came up. 'Pass?' he demanded.

Collins waved a hand at the column of smoke. 'Don't be ridiculous!' he snapped. 'Don't you know what's happened? There has been an attempt on the life of the *Führer*. He has been badly injured. I've been sent to the airfield to get Doctor Morell.'

The man's eyes flickered from Collins to the smoke and then back to Collins. 'I can't allow you through without orders. Wait here.' He turned and strode towards the guardroom.

Damn! Collins glanced at the other guards. There were four of them. They held their machine pistols casually but professionally. The road beyond the barrier looked so inviting. If only . . . no, he hadn't a dog's chance with the barrier stretched across the road.

A large silver Wanderer saloon car came gliding around the corner, through the forest and halted on the opposite side of the barrier to Collins. The vehicle carried a swastika pennant, a silver swastika emblem on the bonnet, and on the other wing of the car there was a checkerboard black-and-red metal flag denoting a *Heeresgruppe* commander.

The warrant officer of the guards had almost reached the entrance to the guard room, was, in fact, already reaching for the telephone by the door, when he suddenly noticed the staff car. He hesitated. The driver of the car sounded his horn. The warrant officer turned and went forward, skirting the barrier pole which, to Collins's frustration, remained in place. The warrant officer examined the passes proffered by the driver, handed them back and stepped away, raising his hand in the Nazi salute. The barrier rose.

Several things happened then. The telephone in the guard room started to shrill. The saloon car glided through the open checkpoint and Collins had a momentary glimpse of a high-ranking officer in an old sheepskin coat and scarf, with his rank badges on his lapels. Next to him was seated a civilian. For a moment the eyes of the civilian met those of Collins. It was *Standartenführer* Rudi Behrens.

Then Collins was gunning his accelerator and tore off along the side of the car and through the still-open barrier, leaving the guards in momentary disorder.

Behind him he heard their cries fade on the wind. Then came a fusillade of shots. They passed dangerously near. One clipped the back of the machine with a clang of metal striking on metal. Collins slewed the motorcycle across the road, managing, miraculously, to retain his balance. Then he was round the corner and streaking down the road towards Rastenburg.

Behind him the SS warrant officer had replaced the telephone with a white face. He screamed for the barrier to be lowered just as Behrens was ordering the car to be turned around.

The warrant officer waved his machine pistol at the Gestapo man. 'Hold it!' he snapped. 'I have personal orders from the *Führer* that no one is allowed in or out. Stay where you are. One mistake is enough for me today.'

'You bloody idiot!' shouted Behrens. 'That man was an Englishman! A spy!'

'In that case, he won't get far. The forests are full of troops. Now you get back into your car and shut up until I get further orders.'

Furious with rage, Behrens spent a few moments describing what he thought of the warrant officer's parentage.

Alarms were ringing all over Wolfsschanze.

In the conference room the *Führer* was issuing a stream of orders – cancelling the birthday press conference; sending yet another message to Himmler's headquarters on Lake Maur, twenty miles away, to ensure that the *Reichsführer* was on his way to Wolfsschanze; and demanding that Streve start making arrests.

Acting on his own authority, Streve had already ordered that the members of the *Britisches Freikorps* be confined to barracks under close guard. He watched them file in with the rotund little *Hauptsturmführer* Gottschalk at their head, wringing his hands in a most unmilitary manner.

At the entrance to the *Lagebaracke,* a group of SS men were beginning to clear up the mangled, twisted wreckage and its grisly contents.

Only when Streve reported that the wreckage had been cleared did the *Führer* venture outside the conference hut.

'Remember,' he admonished Günsche, as they walked across the *Lagebaracke* to his living quarters, where his bitch, Blondi, sat whining for his master, 'remember that no word of this affair is to go beyond Wolfsschanze.'

'It shall be done, my *Führer*. It shall be as if it never happened.'

Hitler paused on the step of his living quarters and glanced towards the gates of the *Lagebaracke* where the explosion had blown a gaping hole in the perimeter fence.

'Send Köhler's family one of my signed photographs. Tell them that he gave his life in the service of the Fatherland and that I hold his memory in great esteem.'

He turned and smiled down at his bitch, reached forward and patted its head. 'No, Blondi. No. We won't go for a walk just yet.'

Günsche saluted as the *Führer* went inside and slammed the door.

Chapter Thirty-Two

Head down, crouched low over the handlebars of the motorcycle, Collins accelerated down the road towards Rastenburg, sheets of mud and slush spraying behind his spinning wheels. He was thinking logically and cooly now. The chase would be in progress and the Germans would surely have telephoned to Rastenburg to stop him. He had to get off this road soon. For a while he tore along by the riverside, alongside the icy torrents of the Guber. Suddenly he came to a crossroads. He skidded his bike to a halt and peered up at a decaying wooden signpost. One arm pointed to Rastenburg, another arm stretched south to Rhein, while another pointed across a small bridge and announced Barten lay in that direction.

'Barten it is!' breathed Collins, pushing forward.

The road to Barten was a mere dirt track, which suited Collins's purpose. Snow and ice still lay thick on the ground, indicating that it had not been used much recently. The signpost had indicated that Barten lay twenty kilometres away. Collins hoped the fuel in the motorcycle would last that long.

But once he reached Barten, what then? He still had to make his way to Korschen, which was, perhaps, another twenty kilometres away. He certainly could not go there until he was sure that he had lost his pursuers. No, the detour through Barten was best. He would have to pick up a change of clothes and some other means of transport soon. His fancy *Britisches Freikorps* uniform would be a dead giveaway. He would have to ditch it.

Obersturmbannführer Streve stood up as Rudi Behrens stormed into his office. Streve was well aware that the Gestapo man held the rank of a full colonel in the SS while he was merely a lieutenant-colonel.

'I am glad that you are here,' Streve began.

'We would have caught the swine had not your guard commander been a congenital idiot!' snapped Behrens, interrupting him.

'He is being disciplined,' soothed Streve.

'Have the members of the *Britisches Freikorps* been arrested?'

'They have been confined to barracks.'

There was a commotion outside and the door swung abruptly open. *Reichsführer* Heinrich Himmler strode in, slamming the door behind him. Behrens and Streve sprang to attention and saluted. Himmler ignored the formality.

'I am going immediately to see the *Führer*. He will ask me questions. I want to be able to supply him with answers,' he said without preamble.

Behrens relaxed a little. 'The assassin was a man named Charles Collins. He entered Germany through Lisbon pretending to be a British Army deserter and volunteered to join the *Britisches Freikorps*. I escorted the man to Berlin but had my reservations about him. My reservations were given in my report to my superior – *Oberstgruppenführer* Kaltenbrunner.'

Behrens laid an unmistakable emphasis on the last sentence. Himmler frowned. 'Who cleared the man?'

Behrens smiled softly. 'The ultimate responsibility lay with the *Herr Oberstgruppenführer*.'

'Kaltenbrunner?' Himmler's face relaxed into something akin to a smile. If heads were to roll it was preferable that Kaltenbrunner's head should go in preference to his own.

Behrens nodded. 'The SD did run a special clearance on him and it seems his story fitted perfectly. Perhaps a little too perfectly in retrospect, *Herr Reichsführer*.'

Himmler gazed at him for a moment. 'Your opinion is that the British planted this man in the *Britisches Freikorps* with the intention of assassinating the *Führer*?'

'It is.'

'So?' Himmler strode up and down, hands clasped behind his back, as he thought out the implications. 'This makes our famous *Britisches Freikorps* worthless,' he said, halting before Behrens. 'Who knows how many agents have been infiltrated into it? Has Collins been executed yet?'

Behrens hesitated. 'Thanks to one of *Obersturmbannführer* Streve's men, I was prevented from arresting Collins when he was making his escape through the checkpoints.'

Himmler glanced to Streve who nodded uncomfortably. 'The man is being disciplined, *Herr Reichsführer*.'

Behind his rimless spectacles, Himmler's eyes narrowed. 'How could that be? There are three perimeters through which he had to pass. What sort of security is that?'

Unhappily, Streve handed Himmler a report. Himmler glanced through it, showing no emotion.

'Collins must be caught at once,' he said, handing the paper back to Streve.

Behrens smiled thinly. 'I think I can guarantee that, *Herr Reichsführer*. Give me twenty-four hours and I will have him.'

Himmler gazed at Behrens curiously. 'You are confident. What makes you so assured?'

'I believe I can accomplish the task,' he replied evasively.

'Very well, *Herr Standartenführer*. You have the duty and

responsibility for tracking down the assassin and his accomplices, if any. The *Führer* will want an account . . . and soon.'

Behrens nodded. 'You can assure the *Führer* that I shall not be found wanting.'

The petrol gauge was reading dangerously low and Collins was still several kilometres south of Barten when he saw smoke among the tall conifers. He switched off the engine and glided the motorcycle to a halt. Then he wheeled it off the roadway and dumped it behind some bushes.

Through the trees he could see the dark outline of a building. It was a large pine-wood cabin, a sort of grand-scale hunting lodge, he thought. Some part of his mind, separate from the rest, registered how beautiful it was, noted the intricacies of the workmanship, its gables and shutters and delicate fretwork over the windows and doors.

Before the steps which led up to a short verandah, a car was parked. A low-slung, long-bonneted Citröen.

Crouching low, Collins crept nearer. The place seemed deserted.

He rose and moved to the driver's door of the car. Damn it! The door was locked and there were no keys in the ignition. They must be inside the house with the owner – whoever the owner was. Well, he could not have good luck all the time. He hesitated, then turned for the house.

At that moment a small sheep dog raced around the corner of the building and started to bark furiously.

Cursing softly, Collins turned to run.

A harsh voice called: 'Hands up! Stand very still!'

He obeyed.

'Turn slowly!'

A stocky, beet-faced man stood in a long military overcoat. He held a Luger pointing at Collins's chest. The man was bare-footed and Collins could see that he wore nothing underneath his great-coat.

'Who are you? What do you want here?' snapped the man.

Collins decided on a bluff. His eyes swiftly taking in the epaulettes on the man's coat.

'*Herr Obersturmführer*? I have been sent to ask you to report to your unit immediately.'

The man frowned. 'What? I've just arrived on leave from Danzig. What does this mean?'

Collins shrugged. 'Orders are orders, *Herr Obersturmführer*,' he smiled. He lowered his hands slowly. 'Well, I'll be off . . .'

'Halt!' the voice was tight. 'No one knew where I was going. What game are you playing? Who are you? Name and unit? You don't sound a German by your accent and . . .'

Collins dived abruptly behind the Citröen.

The German officer let off a shot in his direction.

As he ducked behind the car, he tugged out his Walther PPK. Two bullets! Two precious bullets only!

He rolled swiftly out from the cover, lying in a prone position and aimed the gun. The German, naked except for the overcoat slung over his shoulders, was still standing on the step, smoke rising slowly in the frosty air from the muzzle of his pistol. He jerked round as Collins suddenly presented himself as a target. Collins aimed and shot once. The man's forehead became a red, bloody mess. Without a groan, the man's knees sagged and he slipped to the boards of the verandah. The little collie let out a puzzled whine and trotted across to the body.

There was a scream inside the wooden lodge building. Collins's jaw dropped as a naked blond youth came running out onto the verandah and flung himself down beside the body.

'Franz! Franz!' wailed the young man.

Collins rose slowly to his feet.

The youth was no more than eighteen, perhaps younger. His pretty, almost feminine face, was contorted with grief. He suddenly turned in a crouching position, his lips drawn back over his gums. A vicious bestial snarl rose from his throat.

'Swine! You've killed Franz! You've killed him!' The voice was cracked with hysteria.

Collins felt a welling sickness. 'Get up, son,' he said softly. 'I won't hurt you.'

There was a maniacal gleam in the youth's eyes. With a speed which astonished Collins, the youth flung himself forward, the momentum of his leap carrying Collins off balance onto his back. The gun flew out of his hand. The youth had animal strength. His hands, claw-like, were gripping Collins's throat. For several seconds Collins and the naked youth thrashed about in the snow and slush, the madness in the youth lending him a desperate strength.

Then Collins managed to disengage himself, punching his opponent in the solar plexus. The boy screamed and bent forward holding his stomach.

Collins scrambled to his feet, searching for the Walther PPK. But the youth had spotted it before him and was reaching out for it. Collins dived towards the body of the naked officer, tore the Luger from the stiffening fingers and spun round.

The youth was pointing the Walther towards Collins, finger tightening on the trigger.

Collins hesitated a split second and then fired.

The youth was slammed back into the snow, blood on his face.

Collins found himself sweating. He sat down a moment on the steps, head down, trying to breath deeply.

The collie sat whining at his feet.

After a while, Collins rose and holstered the Luger. Inside the hunting lodge, a fire was blazing in the open fireplace. There was a smell of coffee. In the corner was an unmade double bed. He had obviously interrupted two lovers. Poor, stupid bastards. He searched the place carefully. There was no telephone and no sign of anyone else.

He helped himself to the hot ersatz coffee steaming on the stove, and ate some bread and sausage he found in a cupboard.

Then he went outside and gathered up the body of the youth, depositing him in the bed. He returned to the verandah and dragged the heavier man inside as well. Then he dropped the Walther PPK near the youth's hand. Anyone who came might think they had committed suicide. Perhaps.

He turned and had another cup of coffee.

As he was doing so, he examined the officer's uniform which had been discarded over a chair. The uniform was unfamilar. It was an SS uniform rather than a *Wehrmacht* one. Unlike the usual black, it was in green and silver. On the peaked cap was a miniature death's-head. The black leather belt and holster and field boots were polished almost to the consistency of glass. He glanced at the dead officer. He was about the same build. It took him a few moments to change. The man's uniform was almost a perfect fit. Inside the pockets were keys, indentification and money. Trouble was, the photograph on the identification card looked nothing like him. Well, for the moment he would have to be *Obersturmführer* Franz Steidler . . . until he reached Korschen anyway.

He left the lodge, carefully shutting the door behind him, walked to the Citröen, climbed in and started it.

The collie, sitting dejectedly whining on the top step of the verandah, watched him leave.

Reichsführer Heinrich Himmler was ushered into the *Führer*'s living quarters in the *Lagebaracke*. The Führer was sprawled in an armchair, his face parchment white, his eyes staring and slightly wild. His hands were gripping the sides of his chair. Himmler noticed the knuckles stood out white. He moved forward and saluted. For a few moments Hitler did not appear to notice him.

'My *Führer*?' prompted Himmler.

Finally, Hitler focused on him. 'I want the swines killed!' he screamed so suddenly that the *Reichsführer* took a step back and winced.

'*Standartenführer* Behrens has promised to arrest the assassin within twenty-four hours, my *Führer*,' he replied reassuringly.

Hitler made an effort to control himself. 'The assassin? He has been identified?'

Himmler nodded. 'He was one of the NCOs in the *Britisches Freikorps*, my *Führer*. A man named Collins. Behrens recognised the man as he fled from the third checkpoint.'

Hitler's mouth slackened. 'One of the *Britisches Freikorps*?' he asked, almost vacantly. 'How could this be? Were they not all thoroughly vetted by the Gestapo, by the SD? This is your responsibility, *Reichsführer*.'

Himmler shifted uncomfortably. 'The man was undoubtedly a British agent, my *Führer*. The British gave him an impeccable cover. It checked out completely under the closest scrutiny we could give it.'

Hitler raised a fist and smashed it on the arm of his chair. 'I want the British Free Corps eliminated! Eliminated!'

Himmler tugged at his lower lip and sighed softly. 'Very well, my *Führer*.'

'I want this swine . . . what did you say his name was? . . . I want him executed as a lesson to any other foreign assassins.'

'It shall be done, my *Führer*,' agreed Himmler.

'Wait!' Hitler frowned. 'Wait . . .' he sank in thought for a moment. 'This is all Goebbels' fault. It was his idea to use these British pigs as propaganda.'

He paused.

'Traitors do have their uses. No, do not eliminate them all. The Gestapo and the SD are to investigate each man thoroughly. We must ensure there are no more British agents among them. But no more finances are to be given to them. We have wasted enough time and money. Set them to work. Let them be involved in broadcasting propaganda to England. All idea of using them as a fighting unit of the Waffen-SS will be abandoned. I want to hear no more about them. Is that clear?'

'Perfectly, my *Führer*,' nodded Himmler.

'As an example for his failure, the commander of the unit will be executed.'

'*Hauptsturmführer* Gottschalk? Very well, my *Führer*.'

Hitler sunk back into his chair and waved the *Reichsführer* away.

Himmler saluted and turned to the door.

'A moment.'

Himmler turned to meet the scowl on Hitler's face.

'I want to know immediately the assassin is caught. *Standartenführer* Behrens must do everything to ensure that the man is captured alive. I want a special execution, you understand? I want it recorded on film so that I may see it for myself.'

'It shall be done, my *Führer*,' replied Himmler.

Outside, in the clean, crisp spring air, Himmler leant against the door-post, sweat pouring from his forehead. The pains in his stomach were terrible. God, he must get back to Berlin, back to Doctor Kersten. He needed his osteopath's healing touch. He hoped Behrens would be successful soon. He could not afford to hang round in this god-forsaken wilderness much longer.

Behrens had spent half an hour on the telephone to Kurt Ludecke in Hildesheim. It had been a rewarding conversation.

'The tip of the iceberg, *Herr Standartenführer*,' chortled Ludecke. 'The tip of the iceberg.'

'Explain,' snapped Behrens coldly.

'We ran checks on the activities of Wielen and one of the postmen, who worked with the old man, recalled that a few weeks ago a soldier came to the *Postamt* and asked for Wielen by the name of Uncle Wilhelm. The man particularly noticed this soldier because he wore an English flag in a shield on his jacket sleeve with the words *Britisches Freikorps*.'

'Collins,' muttered Behrens in exasperation.

'We also discovered that Wielen had a daughter named Paula who was executed as a dissident back in '39.'

'I'm not interested in Wielen's past. I want to know his contacts. But things are fitting together. I was sure that he was one of the contacts used by Collins. That ties Collins in with von Fegeleinn's group.'

'You mean Olbricht's group, *Herr Standartenführer*,' replied Ludecke. 'We have established that before his arrest and execution, the Jesuit traitor Olbricht had no less than three meetings with Wielen. In turn we have discovered that Wielen had at least two other regular contacts. One of them was a *Wehrmacht* major in Hanover. He has not been identified as yet, but we are working on it. It won't take long to track down the swine.'

'You said he had two other regular contacts. Who is the second one?'

'A young woman named Lottie Geis. She goes by the name of Else-Else, a singer in a Hanover night-club. Not very important, but probably a courier for the group.'

'So? Has she been arrested?'

There was a pause.

'Not yet. When we went to her apartment, she wasn't there. She left her apartment on the thirteenth of the month, and guess what?'

'What?' Behrens tried to keep the impatience from his voice.

'Her landlady, *Frau* Bebe, said that Lottie Geis had been seeing a lot of some soldier . . .'

Behrens gritted his teeth. 'Who wore a *Britisches Freikorps* uniform?'

'Exactly so, *Herr Standartenführer.*'

Behrens sighed in frustration.

'But that's not all, *Herr Standartenführer.*'

'Well!' Behrens almost shouted at the complacent tone in Ludecke's voice.

'*Fraulein* Geis had the goodness to tell *Frau* Bebe that she would be going away for a week or so to visit a sick aunt. *Frau* Bebe recalls that she used to get mail from her aunt. The postmark was Korschen in East Prussia.'

Behrens stared at the receiver for some moments in silence.

'Hello? Hello?' came Ludecke's voice. 'Are you still there?'

'Yes,' Behrens said drily. 'Korschen, you said? That's a few kilometres from Rastenburg.'

'That's the place,' agreed Ludecke.

'You don't know the name of the aunt by any chance?'

Ludecke chuckled. 'Just try Geis, *Herr Standartenführer.*'

The line went dead as Ludecke hung up.

For several long seconds Behrens sat staring at the telephone and then a smile spread over his face.

Collins was a clever man; but not clever enough.

He picked up the receiver. When the operator answered he said: 'Get me the Gestapo office in Korschen.'

Hauptsturmführer Gerhard Gottschalk did not die in the accustomed manner of an officer of the armed forces of the Reich. He died weeping, screaming for mercy and urinating in his trousers. Gottschalk had never seen a gun fired in anger before, never seen a gun fired at all, for that matter, until the six rifles crashed together sending him, a quivering mess of bloodied flesh, onto the yard before the barrack wall outside the security perimeter at Wolfsschanze.

Gerhard Gottschalk had been happy as a teacher in his small village school in Bavaria; happy until his degree in English had marked him out for a special job with the SS. He was forty-six, married, with two fine children. He did not want to die.

But die he did on a crisp April morning. And he died without dignity, sobbing and pleading with the grim-faced SS officer who commanded his execution squad and who sneered at Gottschalk's last moments of life.

Chapter Thirty-Three

It was dusk when Collins turned the Citröen up the muddy track towards the group of dark farm buildings clustered not far from the banks of the river Guber. He had been able to memorise Lottie's instructions perfectly, skirting the town of Korschen and finding the lane which led to *Frau* Geis's farm. The farmyard was strangely silent as he switched off the engine and sat behind the wheel listening. There were no animal sounds, no lights to be seen anywhere.

He suppressed a vague premonition of danger, climbed out of the car and strode across to the darkened porch. It was a dark night, with snow clouds scudding across the pale moon. He found the door and hammered on it.

There was movement within. Nervously, he let his hand rest loosely on the clip on his holster, and knocked again.

There came the sound of bolts being drawn and the door swung a little way open. A lantern was held up to his face and a male voice demanded to know what he wanted.

'Is this the Geis farm?' he asked.

'Well?'

'Is Lottie Geis here?'

'What do you want with Lottie Geis?' the voice was uncompromising.

There was a sudden gasp from behind the door. 'It's all right, Hans. It's my Karl!' The door was flung open widely and the girl threw herself into Collins's arms.

'Hey,' he protested weakly, trying to disengage himself from her kisses.

'Karl!' she sobbed in relief. 'You're safe. You're all right.'

Collins quietened her and moved inside a large kitchen parlour. An old lamp lit the room, complementing a fire which crackled and danced in a cast-iron kitchen range. The young man who held the lantern shut the door behind them. He was about twenty, tall and fair-haired. He glared suspiciously at Collins.

'Hans, this is my Karl. Karl, this is my cousin Hans.'

The young man nodded, somewhat sourly. 'Lottie did not tell me that you were a lieutenant in the SS *Todt* Organisation.'

Collins grinned wryly. 'I borrowed this uniform without bothering to ask the owner what it represented.'

Hans Geis frowned. 'It is the uniform of the SS Penal Section, the concentration camp guards.'

Collins turned to the girl. 'Where is your aunt, Lottie?'

She pulled a face. 'When I arrived here I found that Aunt Angelika died a month ago. Only Hans is left here trying to run the farm on his own.'

'Does Hans know?'

'He knows we are going to Sweden,' replied Lottie. 'He wants to come too.'

Collins turned to the boy. 'Is that true?'

The youth tried hard to make his face indifferent. 'There is nothing left for me here. The *Führer* is mad. The whole of Germany is mad. Soon the Russians will be here – if not the Russians then the Poles. I want to be a farmer, that's all. But there will be no room for German farmers here after the war. The Poles will claim it as their territory. They will throw our people out. I no longer want to live here.'

Collins bit his lip. It would be dangerous; two people trying to get to Sweden was bad enough, but . . . He caught the look of desperation in the boy's eyes, the expression of pleading on Lottie's face. He sighed deeply.

'I'd better warn you both that I'm being hunted quite vigorously. If we are to go, I suggest we go now.'

Lottie shivered. 'I'm ready, Karl. I have a small bag already packed.'

The boy Hans glanced about the farmhouse kitchen and then shrugged. 'Who needs things anyway?' he said, the catch in his throat betraying the lightness which he tried to force into the remark.

'Right. What's the best way?'

Lottie and Hans exchanged a look and Hans went to the drawer of an old pinewood dresser. He came back with a map which he spread on the table.

'This is Korschen, where we are now. We are on the banks of the Guber. If we can get to Schippenbeil here, we can get a boat. Schippenbeil is a small place where the Guber joins the Alle. Lottie knows it from the old days. My brother owned a boathouse there in which he kept a small motorboat. He stored some gasoline there during his last leave, a year ago. It is all locked up in the boathouse.'

Hans took a key from his pocket. 'I have the key,' he said. 'My brother promised that we'd all go on a fishing trip down the Guber when he next came home. Then we heard he had been killed in Russia.'

The boy paused awkwardly.

'So?' pressed Collins. 'There is a small motorboat with gasoline at Schippenbeil. What then?'

Hans jabbed at the map. 'We go north upriver, north to Wehlau, where the river joins the Pregel, which runs west into Kongisberg itself. From Kongisberg we will either have to find more gasoline and attempt the crossing to Sweden in our small boat, or try to find another, bigger boat.'

'How big is the boat?' asked Collins.

'Two metres long.'

'Not really the sort of thing you'd cross the Baltic in.'

The boy shrugged.

'So what is the best way to Schippenbeil?'

Hans gestured outside. 'You have an automobile?'

'It might be dangerous. They'll be searching for it.'

Hans shook his head. 'Both Lottie and I know a series of farm lanes. We won't have to go near a main road before we reach Schippenbeil.'

'Right,' Collins said. 'The sooner we start, the better.'

'I'm ready,' cried Lottie, picking up a small case.

Hans picked up a satchel, the type for carrying game in. He blew out the storm lantern and opened the door.

There was a sharp explosion from the darkness outside. The door thudded back on its hinges as a bullet smacked into it.

They flung themselves to the floor, Collins struggling to unholster his pistol.

'Sergeant Collins!'

The voice was somehow familar. Collins frowned a moment before placing it. 'Is that you, Behrens?'

'Delighted that you remember me!'

Collins swore volubly. 'I must have led them here like the bloody fool I am!'

Lottie was white-faced in the flickering light of the fire. 'It's not your fault, Karl,' she whispered.

'Are you still there, Collins?' came Behrens voice. 'We know all about your little circle. We know all about *Fraulein* Geis, Uncle Wilhelm and the others.'

Collins felt a deadening feeling of resignation. He had been a fool to believe that his mission could have resulted in anything except failure.

'*Fraulein* Geis and her cousin have nothing to do with it, Behrens,' he called back, knowing it was probably a futile gesture.

In the darkness, he heard Behrens chuckle. 'I didn't think you were an English gentleman, Collins! *Fraulein* Geis and her questionable associates are all traitors. While you, my friend, are a clever English agent. But not quite clever enough. I must ask you to surrender.'

'No!' It was Lottie. 'We shall all be killed anyway, Karl.'

Hans grunted: 'Better to die fighting than die like pigs in a slaughter yard.'

Collins hesitated.

Hans had turned and was crawling to a cupboard. He opened it and took out a double-barrelled shotgun and a box of cartridges.

'There might not be many of them,' he said. 'Perhaps we can fight our way to the car?'

'I shall not wait much longer,' came Behrens's voice. 'I give you precisely one minute.'

'Stay on the floor, Lottie,' snapped Collins, making his decision.

Hans grinned and loaded the shotgun.

Collins gave him an answering smile of encouragement. 'Try to fire only when you know where the target is. Fire at the flashes of their weapons.'

'Your time is up, Collins!'

Collins ducked through the door and fired in the direction of Behrens's voice. Almost at once a fusillade of gunfire came from the surrounding darkness. Collins flung himself back across the threshold of the door.

Hans let off both barrels.

There was a scream in the darkness.

The boy swiftly reloaded.

'I make it about half a dozen of them, maybe less now,' grunted Collins. 'There might be more at the back.'

'The back door is bolted,' Lottie told him.

Collins frowned. 'We'll have to try to make a break for it. It is no use remaining here because we'll be caught like rats. All Behrens has to do is wait for reinforcements to turn up.'

Hans grimaced as a series of pistol shots hammered into the building.

'Your friend Behrens doesn't sound the patient sort,' the boy commented.

'You're probably right,' agreed Collins and pointed: 'What's in that direction?'

'They used to be the pig pens, when we had pigs.'

'We'll make a break in that direction. Maybe we can get away in the darkness . . .'

Something metallic clinked on the step by the door.

'Grenade!' Collins screamed.

Everything began to move in slow motion. Collins strained forward, eyes protruding to the cylindrical object. Lottie shrieked as she saw him reach forward, scoop the grenade up and hurl it back through the door into the night. Shots splattered all around him, as he fell back across the step. There was a loud explosion.

In the silence that followed it they could hear someone moaning.

'I think you've hit one,' muttered Hans unnecessarily.

'Thank God the bastard threw it a few seconds too soon,

258

otherwise . . .' Collins made a wry expression as he heaved himself up. 'Now let's get going before someone else follows the example.'

'They've got this door covered pretty well,' Hans pointed out. 'There's a small pantry window at the side which brings us out into the orchard.'

'Right. Let's get going.'

Hans turned and led the way across the parlour, through another room. The window was small, but not so small that they could not squeeze through.

'You first, Hans. Then Lottie. No questions. Go!'

Hans handed the shotgun to Lottie, climbed over the sill, wriggling through. Lottie, helped by Collins, reached over the sill and handed the shotgun down to Hans. Then she too was through the window. Collins followed. As he did so there came two loud explosions which rocked the house. They could smell the acrid fumes of cordite and hear the crackle of flames from the parlour.

'Not a moment too soon,' muttered Collins, as he dropped beside them. 'Lead the way to the pig pens, Hans. We'll spy out the land from there.'

The boy nodded. As he moved forward a figure abruptly loomed out of the shadows. Collins fired twice. It was almost a reflex action. There was a grunt as the figure crashed into some bushes. Further across the orchard, a torch beam was sweeping in their direction.

'Hurry!' urged Collins.

Crouching low, the three of them scurried through the orchard towards the concrete shelter of the pig pens. They hunched beside them, their breath coming in pants.

'I make it that we have downed three of them,' whispered Collins. 'There can't be many more.'

He stared into the darkness.

'There's another in the orchard,' he gestured towards the sweeping torch beam. 'But where are the others?'

'Can we get to the car before they spot us?' asked Lottie.

The farmhouse had caught fire from the grenades which Behren's men had lobbed into it. It roared and crackled, its dry timbers providing ready fuel, the flames lighting the surrounding countryside as clear as day. Across the yard they saw two men emerge carrying machine pistols.

Without a word, Hans raised his shotgun. The first shot spun one of the men round, the second shot knocked the other man cannoning into his companion. They fell to the ground and lay still.

For a few moments they waited for a reaction. There was no movement. Collins frowned. Had they managed to knock out Behrens and all his men? There was no sound save for the crackling fire and the soft moaning of some wounded man.

'We've done it,' Hans was gleeful. 'We must have got them all.'

'Careful!' Collins cautioned sharply. 'It may be a trick.'

'We can't wait much longer,' protested the boy. 'Those flames will be seen in Korschen and they'll be sending the police and fire brigade out.'

Collins hesitated.

'All right,' he said grudgingly. 'We'll try to make it to the car. The same order as before. Hans first; then Lottie. Keep low and be careful.'

Hans loaded his gun and nodded.

'Go!' snapped Collins.

The boy rose and, bent almost double, he raced across the farmyard towards the Citröen now clearly outlined by the fire.

He had almost reached it when a figure emerged from the shadows. There was a staccato chatter of a machine pistol.

Hans gave a wailing cry, threw up his arms, the momentum of his run sending him smashing into the side of the car where he collapsed and lay motionless.

Lottie smothered a scream.

'Stay still!' snapped Collins.

He jumped up and ran forward, his Luger in his hand.

The Gestapo man heard him coming and spun round, fumbling to bring his machine pistol up.

Collins loosed two shots as he ran forward.

The Gestapo man lurched forward, struggled to retain his balance and crashed to the ground.

Collins halted and walked up, turning the body over with the toe of his boot.

'Stand absolutely still, Collins,' came a cold voice.

Collins felt a chill run through him as he heard the measured tones of Behrens. So, the game was finally lost.

'Drop your pistol . . . now!'

Collins let the Luger fall from his hand.

'You may turn around and raise your hands.'

Behrens stood facing him a few yards away. He held a machine pistol. The casualness of his pose was false. The man's body was as taught as piano wire.

'And where is *Fraulein* Geis?' demanded Behrens.

At least he could allow Lottie to escape.

Collins nodded towards the flaming farmhouse.

Behrens eyes narrowed.

'Ah well, you have fought well, Collins,' he said evenly. 'You are an opponent worthy of my mettle. But now I have to take you back to Wolfsschanze. Somehow, I don't think you will find *Reichsführer* Himmler so complimentary.'

Collins became aware of a figure just behind Behrens. Oh God, no! Mentally he cried out: Get away, Lottie! Get away! There's no need for you to die too.

He forced himself to keep his facial muscles relaxed. 'You are to be congratulated, *Herr Standartenführer*,' he tried to match Behren's evenness. 'You alone managed to survive out of five . . . or was it six?'

Behrens shrugged. 'You and your companions managed to kill six men.'

'That will be difficult for you to explain to the *Reichsführer*,' smiled Collins, mirthlessly. 'You set out to capture a man, a girl and a boy, and you lose all your men.'

Behrens stirred uncomfortably. 'Yet I have still captured you, my English friend, and that is what . . .' He started abruptly. His eyes stood out; his whole body tensed.

Collins uncoiled like a wire spring. He lashed out at Behrens's hand with his right foot, kicking the MP40 machine pistol upwards and out of the man's hands.

Behrens made a gurgling sound, blood started to trickle from the corner of his mouth. He took a pace forward and slumped to his knees.

Behind him stood Lottie, her face working. In her hands was

261

a long-handled pitchfork, its two sharp prongs bloody from where they had sunk into the back of the Gestapo man.

Collins bent forward.

Behrens was still alive. Summoning up some hidden strength the Gestapo man twisted suddenly upwards, hand fumbling for the machine pistol. Collins kicked him in the face. He grunted but continued moving.

Collins turned, searching for his Luger. He spotted it and scooped it up. By the time he turned back, Behrens was on his knees, his face a mask of blood. Animal grunts came from his bloodied lips. Suddenly he spoke clearly, so distinctly that it startled Collins. 'Who will take care of Inge and Jo-Jo?' he said with bafflement in his voice. Then his eyes cleared and he gazed at Collins. The machine pistol was in his hand and he was raising it slowly.

Collins stared at the man in bewilderment.

Behind Behrens, Lottie, crying in desperation, brought the sharp points of the pitchfork plunging into the man's back once more.

Behrens screamed.

The scream stirred Collins to action. He stood over Behrens's threshing body and shot him. Then he turned away and vomited.

It took him a while to regain control of his clenching stomach muscles. He scooped some brackish water from a nearby horse trough and splashed his face.

Lottie was still standing near Behrens's body, the pitchfork in her trembling hands. Collins moved across and gently disengaged the weapon. He took her, turned her round and led her towards the car. The sight of Hans lying sprawled alongside, prompted the floodgate of tearful hysteria to burst.

Firmly, Collins pushed her into the front passenger seat. Then he turned and examined Hans. He had known already that the boy was dead. He smothered his distaste and fumbled in the boy's pocket, taking out the key which the boy had said was that of the boathouse at Schippenbeil.

In the distance he could hear a fire-bell mingling with the sound of a siren from a police car. He trotted back to Behrens's body and scooped up the machine pistol before returning to the car.

'Lottie!' his voice was urgent as he climbed into the driver's seat.

She did not seem to hear him but continued to sob hysterically.

He twisted in his seat and slapped her hard across the cheek. It jolted her into quietness. 'I'm sorry, darling,' he said, 'but we must save ourselves. The police are on the way. Only you know the farm lanes out of here to Schippenbeil. It's up to you now.'

For a moment the girl stared blankly at him. He wondered whether she had understood or not. Then she nodded slowly.

'Down there,' she said, jerking her head across the farmyard.

He started the Citröen and eased it forward, without turning on the lights. At the far side of the house a gate opened into a narrow twisting lane.

'That's it,' muttered Lottie. Her voice was a tremulous whisper. 'Follow the lane.'

Collins turned the car and drove as quickly as he could in the blackness.

Behind them the clanging fire-bell and wail of the police siren grew louder.

Chapter Thirty-Four

For two hours Collins drove the Citröen slowly through the darkness. It was not a total darkness for, although the clouds were heavy, occasionally the moon broke through, reflecting on the sweeping carpet of snow, giving an ethereal quality to the surrounding countryside. He could see well enough to keep the car in the centre of the narrow, winding lane. After two hours, during which he detected no sign of pursuit, he halted the car and turned to look at Lottie. She had said hardly a word since they had left the farmhouse.

He tried to make out the features of her face in the gloom.

'I'll be all right, Karl,' she said softly in reply to his unasked question. 'I thought after Anton died that death would no longer upset me. I'll never become used to it.'

Collins felt awkward. 'I'm sorry about Hans.'

'Do you think it will ever be over?' It was as if she hadn't heard him.

He frowned. 'The war? Yes. Germany can't last much longer. Another year at the most.'

'War.' He could not identify the emotion in her voice. 'It will never be over, Karl. Once this war is over, then there will be another one, and another, and another. It goes on.' She suddenly turned and gripped his hand. 'It could have been you back there in the farmyard. It could have been you!'

He reached across and kissed her gently. 'But it wasn't.' He gave an uneasy glance around. 'We must go on, Lottie.' The girl exhaled in a long, deep sigh.

'How far is it to Schippenbeil?' he insisted.

'Not far. What do you plan to do?'

'Carry on with Hans's idea,' replied Collins, starting the car and easing it forward. 'Go to Schippenbeil and collect his brother's motorboat.'

'But the boathouse is locked. Hans had the key.'

Collins hesitated. 'I remembered the key before we left the farmhouse.'

She made a small sound like 'oh' but said nothing.

After another long silence they came to a rickety wooden bridge which spanned the river Guber. Collins negotiated it without difficulty. Eventually they came to a fork in the road.

'We are only half a kilometre from Schippenbeil, better if we walk the rest of the way,' Lottie said.

They abandoned the car and walked along the now-moonlit road. Soon they were passing dark sleeping houses. Then Lottie pointed to a shadowy pathway which led off between tall black conifers to where they could see the occasional silver glint of the river.

'We are not far from the boathouse,' whispered Lottie.

It was but a moment before they came to a cluster of dark sheds. Lottie pointed silently to the door of one of them. Collins drew out Hans's key and struggled with the padlock. It was rusty and difficult to work, but after several attempts he managed to turn the lock. The doors swung open, screeching on their disused hinges. The noise was enough to wake the dead. Collins broke out into a sweat.

Peering into the boathouse he found he could see nothing in the darkness. Then a stab of light came from behind him. Lottie had produced a small torch from her bag.

The boat was still there, a small boat barely big enough for two. There was an outboard motor wrapped in an oily rag to keep it from rusting.

'Shine the light this way, Lottie,' he instructed her.

The engine appeared to be all right. There was gasoline, just as Hans had said, a couple of large cans which Collins put into the boat.

'Let's push it down to the river,' he said.

It took them ten minutes to traverse the five yards which separated the boathouse from the river bank. They were sweating, grunting and breathless with the exertion. Finally, they managed to launch the craft. Collins held it steady while Lottie climbed into the bow. Then he clambered into the stern. The current took them away from the bank immediately, swirling them, fortunately, in the right direction, for it took him a further ten minutes to start the outboard motor.

It was cold now, bitterly cold, as the little boat chugged across the Guber and into the broader sweep of the Alle. The cross-currents created by the joining of the two rivers were strong. For a few moments he had difficulty controlling the little craft, but eventually they were headed in the right direction. Lottie identified the various towns on the river as they went by: Friedland, then Allenburg, and on to Wehlau, where the river joined the Pregel, whose currents rushed them down to the great Baltic port of Konigsberg.

Dawn had broken an hour before when they reached the outskirts of the town, where the river widened and began to fill with rusting hulks, and the river craft became more numerous.

'I think we'd better leave the boat as soon as we can, Karl,' Lottie said, noticing a boatman gazing at them curiously. 'The river police might start asking questions.'

Collins nodded. The girl was right. They must look a spectacle. A dishevelled girl and uniformed SS officer making a dawn boat-ride. He turned the craft towards a deserted jetty. There was no one about as they tied it up and stamped about to restore the circulation in their feet.

'Well, we've made it to Konigsberg,' said Collins. 'What now?'

'It is some years since I last came here. If we can find a telephone I can call some friends of mine. There was a girl I went to school with, who married a fisherman at Rauschen, a village on the coast just north of here.'

'How do you know they would not turn us in to the Gestapo?'

Lottie shrugged. 'I don't. But what else can we do?'

They walked for an hour until they reached the centre of Konigsberg. It was soon obvious that the city had been under air attack, for the place was strewn with rubble and ruins. There were traces of fires everywhere. Collins presumed it was the Soviets who were carrying out air raids, for Konigsberg was surely beyond the range of British and American bombers. The streets were filled with military personnel marching purposefully in every direction. Convoys of lorries crawled to and from the docklands. Collins caught a glimpse of the waterfront and to his surprise found it full of ships, loading and unloading. The port was a bedlam of movement.

Lottie found a telephone kiosk on Mint Square, the main centre, near the old-fashioned city *Rathaus*. After half an hour she rejoined Collins with a dejected expression. There was no need to ask her if she had any luck.

'The few friends I had here are gone. Hilde at Rauschen, and her husband, were killed a few weeks ago in a Soviet air raid. The others . . .' She shrugged.

'Well,' said Collins, biting his lip, 'let's find a café somewhere and have something to eat and drink. I haven't eaten since yesterday evening. Then we can think of the next step. Perhaps there is a Swedish ship in the harbour. We might be able to persuade them to give us a passage.'

Lottie did not look hopeful. 'Even if we found someone prepared to take the risk, they would want some payment. I only have a few Marks on me. What about you?'

He shook his head. 'Something will turn up,' he said, trying unsuccessfully to inject a note of optimism into his voice.

They found a quiet café near the waterfront, sat at an isolated table in the window, overlooking the harbour, and ordered hot coffee and bread.

'Perhaps we could try a smaller fishing village along the coast?' suggested Collins.

Lottie shook her head. 'We would stand out immediately. And the chances of finding a fisherman willing to run us three hundred odd kilometres across the Baltic are nil. Especially without money.'

'Perhaps we could steal a fishing boat?'

'Can you handle a sailing boat? That's what the fishing boats on this coast are basically. The Baltic isn't just a quiet lake, you know.'

'Well,' rejoined Collins, 'it's better than just sitting here. Someone is bound to start asking questions sooner or later.'

Lottie suddenly tensed. 'It's probably sooner, Karl. Don't look round, but there's a man over by the jetty wall on the far side of the road. I've just noticed that he is staring intently at you.'

Collins felt his nerves tingling. 'Gestapo?'

'He is dressed like a seaman.'

'I'll turn around casually,' whispered Collins. 'If anything happens, pretend that I've just picked you up and invited you for a drink. Get the hell out of it. Understand?'

Lottie bit her lip but nodded.

Slowly Collins twisted round, as if to glance at the seaview.

Lottie was right. A broad-shouldered man in dungarees, a polo-neck sweater, a merchant-seaman's cap and officer's jacket was lounging on the jetty, an old briar pipe clenched between his teeth. A mass of red hair tumbled from under the cap.

Collins's jaw dropped as he recognised the man.

The sailor's eyes widened at the same time. He pushed himself off the wall and began to walk across the road. There was a smile on his features as he pushed into the café and strode to their table.

'Lord above!' the man greeted him in English. 'Is that you, Collins? I thought I recognised you under all that fancy dress.'

Collins simply stared at the genial features of Hennessy.

The first mate of the *Ard Rí* dropped into a vacant chair and smiled at Lottie. 'Hello, miss.' He turned and signalled to the waiter. *'Bier bitte.'*

Collins recovered from his surprise. 'What in hell are you doing in Konigsberg?' he demanded.

Hennessy chuckled. 'Now hell is the right name for this place, and no mistake,' he agreed reflectively. 'The *Ard Rí* has been here three days unloading a cargo. Then we aim to run in ballast for Malmö for another cargo, and on to Dublin.'

Collins started. 'Malmö in Sweden?'

'That's the place,' smiled the Irishman. 'Now tell me, why are you all dressed up? And why did you jump ship in Lisbon?'

The waiter deposited Hennessy's beer. Collins waited until he had gone before he leant across to the Irishman.

'It's a long story, Hennessy. Let's say I have borrowed this suit from a gentleman and now his friends are looking for us, and I don't like what they have in mind for our future.' He paused. 'At the moment we are anxious to get a passage for two to Sweden . . . and I don't mean a first-class booking.'

Hennessy whistled softly. 'I didn't think you were on a tour of Europe for your health. I guess you are working for the Allies, eh?'

Collins gazed at the twinkling blue eyes of the Irishman. He reminded himself that Hennessy was a member of the Irish Republican movement, which would surely make him pro-German. But something in Hennessy's eyes made him nod.

'I thought as much when you came aboard the *Ard Rí* in London,' Hennessy said. 'You were a damned strange Irishman! Well, let me tell you this, Collins, I have three brothers; one is in the American 8th Air Force and the other two are in the British Army. It's a crazy world. I'm a Republican but the Republican movement stands for democracy. We fought against Fascism in Spain. Frank Ryan led the IRA contingent which fought in the Lincoln Brigade for the Spanish Republic. We still stand for democracy and anti-Fascism.'

Collins gazed at him in silence before he said: 'Does that mean you'll help us?'

Lottie had been sitting with a puzzled frown on her face, unable to follow the conversation. Hennessy turned to her and gave a reassuring smile. Then he glanced back at Collins.

'You poor bloody lambs!' he grinned. 'Of course I'm going to help you. I'm a sucker for happy endings.'

Collins leant across the table and gripped the first mate's arm. 'I can't pay you, Hennessy.'

Hennessy growled a protest. 'You benighted English heathen! It isn't payment that I'm wanting. Tell you what, though. When you are nice and safe in that country you call "Old Blighty", tell your friends and neighbours that the Irish aren't all bog-trotting, whiskey-swilling gunmen; and that one day – someday – we really would like our entire country back to run ourselves.'

Collins smiled. 'Anything you say, Hennessy.'

He turned and explained the situation to Lottie rapidly in German.

'What shall we do, Hennessy?' he asked, turning back to the Irishman.

Hennessy was frowning in thought. 'Well, there is no way that you'll be able to get into the main docks. We are tied up in the Charlottenburg dock and sail at midnight. German security is pretty tight, especially around neutral shipping. A couple of escaped POWs were caught trying to get on a Swedish ship early this morning.'

He turned and gazed out of the window.

'I know,' he smiled. 'Do you see that jetty over there, around which all those derelict fishing smacks are tied up?'

'Yes.'

'Can you and the young lady be there at ten-thirty precisely?'

Collins made an affirmative gesture.

'Good. I shall wait off the jetty in the darkness. Do you have a torch?'

'Do you still have that torch, Lottie?' asked Collins.

'Yes. I always carry it because of the black-outs,' replied the girl.

'We have a torch,' Collins told Hennessy.

'Just fine. At ten-thirty give three long flashes out to the point, over towards Pillau at the harbour entrance. See it? Good. I'll flash you once and then come in and pick you up.'

'You're a decent man, Hennessy.'

The Irishman shrugged and climbed to his feet. 'Listen, my English bowsie. We Irish don't hate your country. There's a lot we admire about you. What we hate is the English government in our country. That's a different matter. God willing, I'll see you later.' He sauntered off with a wave of his hand.

Collins smiled at the girl. 'Our luck might hold, Lottie.'

'Please God,' she whispered.

Collins checked what money he had.

'Let's go and have a slap up meal, Lottie, in some out of the way place. Then we can decide how we are going to spend the time until ten-thirty tonight.'

'There are some small restaurants along the Heillingenbeill Strasse, near Mint Square,' she said, as they left the café. 'But I wouldn't have thought you would want to eat so soon again.'

'I fancy a large hot meal,' Collins confessed.

'Well, I know what we can do afterwards.'

'What?'

'Go to the movies, of course.'

'The movies?'

'Who would think of looking for a couple of dangerous criminals on the run in a cinema?'

Collins smiled broadly. 'You're damned right, Lottie. It's a great idea.'

They found a quiet restaurant and feasted themselves on a hot, spicy potato soup, with home-baked bread and sausage to follow, winding up with the inevitable ersatz coffee. Afterwards, they found a cinema not far away and went in. The film was particularly boring. It was called *A Hopeless Case*. The propaganda newsreel was far more entertaining. They left the cinema at a quarter to nine, allowing themselves time to have another meal before meeting Hennessy.

As they left the foyer a heavy hand fell on Collins's shoulder.

'Papers please!'

Collins's heart skipped a beat as he swung round. There was no mistaking the occupation of the grim-faced pair of civilians who stood behind them, their belted raincoats and soft-brimmed hats giving them an oddly sinister appearence.

'We are of the *Geheime Staatspolizei*,' said the first man, who had a thin face and receding chin. 'Your papers please, *Herr Obersturmführer*.'

There was nothing for it but to try to bluff it out.

He reached into his pocket for the identity card of Franz Steidler. The thin-faced man took it.

'Name?'

'*Obersturmführer* Franz Steidler,' replied Collins.

'Unit?'

Collins hesitated: 'I am of the Penal Division of the *Todt* Organisation.'

'Which camp?'

Collins desperately tried to dredge his memory. 'I am stationed in Danzig.'

'I asked, which camp, *Herr Obersturmführer?*'

The Gestapo man glanced at the identity card. His eyes suddenly narrowed. 'This photograph does not do you justice, *Herr Obersturmführer.*'

There was a note of curiosity in his voice.

'It's an old one,' Collins tried to bluff.

'Really? Yet this card was issued only three weeks ago?'

The man's companion was suddenly holding an automatic and it was aimed at Collins. 'We will have to check out this irregularity, *Herr Obersturmführer.*'

He turned to a white-faced and trembling Lottie. 'Papers, *Fraulein.*'

'She is not with me,' interrupted Collins. 'I . . . I just picked her up for . . . well, you know how it is.'

The Gestapo man ignored him. 'Your papers,' he repeated.

Hesitantly, Lottie rummaged in her bag and produced her identity card.

The man glanced at it and whistled softly. 'So? We have orders to pick you up.'

He stepped back and drew out a pistol in imitation of his silent colleague. 'You will walk in front of us, across the square to Gestapo headquarters. Move!'

Collins felt sick, his shoulders slumped in resignation. So close, they had come so close. He felt Lottie's hand clutching tightly at his arm as they moved off under the guidance of the grim-faced pair behind them.

Chapter Thirty-Five

The Konigsberg headquarters of the *Geheime Staatspolizei* was an ugly grey-stone building on Mint Square. A large swastika flag hung over its massive portals and two uniformed SS guards flanked the entrance. The hallway was crowded with people – an assortment of uniformed men and civilians, of harshly shouting officials and guards, of pleading and weeping, and bewildered people.

'Take that corridor on your left,' instructed their thin-faced captor. 'Move quickly.'

They were propelled through the bedlam of the hall and down a corridor. They moved in a dream. But in this dream someone stood halting their progress. It was a man in a dark suit with faintly Slavic features. Collins frowned; the man seemed familiar. With a sinking feeling he recognised him. Manfred Reinecke – Rudi Behrens's assistant.

'Well, well,' Reinecke was smiling.

The thin-faced Gestapo man pushed forward. 'Do you know this man, *Herr Kommissar*?'

Reinecke nodded.

'His papers are not in order, *Herr Kommissar*. And the girl, she is Lottie Geis. We have orders to arrest her, issued directly from the *Reichsführer's* office.'

Reinecke turned and opened the door to a side-office. 'Come in here,' he said to Collins and the girl. 'You may wait outside, Fromm,' he added to the Gestapo man. The thin-faced man, Fromm, frowned, but remained in the corridor.

Manfred Reinecke perched himself on the edge of a desk and motioned them to sit down. 'Well, well. I hear that our volunteer, so eager to serve the Reich, has become a dangerous man. A British agent, no less.'

Collins said nothing.

'*Standartenführer* Behrens was right in his suspicions about you, Collins. Six Gestapo men as well as the *Standartenführer* were killed at Korschen. That's quite a score, Collins. Do you know that all East Prussia has been alerted for you and *Fraulein* Geis here?'

Reinecke waited for a reply and then shrugged.

'You were lucky to get this far. I can't blame you for your silence. However, my colleagues have been known to make even dumb people start to talk.'

He stood up and went to the door. 'Fromm!'

The thin-faced man looked in.

'I am taking charge of these prisoners and personally escorting them back to Rastenburg. The *Reichsführer* will wish to see them personally.'

'Very well, *Herr Kommissar*.'

'Tell them to bring my car to the front.'

'Very well, *Herr Kommissar* . . . *Herr Kommissar?* How many guards will you require for escort?'

'None.'

'But, *Herr Kommissar* . . .'

'You may handcuff the prisoners and give me the keys.'

Fromm nodded. He produced two pairs of handcuffs and fastened their wrists behind them, dutifully handing the keys to Reinecke.

'You will need a driver, *Herr Kommissar*,' he said.

Reinecke sighed.

'Very well, Fromm. Go and get the car.'

By the time Reinecke had ushered them outside, Fromm was waiting in a Mercedes saloon. Reinecke made Lottie sit in the front passenger seat while he pushed Collins in the back seat alongside him.

'Before we take the Rastenburg road, Fromm, I want to stop off at Hafendammstrasse.'

Fromm frowned in the driver's mirror.

'Hafendammstrasse? It's just a bombsite now, *Herr Kommissar*.'

'I know what it is, Fromm,' snapped Reinecke.

No one spoke as the car moved swiftly across the square and through some side-streets into the dockland area. It was the area which had suffered most from the Soviet air attacks. Fromm finally halted the car in a desolate spot, a crumbling wilderness of ruined houses.

Reinecke suddenly took out an automatic from his pocket.

'Now we shall all go for a short walk,' he said evenly. 'You too, driver.'

Collins felt a chill run through his body. So this was it. A lonely spot. A quick bullet. It saved the State time and money. Even so, his racing mind refused to accept the inevitable. If he could signal Lottie. The surrounding buildings were dark. There might be a chance.

Reinecke had eased himself out of the car. Fromm, a grin of anticipation on his face, also climbed out and went round to the passenger door to get Lottie out. The grin on his face betrayed the fact that he knew the outcome of such lonely stops. He turned and dragged Collins out of the rear passenger seat.

'Stand away from them Fromm,' called Reinecke.

The man did so. The gun in Manfred Reinecke's hand barked twice.

With a grunt of surprise, Fromm staggered forward, one hand held out as if to stop Reinecke firing again. Then he pitched headlong on the ground.

Lottie gave a shuddering cry while Collins stared blankly.

'Easy, Collins. Easy,' smiled Reinecke. 'I'm on your side.'

Reinecke took the keys of the handcuffs out of his pocket and walked round the car to free Lottie's wrists. He handed her the keys and stepped back. The girl turned and unlocked Collins's hands.

'What is this, Reinecke?' demanded Collins, as he rubbed his wrists.

Reinecke shrugged. 'You are an Allied agent. So am I.'

Collins stared at him in disbelief. 'Who the hell are you, Reinecke?'

The man smiled in the darkness. 'You don't really want to know that, do you?'

'Perhaps not,' admitted Collins.

'Will you and the girl be all right from here? I would offer you a lift, but I'm heading east and I must travel alone.'

'East?' Collins was incredulous. 'Are you a Russian?'

'Let's just say that I am a member of the German Communist Party working for the Soviets, a member of the German resistance.'

Collins shook his head in bewilderment.

'Incidentally, Collins, you saved us a job by getting rid of Behrens. He was getting close to our group. We were going to eliminate him on his return from Rastenburg.'

Reinecke pocketed his gun. 'Are you sure there is nothing else I can do for you?'

'We'll manage. Just leave us here, Reinecke.'

'Good luck, comrades.' Reinecke lifted his hand in a half wave, slid behind the wheel and accelerated down the empty street.

Collins stood with his arm around the girl for a few moments. He realised that she was crying softly.

'Pull yourself together, Lottie,' he urged. 'We're nearly there. Come on, someone might have heard the shots. Let's get down to the waterfront. It must be nearly time.'

She sobbed quietly but allowed him to lead the way, across the darkened bombsite, stumbling over the rubble and loose brickwork. By the time they had approached a group of houses, she had regained her composure and recognised the waterfront area. Now it was her turn to lead and it was not long before they arrived outside the waterfront café where they had met Hennessy earlier. Collins was able to see from his watch that it was close to ten-thirty. They hurried across to the jetty. Pausing to make sure no one was about, Collins lifted the girl over the short boundary wall onto the wooden construction. Holding her hand tightly, he led the way slowly along the jetty until they could go no further. At the side, iron stairs led precariously down to the water level. They felt their way down the steps until the water lapped just below their feet.

Collins breathed a prayer that the girl had not let go of her shoulder-bag. 'Pass me the torch, Lottie.'

The girl fumbled in the bag and passed him the metal cylinder.

Collins checked his watch. It was a little after ten-thirty now. He tried to take his bearings in the darkness, raised the torch and stabbed at the button three times.

For a moment there was no answer.

Then, almost feet away, came one answering flash.

They heard the sound of oars in rowlocks and then Hennessy's stage-whisper. 'Is it yourself, Collins?'

'Yes. We're both here.'

'Come aboard then.'

A rowing boat bumped against the jetty and a strong hand was held out. Lottie climbed down first with Collins behind her. The dark shadow of Hennessy pushed off with his oar.

'Is everything all right?' whispered Collins.

'As peaceful as a priest's funeral,' came the cheerful reply. 'The *Árd Rí* is getting up steam. She's already had port clearance.'

'Won't we be seen getting aboard?'

'Not in this darkness. We'll come up on her seaward side. The boys have already put down a ladder. Once out to sea they can't stop a neutral ship heading for a neutral port.'

For a while there was no sound save for Hennessy's stertorious breathing as he pulled on the oars. Then he stopped abruptly, head to one side, listening.

The sound of a purring engine came to their ears.

'Get down! Get down both of yous!' snapped the Irishman. ''Tis a bloody harbour patrol vessel!'

He dragged frantically at the oars, heaving the boat towards the giant shadow of a nearby cargo ship.

The little boat bumped softly against the great iron hull and Hennessy flung himself forward, almost on top of them.

The purring sound of the engine grew louder and a searchlight cut through the darkness. It swept along the line of the great hull, sweeping over them. Then the searchlight swept back and seemed to halt a moment on their craft.

Suddenly a banshee wailing started.

'Jesus, Joseph and Mary!' breathed Hennessy. 'An air raid!'

The searchlight snapped out and the engine revved as the patrol boat suddenly sped off.

Hennessy clambered back on his seat, spat on his hands and gripped the oars again.

'Can I help?' asked Collins.

'Jesus, no! You'll only hinder me, and me the champion rower of Dalkey. Twice champion – Blackrock to St Pat's Isle and back. That's me. Christ!'

This last remark came as heavy guns started to open up on the north side of the port. They could hear the drone of heavy bombers.

Hennessy bent his back into his rowing yet the boat gave the appearance of standing still. In the darkness there was no way of judging its speed. Collins had to admire the Irishman; the man was certainly a seaman. He weaved in and out of the stationary ships, managing to hide once more from a racing patrol boat, and finally arriving at the tip of a granite jetty.

'That's the *Ard Rí* across there.'

He gestured to a large black silhouette. Collins felt a curious emotion about the familiar shape. Hennessy began to pull towards it just as the first Soviet bombs fell on Konigsberg.

'I hope our Soviet friends are not too good with their aim tonight,' muttered the Irishman.

Lottie clung fiercely to Collins as the little boat bobbed over the water towards the Irish ship.

Somehow Hennessy managed to find the bottom of the rope ladder, hanging down against the ship's side.

'Is it you, Hennessy?' came a voice from above.

'Sweet mother of God!' snapped Hennessy. 'No, it's Uncle Adolf and a boatload of stormtroopers. Now get ready up there.'

He turned to Collins. 'The girl goes up first. Then you.'

Collins repeated the order for Lottie's benefit. The girl inched forward in the boat and grabbed at the rope ladder. The climb seemed endless but at the top she found willing hands to help her over the rail. Collins came next followed by Hennessy. A smiling seaman guided them along a passageway, down several ladders into the bottom of the cargo hold and through a series of packing cases arranged to make a tiny hidden room.

'Stay here until we clear the harbour . . .' the seaman instructed Collins. Then he disappeared, pushing a packing case over the entrance.

Collins suddenly felt tired. He flopped on a mattress which had been laid on the floor. Lottie remained standing, her arms wrapped around her shoulders. Outside they could hear the sound of explosions, intermingled with the boom of anti-aircraft gunfire. Then the ship began to tremble.

She gasped. 'What is it?'

Collins smiled reassuringly. 'It's the engines, Lottie. We're getting under way.'

It seemed an eternity before Hennessy pushed back the packing case and came in bearing two steaming mugs. He was grinning broadly.

'I thought yous would like to know that we've just steamed passed Pillau Point, out of the Frisches Haf. We are out into the Baltic and Sweden's our next stop.'

'Dear God!' whispered Collins.

Hennessy held out the mugs. 'Celebrate with a cup of hot cocoa. I'll be down in the morning to bring you up once we're out of territorial limits.'

Collins nodded and glanced at his watch. It had stopped.

'What's the time, Hennessy?'

'It's a quarter to one.'

'Quarter to one?' repeated Collins. 'Then it is April the twentieth?'

'What's so special about April the twentieth?' demanded the Irishman.

Collins suddenly started to laugh hysterically as he felt the release of two month's tension. He laughed until tears rolled down his cheeks. He tried to meet the puzzled stares of Lottie and Hennessy.

'Don't you know what April the twentieth is?' he asked, between choking laughter. 'Why, it's Adolf Hitler's birthday.'

Chapter Thirty-Six

April 20, 1944, was not a day that the people of Britain saw as being in any way noteworthy from most other days of the long, grey war years. Only among trade unionists was the day recorded as a black one.

That day, for the first time in London Transport history, a strike of employees had been broken by the use of troops. The Transport Minister, Sir John Griggs, had ordered troops into the capital to take over the function of 1,500 bus drivers and conductors who had gone on strike against the implementation of the new summer schedules. The strike had started despite strong Government warnings and popular disapproval from people who felt that the workers' patriotism was in question. Nowhere was the anger against the transport unions felt more bitterly than in Whitehall, where on Tuesday, 18 April, the House of Commons prepared itself for the struggle against the LPTB workers by passing anti-strike legislation which allowed the courts to impose five years' imprisonment and £500 fines on those who engaged in strike activity. Yet the drivers and conductors ignored the warnings and went ahead with their strike in the early hours of Thursday morning. Troops were sent in immediately to keep the capital's transport system open.

Strike action also took place in Manchester where five hundred men at two gas-producing plants in the city went out that day, leaving 220,000 consumers without gas supplies.

Meeting with his War Cabinet that morning, Churchill was in an angry mood and was sure that the strikes were the result of action by enemy agents or pro-Nazis. He ordered an immediate enquiry into both strikes and asked that action be taken under the new anti-strike legislation.

The great majority of the British people did have a birthday on their minds that day, but it was not the birthday of the

German *Führer*. HRH Princess Elizabeth would be eighteen years old on 21 April and already the newspapers were full of stories of the royal event. As a birthday treat, the princess was taken to a variety show by her parents, King George VI and Queen Elizabeth. The show, entitled *Something in the Air* was running at the Palace Theatre. Afterwards, the royal party went backstage to meet the stars of the show – Jack Hulbert and Cicely Courtneidge.

Something in the Air was a suitable title for what Lieutenant-Colonel Austin Roberts had in mind as he made his way to the radio room in the attic of his Kensington Palace Garden headquarters. Brigadier Kylie was already there, puffing at his old briar. He glanced up as Roberts entered.

'Come to hear Goebbels annual birthday vapours?' he asked.

Roberts nodded. 'I thought we might get an indication from the German radio broadcast,' he said.

The section monitored all German radio networks.

'If anything has happened, we should get wind of it from what little Josef has to say,' he explained as he seated himself beside the brigadier.

On board the SS *Ard Rí* standing out in the choppy, icy seas of the Baltic, Collins, Lottie, Hennessy and the grey-bearded Captain Flynn had just finished lunch in the captain's state room.

'The devil take it,' Flynn grinned at Collins. 'You are the only seaman I've had who has jumped ship on me in one port and become a stowaway in another. It's a crazy world.'

Hennessy gave a broad wink. 'I'll drink to that.'

'What will the two of you do when we put into Malmö tomorrow?' asked the captain.

'Contact the British consulate and get back to England the official way, I suppose.'

'You're welcome to stay on until Dublin.'

'No. Thank you, but we'll make our own way from Malmö.'

Hennessy suddenly grinned. 'I'll tell you what,' he said, getting up and going to the radio. 'You found it amusing that today is Uncle Adolf's birthday. Well, Goebbels is due to sing his annual paean of praise to that illustrious leader of men on the radio about now. I'll expect you'll want to hear it.'

He tuned in the radio.

The birthday broadcast had already begun, with Goebbels speaking about the fluctuating luck and success of great men and nations.

'The *Führer*'s person is the mainstay of both our belief in victory and our honest war aims.

'It may be cheap and comfortable to feast him when he is flushed with easy success obtained without much cost in blood and sacrifice. It is more difficult in a long-drawn-out fight for the life of the nation to stand by the cause firm and unswerving under bitterness and pressure.

'For us, the *Führer* is both the mouthpiece and the executor of the will of the whole people. There has been in Germany from the very first day of this war not a single case of a soldier deserting his *Führer* and laying down his arms, not a single case of a workman laying down his tools.'

Lottie Geis startled everyone with her abrupt laughter. 'He sounds so sincere, doesn't he?' she remarked bitterly.

In his quarters in Hanover, *Major Freiherr* von Krancke, also listened to the broadcast with bitterness.

' . . . not a single case of a soldier deserting his *Führer* and laying down his arms, not a single case of a workman laying down his tools.'

There was a thunderous knocking on his door.

Von Krancke recognised the sound. He had been expecting such a summons for years.

He slipped a hand into his pocket, took out a small capsule and put it into his mouth. Then he walked to the door and opened it.

Two men stood on the threshold.

'I am Kurt Ludecke of the *Geheime Staatspolizei*,' said the younger man. 'You are Major von Krancke?'

Von Krancke bowed his head.

'You are under arrest on a charge of treason against the *Führer* and the Reich.'

Von Krancke lifted his head with a wan smile. Behind him, on the radio, Goebbels was enthusing:

'I have had the good fortune to have been near the *Führer*

in happy and particularly critical hours. He has always been the same. I have never seen him doubting, never vacillating. He is conspicuous among contemporary statesmen by always recognising the perils in time, and dealing with them.'

It seemed a fitting epitaph for von Krancke's failure.

The major drew himself up. 'Long live a free Germany!' He bit hard into the capsule.

Ludecke stared down at the man's convulsing body in disgust. He kicked out savagely at it. 'Treacherous bastard!' he said.

Goebbels' voice was being broadcast throughout the camp.

Helga von Haensel could hear it faintly but could not make out the words. Perhaps Hitler was dead? Perhaps the war was over?

Since von Fegeleinn's death and her internment in Ravensbrück, night had followed day without any differentiation. She had been confined to what was designated 'the Bunker', a prison within the prison. It was a long L-shaped building whose wardress was a peevish little woman with a bovine face and receding chin. Helga von Haensel had been plunged into a world of blackness. At some stage during the endless night, a hatch in the door would open and a mug of watery coffee with a slice of black bread, were thrust inside. Sometime after, a bowl of equally watery soup would follow. But there was no knowing what time it was.

But now she could hear the strident tones of Goebbels' voice echoing and re-echoing above her. Then came the clang of an iron gate and the sound of descending footsteps.

She had often heard such sounds before, sometimes they were followed by screams and dragging sounds. Sometimes there came the noise of beatings, of harsh smacks as leather cut into soft flesh . . . then the demented cries of pain which made her cover her ears and try to smother them. Although she had been a fierce opponent of the Nazis, Helga von Haensel had never fully realised the hell on earth which the Nazi Reich had created.

The steps halted at her door. Two wardresses stood outside. 'Come, Haensel,' one of them grunted.

Countess Helga von Haensel drew the rags of her clothes

around her with what dignity she could muster. 'Von Haensel,' she said slowly.

'Come, *Von* Haensel,' sneered one of the wardresses.

They grabbed her by the arms and pulled her viciously along the corridor, up the stairs and out into the blinding light of day.

Her ears vibrated to the sound of Goebbels' voice.

She was aware of a young *Obersturmbannführer* standing before her. He was a man in his mid thirties, fair-haired and blue-eyed. Curiously, she found herself noting that he had good skin and beautifully shaped hands with tapering, flawless nails.

The wardress cuffed her across the ear. 'Stand to attention in the presence of the commandant.'

Helga von Haensel staggered but recovered her balance.

'I am not in the military,' she replied with spirit.

The wardress raised her hand again, but the commandant motioned her to stop.

He had a paper in his hand and started to read from it in a low monotone. She could not understand. In the background Goebbels' voice echoed on the loudspeakers, drowning the sound of the commandant's voice.

'What is that?'

The *Obersturmbannführer* glanced up in annoyance. 'What?'

Helga von Haensel jerked her head towards the loudspeakers. 'What is happening?'

The commandant allowed a smile to flicker on his face. 'It is the *Führer*'s birthday. I am broadcasting *Reichsminister* Goebbels' birthday speech to the inmates of the camp.'

'Oh,' Helga von Haensel let her shoulders drop.

'It is in honour of his birthday that we have received this special directive from *Reichsführer* Himmler. You are no longer to be held in prison.'

She stared at him in puzzlement, unable to comprehend what he was saying.

'That is right. You will not have to return to solitary confinement. Come.'

He turned and marched off. The two wardresses pushed her forward. They marched from the doorway of the Bunker, through a small gate in the barbed-wire fencing. A short distance away stood a new brick building with its tall chimney belching acrid black smoke with a vile bitter-sweet smell. It reminded Helga von Haensel of burnt pork. She suddenly noticed that she was being watched from behind the wire fencing. Several gaunt scarecrows stood in hideously striped sacking; thin, undernourished creatures that surely could not be human, with their scarred, shaven heads. God, but they were women! They watched her with dead eyes, large, dark and expressionless. They were like spectres out of hell.

They reached a small depression now in which a post stood upright with an iron ring attached to it. It reminded her of a post to which the bulls were tethered on her uncle's farming estate in Silesia.

The commandant smiled encouragingly at her. 'Would you be so good as to walk towards the post?'

Uncaring, unquestioningly, she obeyed, stumbling a little as she walked down the depression. The eyes of the spectre women haunted her vision.

Behind her there was a small metallic click. The SS guard fired only a short burst from the MP40 machine pistol. It slammed the body of Helga von Haensel several yards against the post. For a moment the girl seemed to cling to the post, hands raised in an attitude of prayer. Then she fell inert at its base.

One of the wardresses hurried forward, bent down and then nodded in the direction of the commandant.

'Take it to the crematorium,' the man said turning and walking slowly back, passing the line of pathetic scarecrows who continued to stare through the wire fencing.

Over the loudspeakers of the camp, Goebbels was enthusing: 'The *Führer* is a divine gift.'

The commandant smiled softly, took out a piece of chocolate, unwrapped it carefully and popped it into his mouth.

Roberts and Kylie sat in silence.

'The *Führer* is a divine gift,' Goebbels effervesced. 'Yet even the flower of leadership is not untouchable . . .'

Roberts and Kylie exchanged a quick glance of hope.

' . . . setbacks and defeats fall upon it. Then is the opportunity to live up to itself!

'The *Führer* needs us as much as we need him. Distress and peril have come close to him . . .' Goebbels paused tantalisingly. 'But we believe in him and in his leading us towards victory. He commands – we follow!'

Martial music started to blare out.

Kylie sighed and motioned the operator to turn down the volume.

'We could read a lot into that broadcast,' muttered the brigadier.

'"Distress and peril have come close to him,"' Roberts quoted. 'But it doesn't seem to have come close enough. Collins must have failed.'

'Goebbels' remarks could be an admission of an attempted attack,' Kylie pointed out.

The captain in charge of the communications centre interrupted with an apology. 'A priority one despatch from our agent in Konigsberg, sir,' he said. 'It's a "head-of-section eyes only".'

Kylie glanced at the paper and then he smiled. 'Two days ago someone attempted to blow up the *Führer*'s car. They succeeded, but Hitler was not in it. Instead, an SS general named Köhler was killed with his aide-de-camp and the driver. The blame has been put on the British Free Corps who have been confined to barracks. Their German commanding officer has been executed for dereliction of duty.'

Kylie thrust out his hand to Roberts. 'Collins may not have succeeded in getting his primary target but he's damn well succeeded with the secondary one. The demise of Köhler will be welcomed in several quarters, especially among the Poles. And the British Free Corps has just become as useful as a sore headache to the Nazis.'

Roberts was silent for several moments. 'Is there any word on Collins?'

Kylie shook his head. 'You said yourself that Collins was an ingenious and resolute man. I'm betting that he is going to turn up somewhere soon.'

He turned for the door.

'Well, I'm off to Whitehall. At least I can tell Churchill that Operation Hagen has been partially successful. Make sure all the relevant documents and files are on my desk tomorrow morning. We want to destroy all records as soon as possible.'

Roberts heaved a sigh. 'Goodnight, sir,' he said as Kylie left.

That evening the radio operators who were listening to the broadcasting stations of Occupied Europe were given something to smile about. At 7.15 p.m. Radio Luxembourg broadcast a special programme in honour of the *Führer*'s birthday. Among the speakers was an *Oberstleutnant* Graf of the *Luftwaffe*.

'Those who have had the great fortune to speak personally with the greatest leader in German history,' enthused the *Oberstleutnant*, 'know him . . .'

He was abruptly interrupted by the playing of the station's call sign – the sound of a cuckoo. The *Oberstleutnant* struggled manfully on, trying to ignore the incongruous sound.

' . . . know him to be . . .'

Cuckoo. Cuckoo.

A breathless announcer came on the air. 'Owing to the approach of enemy aircraft we are now closing down.'

Cuckoo. Cuckoo.

The London newspapers observed the next day that it was a fitting birthday memorial for the *Führer*.

Historical Note

A few months after the events recounted here, the German resistance made its last desperate attempt to topple the Nazi regime. On 20 July 1944, Count Klaus von Stauffenberg went to Wolfsschanze and placed a bomb in the conference room near to the spot where Hitler was standing. Of the twenty-four men in the room, four died, three were seriously injured, and the remainder had minor injuries and shock. Hitler walked out of the shattered conference room; his clothes were torn, his hair partially burned away, his right arm hung uselessly at his side and he had a multitude of bruises. But he lived. However, owing to the confusion, von Stauffenberg was able to leave Wolfsschanze believing his mission to have succeeded. German resistance leaders started to emerge into the open only to be arrested.

Von Stauffenberg was shot to death that evening in Berlin with General Friedrich Olbricht, Colonel Merz von Quirnheim and *Leutnant* Werner von Haeften. Von Stauffenberg's last works were: 'Long live Germany!' A few moments before, General Ludwig Beck, given the choice between execution by firing squad or suicide, chose suicide. Later, *Generalfeldmarschall* von Witzleben was executed. *Generalfeldmarschall* Rommel was forced to commit suicide and *Generalfeldmarschall* von Kluge also committed suicide.

Admiral Canaris was sent to Flossenberg concentration camp. Colonel Lunding, a Danish eye-witness, reported seeing Canaris dragged naked from his cell to be executed. Among the many prominent generals executed was also General Artur Nebe, head of the *Kriminalpolizei* (Kripo).

The records of the *Geheime Staatspolizei* show that 7,000

German dissidents, ranging from field marshals, generals to former ambassadors and civilian government ministers, were arrested. Some 4,980 death sentences were carried out. German resistance to Hitler was vigorously crushed.

The *Britisches Freikorps* never became the propaganda weapon which Hitler and Goebbels wanted, nor did it become the vanguard of the fight against Soviet Communism envisaged by John Amery. For the rest of the war they remained overlooked and inactive.

After the war, the men of the Free Corps paraded through the British courts – sorry, dejected and miserable. So pathetic and misguided did most of them seem that few were made to pay the supreme penalty for their treason.

John Amery, son of British Cabinet Minister Leo Amery, who had dreamed up the idea of the British Free Corps and persuaded the Germans to set it up, was found guilty of high treason. Weak, impressionable, at best a foolish young man, he kept an appointment with the public hangman, Albert Pierrepoint, at Wandsworth Prison on 19 December 1945.

Of the Free Corps NCOs, Thomas Heller Cooper was sentenced to death, but the sentence was commuted to life imprisonment; Francis George McLardy received life imprisonment; Ewan Barnard Martin received twenty-five years' imprisonment; Roy Nicholas Courlander received fifteen years' imprisonment and Raymond Davis Hughes received five years' imprisonment.

As for SS *Sturmbannführer* Vivian Stranders, whose job it was to oversee the recruitment for the Free Corps, he had, of course, become a naturalised German citizen before the war. He was therefore entitled to work freely for his adopted country and, after the war, was allowed to return to his university post in Bonn.